It Happened One Summer

By Polly Williams

The Rise and Fall of a Yummy Mummy
A Bad Bride's Tale
A Good Girl Comes Undone
How To Be Married
It Happened One Summer

POLLY WILLIAMS

It Happened One Summer

headline
review

Copyright © 2011 Polly Williams

The right of Polly Williams to be identified as the Author of the Work
has been asserted by her in accordance with the
Copyright, Designs and Patents Act 1988.

First published in 2011
by HEADLINE REVIEW
An imprint of HEADLINE PUBLISHING GROUP

1

Apart from any use permitted under UK copyright law, this publication
may only be reproduced, stored, or transmitted, in any form, or by
any means, with prior permission in writing of the publishers or,
in the case of reprographic production, in accordance with the terms
of licences issued by the Copyright Licensing Agency.

All characters in this publication are fictitious and any
resemblance to real persons, living or dead, is purely coincidental.

Cataloguing in Publication Data is available from the British Library

ISBN 978 0 7553 5884 7 (Hardback)
ISBN 978 0 7553 5925 7 (Trade paperback)

Typeset in Sabon by Avon DataSet Ltd,
Bidford-on-Avon, Warwickshire

Printed in the UK by CPI Mackays, Chatham, ME5 8TD

Headline's policy is to use papers that are natural, renewable and
recyclable products and made from wood grown in sustainable forests.
The logging and manufacturing processes are expected to conform
to the environmental regulations of the country of origin.

For my wonderful mum

Acknowledgements

A big thank you to Imogen Taylor, Jane Morpeth and Lizzy Kremer for all their support. Also Caitlin Raynor, Claire Bentley, Claire Morrison, Ruth Jeffery, Katie Tooke, Laura West and everyone who has worked so hard on this book at Headline. Jane Edwards, thank you for that brilliant conversation last year – it got me thinking about this book in a new way. Thanks also to Andrew and Cath in Cornwall. Much love and many thanks to my mother Julia Williams and mother-in-law Andrea Chase for being so supportive of my work and such star grannies to the growing brood. Finally, a big kiss to Oscar, Jago and Alice – so much love, so little sleep! – and, of course, to my wonderful husband Ben.

Prologue

No one should have to get up at six a.m. on a Saturday morning. And it shouldn't be this stifling, even in August. It was like their skin was oiled, their legs slipping and sliding over each other as they concertinaed beneath the pristine white Egyptian linen that always made Nell feel like she was staying in a hotel. But Jeremy's smart duplex in London's Fitzrovia was better than a hotel and she wasn't checking out any time soon. In fact, she hadn't been back to her flat share in Hackney for days. Jeremy didn't do Hackney.

Nell tried to get out of bed – Cornwall was at least a five-hour drive away, they needed to get going – but Jeremy pulled her back, his fingers walking into the dip between her hip bones. Within twenty minutes he had made her come twice – he was gladiatorial even on five hours' sleep. They showered together in the wet room and Nell knew he was admiring her lean young body as she lifted her arms, slowly, one then the other, and shaved her armpits, ready for her party dress.

After the shower they were properly awake. So they could now speak and reheat the row they'd had the night before. Despite the sex, Jeremy was still pissed off: she'd broken the news that she had a press trip next month, on his birthday weekend, unfortunately. She'd apologised, explained that if she didn't go, her editor would write her off as a non-

1

ambitious homebody. And, come on, it was an all-expenses-paid trip to Miami! Jeremy said *he*'d take her to Miami. Nell said it wasn't about Miami – well, not exactly – it was about work. It was about proving a point, he retorted, throwing a napkin at her plate of Marmite toast. The toast hopped into her lap, leaving sticky brown skids on her petal-pink silk dressing gown.

Fourteen months into their love affair they were having lots of rows, and lots of fantastic make-up sex. Nell knew she'd started to rebel a bit. Jeremy's possessiveness, however tender and flattering, had begun to feel controlling. Worse, she suspected he resented her focus on her career – she'd done well in women's magazines but dreamed of breaking into newspapers – and that it rankled him that he, successful swinging-dick city lawyer, wanted to look after her but she didn't want to be looked after, not yet, anyway. (The babies could wait.) Yes, she loved him. Every bit of him. How could she not? Theirs was a big love, the kind of passionate, sparking Latin love that made you feel alive. It was just that sometimes she wondered if this was enough. Jeremy wanted worship.

Ten a.m. They still hadn't left the flat, making getting up so early completely pointless. Nell was all over the place. Whenever she went home to Cornwall – not often enough, her mother complained – she got skittish, fidgety and forgetful. And it was a hundred times worse going home with Jeremy because she worried about a member of her family doing something off-puttingly dysfunctional. Which was why she couldn't find her make-up remover travel wipes. Or her gold gladiator flats. (She preferred heels but had to disguise that extra inch she had on Jeremy.) Nor could she find the right bra to go with her yellow halter-neck dress. Had she left the damn thing in Hackney?

2

Seven hours, much cursing, bickering and traffic jams later, the mercury was nudging thirty-one. With relief they finally slipped off the motorway and into the Perranortho Valley, weaving their way through leafy narrow lanes towards Tredower House where Valerie, Nell's mother, was hosting the hog roast. An annual event set in her lush semi-tropical garden, it was the one date in the year Nell couldn't easily flake out of, a rounding up of Valerie's closest friends and rivals for a parade of familial harmony. Jeremy's first. Not his last.

They piled out of his convertible and stood, hand in sweaty hand, on the gravel drive. The old stone rectory looked undeniably beautiful even to the most hardened metropolitan. Surrounded by swarms of cabbage whites, bees as big as birds and banks of blooming flowers, everything seemed to be fluttering and in motion, scented, sweating and moist. Suddenly it didn't matter quite so much that Nell didn't have the right bra or that she and Jeremy were irritating the hell out of each other. The day could still be rescued.

In the garden the party was in full swing. A roast suckling pig rotated on the spit with an orange in its mouth, its skin blackening and crisping like burnt toffee. Guests weaved drunkenly across the lawns. Valerie – yet to receive the diagnosis that would flip her world upside down – was animated and pretty in a sky-blue dress, trading gossip and gooseberry-growing tips and somehow working her way around the party without offending anyone. Only Nell noticed when she took five minutes out to sit alone in the summer house at the bottom of the garden, and wondered if she was thinking about Dad.

Circulating at the top of the garden, Corona in hand, was Nell's older brother Ethan. Showing off his twin baby boys and new wife Janet to the rellies, he was chatty, sociable and charming. Nell suspected he'd just done a sneaky line of coke in the downstairs loo.

Heather, Nell's younger sister, was in a less gregarious mood. She sat quietly on a bench beneath a pear tree, sunlight threaded in her blond hair, looking vulnerable and exquisite in a floral maxi-dress. She'd recently split from Damian, the civil servant she'd secretly hoped to marry, and Nell knew she had been dreading the hog roast with all its 'Who's the lucky man?' single-girl agonies.

Nell had a theory. At summer parties and weddings single women split into two camps. One type of woman wears hot-pink or animal print, shows lots of leg and whoops across the dance floor worrying wives and advertising her availability. The other dresses as if she's hitched, avoids dancing and slinks off without saying goodbye by midnight. Heather was the second type. All she'd ever wanted was a meat-and-two-veg love affair, then marriage, the dessert. But somehow the more she wanted it the more single she became.

She needs a gay best friend, thought Nell, as she and Jeremy walked across the lawn towards her. Shame that the only homosexual at the hog roast was Monty, the family Labrador. Then Nell had an idea. Jeremy was Just Gay Enough! He had looks, charm, wore a Ozwald Boateng suit – with pink silk lining – and was much more comfortable in the company of intelligent beautiful women than the lads. He would stop poor old Heather from being hit on by dairy farmers with yellow teeth and, in turn, Heather's company would ease the pressure on her, which meant she could hang out with her old friend Sophie. Genius.

The party zoomed by. The sun blazed. Nell whirled across the dance floor with a peacock feather in her hair, polkaing with the village oldies, smoking a sneaky spliff with Sophie and, because it was so damn hot, knocking back unladylike quantities of sticky table wine, local cider and Pimms. By one in the morning only a small hardcore group (the childless under forties) were still partying.

Nell's breasts ached from all the bouncing about – she'd gone braless in the end – and she was worried that she might have ruined their pencil-test perkiness for ever so she called it a night. Jeremy, excelling in being a Just Gay Enough companion to a much cheerier Heather, said he was too awake to sleep. He'd join her shortly.

At five in the morning Nell woke in her old teenage bedroom with a tongue like dried biltong. She was alone in the bed. Feeling a whoosh of nausea, she leaned over and yanked up the bedroom's wobbly sash window to gulp some air. Outside the dawn sky was lava-lamp pink, the trees vivid green. Trippy, she thought, taking in a lungful of oxygen. And it was then she heard voices in the garden. A low indecipherable murmuring at first. Then laughter, Heather's laughter. Jeremy's voice? Yes, Jeremy's voice. She vaguely wondered if she should go and join them but her brain was fuzzy, and it was so early and she was so, so tired, and, probably, yes, probably she was imagining things.

By ten the next morning, Jeremy's limbs were wrapped around hers again. A smell of bacon wafted under the bedroom door. Forgoing hangover nookie, they stumbled down to breakfast, ravenous. Runny fried eggs. Hash browns. Oily sausages. Toast. Ethan, Janet and Heather were slumped around the battered oak dining table, bleary and smelling of booze; the twins were bouncing in their rockers; Mum, in her striped apron, was pouring a rope of dark brown tea. All as it should be ... until the moment Heather passed Jeremy the wicker basket of toast. Jeremy reached for a piece, and then, as if in slow motion, Nell noticed their fingers touch – a tiny, fleeting touch, a split-second beat of butterfly wings – then part. Jeremy glanced away. Heather looked down at the table. Her neck flushed. A terrible heaviness began to balloon in Nell's stomach. And it was nothing to do with the fry-up.

One

Almost five years later

Ten a.m., Kensal Rise, north-west London. The postman, resentful at being lumbered with the unpopular Saturday morning shift, shoved the letter through Nell's dove-grey door. It landed on the Union Jack coir doormat with a dull thump.

'Love letter?' The man in Nell's bed – Pete? Peter? – grinned – as he dribbled his finger around her belly button.

'Er . . .' Almost certainly a bill or a letter inviting her to upgrade her mobile phone minutes, Nell thought, sucking in her tummy in the vain hope of keeping it flat.

She was aware that he was staring more intently now, as if the possibility of competition had sharpened his appreciation. She felt a corresponding quiver of self-consciousness and rearranged her naked body on to its side. Oops.

Uppermost boob dropping down like triangular bunting. Not a good look. Out of practice. She quickly flipped on to her front – better, less exposed – and as she did so, noticed that the arrow of dark hair around her bedmate's belly button had crusted up like the edges of an omelette.

'Hey, just relax, babes.'

Relax! How much more relaxed could she be? Lying

horizontal, naked but for the sheet she was gripping to hide the stretch marks on her boobs. Maybe waking up next to a naked stranger was something this guy did every weekend? Maybe this was what all people under thirty did. Like Skins! Yikes. She gripped the sheet tighter.

'So you've got to work later? On a Saturday?'

'I have, I'm afraid.'

'You bloody journalists.'

'Boring, I know.' She winced apologetically. Work. Even the word made her tense. She wanted to forget about the newspaper, just for a few hours at least. But the office had taken up residence in her brain like a kind of warped doll's house complete with mini-photocopier and carpet tiles and the matchstick figure of her spiky boss in a black McQueen suit.

Friday had been manic, as always, the hours slipping like minutes, leaving a pile of unedited features that needed to be filed by Monday morning glaring back at her on the desk. There were no longer any keen underlings to palm the surplus work off on. *The London Comet*, like all newspapers, was suffering from crashing advertising revenues. There had been three waves of redundancies, each spreading through the office like a particularly nasty flu, taking a few out each time, and the workloads on the survivors – none of whom suffered survivor's guilt – had dramatically increased.

'Oh, man. Are you sure I can't tempt you to skive off and drink bloody Marys?' He spanked her bottom lightly.

Nell imagined the spank rippling out across her cellulite. She hadn't had sex in over a year. Why couldn't she enjoy it more? What was wrong with her? Yes, she really should be less British and uptight about the whole thing. Channel Catherine Deneuve! Channel *Belle de Jour*! You are a goddess. You *are*. But somewhere inside her a little voice was laughing and whispering, yeah right . . .

'Come on, where do lifestyle journalists hang out on a Saturday morning?'

'Well . . .' she began. The kitchen. Hand in a box of Cheerios. Pore strip on her nose.

'Hey, isn't Portobello market down the road?'

'Not far.' She hadn't been to Portobello for months, possibly years.

'Let's go there! See if you can convert a Hoxton boy to West London.' He nuzzled her neck. 'I warn you. You'll have to use *all* your powers of persuasion.'

'I'm afraid I really do have a deadline.' Thank goodness. He seemed lovely. *This* was lovely. Sexy. Pretty bloody revolutionary, in fact. But . . . well, she wouldn't mind savouring the more delicious sensual details in private without him breaking the spell. Sophie would be waiting for her juicy morning-after phone call. And it was surprisingly stressful all this being-naked-with-someone-you-didn't-know business. It wasn't stressful last night, of course. But now it was morning. The daylight was unforgiving. And she was sober.

It was the last thing she'd been expecting, which was why she'd set off to the party last night in a blue Reiss dress and shocking underwear – Jurassic cheese-wire pale-green thong, Primark T-shirt bra – and a 1970s bikini line. It was a well-connected, fashionable party where everyone had jobs worth broadcasting and even the men passed on the carby canapés. She'd been invited as a Friend of Sophie. (Sophie knew everyone and everyone wanted her at their party. She *was* the party.) Nell had been in a good mood, having had one of those rare successful trips to the hairdresser's in her lunch hour, and having secured, for the first time since she was nine, a fringe. The fringe – heavy, glossy, a bit Daisy Lowe – covered up all her frown lines, did something clever to her cheekbones and made the office swoon with fringe envy. The four pounds she'd shed with the help of the Norovirus two weeks before also helped. Although she was tired – she was always bloody bone tired – she knew she looked OK, plus, there was this distractingly charming twenty-something looking at her mouth when she talked and this had improved her mood immensely.

When he suggested they finish the evening with a drink at a nearby bar she'd dithered – a bar? there was drink at the party – but Sophie had pushed her out of the door, 'The fringe pulled already! Go, Nell, go!' Two hours, five Bellinis later, to Nell's astonishment, they were entangled in a full-on pash-fest back at her flat. She remembered being prudishly surprised that he'd had condoms with him. And, no, she hadn't come. But she hadn't come with anyone since splitting with Jeremy, so it wasn't his fault.

Nell had felt a bit of a hussy. For all of two seconds. Apart from the fact that her hymen was practically growing back, it was a bit late in the day for the coy act now. All that Rules business was for single women who wanted to get married, didn't want to scare off The One and still had to pretend they'd only ever slept with four people. (One of those being another bi-curious heterosexual woman.) Nell didn't want to get married. She wasn't hunting down The One. Indeed, she feared she'd already met him and ballsed up the relationship spectacularly.

'You're lovely, Nell Stockwell.'

'Not the South London tube station,' she said, flattered that he'd got so close. 'Stockdale.'

He kissed her left shoulder flinchingly close to the large mole shaped like Ireland.

'Thanks for inviting Pete back to your lair.'

Pete! She knew it! Must not forget his name again. Very bad manners. She took a closer look at him. Full head of

10

hair. Slanted hazel eyes. Yes, Pete was definitely handsome – not just Bellini goggles – even if it was in a bit of a predictable blokey Ted Baker-shirt-wearing kind of way, like he might be the kind of man who bought gadget magazines.

'Nice place you've got here,' he said, putting his arms beneath his head. His biceps bulged like potatoes.

'We like it.'

Pete's brow furrowed. 'We?'

'Me and my daughter.'

He sat bolt upright and his eyes bugged out.

Oops. No, clearly didn't remember at all. OK, she hadn't gone into huge amounts of detail but she hadn't hidden the fact. Well, not exactly. She was proud of Cass, proud of everything she'd achieved on her own, but stupid as it sounded now, last night she hadn't wanted to draw attention to the fact she was a mum. She just wanted to be Nell, for once.

'Daughter?' Pete pulled the sheet up over his knees. 'Shit. Is she, like, here? In the flat?'

'No. At Dean's.' She twisted on to her side, feeling awkward all of a sudden.

'Dean?'

'Sorry, that's her dad.'

'Right.' Pete scanned the room. 'Right.'

Nell smiled. 'We're not together.'

He frowned. 'You were married?'

'We slept together once.' This wasn't the first time Nell had had to explain this. Better to get it out of the way early on. 'And conceived my daughter.'

'Wow. O-kay.' He groped his balls, as if checking they were still intact and hadn't been snipped off and utilised for fertility purposes. There was a moment's awkward silence. 'God, so you're a *mum*,' he marvelled. 'Sorry. I suppose I wasn't paying full attention last night.' A slow grin spread across his face. 'Mind on other things.' He squeezed her nipple. It reminded her of breastfeeding a baby with teeth. 'Would you mind if I had a quick shower?'

'On your left. Pink fairy wings on the door.'

Pete walked with his legs bowed, big strides like John Wayne. He had high-worked buttocks. A great body, well, a wonderfully male body, which was all that mattered. Hearing the hiss of the shower, knowing he was safely confined to the bathroom, Nell finally started to relax. She wondered if she'd look back and see this morning as a turning point. Not only in terms of her underwear. (Must go knicker shopping immediately.) And, hopefully, her sex life. But maybe, just maybe, after all the years of hard work and the turbulent rollercoaster of single motherhood, she was arriving at a better place? Why, she might even be entering her prime.

Apart from the fact that she had beautiful Cass, the world's most wonderful four year old, she had a fantastic career that was going places, a flat she loved, and she was still nine stone three on a good day. She could spend her money on Colefax and Fowler wallpaper if she so wished – she had expensive plans for the hall – rather than a family estate car. And, yes, Pete was a reminder that she did have a certain freedom, more freedom than married people, anyway. Hell, she could bed men who looked like they'd been born in the *eighties*! Indulge in a no-frills sexual liaison knowing it was never going to end in Chinese takeaways in front of the telly. The married mothers at Cass's nursery couldn't do that, could they? And nor could her sister.

'Hey.' Pete sauntered back into the room, pink towel tightly knotted round his waist. He flung a letter on to the bed's crumpled white waffle throw and winked. 'Your post, Foxy.'

$\mathscr{Two}$

Two hours later, the letter had been opened, half read, thrown against the kitchen wall, then picked back up and read to the end with much teeth gnashing. Woman-in-her-prime had well and truly bolted. So had Pete. The editing hadn't been touched. A howler of a hangover was kicking in. And her brother Ethan had dropped round for coffee, straight into the centre of the storm.

'Good God. Let's not forget that this is The Stockdale Express, Ethan!' Nell held up the letter with shaking hands, steadying herself with her elbows on the kitchen table. 'Mum's annual round robin that goes to *everyone* she knows. Just listen to this.'

Ethan hid his face behind a large mug of coffee. 'I don't know if I want to hear it again actually, sis.'

She started to read anyway. '*Nell is working hard as a journalist as usual – worryingly hard, in my opinion –* blah blah blah. *I don't see as much of her as I'd like . . .* blah. Wait for it. "*Nell, now thirty-seven, remains unattached and although she'll hate me for saying this, would <u>still</u>*" – underlined, Ethan, underlined! – "*make a great wife for somebody out there . . .*"' She looked up at her elder brother in despair. 'Ethan, Mum has actually put out a public appeal – as if I was a kind of emergency disaster fund – for a husband!'

13

Of course they both knew it was made so much worse by the fact that this followed Mum's trumpeting of the 'wonderful family news' of Heather's and Jeremy's (Nell's ex) engagement earlier that month.

'You're winding yourself up. Honestly. Everyone knows what Mum's like.' Ethan grinned his beautiful indie boy grin – still working it one year off forty – and kicked out his high top trainers with their fat caterpillar laces. 'So what if you're single and thirty-seven? You look about thirty-two.'

Thirty-two? Couldn't he at least lie more generously and say twenty-eight? 'Jesus, I'm so pissed off I can hardly speak.'

'Well, you're going to have to. We've got important stuff to discuss.' Ethan checked his black-faced Rolex. 'I'm afraid I've really not got long before I have to pick up the twins from footie practice. If I'm late, Janet will kill me.'

'I know, sorry.' Nell took a deep breath. Ethan was right. Mum's missive had saved the worst for last. They had to discuss it. She looked down at the letter on the kitchen table and skim-read it again: '*Bad news, I'm afraid. My wonderful housekeeper Deng has just announced that she must return to the Philippines for the summer due to family matters. She's been like a daughter to me since my first stroke. I will be at a loss without her.*' It went on to twist the butter knife a little. '*I confess it is getting harder on my own, the practical things mostly. I'm getting terribly forgetful and sometimes the house does seem very big and very empty and the children do seem so far away. But I appreciate that they all have such busy, busy lives – Nell especially – and I take comfort from the fact that at least they're all wonderfully close. I know that if – when! – anything happens to me they've got each other, and lovely spouses to support them. Apart from Nell, who has some terrific girlfriends.*'

'So. Deng. Is. Leaving.' Ethan groaned, resting his chin on his hand. 'Bollocks.'

'Nice of Mum to inform us through the round robin. Liking the personal touch. Or did you know already?'

Ethan took a sip of his coffee. 'Nope.'

'Maybe Mum's just got confused,' said Nell hopefully.

'Afraid not. I phoned Deng first thing this morning. She's going back to the Philippines tomorrow morning. Her boy's not very well.' She was shocked that we didn't know, as she'd told Mum a couple of weeks ago. Mum's obviously been sitting on it. In denial probably.'

Nell's heart went out to Deng, lovely Deng. It had always made her feel terrible that her little boy was living with his grandmother in the Philippines while Deng did the job of mothering *their* mother because they were all too busy and westernised to do it. 'But she's coming back in the autumn, right?'

'Yeah, sure she is,' Ethan said quickly, not meeting her eye.

Nell pinched the bridge of her nose, closed her eyes. No, The Situation hadn't gone away just because she'd had sex this year. She'd woken up in the same old bad dream.

Mum had been diagnosed with vascular dementia not long after her first small stroke – a couple of months after *that* hog roast. She'd had about five small strokes since then, the last the previous month. Sometimes they appeared to be little more than fainting attacks. Other times they were more alarming. And each one diminished a tiny part of her brain. It was, the doctor said, like someone walking through a house flicking off the lights in each room. At the moment most of the house was still well lit but there were signs of imminent gloom, random losses of memory, muscle weakness, and a crankiness of her mood (although, as she

15

was notoriously cranky anyway, this was hard to pin-point). Each time Mum recovered from the stroke – her doctors were always hugely impressed by her resilience – she reached a new plateau. Each plateau was slightly lower than the one before, as if there was a teaspoon less of her somehow. And each stroke aged her terribly. She seemed much older than her 62 years.

Worse, they all knew that the little strokes were rehearsals for The Big One, the killer stroke, which could arrive tomorrow or gatecrash years later. Best case scenario would be that The Big One would kill her immediately. Worst case scenario was that she'd survive with what Mum described as the 'the sentience of a Brussels sprout'. In other words, buggered either way.

'We need to find someone else and fast,' said Nell, snapping into professional hiring and firing mode. 'How about advertising in *The Lady*? She'd love that. She'd feel like a minor royal.'

'Janet's already suggested it.' Ethan rolled his eyes. 'Won't hear of it. She doesn't want a stranger in the house.'

'Shit.' Formidable sister-in-law, Janet – boho mumpreneur with a whim of iron – was the kind of woman who could talk Kate Moss into a pair of Crocs. If she couldn't persuade Mum, no one could. 'But she cannot be at Tredower on her own. She's not even allowed to drive any more, Ethan.'

'Be grateful for small mercies. I don't know who's less roadworthy, her or that rusting heap of metal. I can't believe the old banger is still going.'

Nell raised an eyebrow.

He grinned. 'I'm talking about the car.'

Nell's head began to ache. Her mother was hundreds of miles away, but still, as Ethan noted, 'within the kill zone'. The truth was that as well as making her cross the letter made her feel guilty. And the guilt had the effect of making her feel crosser – with herself, with Mum, with Deng, with her crap toaster that toasted unevenly, with the entire cosmos.

They didn't have an easy relationship. They'd never been the kind of mother and daughter who behaved like girlfriends, swapping clothes, shopping together and giggling when the gay shop assistant asked them if they were sisters. Nell had always imagined that other mothers, normal mothers, were rather like soft floral sofas imprinted with their daughters' shapes. Mum had always been more like a hard-backed kitchen chair with one of its legs slightly shorter than the other, somewhere you could never sit comfortably. And when she said things like 'Nell got the legs. Heather got the looks', it still hurt. 'You don't need to eat so much as you get older, Nell, so I won't offer you seconds.' Not helpful either. Nor when Mum came round to her flat with its spanking new kitchen, stared at her silver American-style fridge, Nell's new ice-crushing marvel, and said in that particularly disarming way of hers, 'Oh.' What an orchestral range of disappointment her mother could convey in that one simple 'Oh.' She'd gone on, 'Do you really need a fridge that size, darling? It's not like you've got a man in the house.'

'Heather …' Ethan instinctively ducked as he spoke. 'She called earlier.'

Just when she thought her morning couldn't get any worse. 'Right,' she said briskly, staring down at her coffee. She couldn't bear to think of her little sister and Jeremy reading the emergency husband appeal in their Surrey love nest.

'Sis, you two are going to have to sort it out. We need to come together this summer.' Ethan's eyes went soft and brown and fluttered appealingly like they always did when he wanted a woman on side. 'This is not the time for unresolved feuds.'

'There is no feud.' She stood up and walked over to the cupboard, picking out a bar of cooking chocolate, the kind that was ostensibly bought for making cupcakes with Cass, but which she scoffed late at night when she got stressed. Because it was cooking chocolate it didn't count. 'Heather and I just don't have much in common these days. Chocolate?'

'Don't have much in common?' Ethan broke off a slab and ate it. 'Apart from Jeremy. Come on, sis. You and Heather used to be thick as thieves.'

She sat down again. 'Well . . .' It was painful to remember those days. She was the big sister after all, the one who'd fought off the school bully in the playground. She'd even shown Heather how to use a tampon because her mother had been going through a depressed distant phase at the time and wasn't bothered. Over the years they'd formed a tight bond. Jeremy had broken it.

'Mentioning Jeremy's name to you is like mentioning the war to a German. We're all running around like Basil Fawlty, "Whatever you do, *don't* mention the war!" But he is about to become your brother-in-law. You can't pretend he doesn't exist. Especially now.'

She looked up and winced. 'I know, but it's *weird*, Ethan.'

'Yeah, for all of us.' He pulled up his sleeves, exposing a bracelet of black Celtic tattoo round his forearm. 'But they've been together ages now.'

'Four years ten months.' One month before Cass was conceived.

Ethan whistled. 'At least you've not been counting.'

'Jeremy's not the reason we're not speaking, Ethan,' Nell blurted. 'That was about her telling Cass off over . . .' She stopped, startled at how petty it sounded. Since Heather and

18

Jeremy had got together almost five years ago – God, had it really been that long? – she'd successfully kept social interaction down to the bare minimum by politely excusing herself with heavy workloads, childcare crises and deliberately clashing holidays but there were still some occasions when they couldn't be avoided. Like Christmas. And last Christmas Heather had insisted on hosting it at her tasteful palace of taupe. There were handmade crackers. Homemade Christmas pudding. (Who makes their own Christmas pudding? That was showing off.) And a very new, very expensive, pale George Smith sofa that Cass decorated with orange felt tip whilst everyone watched the Queen's speech. When Heather – drunk on mulled wine, always a bad drunk – snapped at Cass, Nell had told her to back off in no uncertain terms. Heather had then accused Nell of being secretly pleased that Cass had ruined their new sofa – kind of true – and Nell (who had also quaffed too much to make the Christmas ordeal go quicker) had called her 'unbelievably precious'. It had all melted down from there. They had not spoken since, which suited Nell just fine. She didn't want to have to start now.

'Thank you, God . . .' Ethan looked up at the ceiling and clamped his hands in prayer, 'for not making me female.'

'You'd make a rubbish girl. Too vain. Too hairy.'

'Come on, I'd look great in a bikini.' He stabbed at a crumb on the table with his forefinger, stacked with chunky rings like fat silver tyres. 'The thing is, Heather is right.'

'Heather is right about what?'

'One of us *is* going to have to hang in Cornwall this summer.'

Nell reached for the chocolate again. If only the answer to this problem came in little chunks and wrapped in silver foil. Life would be so much easier.

'You know what I'm saying?'

'Thinking.' She looked up smiling. 'Got it. Heather! Heather can go. It will be a perfect opportunity for her to plan the wedding, source the local suppliers, florists, persuade the rev she's a churchgoer, all that stuff.' Genius.

Ethan put on a high, girlie voice: 'The future Mrs Fisher has builders to supervise – they're doing the loft – and Jeremy can't take time off work. We can't really expect them to separate before the wedding, can we?'

Nell poured more coffee. 'You lot, then?' she ventured carefully, anticipating resistance. 'The twins would love it. And Janet loves Cornwall.'

Ethan's jaw clenched. 'We're Ibiza-ing. Villa all booked. And things are totally mental at the agency. We're filming a big car ad in July.' He nervously drummed out a tune with his fingers on the table. 'Actually,' he began tentatively, 'we were talking—'

'*We?*' Nell had a bad feeling about the plural.

'Me and, er, Heather had this idea that . . .' Ethan hesitated, stealing himself. '. . . perhaps the logical thing is for *you* to go to Cornwall and look after Mum this summer,' he added quickly, as if to get the unpalatable suggestion out of the way. 'You and Cass.'

'You *are* joking?' She laughed shrilly. 'Having me in the house would be the equivalent of drip-feeding Mum full-fat gorgonzola. Imagine what I'd do to her cholesterol levels. Just the sight of me annoys her. And, she'd exhaust herself trying to matchmake me with some poor local.'

'You'd be totally brilliant with her, I know you would. Better than the rest of us. Heather is way too self-absorbed at the moment and too emotional to just get on with it. And even if I *could* go, which I can't, you know I'm just crap, Nell. I'd forget to remind her to take her pills. And the twins would destroy the place in one afternoon.'

She couldn't quite believe what she was hearing.

'You're on the ball, sis. And you know what? For all your disagreements, she respects you.'

Nice try. 'Er, small problem. I have something called a job?'

'Yes, but Dean dishes out too, doesn't he? Couldn't you take a sabbatical or something?'

'No, I cannot! I'm running an understaffed features department. My boss is about as likely to give me a sabbatical as a chauffeur-driven Rolls. She'd only give me compassionate leave if Mum had five minutes to live and even then she'd expect me to take work calls. No, taking the summer off would mean walking away from the job. That would be it.'

And walking away from her job would be like walking away from her life. The point was she had a job not only to pay the mortgage – Dean was far from a meal ticket – but also to keep the brain ticking over, provide a bit of action outside the perimeters of Mr Maker's doodle drawer. And she loved it, most of the time, anyway, even with all the attendant childcare problems and the usual dollop of working mum's guilt. It was a dream job. Everybody said so.

'But it's just you and Cass, sis,' he cajoled gently, as if he were trying to persuade her to take a rejuvenating spa holiday. 'You're free. You've got no ties here.' He dropped his gaze. 'No relationship, I mean.'

So this was what it was all about! Nell flushed, thinking of Pete walking out of the shower naked that morning, the swing of his puckered red balls against his legs, his hairy forearms, the rare welcome maleness of him. 'How do *you* know?' she spluttered indignantly.

'Whoa!' Ethan held up his hands. 'OK, sorry. I mean no one, like, serious.'

21

Nell knew that what he really meant was that there had been nobody serious since Jeremy. 'Why does everyone think that I have a disposable life?'

'No one thinks that. It's just that you're a little unit. You and Cass. She's not at school. You're mobile.'

'I'm not a caravan!' She stood up and crossly paced the wooden kitchen floor. An undaughterly thought rolled off her tongue. 'I hate to say it, but does it not strike you as just *slightly* ironic that we're arguing about who will look after Mum when she wouldn't look after us properly as children?' Instead, it had been down to Dad, when he wasn't at work, which was hardly ever, and a succession of chaotic au pairs, hearty, fun, hairy-armpitted girls from Europe. Once they'd realised the depths of their responsibilities they rarely lasted more than three months.

'Yeah, but she's our mum, isn't she?'

Nell sighed. Yes, she was. She loved Mum, of course she did. But it was complicated. Whereas the love she felt for Cass was pure and transparent like spring water, a whole new emotion she'd never experienced before, her love for her mother was a heavy, sticky, indigestible thing. There were huge swathes of her life, usually when she'd needed Mum the most, when she had been there but not really been there, and her moods would suck everything happy and normal up like a giant hoover and belch it back out again in a toxic cloud. 'Shit. I feel like my head's going to explode.'

'It's called a hangover.'

'It's called a family crisis.'

'It would just be until Deng gets back. Just a couple of months.'

'*Possibly.*'

'Come on, it would go in a flash.' Ethan spoke slowly and quietly in an attempt to seal the deal. 'We'll all come down at weekends and help out when we can. Don't look like that, we would. You know we would.'

She didn't doubt him. But this was the problem. If she stayed in Cornwall all summer how on earth would she be able to avoid Heather and Jeremy? She'd be a sitting duck!

'Look, Nell. It may be her last summer.'

Nell's eyes blurred with tears. A world without Mum was unimaginable. She was an immortal colossus in a muddy green garden apron. 'She'll go on and on. One of those medical miracles that confound doctors. She'll outlive us all!'

'You know that's not true.' He sat forward, brown eyes pleading. 'It's crap, I know. But lots of people have to do this kind of thing at, you know . . .' he swallowed hard, trying to voice the unpalatable truth – 'our age.' *Our age.* Heavens. Even Ethan, the perpetual teenager, had acknowledged it. What stage of life had she stumbled into? She wasn't ready for it. 'I don't think it's fair that you have formed a Stasi-style secret committee and decided – *without* me, you toenail! – that I'm the one who should jettison my career and relocate to the land that time forgot.'

'It really is different if you're married and entrenched with a family. It just is, sis.' He stood up, slung his brown leather man-bag over his shoulder, and kicked the edge of his skateboard so that it flicked off the hall wall neatly into his hand. 'Anyway, it'd do you good to go and chill in Cornwall for a bit.'

Nell frowned. 'What does that mean?'

'You're stressy. You're always stressy.'

'I'm not stressy!' she barked. *Was* she stressy? Wasn't she just busy?

'Listen to yourself,' he said gently. 'I'm a bit worried about you, sis.'

23

'Well, don't be!'

Nell felt a growing sense of disempowerment lapping against her busy London self like cold dirty floodwater at the door of a house. Despite all that she'd achieved – juggling her career with bringing up Cass, owning her own flat, a lipstick-red Kitchen Aid food mixer, migrating from Topshop to Jaeger, having girlfriends who were like a family you could *choose*, grown-up, happy things in other words – she still felt helpless against the thunderous force of her family. Somehow when they were together she regressed. Back to toddlerdom. Or teenagerdom. And it didn't take long in the presence of her mother – even in the mental presence of her, just thinking Mum-centred thoughts did it – to feel like a little girl again, the little girl who was sent to her first day in middle school in a skirt made from old curtains. Green, geometric print curtains that her mother had reinvented in a Friday-night craft group. Curtains that scarred her for life and left her with a phobia of retro prints and anything by Orla Kiely.

'And Cass doesn't get wheezy down in Cornwall, does she?' Ethan pulled his ace.

'Pollution in London. Pesticides in the country,' she rattled off. 'Please don't make this any harder for me, Ethan.'

After he'd gone Nell slumped down on her sofa and looked around her garden flat. *Hers*. A little cocoon in the middle of London. She adored all of it. The mismatched assortment of stripy cushions. The mirrored tea lights and lamps she'd lugged back from Marrakesh. The sliced logs stacked in the redundant fireplace. The posh smellies in white wicker baskets. The stacks of old *Vogue*s.

Even her Joseph and Joseph set of chopping boards, all colour co-ordinated according to different uses. Unlike the septic block of ancient wood on which her mother dismembered rabbits and then, with not even a splash of cold water in between, chopped strawberries or cheese.

Nell's flat was feminine, hygienic and modern and smelled of Diptyque's Fig room spray. Tredower was soggy with memories, damp and smelled of pond.

No, London wasn't perfect. She probably did work too hard. And of course she wished she could spend more time with Cass. But this was her life. And if Deng didn't come back in September, she could get stuck down in Cornwall entangled in some ghastly carer situation and morph into that Little Britain character, the carer in the acrylic jumper and NHS glasses. Worse, Jeremy and Heather would come and stay at Tredower and she would hear them shagging. She might even have to contribute to wedding conversations. No, it didn't bear thinking about. This time she must be strong. Mum would just have to accept a hired carer. Stepping out of her London life, however imperfect, jettisoning her hard-won job and returning to Cornwall for the summer would be an unmitigated disaster for all concerned.

Three

Friday, six days later

'Claridges? That sounds great.' Sounds tricky. Little chance of a babysitter at this short notice. 'I'll make sure someone senior from the office attends this evening.' A twenty-something workie would have to go. 'Great talking to you. Bye, Isla,' she said, trying to bring the conversation with the garrulous PR to a close as quickly as possible – a voicemail from Cass's nursery was now flashing ominously on her mobile. She hated voicemails from the nursery. They usually relayed news of a fall or conjunctivitis or nits. And they always appeared at the worst possible time. Like now, when she was about to usher in the features meeting, which was already running late.

She listened to the message, phone cramped beneath her shoulder as she bundled her notes together in something resembling a professional-looking pile, slipped on her high heels under her desk. As she feared. Cass had a temperature. Nursery wanted her collected as soon as possible. It was nursery policy not to give out Calpol, they reminded her solemnly, as if it was equivalent to administering intravenous morphine rather than the pink stuff every working mother spoon-fed their children like milk. Nell glanced at the clock for the fifth time that minute. Every cell of her body wanted to run to Cass but she knew she had to be careful, very careful. She'd had to take two days off last week when Cass had got wheezy. She'd also had to leave early the week before to get to the nursery play. And so it went on.

Shit. She didn't have time to call the nursery back now. Zara, her editor, a tall, angular woman in her early forties with a helmet of blond hair, wearing a pin-sharp trouser suit and a fixed look of slight disappointment, was standing outside the glass walls of the boardroom, beckoning her over, her gobstopper black cocktail ring glinting malevolently. Shit.

Nell put on her fakest, most professional smile and mouthed, 'Coming!' She glanced anxiously at the phone again. Cass will be OK, she told herself as she walked towards Zara, stomach knotting. Cass will be OK.

'Ah, Nell,' said Zara, not moving aside from the door to the boardroom. It was almost as if she were guarding it. 'Would you mind popping in to the HR office?'

'Haven't we got a features meeting?' Nell's mind was already racing. If she had to go to the HR office, then she could make a quick personal phone call on the way.

Zara hesitated. 'Not right now, no.'

Nell tried not to look relieved. 'Anything I need to know about?' It must be about someone on her team. She couldn't think who, though; they were a lovely bunch. And it was strange that Zara hadn't mentioned anything. Still, she was unpredictable, not the best people manager, they'd had to get used to that since she'd taken over the helm two months ago.

'They'll tell you everything you need to know,' Zara said, smiling tightly and turning on her black cone heel.

'Great.' Nell started to walk up the two flights of steps to

27

the HR office. Something inside started to flutter. Could this be the promotion she'd been working so hard for? Had all the slog, the rushed mornings, the late nights, the working Saturdays, been worth it? How much money would they offer? She must negotiate. Yes, she must. She mustn't be a pushover. Think like a man, that's what Sophie would tell her to do. Think like a man.

But first she had to think like a mother. She stopped outside the HR office and phoned the nursery, reassured them that someone, probably herself, would pick Cass up in the next two hours. Could they call her if she got any worse? Nell could feel their disapproval crackle down the phone. What kind of mother wouldn't rush to their sick child immediately?

She straightened her jacket and strode purposefully into the HR office. The news was delivered quickly. Much banging on about the current economic climate. Six months' pay. At first she stared at him in disbelief, fixated by the flake of croissant crumb on his front tooth, unable to digest what he was saying. Then it hit like a fist. Redundant! And all she wanted to do was to get out of the building, away from the phones, her colleagues, the humiliation. To Cass.

She was still shaking when she got to the nursery. But while Nell was in need of a lie-down in the sick room, Cass was now a picture of pink-cheeked health. Her temperature was down and on sight of her mother she'd miraculously developed an appetite for a milkshake. Nell, not having a reason not to, took her to Starbucks. At the Starbucks counter, blinking back tears, she rummaged through her handbag: iPod, blusher, deodorant, Tampax, packet of raw almonds, spritzer Evian face spray, emergency Haribo, emergency banana ballet flats. Already these seemed like relics from another life. Cass chatted about nothing much quite happily. Nell twisted a soya latte round and round in her hands, winded. How could this be happening to her? Why her?

The more she thought about it the worse she felt. The most inconsequential details of the day started to take on a sinister humiliating turn. Had her colleagues known she was in for the chop when she'd breezed into the office that morning, merrily slurping a coffee and talking about the failings of the Bakerloo line? Had the deputy editor known as they'd both peed in adjacent stalls in the Ladies that morning and she'd done one of those embarrassing pees that seemed to go on for ever? Had the deputy secretly thought, that's the last time you do a long pee in this place, honey? Oh God.

'Mummy? Are you listening?' Cass looked up at her with wide lettuce-green eyes.

'Yes, Cass,' said Nell. She hadn't been listening. 'What is it?'

'Can we do this lots?' She licked the froth off her straw.

Nell tried to smile. 'What, Cass?'

'Milkshakes in the afternoon?'

Nell sighed and hugged her close. 'Looks like it, Cupcake.'

Four

Nell spent the rest of the day utterly wretched. It was a real struggle to keep up appearances for Cass who clearly sensed something was afoot and had become clingy and difficult. Only once Cass was in bed could Nell finally collapse into her own misery on the grey velvet sofa with wine and cooking chocolate and wait for the only person in the world who might be able to lift her spirits. She looked at the clock. Where was Sophie?

Usually Nell was a pro at alchemising spare minutes – those teeny slithers of clock between Cass's naps, late trains and late friends – to catch up on life's uncatchables, hand-washing, emails, Facebook, dutiful phone calls. But she felt only dread at the thought of sharing news of her unemployed circumstances with the world, if they weren't gossiping about it already. A career that had taken over fifteen years to build had been decimated in a three-minute conversation with someone with a croissant crumb on their tooth.

Then the world contacted her. A beep. She grabbed her phone, half expecting it to be a message from Zara begging her to come back. It wasn't. It was a text from Pete. 'Drop round after pub?'

After the pub? How old did he think she was, twenty? She threw the phone on the rug – she wasn't ready to tell Pete either – and flicked between crap Friday-night programmes on the telly, wishing it was Saturday already so that she wouldn't have to face the long, dark insomniac night of the soul that she knew was lying in wait. She began to spiral further down into the depths of self-pity and was only saved from reaching for Leonard Cohen's most miserable hits by a loud *rat-a-tat-tat* on the front door.

'What the fuck!' Sophie burst into the hall in a whirl of Louis Vuitton cashmere, glossy black hair and red 1950s-style sunglasses, clutching two bottles of red wine. She sat down in a poof of expensive perfume on Nell's sofa. 'Can we sue?'

Nell smiled at the 'we' and instantly felt a smidgen less suicidal. She uncorked the wine and poured it into two green knobbly glass tumblers. 'Doubt it.'

'I've just emailed you my lawyer's number. God, these are killing me.' Sophie pulled off a pair of vertiginous heels and tossed them unceremoniously on the floor.

'New?'

Sophie rolled her eyes. 'Credit crunch? What credit crunch? Yes, yes, I know. They were in the sale though. And I'm paying my penance in blisters.' Sophie grabbed her hand. 'Right. Tell me everything immediately, hon.'

Sophie Sweet, Cass's godmother, was Nell's truest friend and had been since they'd first met, aged sixteen, in Cornwall. They'd been inseparable then, making each other snort with laughter about their disastrous love lives, rolling their eyes at anything remotely Cornish and fantasising about the day they could move to London and meet real men like Echo and the Bunnymen's Ian McCulloch.

Without Sophie Nell's life would have taken a different course. There would have been no Cass, for one thing. Because it was through Sophie that Nell had met Dean, funny, history-nerd Dean with his chunky Elvis Costello glasses that

31

would steam up on the dance floor and his white-man hip-hop moves that scared off women in a whirl of helicoptering limbs. Years later, a month after she and Jeremy had split up, on a warm autumn night stirred by a full moon and a bottle of tequila, he'd lunged at her and she'd not resisted. It would be the first and last time they'd sleep together. Forward wind nine months, and, to their collective disbelief, all three of them were in St Mary's labour ward, Sophie bellowing Nell on like a football coach, Dean vomiting into a bedpan.

Sophie unapologetically didn't want her own children – 'I look at pregnant women's tummies and think, cute, but that baby has to get out somehow, honey!' – which made her a devoted godmother. Her career as a TV sales executive was on a roll, and she was truly, madly, deeply in lust with Tom Spoke, aka The Shagster, a TV actor who got repeatedly but sporadically cast as a gangster because of his alpha jaw and don't-fuck-with-me eyes, a man that Sophie's friends and family jokingly deemed 'unsuitable in every way'. Sophie, of course, didn't care. She was not someone easily swayed by others' opinions. Sophie was unembarrasable, fiendishly sociable, loud, politically incorrect, always a couple of stone overweight and always on a diet that never worked. Everyone who met Sophie either immediately adored her or found her insufferable. All her friends felt blissfully chosen.

'Oh, babes.' Sophie slung a soft, plump arm around her shoulders. 'They're so not worth it.'

Nell smiled through a bleary lens of tears. 'God, that's a sign of the times, isn't it? We must be getting old. Crying about careers rather than men.'

'You used to moan about the fact that your boss actually cared what version of Spanx Kate Winslet wore beneath her Baftas gown.'

'The tragic thing is I can't imagine a life without caring

about Bafta underwear now.' Nell sniffed. 'It feels oddly important.'

'Ah, just like a bad relationship,' tut-tutted Sophie. 'Missing all the bits you despised about your ex.'

There was a thump from the floor above. The chandelier trembled. A shard of plaster fell to the floor.

Sophie looked up. 'Miranda from One B?'

'Yet to master coming down from her yoga headstand.'

'Mastering demolition.'

Nell sunk her head into her hands. 'I feel sick.'

'Post-traumatic job disorder.'

'No, I've eaten a whole bar of cooking chocolate.'

'Don't worry, one of your five a day,' laughed Sophie.

'What the hell am I going to do?' despaired Nell. 'There are no jobs. Nada. No one's hiring. The freelance pool of writers is now so full it's overflowing, and with good journalists, too. It's hopeless, Soph.'

'Where's the fighting talk? Come on, Nell. This isn't like you.'

No, it wasn't. But she was hit by the overwhelming realisation that she had no fire left. Not so much as a glowing ember. She was spent.

'You can write that novel you've wanted to write for ever.'

Nell winced. 'Weirdly, writing a novel was so much more appealing when circumstances prevented me from doing it. I know, I know, totally pathetic.'

Sophie refilled Nell's glass. 'Get mad! Get drunk! Get even! Seriously, Nell, a break from work will give you time to reassess things. You've been at full pelt ever since having Cass.'

The word pelt made her feel hairy. Had she been made redundant because she was too hairy? Or wore the wrong shoes? Or because she had Cass's name on the gold necklace round her neck? It wasn't like she was unaware of the division in the office between the mothers and the non-mothers, the latter resentful if they had to carry the load for the ones who tried to rush off at six (guilty as charged), had an excuse to wriggle out of the dullsville evening dos (guilty) and couldn't come to work when the kids were ill (guilty, guilty, guilty). But she'd tried to make up for it in other ways.

'Remember how conflicted you feel, Nell, not being around enough for Cass.'

'I know, I know. But now I'll be around *all* the time.'

Sophie shook her head in exasperation. 'Seriously, Nell, you're a one-woman dynamo, which is why we all love you, well, one of the reasons, but you're knackered. You need to park up for a bit.'

'Like an old car,' she said, fingering her eye sockets, checking for knackered hollows. Yep, craters.

'A lovely vintage sports car that needs a bit of TLC.' Sophie curled her bare feet beneath her and leaned into the sofa. 'You never know, you might even have a bit more time to let that lovely Pete tinker under the old bonnet.' She poked Nell with her bare foot. 'You could even have, like, a relationship? Do coupley things that chart a slow slide from rampant sex to contented nights on the sofa watching *The Wire*?'

'Now *you*'re being ridiculous!' Nell joked, but actually she meant it. She didn't want a relationship, nothing more than what Pete offered, anyway. No, she wanted to be as good a mum as she could, not someone reeling from a string of failed relationships. She'd got real and accepted long ago that no man was going to come along and sweep up her and Cass like birds fallen from the nest. No man that she'd actually want in her life anyhow.

Sophie pulled a bag of cashews out of her handbag. 'Ten calories a cashew, did you know that?' She held one up between finger and thumb and eyed it combatively, as if caught in a battle between good and evil. The cashew won. She ate it, then another ten in quick succession. 'You'll have to go now, won't you? Back to the homeland.'

'Don't.'

'Isn't there a name for your predicament? The sandwich woman or something? A woman caught between the demands of looking after their young family and ageing parents.'

'Sandwich? I feel more like burned toast.' Nell reached for the nuts.

'Exactly. Which is why you must treat it like a long holiday.'

'Listen, Soph. How on earth will I avoid Heather and Jeremy if I'm in Cornwall?'

'Ah, so *that*'s what it's about.' Sophie looked thoughtful. 'Couldn't you see it as an opportunity to sort stuff out with them?'

Nell shook her head. 'What's to sort out? It could make the situation worse.'

'Worse? Like how could it be *worse*? You're not talking to your own sister.'

'Oh, I don't know.' Nell's stomach started to knot. 'Soph, all I know is that when I go back home I remember that night of the hog roast, the one when they got together, I remember it so vividly. And I get this sense that I'm being suffocated. That the house, the landscape, it's all closing in on me.' She shook her head. 'I know it sounds stupid. It's hard to explain.'

'Woo-hoo! And out of the darkness came' – Sophie twiddled her fingers and winged her hand towards her like a bird – 'the steak and mushroom pasty.'

'Sophie, it's not funny. Anyway, it's essential that I'm in London to look for work.' She tossed a handful of cashews into her mouth. 'Absolutely essential.'

Five

The next morning Cass sat on the sofa, small squidgy legs tucked beneath her, Mabel doll in one hand, her weekend bag in the other, glancing at Nell with a look of hurt recrimination. How dare Mummy send her off to Daddy's holiday home in Bridport? Normally she loved it. But today, because she sensed Nell's dark mood and it worried her, she didn't love it. And she wasn't going to make it easy. 'I don't want to go.'

'You love being at Daddy's.'

'But I also want to be with you,' pondered Cass, as if she'd never seen the contradiction before.

Nell sighed.

Cass grinned, spotting a chink in the armour. 'What if I wet my knickers?'

'I'll pack lots of spare knickers.'

'Daddy forgets to take me for a wee before bed.'

'I'll get Freya to remind him.' She gave her a hug. 'Come on, Cupcake.'

They went through this every other weekend. However many times they did it, it always created a tight feeling in Nell's throat. Today was worse. Everything was worse. Even though she swore she'd barely slept last night she'd somehow still managed to have a visceral nightmare about being eaten alive by a giant photocopier. And this morning she felt like her skin had been flayed off. She was dreading Cass leaving, too, knowing she would miss her warm little body slipping into bed beside her at four a.m. and wriggling all night like a baby octopus.

It was imperfect, this co-parenting business. She had learned to live with the bomb in the hold, the possibility that one day Cass might turn around and say she wanted to live with Daddy. After all, Dean specialised in the fun bits – weekends, holidays – not the rushed school run, the tidy-up times, the sitting up in the middle of the night with Cass's asthmatic spacer clamped over her nose and mouth because she was wheezy.

'There's Daddy!' exclaimed Cass, spotting his bulky silhouette through the panes of the front door. She jumped off the sofa. Nell followed her.

'Hi, there!' Dean and his wife of four months, Freya-the-Fragrant-Dentist, stood hand in hand in the doorway, smiling sheepishly, like they might have emerged from a honeymoon kiss.

Cass bundled into Dean's open arms and gazed up at him adoringly.

'Hi, guys.' Nell had a sneaking suspicion that Freya was sizing her up, probably assessing the health of her gums.

'Hello, Nell!' said Freya breezily – wholesome, lovely Freya with her clear baby-blue eyes and swishy subtly highlighted hair. She looked fresh and optimistic in her pink blouse and pressed white linen wide-legged trousers. Like a model from a French clothing catalogue. Whereas Nell, in her fat-day black trousers and dour grey shirt, realised that her outfit bore an unsettling similarity to the John Lewis staff uniform. And she had a hole in one of her grey socks. Damn. She bet Freya would have noticed the hole. Bad gums. Bad socks. Perhaps this was a sign of things to come, now that she was unemployed. Yes, that was it. She would pad around all day wearing holey socks, eating cooking chocolate and developing gum disease.

'You OK, Nell?' Freya asked in that cutesy slightly croaky voice which reminded Nell of Orwell, the green TV puppet from the eighties.

'Fine, thanks.' She could have answered, 'Seriously considering jumping off the top of Selfridges naked', and Freya would have nodded and smiled. She didn't get the impression that Freya ever actually listened to what she was saying, mostly because she was too intent on emphasising to Dean the cordiality of their relations. 'You?'

'Everything's brilliant, thanks!' Freya beamed. And it clearly was.

It struck Nell for the first time that having a proper job, a rather dull-sounding one like dentistry, was super-smart. She couldn't be snooty about it now. As her mother would say, for as long as people eat they will need fillings. Whereas they obviously didn't need someone who could write ironic, knowing copy about It bags and Hollywood plastic surgery fads. No, she wouldn't tell Dean about losing her job. Not yet. Not in front of sensibly employed fragrant Freya.

'You all right, Journobug?' Dean asked Nell, pushing his glasses up his nose. 'You look totally knackered.'

'Dean!' said Freya, nudging him and giving Nell a weary 'Men!' look.

'Oops, sorry. I only notice, because normally you look so . . .' Dean paused, manfully trying to think of an adjective that wouldn't offend or threaten either woman.

'I hear the sound of a shovel digging deeper, Dean. Careful.' Nell smiled.

'Yes, I'll quit while I'm not quite ahead, shall I?' said Dean, cupping his hand on Cass's shoulder. 'And how are you, wee Cassie?'

'Mummy left work to have a milkshake with me!' Cass declared proudly.

'Sounds nice. Took a day off, Nell?' Dean smiled.

'Er, kind of. I'll tell you later.'

Dean's kind, round eyes puzzled behind his boxy black glasses.

'We'll have lots of milkshakes in Dorset, won't we, Cass?' chirped Freya, playing with Cass's long blond hair.

'Can we go shopping for shoes?' asked Cass.

'Of course!'

Nell tried not to bristle. She knew Freya meant well. But shopping for Cass's shoes was *her* job.

'All ready?' Freya beamed, pushing her large tan handbag back over her shoulder.

'Yes!' Cass raced to the door, her reluctance to leave forgotten.

'Not so fast, Cupcake. Come here.' Nell kissed Cass on her freckled forehead and hugged her just a little bit too long and hard. 'I love you.'

'I love you too, Mummy.'

'You girls go,' said Dean, holding Freya's gaze for a moment. 'I'll be five minutes. I want to have a quick word with Mummy.'

'Remind Cass to pee before bed!' Nell called after them.

'No problem!'

Nell watched Freya and Cass walk to Dean's grown-up estate – she still had a single gal's Mini – and was hit by how mummy and daughterish they looked. Feeling a sharp twang of unease, she turned to Dean. 'Is everything OK?'

Dean cleared his throat. 'There's something I want you to

know. And I wanted to tell you before we told Cass.' He looked nervous now.

More bad news, she knew it. They were relocating to Birmingham? Dorset? They were splitting up? They were . . .

'Freya's pregnant.' He beamed.

'Oh my . . . That's such wonderful news!' Nell hugged him. 'Cass will be thrilled to have a sibling. Oh, congratulations, Dean!'

'We didn't think it would happen so fast but we're over the moon as you can imagine and . . .' He started talking quickly, his words tripping over each other, repeatedly pushing his glasses up the bridge of his nose. 'Well, there's something else too. Something I want to ask you.'

'Go ahead.' Nell became aware of an unsettling niggling feeling as Dean's news sank in. She wasn't sure why.

'Well, you know Freya's parents, Maggie and Rich, live in Italy? I told you, remember, near Puglia?'

Nell nodded. But, of course, she didn't remember anything about Freya's parents. Up until now she'd been far too busy working to take much notice of such details.

'Well, they've invited us down for the summer. I'm going to work from there a bit; you know, fly back and forth. Things are particularly quiet for me this summer anyway. And they're not far from the airport.' He grinned his lopsided grin. 'They want her to call them Granny and Gramps, which is kind of sweet, isn't it?'

Er, *no*. She said nothing.

'They're very cool, laid-back people – you'd love them – and, of course, they've got this bloody massive villa, infinity pool, the whole shebang.' He pushed his glasses up his nose with his thumb again.

'Wait a minute, Dean, I'm not sure I understand . . .' She was aware of a new family dynamic forming as they spoke, like one of those wobbly misshapen bubbles blown through a giant wand at a kid's party.

'I know Cass has never been away from you for more than a few days, but she's older now, Nell. She'll be totally fine.' He cocked his head on one side. 'Just a few weeks.'

'*Weeks!*'

'It will give Freya and Cass a chance to really, you know, bond properly, which is so important now that we're going to be a . . . a . . .'

He wants to say 'proper family', thought Nell, digging her fingernails into her palm. 'I understand that, Dean, but—'

'And it will give you a break, free up your weekends to write that novel, fall in love, whatever it is you single ladies do. What do you reckon, Journobug?' He smiled hopefully. 'You haven't got any plans this summer, have you?'

41

Six

Wolvercote, Oxford

In a small honey-coloured stone cottage not far from the village green, April James was seeing her daughter Beth to the front door, spinning out the goodbye and trying to stop herself from commenting on the stripy mini-skirt that was stretched tight – inappropriately tight – over the small swelling of Beth's pregnant tummy. Resist, she told herself. Pick your battles. Nutrition is more important. So she kissed Beth on the cheek – it felt tacky with make-up that she didn't need to wear – and put the Tesco bag in Beth's hand. 'Vits.'

Beth took the bag and peered into it warily. 'You know I can only stomach liquorice and chips at the moment, Mum.'

April smiled hopefully. 'I thought you might want to branch out a bit.'

Beth rolled her kohl-rimmed eyes and shot up one crudely home-plucked eyebrow: she'd honed the losing-will-to-live look to perfection.

'There're some ginger biscuits made by yours truly,' persevered April. 'The ginger helps with the sickness.'

'Nothing, totally nothing helps with the sickness,' Beth groaned.

'Some apples, those green crunchy ones you like. They

used to do the trick with me. Don't look like that. They don't bite back.'

Beth surrendered to the fuss and smiled. 'OK, thanks, Mum.' She curled one foot behind the other and suddenly looked about eleven.

April reached for her. 'Come here, you.'

Beth hugged April back limply, worried about attracting the attention of the neighbours. But she let go of her reluctantly.

'Now you take care while I'm away, OK, love?' Love. When had she started saying, Love? I sound about fifty, April thought. 'You need to drink lots of water – that really does help with the tiredness.'

'Water? I hadn't thought of that. I was thinking more cider.'

April put on her serious mum face. 'Promise me you'll call me if you need me, Beth, any time, night or day. I'll leave my phone switched on at night. And you've got the B. & B. address and numbers and everything, haven't you . . . ?'

'Hello? Mum, you're going on a painting course in Cornwall, not climbing Everest.' April smiled and tried to shrug away the guilt for leaving her family for the summer but couldn't. Also, she suspected that climbing Everest might be easier than trying to relocate that elusive talent she'd once had for art. She was so rusty that even her doodles now looked like a small child's. If you don't use it, you lose it, her art teacher had warned her. She'd been right.

'Anyway, Dad is here. He's not, like, totally incapable.'

April smiled. 'I know, I know, it's just that you're my baby and—'

'I'm eighteen and a—' She almost said 'half' but caught herself. Craning into the hall, she shouted, 'Bye, Dad! Later.'

'Later,' Chris shouted back in a way that was meant to be funny. He was not the kind of man who said, 'Later', and thereby lay the joke.

As Beth agitated to leave, April felt a surge of protectiveness for her child–woman daughter. Not for the first time that day she also felt an electric jolt of shock at the fact of Beth's condition. She reminded herself that Beth was indeed eighteen, not twelve; the situation was unconventional but not disastrous. It wasn't like she had cancer or anything. It would – deep breath – be OK. 'Love you, Beth.'

'Love you, Mum.' Beth switched on her iPod and bounced down the paved front path in her green flip-flops, swinging her bag of ginger biscuits and apples, her slim, pert figure not the least changed by the momentous cellular events unfolding within it. Wrapping her towelling dressing gown tight around her, April leaned against the blue front door, overwhelmed by the sight of Beth, beautiful Beth: she'd always feared those looks would get her into trouble one day. She also felt, and she could barely admit this even to herself, slightly envious of Beth's golden youth, her irrepressible mix of confidence and naïvety. What sort of mother did that make her?

Because April had had Beth pretty young – little short of her twenty-fifth birthday – until recently she had felt they were almost the same generation, sisters as much as mother and daughter. But, now, especially now, she could no longer sustain the delusion. At forty-three, her own fertility was most certainly withering, if it was still there at all, whilst Beth's was like a tree heavy with ripe fruit. April clearly remembered her own mother at forty-three and how she had seemed, bless her, inexcusably ancient and past-it in the true sense of having had all the exciting things having happened to her already. (She feared that this was exactly how Beth viewed her too.)

And even when April *had* been young, she hadn't been as golden as Beth and her gaggle of friends, not even close. Sometimes she'd see them dancing at the bottom of the garden around iPod speakers and they were completely mesmerising, like fairies dancing in the woods. They also seemed older and more assured than she was at that age. It was something about their lack of shyness, their high expectations, the way they expected their lives to shoot up and outwards like stars. They even knew how to dress – she still struggled. And Beth's lot got those glittering grades – Beth's two As and a B were par for the course – despite grazing online most of the day. Of course, it was Beth who had to show her how to set up her Facebook page. While Corin, her eldest – studying politics at Edinburgh, who came home to borrow cash and nail scissors – had chosen the family's new flat-screen telly, neither she nor Chris being up on all the new HD business. Analogue parents with digital kids, Chris liked to joke. Sometimes it felt as if the world was speeding away from them both. And taking the children with it.

'Everything all right, sweetheart?' Chris called from the kitchen, breaking April's thoughts. She smiled. Chris read her mood like no one else, even when they weren't in the same room. That's what happened when you'd been with someone since you were nineteen years old, a kind of dull telepathy.

'Fine.' April joined him in the kitchen, where he sat, one leg crossed over the other, at the painted white table beneath the beautiful seascape print she'd bought and spent a small fortune framing. (Why did frames cost more than pictures? Madness.) It showed a searing cobalt-blue sky, a V of geese, a small red sailing boat on the horizon. Whenever she was feeling down she looked at this picture and felt better. 'I just wish Beth would eat more fruit and vegetables.'

'Oh, I'm sure a craving for something greenish will kick in fairly soon.' Chris poured her a cup of English Breakfast, giving her a sidelong glance.

They sat there silently for a few moments listening to the rhythmic whir of the washing machine, the blackbirds in the garden, the neighbour's lawn mower, the sounds of their life. She wasn't ready for this to be everything.

Chris was.

Surely contentment was a good thing, the thing she paid ten pounds a session to attain in her yoga class? Chris, on the other hand, didn't need to do yoga. He was a natural-born, albeit stiff-jointed, yogi, one of those people happy at the angle he'd fallen in the universe. So why had this contentment begun to irritate? He didn't deserve to be found irritating. The irritation was clearly a reflection on her not him. When she considered the slightly grisly pantheon of her friends' husbands, she knew she'd done well – or got off lightly, depending on which way you looked at it. Unlike most of them, who had begun to sag and bulge in odd places and whose scalps had gone shiny, Chris was better looking now than he had been in his twenties, less gangly; his thicker-set figure, even his salt-and-pepper hair suited him. And he was a good husband, a wonderful husband, actually; kind, funny, loving, mostly rubbish around the house, but that seemed to be par for the course except in the most exceptional households like her friend Pip's. But then Pip's husband – now ex – had turned out to be gay. She'd take the Marigolds, thanks all the same. Besides, Chris worked full time; she didn't. It struck her as a fair trade-off.

There was the sex, of course. Its somewhat sporadic nature. No, they didn't have so much sex these days – did anyone with kids, really? – but she'd never fretted about him playing away or doubted that he loved her. Naïve maybe, but she could see no good in worrying too much, not like some of her friends did. Better to trust and be proved otherwise than be paranoid and ruin what you have, that's what her mum always used to say. Their married life was a good life. It had a happy hum, as if Rolf Harris were whistling very quietly beneath his breath in the background: excellent health – touch wood – friends she'd known since primary school, tennis, book group, weekly yoga class, daily walks on the meadow, Saturday pub lunches at the Trout. This was enough, surely? Why did she have to go and stir things up like an unhinged menopausal person before she'd even had the menopause? Madness.

'She won't eat those apples, you know,' said Chris, glancing over his shoulder as he rummaged through the cupboards in search of his favourite marmalade. (Surely having a favourite marmalade was a sign of middle age?) 'I think you're going to have to back off a bit, April.'

'What do you mean?' She knew exactly what he meant but didn't want it confirmed.

He started spreading his toast, carefully, right up to the edges of the crust. He had a technique for everything. Why couldn't he just smear marmalade on his toast haphazardly like a normal person? 'Beth needs to feel she can do this on her own. The more we all fuss around her the less confidence she'll have.'

'She's pregnant and eighteen years old! I'm her mum.'

'Yes, and she's going to be a mum herself.' He offered his hand.

'Yeah, you're right.' April squeezed his hand. Such a familiar hand with its pianist's fingers, the solid gold wedding ring inscribed with her name. This was the hand that she had gripped until its bones crunched during the births of their children, the hand that had wiped away her tears when Mum

47

had died last year, the hand that had steadied her when a sobbing Beth had shown them those terrifying two blue lines on the pregnancy test.

'Let's forget Beth for a minute.' He spoke more gently. And she sensed the question coming. She'd sensed it brewing all morning. He dropped her hand but held her gaze intently. 'So today's the day, then?'

'I'm meant to be leaving in an hour.' Her voice was apologetic. She couldn't believe she'd booked the ticket. For once her indecision had failed her. 'Were you hoping I'd change my mind?'

Chris blew out air. She could smell toast on his breath. 'I'd be lying if I said no, but you've got to do what you've got to do, darling.' He pulled at the sleeves of his old rugby shirt. 'I'll drive you to the station.'

'Sorry, Chris . . .'

'Don't worry, I'll survive the summer.' He winked, scouring for a joke. 'Somehow.'

'The art course really looks brilliant, Chris. It's in the afternoons, mostly, which gives me free mornings . . .' She stopped, realising she was blathering. She walked up behind him, wrapped her arms round his bristly neck. 'Chris, if I don't do this now I never will. The moment Beth has the baby I'll need to be around, won't I? This is my last gasp for a bit of freedom.' She didn't say she'd had enough of being just April James. Mother. Housewife. Sometime teacher's help. Soon, grandmother! *Things* were stirring inside of her. She wasn't ready to settle in for the long snooze.

Chris took her hands and gently pulled her round to face him. He tucked a wedge of hair behind her ear. 'I need to ask you something, April.'

'You sound serious.' She flicked a toast crumb off his sleeve.

He looked at her searchingly. 'It's not about us, or . . . or . . . someone else, is it, April?'

'God, no! How could you think that?' She laughed, then stopped when she saw that he wasn't laughing. 'Darling . . .'

'It's just, well, I know we haven't had much fun recently, just the two of us. Work's been a bit mad. And Beth's pregnancy has kind of loomed over everything.' He shook his head, as he always did when he mentioned the P word, as if he was still struggling to take in the fact that his nicely brought-up daughter had had sex, let alone was about to have a baby instead of taking up her place at Exeter University.

She was tickled by Chris's paranoia. 'Do I look like a woman who's about to run off into the Cornish sunset with . . . ?'

'A surfing art teacher,' Chris harrumphed, a smile playing at the corner of his mouth now. He looked relieved that he'd asked the question and got the answer he'd hoped for.

'Oh, a lobster catcher would hit the spot,' she teased. 'You know how I love a bit of lobster. With garlic mayonnaise.'

'Try not to sound as if you've actually thought about it! Now, are you sure you don't want to bend me in half and stuff me into your luggage? Promise to breathe in. I could volunteer as a nude model or something, make myself useful.'

April laughed and kneaded his shoulders. 'Such a sweet thought. But you've got to work, keep the home fires burning. I'm not having Beth living in this house alone, with or without Duncan. They'd have one of those Facebook parties that end up on the front page of the *Mail*.' She grinned. 'Anyway, the baton has been passed, Chris. It's going to be your turn to cook and wash up! It'll be a very interesting experiment.'

'My last chilli con carne gave us all food poisoning.'

April smiled. 'Well, you'd better get your act together. I've stuck a list of things Beth can't eat on the fridge, you know, blue cheese and stuff.'

'But she can drink, right?'

'No!' she shouted, then realised he was joking.

Chris stood up and refilled his coffee cup. He looked at her over the cafetière, suddenly serious. 'You may not find what you're looking for. You know that, don't you, April?'

April's fingers twitched on her knee. She'd still not had a reply to the letter, which was gutting, but she wasn't going to let it stop her. There were, she kept telling herself, plenty of explanations. 'Look, I'm not going to push the issue if . . .' She stopped, not wanting to complete the sentence.

'Hmm,' he said unconvinced. 'Don't forget I know you, April James. I know you like the back of my hand.'

April looked away, knowing as she did so that Chris would have noticed her looking away and read things into it. The problem was that April was no longer sure that he *did* know her, that anyone knew her properly, not even herself. And this, she thought, staring into the milky brown circle of her tea, was the thing that was threatening to blow this happy little life apart.

Seven

Mid June

They were now fifteen minutes away from Tredower. Cass, who'd successfully fought sleep for the entire five-hour journey, finally closed her eyes. Her head lolled back against the top-of-the-range car seat that Nell had bought last month and on which Cass had promptly vomited up her macaroni cheese. It still ponged. A box of raisins spilled out across her lap, its contents rolling into the cracks between the seats. Nell switched off the Maisie audio CD that had been driving her slowly nuts. Without the chatter of Cass, the car felt quiet, determined, its destination inescapable.

No turning back now. They were on the road. The hardest bit was over. She'd surrendered to the forces sucking her south and tearfully said goodbye to her lovely home and London life. It felt like she was off on some perilous expedition into the tundra from which she might never return. She felt wholly uprooted, her world stuffed haphazardly into the car's boot, her mother's world already tapping its foot, impatiently waiting. She'd packed comprehensively and efficiently for Cass – every meteorological and medical scenario nailed – and randomly and badly for herself. Waterproof mascara. Make-up remover wipes. Chanel Nº5. Fake tan. Nurofen.

DVDs for long lonely nights. (*Blow Up*, *The Apartment*, *Stepmom*, *Breakfast at Tiffs*.) Frizz serum. Italian cantucci biscuits. Travel hairdryer. iPod. Bikini? Anorak? Both, obviously. Mindful of the all-too-easy slide into *Little Britain* carer persona, she'd also packed various items from her old life, or rather her old future life – the summer she'd anticipated while employed that now wouldn't happen. What was the point in those beautiful Prada wedges she'd bought in March for anticipated glamorous summer assignments if they were *never* worn? Or that Schiaparelli pink summer dress. Or her oversized white sunglasses.

Cass started to snore lightly. Nell gazed at her in the mirror. Bless Cass. And thank goodness she had put the kibosh on the possibility of losing her for the summer to her new, perfect, extended we've-got-an-infinity-pool family in Puglia. She'd struggled with it – she really didn't want to create tension with Dean and Freya – but she knew that this summer could well be her and Cass's one chance to be together properly, quality mummy time without her working. The moment she got another job it would all go back to what it was, the rushed mornings, the bolting back home for bath time, the working late. Yes, Italy would keep. Cass's infancy wouldn't.

Also, if she were totally honest, selfishly, she needed Cass in sniffing distance. The smell of Cass calmed her. And she needed calming. The redundancy had shaken her more than she ever thought possible. She was Nell Stockdale, used to shakes, built for them like a high-tech building adapted for an earthquake zone. But it had knocked her sideways. Taken her by surprise. Sophie invited her to Glasto – she had two VIP backstage passes – but for the first time ever Nell couldn't locate the confidence or desire to hang out with twenty-somethings in fluoro and pirate boots. She'd much rather lock herself in a Portaloo. Ditto the Serpentine party. Or even a cocktail in Shoreditch House where she might have to talk to successful employed people. No, Nell's over-riding urge was to log off, lick her wounds and tug her fringe.

Her wardrobe looked wrong now too. She couldn't wear the smarter tailored stuff from her office days – what would be the point? She'd be masquerading as an employed person. Ditto her cocktail dresses, designer jeans, and shoes with price tags that now she didn't have an income made her eyes water. But it was hard to lose the shopping habit completely, and she feared that to do so meant surrendering to the idea that she'd never work again. So on Friday morning at eleven-fifteen a.m., the exact time she would normally usher in the daily features meeting, she found herself compulsively, sneakily buying a cashmere leopard-print scarf from Net-a-Porter, a compensation prize for everything going pear shaped. The elation of receiving this butter-soft scarf wore off the moment she'd torn open the tissue paper. She was hit by a crashing wave of guilt: she should be trying to spin out the redundancy money as long as possible. Panicked by buyer's remorse, she'd broken open a bottle of white wine, drank two large glasses on her own – bad, very bad, units in double figures – and felt even worse.

The lights changed. Nell stepped on the accelerator, swerved to avoid a hedgehog pancake. It started to rain. No surprise. As soon as they'd crossed the Tamar river the weather had turned, the blazing sunshine swallowed up by an unmade bed of pillowy grey clouds. She could already feel the damp. Whereas in London the weather was incidental to the main business of city living, merely dictating the need for a pedicure or the number of layers of cashmere required, here it imposed itself on every waking minute and altered the entire landscape, mental and physical. It could change in an instant, like Mum. And it dominated everything. (Ditto.)

Valerie Stockdale had Cornwall in her blood. Like her own parents, she had grown up here and was living at Tredower when she met Leslie, Nell's dad, a Bristolian, at a supper party in Truro in the late sixties. Four years later they'd married and left for London, setting up home in Muswell Hill, where Dad worked as a teacher. Nell had loved Muswell Hill, the identity it bestowed: a Londoner with Cornish roots, i.e., mystical cool heritage without the bore of actually having to live somewhere where nothing ever happened and you couldn't get a copy of *The Face*. She'd spent enough school holidays at Tredower missing her London mates to know what the country actually involved and while she did love the sea – duh, everyone loved the sea – she'd always found Tredower to be cold, spooky and crackling with the bad vibes between her mother and intimidating grandmother, who famously got on terribly.

And of course no one had an inkling that Valerie's parents would die suddenly within two months of each other and that Valerie, the surviving child of two siblings (Uncle Pat had died in a yachting accident in 1978 and being gay, albeit in the closet, he hadn't left any descendants), would be left the house, nor that she'd want to move there.

Tredower should have remained a cool, rambling 'We've-got-a-place-in-Cornwall' holiday home. But, unbelievably, Mum ripped them from civilisation and flung them there on a permanent basis. All of them – Nell, Ethan and Heather – devastated to be torn from their friends, sulked and protested endlessly. But it was futile. Neither of her parents lost sleep over it. As Ethan said, things were different then. Parents expected their offspring to 'get on with it'. Like they expected them to sleep in the boots of cars in sleeping bags and walk three miles to school and do paper rounds alone in the dark at the age of thirteen.

The move to the armpit of the universe, Nell later found out, helpfully coincided with the exposure of Dad's affair with Louise Wilkes the blond pottery teacher with the lisp. Her mother wanted to get him as far from *Mith Wilketh*, as she was known to the students, as humanly possible, without actually dropping off the British landmass. Of course, what Mum didn't bank on then was that Dad's new school in Penzance had an even younger, blonder teacher, this time in the English department. Without a lisp. Nor could Nell have foreseen that twelve years after moving to Cornwall, Dad would be driving to the small, pretty cottage of this very lispless English teacher in heavy rain late one Sunday afternoon (whilst pretending to pick up parmesan in Tesco) and that he'd take a bend too fast and spin up and over the hawthorn verge, so that the car would land on its roof in a field and Dad, who rarely bothered with a seatbelt, would die instantly and bloodlessly, surrounded by grazing sheep, Radio Two still blaring from the car radio. Nell often wondered now different their lives would have been had they stayed on the leafy outskirts of London. Dear old Dad wouldn't have been taking a bend in the rain. He'd have been hailing a taxi or hopping on to the Tube. He would have been safe. And, of course, he would be here to look after Mum. And she'd be free.

A lorry hooted. Nell paid attention to the road again. The landscape had started to become horribly familiar. This wasn't the tourist version of Cornwall beloved of West London families bedecked in Boden. Not Rock, or Padstow, or anywhere fashionable with expensive delis that sold pecan brownies for £5 a pop. This was Stockdale land. The motherland, not far from the bottom tip of the country. (And, as the old Cornish saying went, nuts collect at the end of the sock.) Despite all the gentrification in the last decade, this part of Cornwall remained largely as it had been when she was growing up, give or take the odd organic farm shop where you could buy fancy pickle that didn't taste as good as Branston. There was still bungalow after new brick bungalow squatting beside the kerbside with featureless windows displaying the ubiquitous carvings of Nell's most hated animal, the demonic seagull, alongside bad Cornish pottery – usually pimpled with crafty lumps and spots as if suffering from an alarming skin condition – while the twee over-tended front gardens boasted grinning gnomes, vast clumps of pastel hydrangeas – on steroids around here – limp pot plants and honesty boxes by the front gates. Other than the vast aircraft hangar of the regional Tesco, food had to purchased from small, badly stocked general stores, where you couldn't buy the *Guardian* but could buy every single flavour of Walkers crisps and frozen pizzas and Ginsters pasties. And the people! You knew you weren't in London. So many white faces, a paint swatch of beige and pink. And well-fed people, too, a remarkable number of well-fed people, all eating crisps as they pounded the narrow pavements wearing sportswear that they evidently never used for its intended purpose. She couldn't blame them. She always put on the pounds here too. There was something about Cornwall that made you want to eat, as if the sight of the freezing sea programmed the body to fatten up like a seal. And there was also something about being at the very end of the country before it sank into the Atlantic. She'd always felt that. There was no more that England could offer or promise now. Somehow Cornwall answered the question, 'Is this it?' with an icy, sobering 'Yes!'

That did funny things to people's heads, and appetites.

Nell drove over the roundabout, overtaking the wheezing Datsuns and stalling OAP-manned Rovers, passing the tight bend where Ethan had crashed his motorbike years before, breaking his left shinbone in seven places. She smiled at the familiar signs: 'Seals Stairlifts', quickly followed on a left turn with the enticing promise of 'Sunnymede rehabilitation centre', and, five minutes down the road, her old favourite, the weathered maroon sign nailed to an old barn, the ever enterprising, 'Sykes & Co, builder and funeral director'. Welcome to Cornwall, land of Zimmer frames, bad food and Hitchcockian birds, the place where crap cars come to die, thought Nell. Welcome home.

The winding roads narrowed and darkened as she drove deeper into the valley. Finally, she turned into Prickle Lane. With its steep rock verges it was barely passable if you met a car coming from the other direction, let alone a tractor. Dense canopies of trees locked above the lane to create the effect of a giant green polytunnel. Then suddenly, teasingly, it twisted sharply to the left. Nell beeped her horn. A sudden curl to the right, just to really test the old driving skills. And there it was. As it always was.

The sign – Tredower House – white with black lettering, let out its cat-claw squeak as it swung in the breeze on its bent black iron pole. She'd scrawled, 'Abandon Hope, All Ye Who Enter Here', on it when she was seventeen.

The black wrought-iron gate, wonky on its hinges, was already open, like an old mouth. She turned into the drive. Gravel crunched beneath the wheels. Tredower looked down on them, eyeing its exiled daughter disapprovingly. It was an imposingly large Georgian rectory with a sagging roof, its walls and pretty paned window frames covered in a skin of ivy. The exterior walls were three feet thick, walls that tended to keep the damp in and the heat out, walls that parcelled up the world within so absolutely sometimes that Nell would wake in the night and feel like she'd actually dropped off the edge of the world and was living in some kind of dwelling that resembled the hidden bunker in *Lost*.

She glanced at her phone. No signal, of course. It was like being tele-transported back to 1985. The only place in the house you could catch a signal was on the slope in the garden, if you stood on tiptoes and waggled your phone in the air like a mad person trying to catch a butterfly.

'Cupcake.' She gently wiggled Cass's foot. 'Wake up. We're at Grandma's.'

Cass opened one green eye. 'At the seaside?'

'Yep.'

Cass gazed sleepily out of the window. 'Where's the beach?'

'A pebble's throw.'

'Oh,' Cass said, looking puzzled. 'But it's raining.'

'Annoyingly, it does rain at the seaside too, Cass. But, hopefully, not as much as in London.' A necessary white lie. Monty came bounding up, wagging his tail. Cass shrieked with delight and tumbled out of the car into his paws.

'Hey, Monty, you old queen,' said Nell, rubbing him behind his ears. Monty was Cornwall's gayest dog. He displayed no interest in the opposite sex, only other male dogs and, failing that, inanimate objects such as seaweed and dustpan brushes. 'And, look, Cass, there's Grandma!'

Valerie was standing very still beneath the trellised arch that led from the front to the back garden, her orange blouse filling with air like a windsock. Her coarse, wavy hair blew about wildly. She picked a strand out of her mouth and smiled, looking older than Nell remembered, and picked up a bundle of muddy spinach from the low wall beside her.

'Hi, Mum!' Nell said cheerily as she clambered out of the car, taking Cass's hand.

'Hello!' Valerie remained where she was and Nell knew that this was because she wanted them to come to her, not the other way round, and that this was nothing to do with her being unwell and everything to do with the way Mum just was. Cass held on to Nell's hand more tightly. She didn't see Grandma Valerie enough to immediately relax in her company and had secretly expressed a perfectly understandable preference for her other grandmother, known more cosily as Nana, who lived in a small townhouse in Tunbridge Wells and had a glass jar on a shelf stocked with mini Snickers and Twixes for her many grandchildren. Nell nudged her. 'Go on, Cass. Go give Grandma a kiss.'

Cass, being darling Cass, obediently ran towards Valerie, who rested a hand on Cass's shoulder, 'Let me take a look at you. Gosh, don't you get prettier every day?'

Cass stared at the ground, already self-conscious of her milk-blond prettiness. Behind the hedge a row of white pillow-cases on the clothes line snapped in the breeze like sails.

'And look at your cute little nose!' Valerie declared, making Cass squirm again. She addressed Nell, talking over Cass's head as if she wasn't there. 'She's escaped the Stockdale hooter, hasn't she? Lucky girl.'

Nell tried not to grimace. Yes, she had a nose which friends might label 'strong' and which she called two genes short of Rod Stewart's. When she was a little girl she used to fantasise about shaving her Stockdale nose so that it would be like the petite pug nosettes of the pretty girls in her class. She'd never forget the time she confided her insecurities to her mother, who'd merely shrugged and said, 'If you want to do something about it when you're older, you can, darling.' No, funnily enough, that hadn't helped.

Valerie scrutinised Nell. 'You look absolutely shattered. Bad traffic?'

'Snarled outside Bristol.' Nell kissed Valerie's cheek. It smelled familiar, reassuringly of mother; tea and cheap supermarket shampoo. Her mother's white roots were clearly visible, something Nell had never seen before. There was something worrisome about this. Valerie had been home-dying her hair for years, ever since she went grey in her early forties.

'And you're dressed for the city.' Valerie looked down, bemused, at Nell's grey Prada wedges.

'Better to be overdressed than underdressed!' Nell said chirpily, trying to be upbeat while something inside started to sink.

Valerie narrowed her eyes. 'You have a fringe!'

'You like it?'

'Aren't long hair and fringes for younger women, Nell? I thought the rules were that you went short after thirty-five.'

'The rules have changed.'

'I see,' Valerie said doubtfully. 'Well, I better bicarb the slugs off this spinach before they devour the entire crop. You'll love my spinach, Cass.'

Cass shook her head. 'I don't eat green things.'

Valerie looked disapprovingly at Nell. 'She doesn't eat green things?' She meant, 'You let her not eat green things?'

'A new developmental stage, I'm afraid. Lola Adams at nursery doesn't eat green things. And Lola's her best friend so now Cass doesn't do green things either. Don't say anything, Mum. Believe me, I've tried.'

'I've never heard such nonsense. You'll love *my* green things, Cassie, I promise.'

Cass stared down at her feet.

Valerie stooped down to Cass's height. 'Cassie, do you

want to pay a visit to Henny Penny and the hen harem while I make supper?'

'Harem?' Cass looked up at Nell quizzically. Nell winced. She'd have to try to explain that one later.

'She's still not laying, that Henny Penny,' sighed Valerie, picking a slug off a spinach leaf and flicking it away. 'A bloody useless chicken. We've had one egg from her in six months. One!'

Cass looked worried. 'Are you going to eat her, Grandma?'

Valerie smiled. 'It had crossed my mind. But I am a sentimental old thing.'

About chickens and dogs, thought Nell.

Valerie stroked Cass's hair. 'Go on, say hello to Henny Penny. Have a run about, sweetie. Get some proper oxygen in those lungs of yours.'

A dig: Nell was putting a metropolitan lifestyle before Cass's welfare and bringing her up in a smog of traffic fumes.

They watched Cass skip to the back of the garden into the dense, receding shades of green. 'Stay away from that pond, Cass,' Nell shouted after her. Some hope. All children were drawn to that black, lily-padded pond in the depths of the garden. Despite repeatedly asking Mum to fence it, she had not. Valerie didn't believe in indulging children, in the name of safety or otherwise. No, she was a great believer in the adage that 'Children learn by their mistakes.' This accounted for the fact that Ethan had enjoyed a broken leg, twisted wrist and a snapped rib, all by the age of eighteen, as well as countless bloody noses. It accounted for the fact that Nell could go out when she pleased from the age of about fourteen and become acquainted with cigarettes, Thunderbird – chased with cough medicine, obviously – and sex before she was legally allowed to drive. And it probably also accounted for the fact that Heather, who had grown up in a unchild-proofed world full of hazards, now seemed scared of anything out of her very limited comfort zone (flying, diving or being single) and was determined to live the safest life she could, which, in her case, culminated in moving to Surrey with a city lawyer.

'Come on. We need a brew,' said Valerie.

Nell hesitated, worried about the pond.

'Nell, the pond is about six centimetres deep!' said Valerie, reading her daughter's frown.

They walked down the The Path of Pain, so called because of its bordering clumps of lavender alive with tetchy bees. Through the trellis, the warped wooden gate. Nell pushed open the back door. Inside the house the temperature immediately dropped. She could feel the damp. The thickness of the walls. The depth of family history caged within them. She knew every wooden board, every telephone cable, every bloom of damp so intimately it was almost like gazing at her own body in a mirror. Nothing had changed here, nothing ever changed here, it just got older, like the rest of them. She stopped for a moment, while Valerie bustled through to the kitchen. There was a scattering of dandelion clock on the tiled hall floor near the front door, as if the garden itself was blowing in reminders of passing time. And for a moment, as she stood there in that square cornflower-blue hall, she could almost hear them as they were, shouting children, mumbling teenagers. She could see Ethan kicking a ball off the walls, knocking off Grandma's watercolours, Heather telling him off, her own younger self giggling. She could see their tiny feet poking out of the bottom of the long velvet curtains, hear the rustle of sweet wrappers as they huddled together with comforting lumps of sugar during those long 'holidays' at their grandparents while Mum would bolt herself in London, 'ill'. She smiled, remembering the time she dared Ethan to paint the living room with the absinthe-green paint they'd found in the shed while their parents were away. She pushed open the door to the sitting room. It didn't look so vivid now, although you could still see Ethan's crude brush strokes.

'Aren't you coming through, darling?' her mother called from the kitchen.

'Yes, yes. Sorry. Miles away.' She hurried through to the kitchen and was immediately struck by how dilapidated it looked too, which made her sad because the kitchen had always been the pumping heart of the house: it was in here that Grandma Penelope had mashed Mum's first foods, where Mum cooked Sunday roasts, made the nibbles for their father's wake. But now it looked tired and 'dated' as an estate agent might mutter beneath his breath, whisking his clients sharply away to a better room. The wooden worktops were warped and black behind the leaking kitchen taps, the displayed blue and white Cornish crockery looked grubby. A kitchen roll stood dangerously close to the gas hob. For some reason there was a sock on the draining board. And there was something a tad depressing about the old jam jars full of copper change, the white fridge – only people over sixty liked white fridges – the badly washed-up kitchen utensils. Nell was hit by a powerful urge to scrub it all new again. She made a mental note for the kitchen to be high up on the To Do list as soon as she'd unpacked. 'I'll make the tea, Mum. You sit down.'

Valerie looked up at her sharply, those famously bright green eyes flashing in the tanned folds of her face. 'You're speaking to me like I'm one of the girls in your office.'

'Sorry.' Was she? Cripes. 'Bad habit.' Something in her twisted. It was Friday. The girls on her desk at work would be eating Kit Kats or bags of raw almonds now, gossiping and checking the rolling afternoon news, looking forward to the weekend, making plans. Well, at least tomorrow would be Saturday. At least then no one else was working either.

'And, let's get this straight from the off, Nell, I'm not in the least incapable,' Valerie said firmly, wiping her hands on her red striped apron. 'I need a bit of a hand. Not a nursemaid.'

'I know, Mum,' Nell said softly, taking care not to use her default job voice.

'It's lovely that you want to holiday here for the summer but don't imagine you can fill Deng's shoes,' Valerie added briskly.

Nell laughed. 'I don't, Mum!'

'We'll have to muddle through, won't we?'

That clipped tone. That pulling back. It hurt every time. Nell felt a wash of sadness that Mum wasn't more grateful. No, not grateful. She didn't want gratitude, just some kind of acknowledgement that she wasn't on bleeding holiday. She sat down on one of the old wooden ladder-back chairs, its seat shiny from decades of shifting bottoms. She watched as Valerie rolled back her blouse sleeves, exposing her rounded and liver-spotted forearms, and plunged the muddy spinach into a bowl of water. An engorged slug floated to the surface. She picked it up, oozing between her fingers.

Nell looked away. She found the daily invasion of creatures in Cornwall difficult to cope with; the little grey mice that scuttled along the skirting boards, the enormous powdery moths, the wheeling mosquitoes and the armies of spiders that pranced around the baths, eyeing her up, daring her to flush them away, which she didn't, partly because she was scared they'd jump up and grab her hand in a kind of revenge suicide attack but mostly because she didn't want their death on her conscience. She was, in other words, an utterly hopeless country person in every way.

'So you've lost that job, darling,' Valerie said, dunking the spinach again, looking up.

That job? There were worse things, surely. She wasn't a corrupt banker. A grave robber. Or one of those people who employ illegal cockle pickers and pay them two pence an hour. 'Everyone's making cutbacks, Mum.'

'Well, not such a bad thing. You worked too hard, darling. Working hard doesn't suit women,' she added with the blitheness of a woman who had never had a proper career, or had to work. She'd inherited the house, so they'd been more than comfortable on Dad's salary. 'Terribly ageing. I always worried about – what is it they call it? – burnout, I think. Sounds dreadful! Ethan's been worried about you, darling. Says you've been a right stresshead.'

Thanks, bro. 'Mum, I need to work, and I want to work.'

'Well, you could be a florist.' Valerie looked up hopefully. 'Or a doctor.'

'Mum, I would be the world's worst florist. I would kill all the flowers stone dead within hours. And, hate to break it to you, but I studied anthropology, not medicine.' She looked down at her Prada shoes and was struck by how wrong they looked suddenly – out of place, flash, braying outsiders. Still, better them than her mother's gardening clogs.

'More's the pity. You could have met a nice doctor.' Valerie shook her hands dry, then filled an ancient, chipped brown teapot – a relic from Nell's own childhood – and poured milk into the mismatched mugs. Nell didn't take milk in tea, hadn't taken milk since she was about sixteen. She never quite knew if her mother did these things on purpose to get a reaction or if it was the illness.

Valerie shook out half a packet of chocolate chip biscuits on to a small floral plate. 'I see you've put on a bit, darling.'

65

'Don't say that when you're loading up a plate of biscuits!'

'If your own mother can't tell you, who can?'

'I'd rather not know, thanks all the same.' Anything to avoid a diet. The moment the word 'diet' popped up in her brain she instantly gained seven pounds.

'It's good to have a bit of fat on your cheeks as you get older.' Valerie pulled at her plump sun-freckled cheeks to emphasise the point. 'Do you remember that girl Sally Brown from your sixth form? Bumped into her the other day. *Terribly* thin around the face. Not attractive, not at all. Very horsey. A lot of those forty-something newsreaders have the same thing – what's her name, thingy from ITV?' She took a sip of tea. There were black crescents of mud under her cracked gardener's fingernails. 'Now Sophie won't have that problem, will she? There's a girl who carries a few extra pounds like a 1950s bombshell. How is dear Sophie? Any sound of wedding bells yet?'

'No. Still seeing Tom though.'

'Seeing?'

'Dating.'

'I don't understand, I really don't.' Valerie dabbed at her lips with an old linen napkin. 'Granted, it's different if you've got a child in tow, like you. *Much* harder to find a husband.'

'Maybe I don't want a husband, Mum. Radical, I know.' Hold the sarkiness, Nell told herself sternly. Mum is ill.

'Don't want a husband? Every girl wants a husband.'

'I'm not a girl, Mum. I'm thirty-seven years old!' Blood pressure rising.

'Even more pressing, then.'

Nell laughed, a high, hamster squeak of a laugh. If she didn't laugh she'd scream. If she had to listen to this all summer, she'd go round the bloody bend. She'd join a convent or something just to shut her up. She'd become a lesbian. Marry a sheep. Anything.

'You may laugh now, darling. You won't be laughing when you're in your late forties and your face is cracking faster than this kitchen ceiling. Just remember, a career won't keep you warm at night. And it won't put up shelves or fix the washing machine either.' Oh God. This was all turning out exactly as she feared. She stared determinedly out of the rain-stained kitchen windows, to the shock of green beyond; hills, trees, more trees. Green. Green. Relentless green. Like living inside a cabbage.

'A top-up?' Valerie refilled their mugs. 'Gosh, how long has it been since us two had a nice cup of tea together?' She sighed dramatically as if two world wars had passed in the interim. It had been three months. 'Now. How's the flat? Have you killed off those herbs I gave you yet?'

'No,' lied Nell. Parsley, rosemary, sage, all died long, lonely deaths.

'And what about that little painting I sent you? I bet it looks beautiful above the fireplace.' She took a bowl of pea pods from the worktop and started shelling them.

'Gorgeous.' Another lie. It was an *awful* painting, very amateur, depicting a seascape with the regulation red fishing boats. Nell had a particular aversion to bad seascapes. But she daren't give the picture away in case her mother came round and asked about its whereabouts on a visit, so it had to lurk, taking up badly needed storage space, at the top of the airing cupboard.

'I was just thrilled to pick that up at the WI fair. Three pounds, I got it for, Nell, can you believe it?'

Yes, she could, actually. She tried to wipe a streak of mud off her black jeans. Just through the door and she was muddy! God, she hated the country.

'I thought it could replace that dreadful photograph of those men in drag.' Her pea popping speeded up, became more purposeful as she warmed to her theme and the tension between them tightened.

The 'dreadful photograph' was Nell's trannies-in-back-of-New York cab signed print.

'You've got to take it down, Nell. It will put men off,' she said, popping a pea so hard it shot across the table and hit Monty on the nose.

'I don't think it's been the deal breaker yet.'

'Well, I mentioned your predicament in my round robin. You never know.'

'Mum, please don't write something like that again! *Ever*. And it's not a bloody predicament! Not having a job is a predicament!'

'There's no harm putting the word out that you're single.' Valerie shook the bowl of peas a little crossly, bundled up the empty pods, and tossed them into her rank composting bucket. 'You can't go on like this, dear.'

Nell felt the red mist descend. How long had that taken? 'What do you mean, *this*?'

'Time to settle down, Nell. You can't use Cass as an excuse forever. Or' – she raised an eyebrow – 'your job.'

'Mum . . .'

'Shoot me down for not being "modern",' she said, making annoying quote marks with her fingers, 'but the traditional family unit works.'

Nell spluttered out her mouthful of tea. Like it worked for us lot!

'Look at Heather, how happy she is now she's got a diamond ring on her finger.'

Was loss of sensitivity symptomatic of the dementia? No, Nell decided, she's always been like this. She rolled a pea

68

back and forth between her fingers. Concentrate on the pea, the round, green pea, she told herself. Breathe. But she couldn't breathe. The air felt thinner at Tredower. Like the house was perched about six thousand feet above sea level, despite being in a valley.

'If you weren't so proud and headstrong and convinced you're right when you're wrong, you could have another go at things, as Dean has done, finding that dentist. Nell, *you* could find a dentist!'

'What is it with you and dentists and doctors, Mum? I don't want to find a bloody dentist.' She groaned. 'I can't imagine anything worse! I *hate* dentists!'

Valerie shook her head. 'It's not becoming to be bitter, Nell.'

Nell slapped her forehead in exasperation. 'I meant that I don't enjoy having someone excavating my mouth. Not that I don't like Freya. I do like Freya.'

'She sounds very nice. Cass likes her, that's the most important thing. She says she's very pretty.'

'She is pretty. She is also pregnant.' Nell walked to the window and watched Cass, who was crouched near the chicken pen.

'Oh.' Valerie looked puzzled. 'Pregnant? But they're not married.'

'Mum, they married last year.' How could her mother have forgotten that? Exactly the kind of muddle the doctors had warned them about, she realised.

At that moment Cass rushed into the kitchen, pink cheeked and excited. 'Henny Penny sat on my knee. Come and see, Mummy, come and see!'

'You go, Nell,' said Valerie. 'I've got lots to be getting on with. No, no, I don't need help, not in the kitchen. Please don't fuss. Not gaga yet, am I? Just bring your bags in from

69

the car. Mind the paintwork. I've put you in Ethan's old bedroom so Cass is in the one next door.' Valerie stood up and prodded a few different buttons on her radio, looking for Classic FM. She couldn't find it and settled for Radio 3 instead. 'Right. What's the time?' She peered up at the wall clock. 'Bloody thing is running slow again. Remember that, always add twelve minutes, or you'll be permanently late. Oh, and Nell . . .'

'Yup?' Try not to sound weary.

'One other thing, darling. Heather likes the bedroom at the front. Would you mind checking that there are fresh sheets? I do find that airing cupboard tricky. Deng's domain, you see.'

Nell froze. 'Pardon?'

'All those sheets, so difficult to reach.' Valerie snapped the leafy top off a muddy carrot.

'Heather? Is Heather coming?'

'Oh, didn't I mention it?' said Valerie breezily. 'Yes, Heather and Jeremy.'

'*Jeremy?*'

'Short notice, I know. Heather's a bit late because she's been sitting for an artist, someone who draws naked pictures of ladies from behind for their husbands. Nothing tasteless, apparently; you know Heather.' She shook her head, bemused. 'She wants someone to capture her figure before she gets pregnant or some such nonsense.'

'But Mum, you should tell me these things . . .' And I wouldn't have come!

'Look, we all know I'm not going to be around for ever, darling.' Valerie gave her a stern look. 'I've told Ethan and Janet that they must come this weekend too.'

Something mischievous glinted in her eyes. 'There are things, important things, that need to be discussed.'

Eight

Under the duvet, 2.45 a.m.

Things I must accept that my mother will never understand about me:

- Why I buy Falke socks at £14 a pair rather than a multi-pack from Marks and Spencer.
- Why I return vegetable peelings to the council's recycling lorry rather than composting them in the garden in a green stinking bin or – heave – a wormery.
- Ocado. Why pay for stuff to be delivered when there is a supermarket ten minutes down the road, a trip to which offers me the chance to 'stretch my legs'?
- Why I need an icemaker on my fridge, unless I'm pretending to be American.
- Why I tell Cass I love her all the time, unless I'm pretending to be American.
- Why Cass needs a lime-green booster chair of Swedish origin rather than an old cushion on top of a normal kitchen chair.
- Why anyone would spend £200 on 'slippers', i.e., Ugg Boots.
- Why I didn't marry Jeremy while I had the chance and

consider myself 'a very lucky girl'.

- Or resort to Plan B and use the pregnancy to get Dean to marry me and consider myself 'a very lucky girl'.
- Why I avoid family get-togethers, even now, when all the water has flowed under the bridge as far as Jeremy and Heather are concerned and we all need to 'put our best foot forward'.

What I don't understand about my mother:

- Why she has firm principles about organic eggs but not about sending out defamatory, incendiary round robins to all and sundry about her daughter.
- Why she finds it so much easier to write 'Love, Mum' on a birthday card than say 'I love you.'
- Why she trusted seventeen- and eighteen-year-old au pairs from Germany and Hungary to bring up her children but will not trust a trained professional to look after her.
- How she felt when Dad had his affairs.
- How she really felt when Dad died. 'It could have been worse,' was one of her best lines. Er, like, how?
- What it really feels like to know that you are slowly going to go bonkers and then die.
- How she can bear to embrace Jeremy as her future son-in-law. Considering.

And other miscellaneous stuff that keeps me awake at night:

- Why my biggest fear is that I am turning into my mother.
- Why I sometimes see my mother in Cass and this, curiously, makes me happy.
- Why I still want her approval, even though, as she is

always reminding me, I'm three years off forty, have given birth and have five grey hairs.

- Why I am lying on a dusty old bed next to my wriggling daughter in Cornwall, rather than lying on my Tempur mattress in London next to born-in-the-eighties Pete . . .

Nine

April licked her finger and turned the last page of Elizabeth Gilbert's *Eat, Pray, Love*, wishing she hadn't got to the end already. Why hadn't she done a Gilbert, even a Gilbert-lite, chanted and eaten and fucked her way round the world, *before* settling down? But she'd always been in such a hurry. She'd wanted marriage and babies since she was a little girl and had settled early, compared to her more dynamic contemporaries, with her teenage sweetheart. It was only now that she'd begun to question her choices. In fact, she'd begun to question everything since her mother had died. No, she couldn't do a Gilbert. But she could do *this*. April flexed her toes in her once white, now scuffed grey, plimsolls. Her body was stiff from sitting in the cramped train seat – five hours already – and bloated from snacking on Maltesers – family pack, shame on her – and four terrible cups of Great Western tea. It hadn't helped that she'd got a bit of a bum seat, in the middle of a loud, noisy family with two squabbling kids and a crying baby. She'd felt sorry for the mother, poor harassed thing, and had offered to jiggle the baby on her knee to give her a break, rather hoping she'd refuse the offer as people usually do. This one didn't. Boy, did that baby have a good pair of lungs! Every time he howled it brought those befuddled baby days back in vivid acoustic detail and she wondered how on earth Beth, barely out of childhood herself, and Duncan, ditto, would cope. On the other hand, the baby also smelt deliciously of maple syrup and he was such a soothing, warm, dense lump on her knee. Anyway, she'd since learned that those noisy, sleep-deprived early years weren't the hardest. She'd take a cross baby over a stroppy teenager any day. And she'd rather listen to a screaming baby than her own baby boy – albeit a twenty-year-old one – having sex with his girlfriend in the bedroom next door.

Wiping crumbs off her jeans, she gazed out of the window at the view rushing past. It seemed so familiar, probably from those episodes of *Coast* which she'd re-watched endlessly. (She had a crush on that grumpy soft-spoken Scot with the long, dark, medieval hair.) She wasn't sure when she'd last been to Cornwall in person, if ever. They'd never taken the kids to Cornwall, on account of Chris's parents' place in Devon, which was nearer, free and came with willing baby-sitters. While her own parents had always gone to Ilfracombe with the Gullivers from Aylesbury, because they had a daughter her own age, and Mum had always tried to compensate for her being an only child by holidaying with the rather dull Gullivers. April licked the last smear of Malteser chocolate off her little finger. The chocolate tasted junky, too sweet now, nothing like those first few delicious mouthfuls. Funny how too much of anything made you lose a taste for it. Well, everything apart from a nice cold glass of wine, obviously.

There was a grinding noise as the train began to slow on the track. They were stopping? Already? Despite having sat there for hours she was, of course, now totally unprepared for her arrival. She scrambled to get all her things together – how was it possible to lose so many things in one square foot of seat space? – and rummaged through her handbag for her hairbrush, combing out her long hair – hardly a crowning glory, but her new highlights were pretty – guided by her reflection in the train window. Seeing herself in such an unfamiliar mirror was a jolt. She had mirrors she favoured at home – the tinted, elongating ones – and ways of angling her head and pouting her mouth that were more flattering than others. But straight on like this? Just another forty-something woman with highlights wearing Boden, she realised with a heavy heart.

The train screeched to a stop at Penzance station. With her over-stuffed red holdall at her feet, April sat on a wooden bench outside the station to consult the large map that wouldn't unfold properly and flapped flamboyantly in the wind like a flag saying, 'confused tourist!' She dug into her jeans' pocket and with some effort yanked out the page of notepaper with the name and address of the B. & B. that she'd booked last month, a little cavalierly. She prayed it wasn't a complete fleapit.

The street was narrow and smelled of chips. The B. & B. was an old fisherman's cottage with wobbly whitewashed walls. No sea views, of course, not for that price. But once inside she was pleased to see it was clean – she was a stickler for clean, when it came to foreign beds, you never knew who'd been there before you – if a little damp; more than adequate for its purpose. The room was small, as the landlady had warned her. But it had a fantastic desk for sketching, as promised. And the bed had some bounce. She sat down on the skiddy floral eiderdown, trying to take in the fact she was here, alone, in Cornwall! Gosh. She'd actually done it.

Feeling like a teenager away from home for the first time, she dutifully called Chris, disturbing his supper of boiled eggs, pitta bread and lager, bless, then Dad in Spain, instructing him to phone Beth every other day so that she didn't feel neglected. She texted her best friend Mandy – 'The mid-life crisis quest begins! Say hi to book group' – who also had an instruction to keep a beady eye out for Beth, then unpacked her clothes, hanging them up on those maddening fixed hangers. (Who were these people who nicked hangers?) When she saw the hotchpotch of clothes hanging up, it became clear that, somehow, she'd managed to pick out everything in her wardrobe that didn't actually go with anything else.

Curious about the rest of the B. & B., April clattered down some narrow stairs to the lobby and through a creaky blue door into the patio garden, which was tiny but idyllic, with heavenly lilac wisteria draping from the bulging whitewashed stone walls. A row of spiky palms in pots, a mossy garden-centre Greek goddess statue. She took a deep inhalation of the scented air. Sea. A breath of sea. And maybe chips. She smiled. This was, she realised, the first time she'd been away on her own for *years*, if not ever. Relishing not having to ask anyone else what they wanted to order first, she ordered a cream tea from Joy, the proprietor – a bustling, jolly woman in her sixties who looked like she'd ingested many cream teas in her time – and happily unfolded her map of Cornwall.

'Can I get you some more?' asked Joy, waddling over the moment the last mouthful of scone hit her stomach.

She felt herself flush – it was weirdly embarrassing being waited on when you were on your own – and was tempted to order more just to avoid hurting Joy's feelings, but, no, that was ridiculous. 'I really shouldn't. But they're completely delicious, though, thank you, thank you very much.'

'The weather's going to turn,' said Joy with authority, not looking like she had anything more pressing to attend to. 'I'd take your anorak when you go out, if I were you.'

April glanced up at the sky. It was blue directly ahead but clustered with ominous grey clouds to the east. A little part of her was secretly relieved that the weather was going to cool. She found hot-weather dressing stressful. Hers was not a holiday body.

'Going to the beach, are you?' Joy stared at her, sizing her up, as if trying to work out what she was doing here on her own. She glanced down at her left hand checking out April's wedding ring. 'Making the most of the sunshine?'

April hesitated. Where *was* she going right now? She didn't need to enrol on the art course until tomorrow. And . . . yes, a beach would delay the inevitable a little bit. 'Yes! Yes, I am.' She pointed to a small wedge of yellow on her map near the house she'd marked with a cross in red Biro. 'This beach, is it nice?'

The landlady bent over the table and squinted. April recognised her cakey smell: self-raising flour, caster sugar.

'Oh, that's Perranortho Bay, that is,' said Joy, stabbing a pink finger at April's map. 'Lovely, bit off the beaten track, mind. But you won't get the crowds there.'

'Sounds perfect.' April dug into her handbag for her purse. Did she pay now? She was hit by a wave of social clumsiness.

'I'll put it all on your bill, don't you worry,' said Joy, patting her shoulder in a manner that felt slightly invasive. 'You have a nice time, now. And don't forget that anorak!'

No one would forget April's anorak. It was an unforgiving bright orange with neon yellow elbow patches and a giant hood – there hadn't been a great choice in the women's section at Millets. Staring at herself in the bedroom's wonky mirror, she noticed that the orange anorak gave her skin a strange satsumaish hue, a look not helped by the fact that her hair had started to frizz into curls in the damp air. She attacked it with a hairbrush then pulled on her tan leather sandals, swung a small, red nylon rucksack – a freebie from the local gym she never attended, put to use at last! – over her shoulder, and set off purposely to the bus stop on the promenade.

Even the buses seemed to go slower here – well, until they took a hairpin bend, a manoeuvre that for some reason made the driver recklessly speed up. She stared intently out of the bus window, trying to pull the Cornish seasidey details deep inside of her for ever so that she had a surplus in case she never returned; the random smells of fish, some fresh, some rotting, the peaty bonfire smoke, the diva calls of those shockingly massive seagulls, the clouds of dreamy hydrangeas, even the endless squashed rabbits. She didn't want to miss anything, not a bit. Finally, the bus dropped her in a small village where she could smell the sea even more strongly and, tantalisingly, could taste salt on her lips. Feeling free and adventurous, she followed the signs to the bay, down a narrow lane fluttering with butterflies that looked like those kind of fancy hair accessories you'd wear to a wedding. It went on a long way. And she needed to pee. Just when she thought she'd taken a wrong turn and was considering squatting in the hedgerows to relieve herself, she reached a small car park, and, thank goodness, toilets. (It's all very well being free and adventurous, but a woman needs toilets.) There was also a little café – a cute wooden shack painted blue, like something from a fashion shoot in a magazine – and a sloping stone slipway that led to . . . a most glorious beach! Heaven.

'Oops, sorry!' A woman knocked against her as she hurtled past, hand in hand with a little girl, a little slip of a blond thing in a wet suit, and a jumpy brown labrador. The woman's face was obscured by enormous white sunglasses and a billowing swathe of leopard-print scarf. Incongruously glamorous, April thought, watching her running and skidding down the slipway towards the beach, trailing a tail of scarf. She waited to create a polite distance.

Watching them recede into the distance, April sat down on the slipway wall beside the beach, slipped off her sandals, and swung them in her hand. She wanted to be earthed. To her delight, just as her bare foot touched the soft, marshy sand, the sun came out blazing. It was like stepping on a light switch! She walked on a few paces before turning to admire the short trail of her footprints in the sand. Like those babies'-feet plaster mementoes, they were proof that she'd arrived.

Ten

Nell climbed up to the highest rock she could find, whirled her iPhone in a figure of eight in the air, trying to scoop up any low-flying phone signals. Just when she'd almost given up . . . Ping! Result! She glanced at her phone excitedly. Four new emails. Four! She sat down on to the rock and opened them up excitedly. Two sweet 'miss you' emails from Sue and Kathy, two old colleagues. A forwarded invite to an Anya Hindmarch sample sale from gay Dave on the fashion desk. Something from her bank, or a crook pretending to be her bank. Nothing from Pete. And, glaringly, no one begging her to come back to work, telling her they'd made a terrible mistake, or even asking her to freelance. Dispirited, she shoved the phone back into her handbag and her mind instantly snapped like an elastic band to Jeremy and Heather. She wondered where they were, imagining their slow trail through the country marked by red pin flags like the march of an invading army on a military map. Bristol? Bude? Mumbai would be preferable. God, she could kill her mother sometimes. (A lot of the time.) Why on earth didn't she warn her?

It had been five years. The old wounds should have healed and sealed. She'd tried hard, so bloody hard, to un-forget Jeremy. But she still remembered how they used to make love

– he liked her sitting down on the bed, him standing, pushing into her, because this masked the disparity in their heights. She remembered the exact groan he made when he came, somewhere between a wolf growling and a washing machine coming to the end of its cycle. She remembered his laugh, his jokes, their private jokes, his taste in books – thrillers, wine guides, political memoirs – and telly – *Newsnight, Have I Got News for You, Later with Jools Holland* – the way he liked his coffee (black, one brown sugar) and the way he always used to break wind in the shower, thinking that she couldn't hear him over the hiss of water. (She could.) But most of all she remembered the way he always used to call her 'the missus', when with his mates, which in hindsight took irony to a whole new level, considering he was about to get hitched to her sister.

A shaft of dazzling sunlight swung across Perranortho Bay like a ship's boom, jolting her out of her thoughts. Nell adjusted her sunglasses and squinted towards the horizon. Cass was carefully paddling along the frill of the shoreline – she was nervous of the sea – and pulling an enormous plume of seaweed behind her, a silhouette in her black wetsuit. Monty was trying to hump the seaweed.

Nell waved, happy to see Cass on a beach, rather than a sandpit in an inner-city playground. And it really was a wonderful beach for children with its rock pools and caves and massive sands at low tide. Even she'd loved it as a moody teenager, particularly in winter when the wind and the bleak colour palate reflected her own state of mind and gave her a dramatic elemental stage-set for a bit of navel gazing, as well as lending her hair a grungy texture that no Superdrug hair mousse could ever replicate. For a moment she could almost see her seventeen-year-old self walking down the beach, blowing out puffs of Marlboro Lights, glancing back at her as she was now – thirty-seven, a mum – and not registering her. Back then nobody over the age of twenty-five registered. And mums were particularly yawnsome.

The bay hadn't changed much. It was still mercifully free of the crowds. The area's tourists decamped with their windbreaks and frisbees to nearby Marazion. Only the more knowledgeable ones, seasoned surfers and locals, came that extra few miles down those narrow winding lanes to the bay. The crashing surf and riptides helped too, swallowing the sweep of beach whole at high tide and with it the possibility of picnics and sunbathing. So it remained underdeveloped, a little wild, refusing to tow the 'family fun' line. There was no coach park, no bucket and spade shop, just toilets, inconveniently far from the beach, a small car park where you frequently got boxed in, and the shark-blue shack café with seating in the bracing outside only. It did good coffee and good cake. And that was what mattered. In fact, she'd kill for a latte right now.

'Cass!' she called again, but her voice was blown off course by the wind. Tying up her leopard-print career-rebound scarf, which, she'd realised, itched – scarves that cost a hundred and thirty pounds were not meant to itch! – she ran towards Cass in her bare feet. 'Ice cream?'

'Yes, please!' Sand and salt twinkled like glitter on the tips of Cass's lashes.

'Come on, beautiful. Let's hit the café. Monty, get off, you sodden old mutt!' She gave the dog a nudge with her foot. She swore he understood the words, 'ice cream' too.

In the café garden 'Rhythm is a Mystery' – an old rave anthem from the early nineties – was playing, setting the pace for the toe tapping of the clientele in the garden: a table of surfers, a family with two blue-lipped boys eating ice creams, and a solitary lady in a bright orange anorak eating an extremely large piece of chocolate cake, her tangle of thick blondish hair alive in the wind, obscuring her face. Yes, it looked like the lady she'd nearly trampled on the slipway.

Nell and Cass sat right at the back of the garden, cuddled up on the old oak bench beneath the pine tree where blue tits and other teeny brown birds clustered in its dense branches to shelter from the wind. Cass concentrated on licking her vanilla ice cream. Nell sipped her coffee, looking up through the branches of the tree at the capricious sky. She rubbed her arms. Where was global warming when you needed it?

'It'll blow over as soon as it's got this little number out of its system.'

Pardon? She glanced at the man warily. He was tall, scruffy, lightly bearded in the manner of a pop star who wanted to be taken seriously. Hard to age. Early forties, maybe? His shaggy hair – brown, bleached bright blond at the tips, surfer-style – resembled an old string mop head that had dried in the sun. He was wearing an orange fleece that made her eyes hurt, mirrored Ray-Ban sunglasses on a cord around his neck, knackered blue jeans belted with what appeared to be a bit of string. Only in Cornwall.

'I hope you're right.' She smiled tightly and clipped her voice so that he didn't take her response as an invitation to chat.

'Do you mind if I sit down?' He smiled at her, a boyish grin, a bit lopsided. His teeth looked very white against the deep tan of his face, the kind of deep tan that only surfers or sailors ever achieved.

Attractive or not? Not. Too many teeth. Scraggy. He reminded her of someone, though. Something to do with the long limbs, the gangliness combined with his general largeness of scale. Those hands were like frisbees. She'd got it! The BFG. The Roald Dahl character. 'Not at all,' she said, minding quite a lot as she shuffled along the bench.

Monty watched him intently with his chocolate-button eyes, head on paws, one ear cocked up. The man started to smoke a thin, hand-rolled cigarette. He kept trying to blow the smoke away from her and Cass but the wind kept blowing it back again. Nell couldn't help but smile. You couldn't pee into the wind. You couldn't smoke into it either. Did this man know nothing?

'I give up.' There was a sizzle as he dunked the cigarette into his paper coffee cup. 'Sorry to blow fumes in your faces.'

'We're almost done anyway.' She drained her coffee. She wasn't going to hang around.

'Come down from London, have you?'

'Is it that obvious?' She couldn't help but be pleased that she'd been identified so easily. She would have been a bit concerned if he'd asked her if she came from Redruth.

'You've dropped your Oyster card.'

'Oh, right,' she said feeling silly. Clocking that her handbag had come unzipped, she bent down to pick up the yellow plastic pouch. Now that she was on shoe-level she noticed he was wearing Converse trainers, bright canary-yellow Converse. She felt a ruffle of curiosity. The only thing a local man might wear in canary-yellow was an anorak or a life jacket. Still, he was wearing a fleece, very Cornish. And his belt was definitely a bit of string, which suggested native, or perhaps wannabe native, which was worse.

The man's feet twitched, as if they knew they were being sized up. 'They're the wrong colour, aren't they?'

Nell smiled. 'Makes a change from the ubiquitous black ones.'

He tapped his foot in time to the music, the yellow left foot waggling up and down like a giant banana. 'Oh yes, I was being purposely fashionably individual, rather than just buying the last pair in the shop in my humungous size.'

Humungous. Nell tried not to think about that old adage about men with big feet.

Oh no, Monty was starting to eye them up now. That was all she needed.

'Your shoes look like boats,' said Cass matter-of-factly, drilling the point home.

'Lifeboats?' laughed the man.

Cass shrugged. 'Just boats.'

He laughed again. It was actually a nice laugh, not a loon laugh, but the kind of laugh she imagined would be the same if he'd known you all his life or for five minutes.

'It's raining, Mummy!' Cass cupped her hands to catch the raindrops. 'Can we go home?'

Sure enough fine droplets of rain had begun to fall in a fine mist, like a collapsing cloud. She turned to the man. 'Your weather predictions were wrong, I'm afraid.' She couldn't resist. 'Come on, Cass, time to hit the road.'

'I'm never wrong.' He grinned as they started to walk away. 'Apart from when it comes to shoes.'

Nell got to the car park just as the rain came down harder, much harder. She dug into her handbag for her key. Not there. She dug into every pouch, every blasted concealed zipper that added so much to the cost of these bags. Not there. Fuck.

'What's the matter, Mummy?'

'I appear to have lost my car key, Cass,' she said with a calmness she didn't feel. It was the voice she'd honed in journalism, a good tone for breaking the news to editors when big stories had fallen through.

'Are you sure?' Cass looked worried. She was not a child who thrived on the unpredictable or unexpected. And the rain was cold. 'Then how will we get back to Grandma's?'

'We'll find them. Come on, let's retrace our steps. They must be in the café, where I dropped the Oyster card.'

'But it's raining.'

'We'll put on your anorak.'

'It's in the car.'

'Have this, honey.' She pulled off her denim jacket and slung it over Cass's tiny little shoulders, and they ran through the rain back to the café. The only customer left was the solitary lady in the orange anorak who was holding a yellow stripy umbrella above her head and staring up at the pine tree, mesmerised by the birds in its branches. No sign of the goddamn key!

'The beach,' Nell declared, trying to sound confident for Cass's sake, but knowing it would be easier to find a seal sunbathing than a key. The tide was coming in fast now. 'It's got that little orange fluoro key-ring on it. Do you remember that, Cass? That's what you need to look for; a little fleck of orange in the sand. The colour of . . . of an orange Fruit Shoot.'

'But it's raining, Mummy. I'm cold.'

'Come on, let's pretend that we've been swimming in the sea. If we'd been swimming in the sea, we'd be wet and cold. But we wouldn't mind, would we?'

Cass looked at her like she was mad. 'I would.'

'Luckily you're wearing a wet suit, Cass.'

Unluckily she wasn't. The rain had sodden her white gossamer-thin T-shirt and it had gone transparent, revealing two formidable D cups of her flesh-coloured bra. Her shoes were ruined. Her dry-clean-only scarf sat like a wet towel around her neck and her eyes stung with streaking mascara. There was a crack. Out at sea the sky flashed halogen yellow.

'Thunder!' shouted Cass. Her bottom lip started to quiver.

'One last look, sweetheart.' Hand in hand, they ran the stretch of the beach to where Cass had been playing with the seaweed earlier. Nothing. Then a frill of waves reclaimed the sand around their feet, a big, wet, salty kiss goodbye to her shoes. She miserably plumped down on a rock. She'd been defeated by her job. By her mother. Now by her car key. 'OK, it's a plan B situation, Cass. I'll phone a taxi.'

'Look!' said Cass, pointing to the top of the beach. A figure was pounding down the slipway. 'Someone's coming!'

Nell recognised the yellow shoes immediately. He was running towards them, all flying limbs and hair. When he reached them, Monty jumped up at him excitedly, leaving sandy paw prints on his jeans. 'Looking for this?' He held out the key.

'I am! Thank you so much!'

He wiped the rain out of his eyes and grinned. 'Hopefully, I've saved one more marital honey-I-lost-the-car-key row. You'd be surprised how often it happens.'

'I'm not married, actually,' said Nell quickly, too quickly. 'Where did you find it?'

'A nice lady handed it in.'

Nell looked at him blankly. 'Handed it in where?'

'To my caff,' he said, nodding towards the cliff side.

'*Your* caff? I thought—'

He stuck out his frisbee hand. 'Michael.'

'Nell.' She caught his eyes flickering over her top and, realising immediately what he couldn't help but look at, crossed her arms over her chest. 'I'm so grateful. But I thought Tom owned the café, Tom Willis? His wife ran it, a lady called Sheila?'

'They emigrated to Canada last year and sold it to me.'

'Oh right.' Nell wondered what kind of man would want to run a glorified shed on a beach. Then she reminded herself that it was a job and people needed to work in Cornwall; there wasn't much of it about. And that she shouldn't be snooty because she didn't have a job at all.

'You know this beach, then?'

Nell noticed his eyes were shadowy grey-blue, much like the sea. 'Moved here when I was sixteen.' She smiled. 'Left as soon as I could. Not a very long episode.'

Cass pulled on her hand. 'Can we go now?'

'You're from London too?' Nell asked. Oh no, it had started happening! She was doing that Cornish thing of initiating conversations with strangers. She must stop it at once.

'How did you know? Is it my shoes?'

'You recognised my Oyster card.'

'Ah, yes.'

'*Mum*,' hissed Cass, pulling on her hand again. 'Can we go? The sea's coming in.'

Nell looked down to see the waves creeping up on them again.

'We'd all be swept away if someone sensible wasn't keeping an eye out,' said Michael to Cass.

Cass shyly looked away. They walked up to the slipway together. As they reached the main path and the entrance to the café, the sky cleared and a bright sun blazed.

Michael winked at Nell. 'Sunshine. My weather predictions were correct you see.'

'For now.' Nell smiled. 'Is the lady who found my keys still here? I really must thank her.'

Michael looked around, scratched his mop. 'Nah, looks like she's gone. I think that's her walking up the lane. Yes, it is.' He pointed to the woman Nell had seen earlier in the orange anorak, the one she'd collided with on the slipway. She was walking away from them. Then she turned a corner and was gone.

'Michael.' They were interrupted by a pretty girl with a nose ring. 'The wife's on the phone.'

'I've got to go too,' said Nell quickly. So he was married. Aha. She should have guessed. Seagulls outnumbered single men by a ratio of about a thousand to one in Cornwall. 'Thanks, again.' She and Cass walked back up the lane, steaming in the sun.

'Look who it is, Mum!' squealed Cass, pulling on her sleeve and pointing towards the car park.

Nell froze. A woman was leaning against her Mini, bum resting on the bonnet. White dress with a poppy print. Matching red sandals, the kind of large tortoiseshell shades that were once the preserve of fashionistas and now did a roaring trade at Next. Oh God. It couldn't be?

Eleven

The sight of her sister, so little and blond and so shockingly familiar, floored Nell. For one terrible moment she thought she might cry. She glanced around uneasily. Where was Jeremy?

'Hi.' Heather squinted and smiled, studying Nell's face for something. She pulled her raffia bag over her small, toned shoulder.

'Hi.'

There was a long pause of awkwardness, made more awkward by the fact that they both knew that their awkwardness was a post-Jeremy phenomena. Before that they'd always been thoughtlessly physical, holding hands as little girls, hugging easily as adults. Nell felt strained and self-conscious, as if they were both being watched and judged by the God of correct sisterly conduct.

'Mum said you were here.' A flush stole over Heather's collarbone. She was smiling so hard it made her neck go sinewy. Yes, she was clearly uncomfortable. (As she should be.) And for all her grooming, she looked tired. (Good!)

'We arrived a bit early and . . . I . . . I thought it might be nice to, you know, meet before we . . .' Heather hesitated. 'Jeremy's having a lie down at Tredower after the drive,' she explained quickly.

Nell relaxed a little. 'You've lost a load of weight,' she said, directing them away from the quicksand topic of Jeremy on to the safer ground of weight loss.

'I've been training.' Heather tucked her shiny curtain of blond hair behind her ear. 'Running, actually.'

'Running?' Jeremy must have got her into it. He was a runner. An image of them running alongside each other hand in hand like one of those annoying marathon couples in matching charity T-shirts flashed through her mind. 'Wow.'

'Gosh, doesn't Cass look like Mum? Those lovely big green eyes.'

Cass curled one foot behind the other. 'I go to big school in September, Aunty Heather.'

'That's totally amazing!' Heather fingered her dress. Nell noticed that her nails were manicured in a tasteful shade of nude. Annoying. 'And you look well, Nell. Love the fringe.'

'Thanks.' Nell smiled. 'I don't think the fringe loves the salt air though.' Heather laughed. A crashing silence. Someone needed to lead the situation before the subject of Jeremy popped up in the conversation again. 'Um, we were just heading back, actually.'

'Oh, no, really?' Heather's face fell. 'I guess I got here a bit too late.'

'Afraid so.' The words hung there, inescapably loaded.

'Not even a little stroll along the coast path before we head back?' Heather cocked her head on one side and Nell knew she was trying to charm her. 'Please.'

'Come on, Mum,' chirped Cass, tugging at her hand and making it impossible to refuse. 'Let's go with Aunty Heather. It's sunny now.'

The small, stone-strewn path weaved up the cliff on such a sharp gradient it made their thigh muscles burn immediately. Walking up into the windy horizon was just what was needed, Nell realised; much less intense than sitting on a sofa facing each other over a deathly cup of tea. 'How's life?' Nell panted as she skidded in her impractical sea-sodden sandals.

'We've done our kitchen.'

That wasn't the question! Or maybe it was. Maybe when you settled in the 'burbs your wellbeing depended on the grade of your Poggenpohl kitchen.

Heather stopped to catch her breath, holding her straw hat on her head in the wind. 'And we're in the last stages of the loft, too. We've done that since we, last, um, spoke.'

That meant five bedrooms. Nell couldn't help but compare that with her own two-bedroomed flat. Why on earth did they need *five* bedrooms?

'I never imagined I'd live in such a big house,' said Heather apologetically, digging herself in deeper. 'It's silly really.'

Yes it was! Nell couldn't look at her. She hated her furiously at this moment, hated her all the more for remembering how much she also loved her.

They were near the peak of the cliff top now. Immediately below them was an angry spit hole where waves collided and smashed. They used to come here as teenagers to escape their parents. Armed with a big family bar of Dairy Milk and a couple of cans of Diet Coke (they never saw the calorific contradiction) they'd hurtle up the path with the speed and carelessness of youth and sit right here, feet dangling dangerously into the spit hole, giggling and gorging on chocolate and discussing their romantic futures, the only future that mattered, obviously.

Heather hungered after the suburban, even at the age of twelve though they didn't have the word for it then. For her marriage was always *the* happy ending, despite all the evidence to the contrary helpfully provided by their parents. Her perfect man? She had posters of a-ha's Morten Harket on her bedroom wall.

Nell's walls were covered with pictures of The Doors' late Jim Morrison, perfectly rugged, perfectly dead, so he couldn't go on and disappoint anyone and grow a pot belly or enter *The Eurovision Song Contest*. The perfect man whom Nell sketched out would do 'something creative', and frequent dimly lit clubs where people smoked and talked about books. He'd agree with her that marriage was a sham cooked up by oppressing traditionalists but would want to marry her anyway.

All of which begged two questions. Had they both seen entirely different things in Jeremy? And what exactly had Jeremy seen in each of them?

Heather shielded her eyes from the sun with her hand and looked at her intently. She seemed thinner, smaller up here, like a small flightless bird the wind might pick up and blow off the side of the cliff. 'Nell. I . . .'

Nell could tell from the tone of her voice what was coming and wanted the conversation over as quickly as possible. She stared determinedly out to sea, smiling benignly but refusing to meet Heather's eye.

'I really appreciate you coming down to look after Mum this summer. We all do.'

Nell shrugged. 'Someone had to do it.'

'I think we need to pull together now, don't we? What, well, with you being down here . . .' She smiled nervously and ruffled Monty's ears. 'You're not going to be able to avoid me and Jeremy much longer, are you?'

Nell's internal Jeremy sonar was screaming at high pitch. She could sense he was near. Taking a deep breath, she walked towards the house into the white noise. And there he was.

Back to her. Pink shirt. (She'd always secretly feared that he might turn into the type of man who wore pink shirts.) His stocky, short – five foot eight – frame was outlined in the bulge of a deckchair; small, tight buttock cheeks, the spine of his back like a row of buttons, those tense square shoulders which he bulked up at the gym to compensate for his low stature. He had all the male Napoleon-complex insecurities and alpha male posturing that came with it. OK, he was still bloody handsome, no denying it – he and Heather made a pretty pair – but satisfyingly, she couldn't help but note that he'd lost some of his seal-black hair since she had last seen him; the skin on his olive-skinned temples gleamed in the sunshine like the sides of a helmet. He was also wearing stiff bright blue jeans. Jeremy Clarkson denim! How the mighty had fallen. No, she didn't want him. Of course not. But something deep inside her responded to him nonetheless. He would never be neutral. Just a brother-in-law. Damn. Her stomach knotted tighter.

Jeremy caracoled round as if he recognised Nell's step on the paved path. 'Hey!' That brilliant white smile. Those terrible jeans.

'Hey,' she replied and blushed.

He stood up. And she was aware of her height again, as she always had been with him, upsetting the dynamic of their relationship with that extra inch. Jeremy initiated a kiss, and because she jerked nervously and because of the disparity in their heights, he missed the benign spot on her cheek and the kiss landed too close to Nell's mouth, his soft lower lip skating over the corner of hers. They both leapt back. Jeremy tried to hide the faux pas by standing with his legs wide apart like a compass. All awful, made more awful by the knowledge that everyone was watching.

Something began to ring in her handbag. 'My phone?' she

stuttered in disbelief. A signal! She'd caught a signal. She loved her phone so much at this moment that she could have married it.

'Your phone,' he repeated.

'Excuse me.' She flung herself behind a bushy hedge of rosemary. No number was showing up. But she didn't even care if it was an insurance company doing a survey. She'd be delighted to answer all their questions. 'Hello?'

'Stressed?'

'Sophie!'

'Just phoning to see how the odyssey is going.'

'Well, I haven't thrown myself off a cliff. Yet.'

Sophie laughed. 'And how's your lovely ma?'

'Surprisingly well, actually. No more nuts than usual.' Nell lowered her voice. 'But you won't guess what she's gone and done this time? She's only invited Heather and Jeremy for the weekend!'

'Oh. My. God. That's going to be interesting. Ooh, would love to be a fly on the wall.'

'Be my fly. My mosquito. Anything. Come, please, Sophie. Bring The Shagster if you like.'

'I'd love to. But I've got a date in his gypsy caravan in a boggy Welsh field. We're heading up there this afternoon.'

'Can't you wheel the caravan down the M5 or something instead?'

'Unlikely, considering the caravan hasn't actually moved off that field in eight years and is missing a wheel. We sleep on a slope, Nell. Ever tried having sex on a slope? It gives you motion sickness.'

Nell suddenly missed Sophie tremendously. Not only did she miss Sophie, but she also missed everything she represented: London; cold white wine drunk on Sophie's sun-warmed patio; the slick, witty people she knew; the fast urban life that stopped you getting too morose and made you look forward rather than backwards; work; hell, the smell of traffic pollution in the morning; the parade of snarling staffies on the overcrowded pavements like an urban parody of Crufts. Anything but this.

'Oh, by the way,' Sophie added, 'Pete emailed *me*!'

'Pete?' Nell frowned, puzzled. 'My Pete?

'Your Pete. Very odd. He had obviously tracked me down through our Ladbroke Grove party friends. Just thought I'd mention it. I know you aren't *at all* interested in taking things further.'

'Really? What did he want?' Nell clamped the phone harder against her ear.

'Your email address, of course. He'd tried to phone you a couple of times yesterday but hadn't managed to get reception.'

Committing to their state of non-commitment! She was oddly touched.

Nell heard her mother calling from the other side of the hedge. 'Nell! Nell! Can you hear me? I need you and Heather to finish popping those peas.'

Nell held the phone up in the direction of her mother's voice. 'See what you're missing?'

'Pop those peas, babe.'

'I need a pea shooter, preferably one that fires fifty rounds a second.'

'Go, Nell! Go get them between the eyes.'

Twelve

Nell was tempted to use her officious work voice. She knew it was still in her somewhere. Although she wasn't convinced that her little nephews, Nat and Cosmo, would respond to it. They probably wouldn't respond to the bark of a military general. So she bit her tongue and wondered how long it would be until someone else – a parent would be the obvious choice – said something about the twins' behaviour at the meal table.

Nat kicked Cosmo hard on the shin. Cosmo yelped, flicked his fork and splattered gravy across his twin's cheek. Monty, who'd been hoovering up crumbs beneath their feet, took refuge beneath the table. Cass stared in shy awe. Still no one said anything. No, the twins' bad behaviour would be tolerated until Queen Janet, and only Queen Janet, acknowledged it as more than boyish high spirits and would, perhaps, discipline them in a way that did not damage their self-esteem.

Nat escalated the provocation, leaping up on to the long oak dining table and running its length in bare feet, kicking up bread rolls, padding through a dish of olive oil, before Cosmo grabbed his foot with his right hand, held it fast and stabbed his ankle with a fork. Cass watched open mouthed.

'Ethan,' mouthed Janet, eyes flashing. 'The boys.'

Ethan fortified himself with a gulp of red wine and then bellowed, 'Get down, Nat. Now!'

Nat giggled and kicked Cosmo with his bare foot. Cosmo plunged the fork into him once again. Nat yelped.

'Boys!' said Janet firmly, without shouting. The strings of gold necklaces shook like cutlasses over her ample cleavage. 'I do not want to have to tell you off, do I?' Her voice was barely a whisper. Chastened, Nat got down. Cosmo withdrew his torture implement.

'Thank you,' said Janet, shooting a hard glance at Ethan. Nell couldn't help but wonder what her brother had done to deserve that skewer of a look. She felt a flash of protectiveness. However annoying Ethan was – pretty bloody annoying, actually – he was still her big brother, childhood comrade in the dark times, someone who *understood*. OK, he'd had a history of 'going off the rails', as the family called it. Incidences involving drugs and minor skirmishes with the law and AWOL 'gap months' in India when he was in his early twenties. But Janet had worked wonders, rehabilitating Ethan from a non-committal womaniser and adrenaline junky to a husband and dad of irrepressible twin boys six years ago. True, he sometimes kicked against it, like the time he sold the family estate car and bought a Porsche in a thirty-fifth-birthday identity crisis. Or the time he disappeared on a coke-fuelled bender on a stag do in Ibiza and turned his phone off. But fatherhood – the responsibility of his own family, as opposed to playing the lovable rogue in his old one – had shocked him into behaving. He'd even stopped smoking and started eating German muesli.

Still, things seemed tense between them at the moment, Nell decided. Something crackled and not in a good way. Janet had shot him quite a few evils over the buttered beans. She looked cross. It was that silent, killer type of marital

99

crossness, the protruding part of a giant submerged iceberg. She masked it well, of course, with her lovely, soft voice honed to rich depths by years of ashtanga yoga breathing exercises. And that face.

Janet had the kind of face that you might find dreamily staring out from a 1970s soft-rock album cover: high cheekbones, clean jaw, freckles and streaky blond luxe-hippy hair parted in the middle like the pages of the glossy fashion magazines Janet used to work on in her twenties. (Nell suspected that beneath it all she was as ambitious and steely as any coiffed North London pushy banker's wife.)

Everyone agreed Ethan had miraculously lucked out in snaring Janet. Not only was Janet beautiful – all of Ethan's girlfriends were beautiful – but she also had substance. She ran her own business with a friend, a small eco gift catalogue called Muffin that stocked, among other things, fifteen varieties of hemp cloth bags in tasteful shades of taupe. She was a one-woman crusade for localised, carbon-free living. There was the small problem of her penchant for foreign holidays – cue much off-setting and donations to dodgy tree planting schemes in the Amazon – and the rather too visible ideological inconvenience of the family's four-by-four. But she donated 4 per cent of her business profits – this got Nell every time, couldn't she at least round it up to 5 per cent? – to organic rice farms in Sri Lanka. Her vision was global.

So why was this quite so annoying?

Nell *tried* not to find Janet annoying. She admired her – her recycling put her to shame. She respected her – hats off to any mother of twins who managed to look like Sarah Jessica Parker's prettier sister. And she had domesticated Ethan, where every other woman had failed. But somehow Janet was not a girl's girl, not the kind of woman one could trust with the shorthand of rules that proper girlfriends or, Nell thought, good sisters-in-laws abided by: thou shalt not say your sister-in-law looks tired; thou shall not always take your mother-in-law's side in a family argument; thou shall not try to outshine your sister-in-law at mother-in-law's house by faking newly acquired interest in the vegetable patch and offering to chip the prehistoric splatters of lentil and hock soup off the Aga.

Sometimes Nell harboured darker doubts, unmentionable doubts, mostly about the way Janet's recent super-energetic attentions had coincided with her mother-in-law's worsening condition and her placard-round-the-neck declaration that 'the end was nigh'. She worried that Janet, with her apprecia-tive eye for Mum's collection of antiques and quirky knick-knacks, and her material ambitions for her own family, was circling. Nell felt horribly guilty for thinking such things. Maybe she was just jealous of Janet's long legs in tiny, cut-off denim shorts. Or her beautiful West London home. Or something.

'I'll get pudding, shall I, ladies?' Janet smiled, flashing her beautiful gummy smile.

Ladies. It made Nell feel like they were taking tea at Balmoral.

Janet stood up to her full willowy height and went into the kitchen, appearing a few moments later with the steaming crumble. 'Ooo!' she marvelled. 'The kitchen is transformed, Val! You've been busy.'

'It is looking much more hygienic, Mum,' said Heather approvingly. 'I noticed too.'

'Not me, girls. Nell has been working like a demon since she got here, flapping around, sorting things out . . .' she frowned – 'throwing my things away.'

'Mum, it needed to be done. You cannot keep Marmite with a sell-by-date of 2001 or green curry paste from 1998!'

'Why ever not?'

'You'll get food poisoning.'

Heather laughed and plaited her hair loosely with her fingers.

'Nonsense.' Valerie picked up the silver serving spoon and dug into the crumble, tilting away from the spume of steam. 'Right, it's rhubarb from the garden. About two hours old, so not quite past the date stamp. Any takers?'

'Ooh, yes, please. That smells *so* good,' sighed Janet, sounding embarrassingly sensual. 'It's got that wonderful sweet sour yin yang thing going on, hasn't it?'

Yin Yang? Rhubarb? Honestly. Nell suddenly missed being able to exchange knowing looks about Janet with Heather. They'd once been able to pipe hours of conversation into one wordless look.

'Yuck!' said Nat. 'It's like stringy snot. I totally completely *hate* rhubarb.'

Child off message! Child off message! Nell struggled not to smile. She could see Heather's lips twitch too.

'You do *not* hate rhubarb,' Janet informed him.

Valerie ruffled Nat's hair. 'Boys, there's some chocolate ice cream in the freezer.'

'From the turn of the century,' deadpanned Ethan, putting his arm around his mother and giving her a squeeze. Nell was struck by how big and beefy her brother looked in comparison. How bizarre that Valerie had once carried Ethan in her womb. It seemed impossible, like an impala carrying a buffalo, a jump of species.

'Ice cream!' The twins leapt up from the table before their mother had a chance to overturn Val's decision. Cass hesitated, glancing at Nell for approval. Nell smiled at her daughter's sweet obedience. 'Go on, Cass,' she said, nudging her gently. Monty followed Cass, tail wagging, much preferring her to her loud, intimidating cousins.

'Do the honours, Ethan, please,' said Valerie, tapping her dessert spoon on the side of her glass. 'I think we are all going to need a drink.'

'At your service, Mater.' Ethan sloshed wine into everyone's glass, apart from Heather's – she put a hand over hers and glanced at Jeremy.

Nell wondered if she'd done it to please him. He wouldn't want his fiancée drinking much, she suspected. His puritanical streak had driven her mad and had had the perverse effect of making her want to hook herself intravenously to a wine bag out of sheer bloody mindedness. She stole a glance at him too and was embarrassed to see that he was already looking at her. Those intense intelligent black eyes. Damn him. Quickly she looked away.

'Welcome back to the nest!' said Valerie with unexpected cheeriness, holding up her glass. 'To the Stockdales! A toast.'

'To the Stockdales!' Everyone chimed, raising their glasses.

'To our favourite nest, Mum.' Ethan grinned, bending over and giving her a kiss on the cheek.

Nell glugged her drink. Dutch courage. It was too weird. Like. Nothing. Had. Happened. She sneaked a glance. Yes, he was smiling at her again.

'Now. Are the rascals settled?' Valerie glanced behind her to check that the children were absorbed in the television. 'Good. Now we can talk.'

Heather, Ethan and Nell exchanged puzzled glances. Something about Mum's tone of voice.

'As you know, I'm going to pop my clogs,' she said, matter-of-factly. 'Maybe tomorrow. Maybe next year.'

Nell spluttered on her mouthful of crumble.

'Please don't, Mum.' Heather pressed a napkin to her mouth in distaste.

'No point sugaring the pill, Heather,' Valerie said, her green eyes glittering with something close to mischief. 'I'm not going to be here for ever.'

Oh God, thought Nell. She's actually enjoying this.

'I've had to think about what I'm going to do with Tredower.' She gestured around her. 'Your family home.'

Janet visibly tensed, sitting up straighter, her jaw clenched. Nell was sure she could hear the sound of her fingernails digging into the oak dining table.

'Stupidly, I didn't give it to one of you before I got ill and foxed the tax man. Regretfully, now, that is no longer possible.'

Janet glared at Ethan. Ethan looked away quickly.

'But then, to be honest, I thought my organic veggies would hold off the strokes for a fair bit longer,' Valerie said, her eyes softening. 'In fact, a part of me still believes there's a strong possibility you'll have to throw me off Land's End at one hundred-and-four like an old Aborigine woman. I'd hate to become a burden.'

Ethan released a short snort of laughter. Janet glared at him again.

'But that would get you into all sorts of trouble with the law, I believe.' She took a sip of wine. It left a moustache of red on her upper lip. Nell knew Mum would hate to be talking like this and have a smear of wine on her lip. If they had a more intimate relationship she would have been able to silently indicate the need for a discreet napkin wipe. But this wasn't the case. 'Luckily for you lot, it looks likely that I'm going to be dispatched a little earlier than that.'

'Jesus, Mum!' protested Heather. 'Dispatched! You're not a parcel.'

'In a way, we are all mere parcels,' Valerie declared with some pomp, enjoying the authority her illness lent on such matters. 'Some of us go first class, others take longer. But we all end up in the sorting house.'

Ethan started to laugh. 'Let's just hope it's not the one in Penzance or we'll all get lost in purgatory.'

'Grow up, Ethan,' said Heather. 'This is serious.'

Valerie patted Heather's hand as if she were a simple child and turned to the rest of them. 'But, still, there is the matter of power of attorney.'

Everyone twitched at the mention of the elephant in the room. Nell suspected there was a herd not far behind.

'Janet and Ethan have made a very good case that it should be them . . .'

They had? When? Heather turned to Nell and widened her eyes in outrage. Nell smiled briefly in acknowledgement but, not wanting things to implode before she had time to think it through, ducked out of the collusion and looked down at her plate. Their dining-room table had always been like this, a military airspace where looks were exchanged like mortar fire and allegiances switched, battles won and lost. When they were little it was all about ownership of the last ginger biscuit or their mother's finite crumbs of attention, now it was the house.

Valerie shrugged. 'I see no reason why not. So that's that, then. If I completely lose my marbles, girls, Ethan will have control of my affairs.'

Heather went bright red and took a sharp intake of breath.

'Heather,' said Ethan softly, reaching out and touching her hand. 'Don't look like that. I'm always going to look after my little sisters, aren't I?'

'But it should be someone who's good at things like that. Someone with a clear brain. Nell. Or Jeremy,' stuttered

Heather. 'Not . . . not . . .' she stopped, intimidated by the just-you-dare look on Janet's face.

'He *is* the eldest, darling,' said Valerie, as if this was all that mattered.

He was also a man, Nell thought, the flawed, lovable golden boy. Demonstrative, uncomplicated, loving; a bit like a dog. And Mum had always preferred dogs to human beings.

'There is also, of course, the question of *who* is going to get Tredower after I die,' added Valerie, atomising the remains of their lunch.

Silence.

'Who?' said Heather eventually, gripping her dessert spoon so tightly that her fingertips went white. 'Mum, I'm not sure we quite understand.'

'Well, I've been thinking about it rather a lot,' Valerie said casually, as if they were discussing fundraising for the church roof. 'I've had a lot of time to think, all these long days on my *own*. And I realise how much I'd love the house to remain in the family.' She cleared her throat. 'I don't want this house cut up like a Victoria sponge.'

'But Mum . . .' Nell felt confused, and cross. She had never dwelled on her inheritance – there was something distasteful about that – but she had assumed, surely they all had, that when the time came, Tredower would somehow be divided up equally. There was no money in the family, no savings or assets. It was all tied up in this house, a house that had once been a beautiful but remote rectory and now, due to Cornwall's new-found fashion status, had earned more over the years than the rest of them put together. Despite all Mum's lady-of-the-manor posturing, she'd never be able to afford this place now, not even if Dad were alive. In fact, none of them would.

'I know that one is not meant to have favourites,' Valerie continued, implying that she did. 'So it's difficult, terribly difficult.'

Jeremy coughed. He looked like he'd rather be anywhere else.

'Sorry, guys. I know it's a bit of a tricky old subject. But I'm hoping there will be a way of deciding who wants to take Tredower that will work for everybody.'

'Don't worry, Val. I'm sure we'll work it all out. Lots of families still stick by the system of primogeniture, don't they?' Janet looked up at the blank stunned faces. 'The inheritance by the eldest son. I mean, ladies, isn't inheritance really just another form of recycling anyway? Aren't we all getting our knickers in a twist here?' She saw Nell and Heather's thunderous faces and started to backpedal. 'Anyway, the point is, as I'm sure everyone would agree, these little details are not things you should be worrying about right now, are they?'

'No, no they're not.' Heather's hand gripped her water glass so hard veins bulged up beneath her skin. 'It's premature, Mum. Really.'

But it wasn't. And everyone knew it. They'd all swept it under the carpet for far too long.

'The problem we have, guys, is that Tredower would not suit *everyone*.' Valerie scraped the last bit of custard from her bowl. 'Nell, for instance, detests the countryside, as much as I love it. She'd much rather be flying across London in her high heels, wouldn't you, darling?'

Nell bit her tongue. Stay calm. Don't rise to it. Remember. Mum Is Ill, not just a pain in the arse.

'Heather, well, you and Jeremy will probably have a family one day,' said Valerie.

Heather frowned, unsure where this was heading. She exchanged a worried look with Jeremy.

'But you might not, my darling. You're not getting any younger.'

Heather's smile crashed. 'Mum, I'm only thirty-three. And we absolutely want children. Don't we, Jeremy?'

Jeremy nodded quickly, embarrassed.

'Good, good. This is a house that should be enjoyed by children, I think, I really do,' said Valerie, turning the stem of her wine glass round with her sun-mottled fingers.

'I'm sure our brood will grow, Val!' said Janet, shooting Ethan a dark look.

Ethan, whose response to family tension had always been to drink too much and make tactless jokes, said, 'Ta, Ma. We'll take it.'

Valerie smiled indulgently at Ethan. 'Not yours quite yet, darling. I'm going to propose a bit of fun.'

Fun. That could only mean one thing: the polar opposite. Nell's heart sank.

'Mum,' said Heather, her face ironed with anxiety. 'Nothing so far is really sounding that much fun, to be perfectly honest.'

'Oh come on, a bit more gallows humour wouldn't go amiss, Heather.'

'Gallows humour!' muttered Heather, putting her glass to her cheek, hiding her face from Valerie. 'What the . . .' she mouthed to Nell.

Nell winced. 'I know,' she mouthed back. 'Talk later.'

Valerie picked a string of rhubarb from between her teeth. 'I want all of you to go away and really think about whether you want this house or not. It needs a lot of love and *a lot* of money thrown at it – the roof needs rehatting – and it's not for the faint hearted. I want you to think about how you'd use the house, what you'd do with the veggie garden, everything.' She took a large sip of wine and cleared her throat.

'*Then* I'll decide. It seems like quite the fairest way to me.'

Janet put her wine glass sharply down on the table. 'But Valerie,' she smiled icily, nostrils flaring, 'perhaps the element of competition is a little unfair. Doesn't Nell have a bit of an advantage, being here all summer?'

'Excuse me!' blurted Nell, incensed. Like she wanted to be here!

'Come on, Janet,' said Ethan, putting a hand on her slim arm, trying to calm her down and smiling apologetically at Nell.

'Janet, the reason Nell is here is because she's the one person who's taken time out to look after Valerie this summer,' said Jeremy dryly.

All eyes were on him. It was the first time he'd volunteered to speak during this conversation. And to come out on Nell's side like that! Well, well.

'If you think I need looking after, you are much mistaken, Jeremy!' snapped Valerie as if he'd suggested something outrageous. 'Nell is relishing the opportunity to recuperate in the fresh seaside air with little Cass now that she's finally rid of that terrible job in London, aren't you, Nell?'

Nell felt her blood pressure rise. 'Actually, Mum—' she growled.

Ethan kicked her sharply under the table.

'Er . . .' stuttered Nell, the words gagging in her throat. How she wished she was back in her little flat at this moment. How she wished she had her job back, her old life back. Sophie. Pete. Sushi boxes. Minkie deli's brownies. Starbucks soya latte. 'It's lovely to be home.'

'As I thought,' sniffed Valerie, satisfied. 'Now, darlings, anyone for a Nescafé?'

Thirteen

Stop stressing. Calm down. *Breathe*. You are not entirely isolated from the civilised world. You have a phone. Of sorts. She turned over the mobile she'd borrowed from Mum's whole-lot-of-crap drawer in her hand. It was brick-like, about eight years old, and resembled a phone in the same way a clog resembled a Lanvin ballet pump, but it was connected to a more reliable service provider and at least insured she could receive a phone call even if the wind was blowing in the wrong direction. It was only when she tried to fit it into the sandy inner pocket of her handbag next to her iPhone and had to take the iPhone out that she realised that she'd unwittingly got a signal. Yay! Three new emails, in fact. Twenty-first-century communication. She hadn't fallen off the edge of the world after all.

Dear Nell Not-a-Tube-Station,
How u doing? Miss our nites of passion. Got pissed last Thursday and totally forgot that you were in Cornwall, staggered round to yours in hope of a friendly coffee ☺ but you'd shut up shop! Lovely Miranda from upstairs had to scoop me off doormat. Anyway, when you back, Foxy?
Pete x

Foxy? Hmm. And perhaps his spelling of 'nites' shouldn't matter but it did somehow. And, also, come to think of it, she didn't really like the idea of him making himself known to the neighbours either. Jesus, what would Miranda think? Nell knew if she was in London she'd be unable to resist pointing out to Miranda that Pete was, you know, just a casual fling, nothing serious or anything. But *was* he a fling? Was this the correct description now that they were in nickname territory?

She scrolled down to the other two emails. Oh. An invitation to send off her bank details to claim an inheritance. Kind of ironic. An offer of cheap Viagra. Like she'd need that down here.

Glaringly, *no* work mail. Nothing from her colleagues. All those people who'd so recently flocked around her, complimenting her on her shoes, her fringe, her feature ideas, as if they really meant it. She guessed that they were really busy, and maybe a bit embarrassed. Still. They'd all moved on pretty bloody quickly, hadn't they?

Nell missed work. She missed being paid. She was chomping through her redundancy money quicker than she should. She missed having something to feel stressed about – something you were *allowed* to be stressed about, like long hours, tricky bosses or a nightmare commute. Spooky country silence, ill mothers and earwigs didn't quite cut it. And she was surprised, rather childishly perhaps, that she also missed her work being recognised, rewarded and noticed. No one seemed to appreciate what she'd been doing at Tredower. Sure, Janet and Heather had cooed at the reorganised kitchen but that was it. There was no recognition of how much time and effort was going into other stuff, like the August hog roast – she was tackling it as if it were an industry party attended by Michelle Obama – or the diarising of her

111

mother's medical appointments, the follow-up calls to the doctors or the house administration – insurance, boiler checks, council tax – that had been neglected for months and made tearing off her own fingernails a comparatively joyous activity.

'Ready for the beach?' Janet walked into the sitting room in candy-pink Hunter wellies, a Breton top, jeans and a honey-coloured cashmere poncho. Unlike Nell, who was still defiantly stomping around in those ridiculous Prada wedges, she'd got her Cornish chic look down.

'Cass is just talking to Dean on the phone. Won't be a minute.' Nell leaned forward on the sofa and peaked through the door to get a glimpse of Cass hopping excitedly from Croc to Croc.

'No rush. We're all still waiting for Ethan anyway.' Janet rolled her eyes. 'I spend half my life waiting for Ethan.'

'He is, I'm afraid, constitutionally late. He was even born late, missing his due date by three weeks. And he's got later ever since.'

'But what is he *actually* doing up there, Nell? How long can it take one man to shower?' She rolled her eyes in exasperation. 'I just don't understand.'

'I'd count yourself lucky he has any personal hygiene routine at all. He never used to.'

Janet laughed, but her lovely sapphire eyes looked suspiciously pink and rheumy. Was something up?

'Everything, OK, Janet?' she asked hesitantly.

Janet looked startled. 'Why wouldn't it be?'

'I just noticed a bit of . . .' Nell felt silly. What did she know about marriage? She was the only one out of all the siblings who seemed incapable of having a proper relationship. 'Sorry.'

Janet opened her mouth to say something then seemed to

112

change her mind. 'I think this situation with your mum is getting to Ethan.'

That wasn't the answer to her question but Nell felt she couldn't push it further.

Janet leaned back on the old Chinese cabinet behind her. It creaked loudly. 'Oops! Too much crumble.'

'Don't worry about that old thing. It's heading for the junkyard soon.'

'This? You're joking?' Janet pulled out a drawer, then pushed it back gently. 'It's a lovely piece.'

'Well, maybe Mum will decide to donate it to the local home for ageing organic carrots or something,' Nell quipped.

Janet didn't laugh. She sat down next to her on the sofa, and spoke in a low, collusive whisper. 'I've been thinking about all that stuff at lunch.'

'I don't know about you but I certainly got indigestion afterwards.'

Janet winced. 'Well, it's a tricky situation. It must be horribly stressful for you. I know it is for Ethan. He hates all this kind of stuff. He gets so upset, bottles it all up like men do but I know how much it worries him.' She cleared her throat. 'I've been thinking, how about we come to some private little agreement or something? That way we can keep it civilised.' Her voice was very low now, sing-song, hypnotic, her eyes soft and totally focussed as though Nell was the only person in the world who mattered. She felt herself falling under Janet's spell. 'Would you consider approaching things from a different angle? You know, working things out between ourselves, finding a different way to split the assets? Just think how much stress it would save, Nell.' She lowered her voice further. 'We could hammer something out, just me and you.'

Was Janet suggesting they clique together and exclude

Heather, or was it just an unfortunate turn of phrase? 'Sorry, Janet, but I really do think the fairest thing would be for the house to be sold and divided equally.'

Something in Janet's eyes hardened. 'But your mum doesn't want the house to go out of the family. I'd be the same. Wouldn't you?'

'Which twin would you leave it to, then, Janet? Nat or Cosmo?'

Three days later, Tredower felt as big as a two-up two-down terrace. Every bedroom had been farted in, every toilet seat peed on. They all needed to escape to avoid killing each other. The beach café, if you were Nell; dawn yoga, if you were Janet; two-hour cliff runs if you were Jeremy and Heather; even Monty had taken to gnawing his favourite old pink fluffy slipper alone in the refuge of a deckchair. When they were all together the beach became the obvious place to hang out as it offered room for egos, childhood resentments and love triangles to roam freely, kick back and enjoy the rain.

However, this morning the sun was blazing.

'Don't even try and keep up, pussycats!' Ethan yelled, slamming the car door and revving the barge-sized Volvo out of the drive. Heather and Jeremy followed in their silver Audi, which also contained Valerie, Jeremy accelerating to keep up with Ethan, competitive as ever. Nell shook her head. Boys and their toys. Hell, they could speed all they liked. She'd take her time.

At the Perranortho Beach car park she waved at Ethan. He looked up from fiddling with his video camera – did he want their mother to live on for ever as a video download or something? 'Took the scenic route, eh, sis?'

Nell walked towards them all, their group a loud skirmish in the middle of the otherwise quiet car park. The twins were fighting over fishing nets, Monty leaping up and trying to join in. Valerie was cursing the bit of gravel stuck inside her Birkenstock. Heather was battling the breeze for her straw hat while Jeremy sedately dug his hands into the pockets of his cream chino shorts, looking like an American politician holidaying in Cape Cod. His eyes darkened when he saw her. Something in the air crackled.

Nell offered her arm to Mum as they walked towards the beach, trying to put as much distance between them as possible. But as they walked she couldn't help but remember all the times she and Jeremy had walked down this slipway hand in hand in their previous incarnation as a couple – the bank holidays, the dirty weekenders, the summer dashes down to the coast in his old convertible.

They passed the café. Not many people there at all today, bar a couple of tables of rowdy, beautiful teenage surfers, all golden and statuesque like they might have dropped off the roof of the Sistine Chapel. The girl with the nose ring was carrying a tray of mugs towards their table and the boys were intently studying her small neat figure in its clingy black skull print T-shirt dress. No sign of the BFG.

'I'm really not a fan of those nose ring thingies,' said Valerie, glancing at the girl too. 'This café has changed hands, you know.' She sniffed. 'You can tell.'

'I met the new owner. A guy called Michael.'

'A wealthy man, that Michael chap.' Valerie smiled knowingly, always pleased to have pinned down the local gossip before anyone else.

'You sure? He doesn't look like it,' said Nell, remembering his string belt.

'Pat Patterson knows of him. Tried to buy The Rectory down in Penzance. Apparently he drove past and had the gall to knock and ask them if they were selling! Imagine.'

115

Ethan came up beside them, surfboard over his shoulder. 'Another rich doughnut trying to find himself in Cornwall? Give me your wedge, mate. Then you can really live the simple life.'

'At least you're not bitter, Ethan,' said Nell.

A warm spot of soft sugary sand at the very top of the beach became their HQ for the afternoon. The children ran off towards the surf as soon as they arrived, carrying a jumble of buckets and spades and nets. Monty flirted with a boa of seaweed. To an outsider they must look like any other nice middle-class family, rather than one purposely pitted against each other by some crackpot scheme of their mother's, Nell thought, feeling a fresh flush of anger at the inheritance proposal.

'Towels. That's what we need.' Heather, summery and pretty in a floral tea dress, rummaged through her beach bag and carefully laid out some fraying colour-washed towels from the depths of Tredower's linen cupboard which Nell recognised from her childhood.

Janet pulled a green kaftan over her head, revealing a chocolate-brown bikini and toned stomach that showed scant evidence of ever digesting a pudding let alone gestating twins. She lay back with a sigh. 'Ah, hello, sun.'

'Right,' said Ethan, scratching his balls inside his floral surf shorts. 'I'm going to get these babies wet.'

'Don't you want a nibble of lunch first? It's gone one,' said Valerie, peaking inside the wicker basket covered with a gingham tea towel, picking out a grape.

'You're meant to eat *after* swimming, Mum,' muttered Heather.

'I'm still digesting this morning's fry up.' Ethan patted his hairy belly. 'You coming, Janet?'

Janet looked away coolly. 'Not yet.'

'Jeremy?' asked Ethan, glancing back at Janet, as if trying to second-guess his wife's mood.

'Um . . .' Jeremy hesitated, eyed the churning sea warily. 'It looks bloody cold, Ethan.'

'Don't you dare wuss out on me,' said Ethan, giving him a karate kick with his foot.

'You must swim, Jeremy, really,' said Valerie smiling. Her mood always lightened the moment they were beside the sea. She tugged up her denim skirt to reveal one varicosey tanned calf to the sun. 'Enjoy the sunshine while you can. I'm certainly going to.'

'Go on, sweetheart,' said Heather, resting a hand lightly on Jeremy's bare foot in a gesture of casual possession. 'You'll like it once you're in.'

Nell watched with interest. She knew Jeremy wasn't the outdoorsy type. That he liked to swim in pools, preferably pools kept at a toasty twenty-two degrees. That he liked teak sun-loungers not sandy towels.

'No pressure, then,' Jeremy said and then, shockingly, started peeling off his shirt. Nell took a quick intake of breath. She hadn't seen his near-naked body since they split – until this summer she'd successfully managed to avoid family beach trips where disrobing might be required. Gulp. The shirt was off. Bloody hell.

He was in good shape, only slightly rounder in the middle. More hair on the shoulders. And she couldn't help but notice – *no one* could fail to notice – the improbably large coil of penis in his tight swim shorts. She became aware of Heather watching her watching his swim shorts and quickly applied herself to rummaging in her bag for sun cream.

'Just us, ladies,' said Janet, flipping down her sunglasses. 'No children. No men. Bliss.'

'Isn't it? And you know what? I'm hungry again,' groaned

Nell. 'Since leaving London I've developed the appetite of a shire horse.'

Janet lay back on her towel. 'The air. I reckon it's the air. The pollution in London air must be an appetite suppressant.'

Nell laughed, peeked into the picnic basket. Inside were a few bread rolls, a sweating lump of Cornish yarg cheese, garden-grown strawberries and grapes, not exactly a feast. She had wanted to pack it up herself but Mum had insisted. She'd known it could go either way. As a child she'd get a huge home-made iced cupcake in her lunch box one day, the next she'd find a stale Marmite sandwich and a stick of muddy celery.

'Don't wrinkle your nose, Nell!' exclaimed Valerie.

'I'm not.' She unwrinkled her nose.

'I suppose you've got used to expensed fancy work lunches,' Valerie added with a small sniff.

'Absolutely not,' she lied. 'This is perfect.'

'Let's nick Ethan's beers,' said Janet, breaking open cool box and passing them round.

'God, I so love this cheese,' said Nell, slicing a small wedge off the Cornish yarg and washing it down with a heavenly swig of cold beer.

'We must save some for Jeremy. He *loves* Cornish yarg,' said Heather, rubbing a large dollop of sun block into her legs. (Heather didn't like to tan, which was why she looked about fifteen. Nell used to use cooking oil.) 'Anything Cornish, in fact,' she added unnecessarily, leaning back on the towel, hat over her face to protect it. 'Look, he's in the sea!' She laughed. 'I knew he'd go native.'

Jeremy stood next to the ocean, dipped his toe in and yelped. Ethan started wading towards him splashing water. Then dunked him.

'Funny,' sighed Valerie. 'Whenever I think of Jeremy I think of him at a desk in the city.'

Nell spluttered, trying not to laugh. Sometimes her mother, quite unintentionally, got right to the heart of things.

Heather pulled her straw hat further down over her face.

'Oh don't get me wrong, darling. He's a catch, all right.' Valerie tore off a bit of bread and stuck a creamy lump of cheese on top of it. 'You did well there, darling.'

Everyone tensed. Nell could feel it. It was coming. She needed to steer the conversation off the prickly terrain of Jeremy as quickly as possible.

'Your turn next, I think, Nell,' Valerie said on cue.

The remark hung in the air like a column of itchy sand flies.

'You're not forty yet. You've got a bit of time.'

'Mum!' Nell exploded. 'Please.'

Valerie bit the head off a strawberry. 'I always seem to say the wrong thing.'

Heather's fingers drilled anxiously into the blond sand.

Janet shot Nell a sympathetic look from behind her shades. 'Perranortho Beach has to be the dreamiest beach in the world,' she said, gamely trying to pull the conversation into shallower waters. 'I love the grasses on the dunes. It feels secret, so much like a secret smuggler's beach. It must have been amazing growing up here, having it on your doorstep.'

Nell gave her a small grateful smile.

'Nell used to come and sulk here as a teenager, didn't you, darling?' said Valerie. She understood sulks, having mastered the art herself over the years.

'Among other things,' said Heather coyly, a smile playing around the corner of her mouth.

'I have two words for you, Heather,' said Nell. 'Caspar Jones.'

119

'Shuddup.' Heather pulled her hat further down on her head so that only her chin and her smiling mouth were visible.

'*Ooo*. And who is Caspar Jones?' Janet sat upright.

'Heather went skinny dipping with this boy, Caspar . . .'

Heather groaned.

'Heather skinny dipping?' exclaimed Janet.

'Oh, she has a hidden wild side, all right,' said Nell wryly. 'Or used to.' She couldn't resist that. 'Anyway, to cut a very long story short, they went skinny dipping and some of the guys at school thought it would be hilarious to nick their clothes.'

'It was a very long walk home,' mumbled Heather beneath her hat.

They all started to laugh, and for a moment the sun and the sand and the nostalgia cleared the air (and all thoughts of Jeremy's penis from Nell's overheating brain). They sipped beers and watched the children playing happily, the mound of their sandcastle taking shape spade by spade. Nell smiled: they looked like so many photographs of her and Heather and Ethan as children, on the same beach, with spades and buckets.

'I used to come here on my own too. Do you remember that funny old time I spent the night on the beach, Nell darling?' Valerie said suddenly.

Nell stiffened. How could she forget?

During one of her mother's particularly 'bad patches', as Dad always referred to them, Mum had disappeared one summer's night. He had gone to bed late and found the bed empty. They'd searched the gardens, the lane, even the vegetable patch, in case she'd decided to do a bit of drunken late-night gardening – not unheard of – but there was no sight of her. As dawn broke, Dad had started to panic, until he thought of the beach. Just a hunch, he'd said. He was right. There she was, the frill of her silk nightie sticking out like a tutu beneath her old Barbour, as she paced back and forth along the sand in her wellies. She'd been crying, her eyes red and sore. But she'd smiled when she'd seen them, relieved to be disturbed. Nell had asked her what was wrong. 'The past won't go away, it won't go away,' was all she'd whispered. Nothing more. Dad shrugged his coat over her shoulders like he understood everything and led her back to the car. The incident was never referred to again. Nell was puzzled as to why, suddenly, after all these years, her mother had brought it up. Maybe the illness again. 'I don't really remember, Mum.'

'I'm going for a dip,' Valerie said briskly, getting up from her towel and closing the conversation as fast as she'd opened it. 'Coming?'

'Too cold for me,' said Nell, wondering what the sea was going to do to her fringe. She'd been paddling with Cass but had yet to go for the full icy submersion. And she certainly wasn't ready to strip down to her bikini in front of Jeremy.

'I'm warming up to it,' said Heather. 'Later.'

'Sure! I'll keep you company, Val.' Janet leapt up, the tassels of her bikini flicking off the sides of her smooth brown thighs. She had that particular public school girl heartiness, unfazed by the iciest of waters. It was one of the things that particularly endeared her to Valerie.

Nell and Heather watched them walk down to the sea, the dumpier older woman in her turquoise swimming costume, the lithe younger woman in her bikini, chatting easily.

Heather turned to Nell, blue eyes flashing. 'Don't you think she could ease off the perfect daughter-in-law act for just *one* minute? I mean honestly.'

'You sound jealous.'

'I'm jealous of her legs.'

'Is it my imagination or are they actually getting longer as she gets older?' marvelled Nell. 'Maybe there's some secret West London leg-lengthening machine I haven't discovered yet.'

'Yes. It's called Pilates. And I tell you what, Nell, her legs are the least of our worries, now that Mum's set up a kind of . . .'

'. . . it's a knockout.'

'Exactly. Janet's only going to get worse. She's probably been working on some PowerPoint presentation all week.'

Nell leaned back on her elbows. 'Heather, in the end Mum will do what she wants to do. This is all about her retaining control, isn't it?'

Heather shadowed her eyes with her arm. 'You reckon?'

Nell suddenly noticed Heather's toned arms. 'Get you. Your trainer is obviously worth the fee.'

'Why?'

'You've got Hollywood arms. And . . .' she peered in closer. 'Heather, do you *wax* your arms?'

Heather blushed, quickly put her arm down by her side. 'Only for holiday. Jeremy's not keen on—' She stopped, opened one eye. '. . . hairiness.'

'Oh.' The conversation could go either way, dangling like a car caught on the cliff barrier. She could say something about him not minding *her* being hairy. Or she could sympathise in a sisterly manner as if he had never been her boyfriend. Or she could say: 'Oh, it's a slippery slope, Heather. You start waxing your arms, then it's your armpits, and before you know you'll be ripping hairs out of your nostrils before breakfast.'

'Stop it.' Heather started to giggle, swivelled on to her side and peered up at Nell. It felt as if the atmosphere between them was crankily shifting a gear, the sound of rusty cogs turning again. 'I'm sorry,' she said quietly. 'About blowing up about the thing with the sofa. You know. The crayons.'

Nell shrugged, swatted a sand fly off her foot. 'I'm sorry that your sofa got vandalised.'

Heather wet her lips with her tongue. She opened her mouth to speak but no words came out. She tried again. 'It's like old times, isn't it? You know, me and you, refusing to swim, tolerating Mum, Ethan showing off, these sandy picnics.' She bit her lip, as if trying to stop herself crying. 'I've missed this.'

Nell was too proud to say she'd missed it too.

'Nell, can't we be grown-up about it all?'

'What, Heather?' But she knew exactly what.

'Jeremy.' She looked down at the beach, unable to meet Nell's eyes. 'I feel like, even after all this time, it's an . . . an issue.'

Nell stared out at the horizon, unsure how to respond. To her horror her eyes filled with tears. She looked away, towards the cheery blue café. 'I'm dying for a coffee, Heather. Can I get you one?'

The BFG was there now. Nell could just make him out as she walked towards the café hut, salt-and-pepper curls lifted off his hair by the wind, khaki fleece tied around his waist. He was tall but he didn't stoop. She liked that.

'A coffee and an apple juice. Thanks.'

'Coming up.' Michael didn't acknowledge her. She felt a dip of disappointment. He turned to the fridge, pulled out a carton of apple juice, skidded it along the counter top. 'Milk?' Then he looked up. His expression changed immediately. 'Hey, isn't it—'

'The idiot who lost her car key.'

'Nell?'

'Excellent memory.'

He sloshed some coffee into the paper cup and shoved it casually towards her. 'On the shack.'

'Really? Thank you very much.'

He looked at her for a moment too long, as if weighing something up. 'But it comes with strings attached.' He turned around. 'Annie?'

The girl with the nose ring looked up, wiped her hands on her apron.

'Hold the fort, will you? Going for a ciggy.'

No, she needn't go straight back. Heather could wait. Nell sat next to Michael on the bench in the café garden beneath the pine trees. He rolled a cigarette and licked the papers. The sea was a gentle roar behind them and the sun was bright. 'Rumour has it that you tried to buy a house off the Pattersons of Penzance.'

Michael blew out a cone of smoke. 'Ah, word gets around.'

'My mother lives up the road. And she likes to think she knows everything and everyone.'

Michael laughed. 'Mothers do, don't they? You're a mum. Don't you know most things?'

'It's daughters who know everything. Just ask my four year old.'

Michael laughed again. She felt it as a warm exhalation of air on her bare shoulder where her black vest top met her bra strap. 'Who's your ma? Do I know her?'

'Valerie Stockdale? Lives at Tredower, old rectory down in the valley.'

Michael scratched his head. 'Wait a minute. Tredower, Tredower . . . Not that big old hunk of a house with ivy-clad windows?'

'That's the one.'

'You know what? I've driven past many times, especially when I first arrived down here and kept getting lost and reversing into your driveways in my exhaust-spluttering soft top, asking people if they'd sell their houses.'

Nell raised an eyebrow. Was he trying to show off? She wasn't easily impressed, certainly not by soft-top cars. Well, only a little bit.

'I'm now disguised in a Volvo.' He drew on his cigarette. 'Mud-splattered wheels and everything.' He grinned. 'You'd never know.'

'Did you find a house?' she asked, curious.

'Sure did.' He pointed to the hills above the cliff.

Everyone knew the modern glass box, nestled into the hillside, sometimes sinking into the greenery completely in certain lights, other times glittering like a jewel. Built about ten years ago by an architect, it had had a series of owners since – none of them natives, of course, well beyond their budgets – and had divided local opinion along the usual traditional-versus-modernist lines. Nell had always been curious about it, wondered what kind of person might live in that house. And now she knew. 'My brother says it looks like a microwave that's landed on a tree,' she said before she could stop herself.

Fortunately, he didn't take offence and seemed to think this funny. And as he laughed she noticed his sandy lashes, the way they collided chaotically like they were all growing in different directions at once. She noticed the sag of skin above his eyes, a sag that in a woman would be a sign of ageing but, unfairly, in a man just added character. They didn't speak for a while, but sat, oddly comfortably, staring out at the denim sea, the blue tits fluttering tamely in the tangle of tree above them. She looked at her watch. She must

125

get back. Heather would be waiting for her apple juice, wondering what on earth had become of her. Yes, she absolutely must.

'That lady who found your keys?' Michael said suddenly, as if sensing that she was readying for departure and deterring her.

'Oh yes?' She slung her bag over her shoulder and shuffled her feet apart, ready to stand up.

'She was here again yesterday. I gave her a coffee on the house for her good deed. And a piece of honey cake. Very nice lady she was, too.'

Very nice lady. Nell tried to remember: was the woman attractive? Yes, she seemed to remember, ordinary but wholesomely pretty. She put a little note next to Michael in her head: 'Man who gives out freebies to female customers.' Aha, wolf in fleecy clothing. She had the BFG sussed. Only taken two meetings. This was one of the benefits of having clocked up three decades of romantic experience. She could slot men into different genres very quickly, as if they were all different types of fiction sitting on a library shelf. (Jeremy had always been a dark, intense page turner.) Bets on that the BFG fell into the commercial humorous light fiction camp. A great beach read. Nothing weightier, she decided. She thanked him for the coffee and half walked, half skidded down the slipway in her wedges, for some reason the sound of Michael's laughter still ringing in her ears like a bell.

Fourteen

April slid her drawing pad into her art folder and carefully slotted it into the well of the new hire car. Yes, she was embarrassingly amateur, stalled at the sketching standard of a teenager, but she was thoroughly enjoying herself. Its pointlessness gave her pleasure. And as each brushstroke became more assured, her use of colour bolder, she began to feel more like the old April, the April who had existed before marriage and kids, before she'd been diluted, then diluted again like a homeopathic tincture until only a memory of her original molecular structure remained.

Her teacher Bea, a woman in her seventies with long, wild silver hair and an actual paint-splattered smock, twinkled with convincing enthusiasm at her work. Bea made her feel that there was nothing better she could be doing with her time: 'You can't paint when you're dead, April!' April repeated this like a mantra whenever she felt silly or selfish. Also, if she was being perfectly honest, the art course gave her a compellingly good excuse *not* to do the thing that had brought her to Cornwall in the first place. Every day the course seemed to conjure up another acceptable reason – drinks with the other students, an evening swim, a quick sunset watercolour – not to get in the hire car, not to go to that place marked with a red cross on the map and an even bigger cross in her head.

Chris was right, though. She'd come this far, hadn't she? No point bottling out of it now. She couldn't go back to Wolvercote with just a clutch of watercolours to show for the summer. No more procrastinating. She took a glug from her bottle of Evian, feeling like a cowgirl swigging from a hipflask, and hit the accelerator hard.

The engine stalled. April restarted it, remembering that she'd never been a super-confident driver, one of those people who couldn't drive in France or in anything bigger than a Clio. Chris had sat in the driving seat as a matter of course. What did this say about her marriage?

Suddenly, as if in response, the car revved. Her scalp prickled. She was no passenger now! Oh no. She'd just drive past the house, get a glimpse of it through the trees. It wouldn't look too suspicious. Nobody would see her. That might be enough to satisfy her, just seeing it.

At first she drove nervously, shoulders hunched up to her earlobes, heart pounding every time one of those insanely large tractors tried to pass on those narrow lanes made for pygmy horses. Then, emboldened by the fact that she hadn't yet crashed, she got more confident and started to speed up a bit. The wind fluttered in through the open window, making her pink silk scarf whip softly against her cheek.

Suddenly. A double take. Tredower House! The sign flashed past, unmistakable, black lettering on a swinging, white board. She panicked, floored the gas, her whole body leaning windscreen-wards, as if to get away from the house and its swinging sign and everything it might mean.

But there was another part of April that set her jaw, slammed on the brakes and started to reverse slowly down the lane. Her palms were sweaty on the steering wheel. Her feet felt heavy, as if blood was pooling in them. For a moment she thought she was going to have to stop the car and have a breather. Then the moment passed and she was OK again.

She stopped opposite the gate and stared into the drive, eyes widening, mouth dropping open. The house was far grander and more beautiful than anything she'd imagined. It was also much wilder, embedded in the tangle of surrounding vegetation like a tooth in its gum.

She glanced uneasily at the house's windows. Open but no signs of life, thank goodness. One car in the drive, a rusty, muddy VW, stickered with bird poo and leaves. But . . . oh, a child's pink scooter leaning against the front door. A skateboard. Surfboard. Young children must live here?

She reversed a bit further to improve her view. She could now see through a pretty wrought-iron gate that led from the front to the back gardens. There was an open patch of lawn. A deck chair. A wooden table. *And* . . . three mugs on the table, a magazine open, its pages riffling in the breeze! April froze. As if they'd all been here a moment ago but had now vaporised like ghosts on the *Marie Celeste*. She started to reverse, too fast.

Beep! Beep! *Shit.* Looking over her shoulder, she stared down the snout of a black four-by-four in the lane outside the house. A man was thumping his horn. Beside him, she glimpsed a blond woman, her hand pressing on the man's arm, as if to hold back the beeping. April raised her hand in apology and sped away. It was only when she checked her mirror that she saw the car turning into the drive.

Fifteen

OK, it was an idyllic scene, Nell acknowledged, but only if she blanked certain things – i.e. people – from the picture. And if she forgot about the fact that Monty had chewed one of her Prada wedges like a rubber bone this morning. That her mother had torn off half of her notebook – with its critical hog roast countdown list – and used it to light the barbecue. That rather than risking the terrifying blue-rinse factory, A Cut Above!, in the neighbouring village she'd trimmed her own fringe and now looked like she'd been mauled by the lawn mower. That she'd excitedly opened an email from work, thinking it might be a glamorous freelance assignment and it was an old colleague wondering if she had any first-person stories about 'burnout' she could pitch.

So, yes, apart from all this, it was idyllic. The weather had certainly cheered up. After a violent rain shower earlier, the air had cleared and a rouged sun was sinking behind the apple trees at the bottom of the back garden. Janet was having a bath, her Mongolian throat singing music warbling out of the open bathroom window. Monty lay on the lawn, one paw outstretched, eyes half closed in camp sufferance. Circled by the large logs that served as benches, Ethan was lazily nudging smouldering charcoals in the stone barbecue, his tattooed torso bare, his shoulders a little pink, a Corona in his hand. The children whooped around him, trying to compete for a reaction, Cass cartwheeling across the lawn, the twins fighting over the tractor, a lethal toy from the seventies constructed from sharp bits of rusty metal. They dragged the tractor repeatedly to the very top of the steep slope at the back of the garden and then ricocheted down, screaming with delight.

Thankfully, Jeremy was nowhere to be seen – nor was Heather – but Nell still couldn't quite relax, knowing that he was in the zone and likely to reappear at any moment. She'd successfully avoided being alone with him thus far, but still found it intensely stressful being in the same room as him, even with the others around. It was like she had nothing to say to him and everything to say to him at the same time. And she feared that if she did actually start to speak to him she might never stop and she'd want to bang him into the ground with her handbag like a tent peg.

A blood curdling yelp. Cass! Nell leapt up. Cass was on the ground. But, no, no blood. No injury. *Yet.* Nell tried to remain nonchalant. She wanted Cass to enjoy the rough and tumble of her cousins while she could. In London she spent too much time sitting on the velvet sofa with her and Sophie like she was four going on thirty-five. Not taking her eyes off Cass, mentally preparing to flee to A & E at any moment, Nell sat back down, picked a large mint leaf from her glass of Pimms and sucked it.

'I hope you don't suck your mint like that on a date, Nell,' said Valerie, walking up behind her in a blowsy seventies-style floral dress and wide straw hat. She looked ruddily well. You'd never know. Which made it all the more heartbreaking somehow.

'Worse, I'm afraid.' Nell got up. 'Here, have a seat, Mum.

131

I'll sit on the grass.' She sat down cross-legged on the springy green lawn.

'Thank you, darling. Oh look!' she said, levering herself into the chair. 'Look at Janet.'

Janet, unmissable in a hot-pink maxi-dress, was standing by the back door waving.

'What a gorgeous frock!' exclaimed Valerie. 'Pink is her colour, isn't it?'

Annoyingly, every colour was Janet's colour.

Janet sashayed across the lawn, the dress flapping around her tanned ankles, washed wet hair trailing down her back. Nell watched her talking to Ethan at the barbecue. Ethan bent his head down and headbutted her shoulder affectionately. She turned away from him, a proper cold shoulder.

'Have you thought about wearing dresses more?' said Valerie, eyeing Nell's grey cut-off jeans disapprovingly. 'Keep the jeans for when you've got a ring on your finger?'

She had fifteen pairs of jeans. Skinny. Bootleg. Black. Blue. Grey. White. She couldn't imagine a world without jeans. 'Mum, it's not 1955.'

'I suppose.' Valerie's face lit up. 'Why don't you put those jeans to good use, then, and do the attic?'

Nell's spirits sank. All very well, shipshaping Tredower. But the attic? Mice lived in attics. Spiders lived in attics. Mountain ranges of Stockdale crap lived in attics. 'And what needs doing up there?'

'What doesn't?'

'Has anyone been up there this century?'

'Heather had a poke about, tried to find some vase or other at Christmas. Other than that it's been years, probably. It always spooked the living daylights out of Deng. She refused to go near it. Yes, it'll be interesting to see what's up

132

there. Lots of family skeletons, I should imagine,' she added with a smile. 'Oh, hi, Heather!'

Nell turned to see Heather standing behind them, silent on the grass with her bare feet. She looked worried. 'What's in the attic, Mum?'

'You know better than any of us. You were the last one up there, darling.'

'Yes, I guess I was.' Heather flushed. 'It's just a lot of rubbish. I wouldn't bother going through it,' she added quickly.

'That's precisely why I want Nell to do one of her thorough clean-outs, give it an editor's eye.'

'A loft detox.'

'I'll help,' said Heather unexpectedly. 'When are you going up?'

'Er, tomorrow? Unless it's a beautiful day that we don't want to waste not lying on the beach.'

'OK,' said Heather, fingering her yellow sundress. She looked stressy. Nell wondered if she'd had a row with Jeremy. Or maybe, understandably, the inheritance stuff was getting to her.

'Don't hover, Heather,' said Valerie.

Heather sat down on the grass, pulling her dress carefully over her knees and cradling the soles of her bare feet on the palms of her hands.

'Hey, what's up?' Nell asked.

Heather's smile didn't reach her eyes. 'I'm fine.'

Nell frowned. 'You sure?'

'Well . . .'

'What is it, darling?' said Valerie, pushing up the brim of her hat, eyes narrowing.

Heather frowned. 'Oh, I don't know. It's a funny one. Maybe I'm being neurotic . . .'

'What?'

'Well, I just popped out to pick up some papers and when I came back there was this lady staring into the house from the road, just staring. There was something about her . . .' Heather bit her thumbnail. 'When she saw me she scuttled off quickly. It just struck me as . . . I don't know, *odd*.'

'Probably just a rambler. A nosy bunch.' Valerie fanned herself with her hat. 'The Americans are particularly bad.'

'Yes,' said Heather, staring anxiously into the mid-distance. 'I'm sure you're right.'

The woman didn't reappear and was not mentioned again, although Nell didn't think Heather had forgotten her. For the rest of the day she seemed preoccupied, staring off into the mid-distance, occasionally twitching the hall curtains to check that nobody was in the drive.

The sun dropped. But it remained a balmy, delicious summer evening, the sky jumbled with stars, the wind tugging at the flames in the hurricane lamps, carrying with it the smell of earth and sea and woodsmoke.

Away from the barbecue, the air was cold in that knife-clean way that cloudless coastal summer nights were cold. Nell heaved a sigh of relief. The weekend could have been a lot worse. No disaster had unfolded. Janet hadn't mentioned her Tredower plans for at least two hours – Nell suspected Ethan had had words. Cass and the cousins were getting on brilliantly. And things had been perfectly civil with Jeremy. (Bastard.) Better still, no mad glitches from Mum, not so much as a memory lapse today, so they could all pretend she wasn't ill and that what was happening wasn't.

They sat on the circle of gnarly logs around the embers of the barbecue, huddled up beneath musty woolly blankets. Jeremy was quiet tonight, Nell noticed, and undeniably absurdly handsome in the light of the flickering fire, taut, masculine; all he needed was a rifle over his shoulder. Occasionally he'd glance up, catch her eye. She tried to look away immediately but sometimes she couldn't help but let her eyes linger for a second or two.

Nell took one of the chocolate fingers from the box. How good were they? The nursery sweetness flooded her with memories of her childhood, midnight feasts, birthday parties, the way Dad always used to make sure they had treats when Mum was 'not feeling well', spoiling them to compensate. At the time it seemed a good deal. A Wagon Wheel for a moody mum? Every time, thanks.

She bit into the chocolate finger again but this time was jolted from her sugary nostalgia by the conversation taking a tricky turn, striding down the aisle to The Wedding. Suddenly the chocolate didn't taste so good. Numbers, Heather was saying. How impossible it was to limit the guest list. And how hard it was to keep the costs from spiralling to Peter and Jordan proportions. It wasn't like she wanted anything totally extravagant, was it? That would be bad taste.

Nell put the chocolate finger down – yes, a bad taste in her mouth now – and said nothing because whatever she said was going to sound loaded. Heather got on to dates. The following April was most likely, they were both too busy before then. A marquee in Tredower garden would be beyond perfect. Heather sighed and leaned back into the gap between Jeremy's knees. Valerie refilled their glasses.

'Er, losing the will to live over here,' groaned Ethan, putting his hand up. 'No offence, Heather. But there is a limit to how much wedding talk a man can stomach and I think we've just exceeded it.'

Nell gave him a small, grateful smile, knowing that he had intervened on her behalf.

Ethan discreetly pulled out a plastic bag full of weed, large

Rizlas and a pocket of rolling tobacco, laying them out behind a row of beer bottles on the slab of stone barbecue.

'Ethan!' hissed Heather, sitting bolt upright. 'Not here!'

'Oh. What's that?' said Valerie, curiosity piqued, peering from behind the bottles. 'Oh, Ethan! Honestly.'

'Put it away, Ethan.' Janet rolled her eyes.

'It's all right Janet.' Valerie smiled indulgently. 'I've tried giving him a piece of my mind in my time . . .' she raised an eyebrow – 'when I had more pieces, but it never worked, not in the slightest. I'd even go so far as to say my disapproval fanned his flames.'

'Can I take this opportunity to apologise for my youthful self?' Ethan grinned, not looking the least repentant.

'You mean the one who made Pete Doherty look like Aled Jones?' snorted Heather. She had always been the straightest of them all and the least forgiving of Ethan's past escapades.

'Yeah, that's the one,' Ethan said, clearly wondering whether to proceed with the spliff rolling now that all eyes were on him.

Especially Jeremy's eyes. Yes, deeply unimpressed. He wasn't a man who had ever, as far as Nell knew, taken anything. Worried about losing control, probably. Nor was he someone who did something just because everyone else was doing it. She'd once found that very sexy.

'Boys will be wild,' muttered Valerie, draining her glass of wine. 'Anyway, Ethan's naughty side is like ground elder. Just when you think it's been eradicated it pops up again. Aren't I right, Janet?'

'Nail on the head,' said Janet, shooting Ethan an unreadable look.

'Besides, surely there are worst things in the world than cannabis,' continued Valerie. 'I read stories about teenagers taking all sorts of things these days, things like hedgehog tranquillisers!'

Nell caught Heather's eye. They both laughed.

'It's horse tranquilliser, Mum,' explained Nell. 'Ketamine.'

'Really? Why on earth . . .' Valerie shook her head. 'Some people believe that cannabis can actually help with illness, however.' Her voice slurred slightly and Nell suspected she'd drunk too much. This was not good. Valerie was meant to watch her alcohol units, i.e. Nell was meant to watch Valerie's alcohol units. She hadn't.

'I think that's for arthritis, Mum,' said Heather quickly, lest she get any silly ideas.

'Maybe I should try it? It's been about thirty years since I had a puff.'

'No!' declared Heather and Nell in unison. Janet giggled. Jeremy struggled not to look appalled.

'Don't stand on ceremony, Ethan. Pass it over. Honestly, do you not think what the doctors stick into my arm these days isn't a whole lot stronger than this stuff?'

Heather's eyes widened. 'She's been drinking,' she mouthed. 'Don't.'

'Heather . . .' said Valerie, with a new, brittle edge to her voice. 'I refuse to be treated like an ill old person. And I am not in the least tiddly!'

Ethan hesitated, licked the paper, lit it, then passed it over.

Valerie took a lug and spluttered violently.

Heather leapt up and clapped her on the back. 'Oh God, Mum. Are you OK?'

'I would be, if you weren't thumping me on the back like an old rug. For goodness' sake, calm down.' She handed the spliff quickly back to Ethan. 'Not for me, darling. But I'll try everything twice.'

Janet laughed, slung an arm over Valerie's shoulder and hugged her towards her with an easiness that Nell couldn't help but envy. 'Oh, Val,' laughed Janet, 'you're a hoot.'

'The thing is . . .' Valerie continued, still coughing slightly, 'fill my glass up, Janet. Thanks, darling. I know that the village ladies would be appalled. But none of it matters, you know, what other people think.' Her voice dropped to a whisper and her eyes narrowed and darkened. 'I realise that now. I wish I'd realised it years ago.'

Ethan and Nell exchanged anxious glances. Nell felt a lump in her own throat. It tore her apart to see these raw glimpses of regret. They came from dark, secret parts of her mother's life she knew nothing about.

'I just should have said bugger the lot of you!'

'About what?' Janet probed.

Valerie suddenly looked bewildered, as if she had no idea how she'd got into this conversation or how she was going to get herself out of it. She looked at Nell helplessly.

'Come on, Mum. I'll take you in,' Nell said, offering her hand. 'I'll make you a cup of hot chocolate.' They'd all gone too far. They'd been irresponsible. Mum shouldn't be drunk. Or stoned. Jesus. What kind of family were they?

Valerie didn't take her hand. She stared into the embers, her mind elsewhere.

'Come on. You're tired.'

'I don't need to be told if I'm tired or not, thank you, Nell.' Valerie's voice was notably slurred now, her eyes wild, the embers of the barbecue reflected in them like chunks of sun.

Nell got a horrible sense of foreboding. Something was wrong. And if it wasn't yet wrong, it was about to become wrong.

'I haven't been the best mother, have I?' She turned to

address Jeremy directly. 'Ethan's wild days, I'm not sure Leslie and I dealt with that very well, and as for Nell . . .'

Oh God. Where's this one going? Nell looked at Ethan in panic.

'. . . her addiction to work and *still* single. Heather—'

'Mum, that's enough,' said Nell.

'Val.' Janet leaned forward and spoke in her softest, most hypnotic voice, as if she were lulling a small child asleep. 'You've done a great job. You really have.' She shot Ethan an inscrutable look. 'I haven't returned the end product yet, have I?'

'And you, Mr Jeremy Fisher?' said Valerie brightly, warming to her theme.

Jeremy froze.

'You think you got the right one, do you?'

Nell daren't look at Jeremy. Or Heather.

'They're lovely girls, my daughters,' continued Valerie, rubbing her hands together and holding them up to the heat. 'I don't know which one I'd choose. Feisty old Nell? Tricky middle child. Hard work, wilful but clever, very clever, I think, despite the grades at school. Or soft-centred Heather? A natural blonde, no less!'

It felt like her mother had got a boil and lanced it there and then.

'Right, come on, Ma,' said Ethan cheerily, prising her off the log and trying to take control of the situation. 'Time for bed.'

But it was too late. In a flash, Heather had leapt up and run away into the garden's bushy blackness. Jeremy jumped up to follow her.

'Oh dear,' said Valerie, looking at Ethan, puzzled. 'Did I say the wrong thing?'

Sixteen

'What colour knickers are you wearing?'

'I'm not wearing any.' Well, it was the honest answer. Gripping the brick phone between ear and shoulder, Nell looked at the clock. Midnight. Six hours before Cass woke up. She needed to sleep or she'd be demented tomorrow.

Bedclothes rustled. 'Yeah, baby, yeah.'

Nell shut her eyes. 'Please don't do that.'

'What?'

'That voice. That Austin Powers thing.'

Silence.

'Sorry, I don't *not* like your voice,' Nell said quickly. She sat up and propped herself up on the pillow. 'It's just accents. I'm not that into accents – fake ones, I mean.' She hadn't realised this fact until this moment. She tried to stifle her yawn. The evening had completely drained her. She craved the oblivion of sleep. 'Pete, sorry, but do you mind if—'

'Silk sheets? Or on a chaise longue? Beneath the stars, your peachy arse on the cold, striped lawn?'

'No, Pete.' Nell hugged the duvet tight. 'It's chilly in the house right now, let alone outside in the muddy garden.'

'But . . .'

'I'm in Ethan's old bed. He's my brother. And the bed smells of him. And that's really not a good thing.'

'Do you have to ruin things? I was getting into that.'

'Sorry, Pete. This is all a bit weird. The thing is . . .' this should get him off the phone – 'my mother is asleep across the hall.'

'Oh.' Pete was silent. He didn't like to talk about Valerie, or why Nell was there in Cornwall, as if the subject itself was too intimate for their level of non-commitment.

'There's also a possibility that I'm too old for phone sex.'

'Too old? How old *are* you, Nell-I'm-Not-a-Tube-Station?'

'Old enough to need my sleep.'

'When are you back, anyhow?' he asked impatiently. 'There's a limit to how long a red-blooded male can wait for his lady.'

He was waiting for her? 'I'm not sure.'

'Well, if you're feeling horny, call me, won't you?'

She smiled. There was something sweet about his puppyish enthusiasm. 'I will.'

'Night, Foxy. Sleep tight. Don't let the bedbugs bite.'

'You have no idea how apt advice that is.'

It was one o'clock in the morning now. And she was still awake, her brain a carousel, thoughts rising and falling like crazed, wooden horses. This was ridiculous. Having insomnia while she was working in newspapers and living in inner London was one thing. But having insomnia in a Cornish rectory that didn't even have any Wi-Fi was quite another. She swivelled around in her bed, trying to avoid the spring stabbing her left buttock and dwelling on the strange turn of events that evening at the barbecue.

Poor Heather. For all her faults Nell knew she didn't have the bark-thick skin that she and Ethan had developed when it came to their mother. None of them had seen her since she'd run off. Jeremy had come downstairs all protective and husband-like and said that Heather had a migraine and didn't want to see anyone and they would be off early the next morning to avoid the bank-holiday traffic. Valerie, seemingly oblivious to the part she'd played in their early departure, cheerily muttered something about it being a very good idea to miss the traffic and that she'd pack them some fruit loaf for elevenses. The crazed carousel started spinning faster. Jeremy. What an enormous relief that he was leaving. Finally.

Nell swung her legs off the bed. Hugging her duvet around her, she padded to the window and parted the linen curtains. A polka dot of ivy suckers clung to the panes like the feet of exotic frogs. A spider swung from drapes of web. The sky was matt-black, eerie tonight. For some reason she thought of the woman Heather had seen staring at the house earlier, and shivered.

Nell reached for her grandmother's old quilted Liberty print dressing gown hanging on the bedroom door. Threads were coming loose on the cuff but apart from that, age had only softened it deliciously. Pulling it on she felt comforted. Weirdly it still smelled a bit of Grandma, lipstickey and cakey, in the way that clothing that was particular to a person did absorb something of its original owner, however many times it was washed (which was why she didn't like vintage with its stranger's skin cells embedded in its threads).

Penelope, Valerie's mother, had been famously strict, religious, but she had a dry, mischievous sense of humour, and a slightly incongruous love of hats. She was not, as Valerie had frequently told her, as if it were a fact as indisputable as the laws of gravity, a good mother herself. But Nell had always thought her a cracking granny, funny, caustic at times, never boring and not nearly as terrifying as

142

her grandfather with his short temper and red beard that exploded from his chin like fireworks.

Even now, all these years after her death, another generation along the line, there was a huge sludge pile of Stuff between Valerie and Penelope that was unresolved, and, now that Grandma was dead, would for ever remain unresolved, Nell reflected sadly, tying the silk dressing-gown belt.

She padded down the creaking corridor, glancing at Mum's bedroom – the very same room Grandma had given birth to her in, years earlier – and peeked into Cass's. It was far smaller than Cass's bedroom in London, with a low ceiling and small paned window and no storage space. But Cass loved it. Something about the proportions made her feel safe: she had already stopped creeping into Nell's bed. (Secretly Nell rather missed this.) In the gloom she could just make out Cass's shape, a small, sighing lump under the duvet, and, wonderfully, no wheezing. The sea air really was brilliant for Cass. There was no denying it.

Nell hovered by the door, wondering whether an adult Cass would lament that her mother and grandmother never resolved their issues. One day it would be too late for them, as it had been for Mum and Grandma Penelope. And that day probably wasn't too far away either. Nell blew Cass a kiss and shut the door gently.

Now what? She didn't fancy going back to bed. Ah, an idea. She'd nick one of Ethan's cigarettes and have a sneaky smoke outside! It would be like being a teenager again. She'd smoke in honour of Grandma Penelope, who had been partial to the odd ciggie herself.

She crouched down in the hall and just about managed to squeeze her size-six feet into Janet's size-five pink Hunter wellies. When she opened the glass conservatory door the night billowed into the house. She sat down on the stone step, lit the cigarette. It tasted horrible.

The house sign swung and squeaked on its post, picking up momentum in the wind. The night got a shade darker. Like dropping deeper beneath the ocean in a diving bell. She'd forgotten how all-consuming the night was in Cornwall, blanketing the familiar and raising a curtain on a whole new theatre of bats and owls and alien noises. Heather had been so scared of these noises as a child, convinced they were ghosts. Whenever they stayed at Tredower as children she would creep into Nell's bed at night, her fragile, warm body spooned against her own, the two of them united against unidentifiable terrors outside the dusty blankets. Even when they were teenagers they sometimes still slept in the same bed, using the excuse of falling asleep chatting.

Mum being Mum had always been wholly unsympathetic to Heather's nocturnal anxieties. 'It's the real stuff that happens you need to be scared about, Heather, not ghosts,' she would say sternly. And Mum herself was certainly fearless. Nell remembered one notably nutty phase – so many to choose from! – when Mum had a habit of going off on night-time walks alone in the woods. Dad knew it was futile trying to stop her, or maybe he thought she needed the walk. Because Mum always came back calmer, having released some of that restless energy that seemed to torture her for some days for no apparent reason. Nell blew out another rope of smoke and it scarved into the air like the memories in her head.

'Mind if I join you?'

Nell jumped. A short, stocky figure standing behind her in the dark, unlit hall. Jeremy! Oh God. *Jeremy*.

'Can't sleep.' Jeremy sat down beside her heavily. There was a boozy smell. Striped flannel pyjamas? He never used to wear pyjamas in bed. He used to sleep butt naked.

'Nor can I. How's Heather?' She tried to sound concerned

and sisterly and normal. But her heart had started to drum.

'Fast asleep now.' He spoke softly. 'She'll be OK.'

'I don't know what got into Mum earlier. I'm sorry.'

'It's not just that. Heather was in a funny mood anyway. Keeps going on about this woman she caught staring at the house. No. Don't ask me. I've no idea why she's in such a state about it either.'

Nell frowned. Heather had always taken quite instinctive dislikes to people, especially as a child. Certain people worried her. It was as if she sensed things that other people didn't. Nell didn't say all this to Jeremy, though. Somehow it didn't feel right, their discussing Heather behind her back.

'Can I have a puff?' he asked.

'You don't smoke.'

'Aren't normal rules suspended at Tredower?'

She smiled. He'd certainly bent a few in his time.

'Anyway, you don't smoke either,' he added wryly. 'Or have you taken it up since taking Fleet Street by storm?'

'No, I don't smoke. And, as you know, I'm unemployed now.' Nell passed him the cigarette. Their fingers touched, leapt apart. She became aware of his pyjamas and randomly wondered how many layers of clothing lay between her bare flesh and his. A dressing gown. A nightie. Pyjamas. Three layers. Then nakedness.

'I can't imagine you'll be out of a job for long.' Jeremy inhaled and tried not to cough, which only made the cough worse.

'Not as easy to kill yourself as it looks?'

Jeremy handed the cigarette back. 'You know I never learned the fine art of smoking as a teenager.'

Those subtly inclusive words 'You know' were oddly soothing, an acknowledgement of sorts. Now it was just the two of them they didn't have to pretend that the past had never happened. Nell put the cigarette to her lips. It was wet with Jeremy's spit, which seemed inappropriate somehow. She ground it out on the stone step.

'It's not me who wants to inherit this house, Nell.' He fisted his hands and knocked his knuckles together. 'I want you to know that.' There was a smile in his voice. 'In fact, I can't imagine anything worse. What would I do in Cornwall?'

'Surf?'

'I wouldn't want to show up all the other surfers with my moves.' He ran his fingers through his tufty hair, the light from the hall reflecting off the glacial retreat of hair on his temple, reminders of the years they'd spent apart. 'Unfair competition.'

Nell laughed. 'You'll have to come up with some corkingly bad ideas for Tredower's future to make sure she doesn't inherit it, then.' She sneaked a glance at him. His profile was black against the blue shadows, graphic, Roman, a sexy tension between the masculine cleft of his chin and the generous, almost feminine mouth.

'I've been working on them.' A small, low laugh caught at the back of his throat. 'Drug rehabilitation centre?'

'That might actually appeal to Mum in some perverse way. I wouldn't risk it.'

'A centre for GM research?'

'More like it.'

'Sell the site to McDonald's?'

'That would clinch it.' She laughed and felt a pang for the jokes they used to share and what had been.

A bat zipped in front of them, carving out a figure of eight against the silver-black of sky. The trees rustled gently. She became aware of a fizz in the air. She must go to bed now. She must walk upstairs. Back to her life. Back to Cass. Her toes twitched inside Janet's wellies, readying them for movement. But she didn't move. Something was stopping her.

'I'm sorry,' he said suddenly, turning to face her. His dark eyes glittered. A muscle twitched in his cheek. 'I never meant to cause all this . . . this tension.'

She shrugged, trying to look like she didn't care less.

'I'm truly sorry, Nell. From the bottom of my heart.'

'Will you *stop* apologising?' The words bolted out of her with unexpected force and hung accusingly in the air. She closed her eyes and pressed the tips of her cold fingers against them. And it was like it had happened yesterday, not five years before. She pressed harder to make the memories go away. She couldn't.

That empty space next to her in bed the night of that hog roast. The sound of her sister's laughter in the garden. The touch of their hands on the toast basket. Heather looking down at the table. Her own intuition telling her, *knowing* something was wrong. And it got more wrong over the following week. Things had got tenser and tenser between them, until, five days later, it all exploded. She'd got stuck at some deathly aromatherapy press launch and had to cancel dinner at the last minute. He yelled at her for being uncommitted and selfish. She screamed at him for being controlling, for not understanding the demands of her job, for being so fucking *Jeremyish*. Then he really crossed the line.

He said she was just like her mother.

That was it. She ended it spontaneously. There and then, holding a goodie bag full of aromatherapy candles – she could no longer stomach the smell of ylang-ylang – with tears streaming down her face. Enough, she said. Enough. Even as she said it she didn't know if she meant it.

The last thing she'd been expecting was for him to look

147

her in the eye with devastating calmness and say, 'OK.'

The following week she'd wandered around in a daze, burst into tears during a features conference, totally unable to comprehend the enormity of what she'd done. Had she actually just dumped the man she loved? She'd go round and round it all in her head, boring friends to death. Maybe what they really needed was a bit of time apart, room to breathe? Maybe they weren't suited? They'd always been an unlikely couple, everyone said so. But if so, how come they had such good sex? Or maybe he didn't love her, because if he did love her, why wasn't he begging her to come back? When he didn't return her phone calls – she always made them after she'd had a night out drinking and listing his faults to girlfriends, then come home and missed him horribly – she assumed he was licking his wounds, the proud, hurt lion. He loved her last week. So he couldn't not love her now, could he? Their kind of love didn't switch on and off like a garden sprinkler. He'd phone her, surely. But the days passed and he didn't phone her. So she phoned him. He didn't return her call.

And then she heard.

It took a while to percolate. She couldn't believe it. Jeremy and Heather? Jeremy and her fucking – younger, prettier, *shorter* – sister were dating? A state of emergency was declared. Ethan was dispatched to Heather's flat to make her see sense, understand the delicacy of the situation.

And Heather did the right thing. She finished it.

But it almost finished her. Her weight dropped to seven stone. She cut off all her long blond hair. She got stress-induced shingles. After a couple of weeks, Ethan gently informed Nell that they'd got back together again. Heather had told him she'd struggled with it, torn herself apart trying to deny her feelings, but couldn't. She was powerless against the force of their love. And anyway, Nell didn't want Jeremy.

She'd dumped him, hadn't she? Nell couldn't own him for ever. Exes didn't come with copyright.

Heather had phoned Nell for her blessing not long after. She was embarrassed and apologetic but unable to mask that loved-up giddiness that made Nell feel sick to the pit of her stomach. And, of course, she'd insisted nothing had happened until *after* Nell and Jeremy had split. Nell screamed at Heather. Heather sobbed back, insisting again and again that they'd just hung out and got to know one another at the hog roast, nothing more. Nell hung up, slumped down the wall and bawled like a baby on the floor. Then she drank half a bottle of vodka and Sophie had to hold her hair back while she was sick into the toilet. That same weekend she had rebound tequila sex with Dean. The condom slid off inside her. And, thus, inconceivably, the walking, talking little marvel that was Cass was conceived. All their fates were suddenly sealed. And she hadn't touched tequila since.

'You all right, Nell?' Jeremy leaned in closer. His breath was warm on her cheek. It smelt of red wine and how his breath used to smell on Sunday mornings before he'd had his daily power shot of caffiene.

'Tired. I'm going to hit the sack.' She stood up quickly, prised the heel of one wellie against the toe of the other to extract her foot. But her foot remained stuck. 'Argh! Bugger this boot.'

'Nell . . .'

Something about his tone of voice stopped her. She looked at him. He was staring at her intently, like he might be about to murder her. Or he wanted to fuck her brains out. She couldn't be sure which.

'I miss you, Nell.'

'*What?*'

'I miss you.'

149

How was she meant to respond? *How?* She could taste tears in the back of her throat. She must not cry. Never.

'I know I shouldn't say it but it's true.' Jeremy's voice broke. 'I miss hanging out with you.'

To her mortification she couldn't stop the tears then. She wiped them away on the dressing-gown sleeve and struggled harder with the boot with clumsy fingers. She realised with a horrible, stabbing pain deep in her abdomen that she missed him too. But she'd never admit it. Never. She had to get out of here and fast.

'Here. Let me.' Jeremy held Nell's right boot tightly. His grip was firm, and to Nell's surprise and horror, it sent an electric tingle up her ankle, her calf, her thigh. Her bare foot flew out of the boot. It looked naked. He stared at it. She wished she were wearing socks.

'I always loved the way your second toe is longer than the big one.'

Nell quickly yanked off the other boot. Two bare feet now. Jeremy slumped against the doorframe, head tilted back, predatory eyes fixed on her with a sexual hunger that flattered as much as it appalled.

'It's nice just to have a chance to look at you properly.' He bit his thumbnail, still watching her. 'I feel like I can't even look at you now. Heather gets jealous.'

Heather jealous? It was the first time Nell had ever considered the possibility that Heather was jealous of *her*, of what she and Jeremy had had. Heather would be the one to march him down the aisle, after all. They were the beautiful couple, the ones with the future. She was a footnote.

'Nell …' he began.

'No.' She shook her head. He couldn't do this! Damn him. 'Goodnight, Jeremy,' she said and meant it. But then, rather than striding purposefully away, she hesitated. And Jeremy's right hand reached right into that hesitation, wrapping his cool, thick fingers over the tender, tingling skin of her bare ankle in heart-stopping slow motion. All her blood rushed to that ankle, away from her head. She couldn't think. She could only throb with a million feelings, the two of them – unfinished exes, fated and doomed – captured at a terrifying junction of possibility, the place where his hand touched her skin burning like a new tattoo.

Seventeen

It was not even nine-thirty. The tourists were still sleeping. And the promenade was emptier than April had ever seen it. She anxiously paced along in the shadow cast by the spire of St Mary's church, sea spray flicking up through the iron balustrades. She reread Beth's text as she walked and her blood ran cold: 'bad news Mum. Fone me asap.' She pressed redial. Voicemail again. She couldn't get hold of Chris either. He was probably cycling to work. Bad news. Bad news. What could it mean? Her orange anorak flapped open like a tent and a lick of icy spray caught her cheek. She pulled the anorak hood up, glanced at her watch, feeling near hysterical. Yes, to hell with it, she would run to the station and jump on a train if Beth's lack of communication went on any longer.

Then the phone rang. '*Beth!*'

'All right, Mum.' Beth's voice was very quiet.

'Are you OK? What's the matter? Why haven't you picked up your phone?' blurted April crossly. She wasn't cross, just relieved to hear Beth's voice.

'Sorry. Sorry. I needed some time . . .' Beth's voice began to crack.

April felt pure, cold, maternal dread, that dread that stops breath, freeze-frames the moment to a horror still that she'd remember for ever. Beth. Her baby daughter. Something had happened. She'd *let* something happen. Whatever the bad thing was it was April's fault. All these thoughts trammelled past in one second's pause. 'Oh sweetheart, what is it?'

'Mu-mu-mum . . .' sniffed Beth. 'The scan . . .'

The scan. April collapsed on a promenade bench. There *was* something wrong with the baby. 'Whatever happens you'll be OK. I promise you. We'll deal with it together. You're not alone, Beth.' She pressed the phone harder against her ear, as if this would move her closer to her daughter somehow, protect her from the cards life had cruelly thrown. Downs? Edwards Syndrome? 'Go on, love.'

'There . . .' explained Beth, sniffing – 'there were two green blobs on the screen.'

April frowned. 'I don't understand.'

'Twins.'

'*Twins!* Oh my God!' April yelled, crushing her hands to her mouth. Passersby turned to stare. Bloody hell. 'Oh, Beth. Oh love, I thought you were going to say something so much worse!'

'My life's over.'

'Beth, it is not.' April's brain scrambled together the right maternal spin. 'Listen, your life is just beginning! It'll be hard work. But we'll all help out.' Twins. Crikey. 'You'll be OK, I promise.'

'I've totally screwed Duncan's life.'

'Nonsense. He'll rise to the challenge.' He'd better. Duncan adored Beth but he was only nineteen, currently working in the lowliest position in an Oxford marketing company while he worked out what to do with his life. Well, life had worked it out for him. 'Have you told Dad yet?'

'No!' said Beth sounding terrified.

Chris would have kittens, no point in pretending otherwise. 'Do you want me to tell him?' April asked softly.

153

'Thanks, Mum.'

'Don't worry about the old bear. He'll get his head around it soon enough.' She zipped up her anorak, snapped into efficient-mum mode. 'I'll be on the first train home.'

'No! I don't want you to, Mum. You'll miss the last bit of your course and . . .' Beth hesitated, unsure how to phrase it.

'Don't be silly. This is far more important! I'll get the over-nighter.'

There was a pause down the line. 'No offence, Mum. Don't take this the wrong way, but, like, what are you actually going to do down here?'

'Just be there?'

'I don't want you to come back just for me.'

April began to feel hurt. Did Beth not want her own mother with her at a time like this? What had she done this time?

'How about I come to Cornwall?' said Beth, leaping into the taut silence. 'I've got a couple more appointments at antenatal then I could come down in a week, or the one after? I wouldn't mind a break, to be honest, Mum.'

'That would be . . . just *lovely*.' Something warm and hopeful bloomed in April. Was she going to get her daughter back? Would the birth of the twins bring them together after the rows and sulks of Beth's teenage years? God, she hoped so. She missed Beth. She missed the unconditional love of her children. She'd never developed the thick skin of her friends who'd laugh and roll their eyes as their seventeen-year-old babies pulled away from them, cringed at them, flew perilously from the nest. 'We'll eat ice creams and sit on the beach and talk double pushchairs. We'll spoil ourselves rotten.'

'Pushchair talk freaks me out a bit.'

'OK, no pushchair talk, promise. I'd love to have a bit of

company. I'd love to show you where I've been this summer. I've found the most beautiful beach, Beth. It's this perfect little bay with just this gorgeous café and all these birds in the trees.' She knew she beginning to gush. She could almost hear Beth's 'whatever' in her head. 'I've made friends with the owner, Michael. A surfer, you'd love him . . .'

'Ooo,' laughed Beth. 'Michael. The surfer. Watch out, Mum.'

April blushed, grateful her daughter couldn't see it. She must be more careful what she said. It was hard not to sound a bit Shirley Valentine. Difficult to put it into words, even to her girlfriends, how nice it was to meet someone new, someone not connected to the kids' school, not a parent, not on the residents' committee, not a colleague of Chris's or someone in Wolvercote. Yes, a man. A man! And why *shouldn't* she make friends with a man? It wasn't like she was about to have an affair. Michael was one of the warmest, twinkliest-eyed people she'd ever met, completely non-judgemental. She liked that he knew nothing about her. Chris would like him, she was sure of that. Maybe she'd get a chance to introduce them one day.

Or maybe not.

'Right,' she said quickly, realigning her thoughts. 'I'll speak to Joy, she's the landlady at the B. & B., a sweet lady, rather large . . .' A seagull picked a large chip bloodied with ketchup from the pavement. It flew up, swirled close to her head, then swooped away. April followed its path. And that's when she saw it.

'Mum? Are you there? I think the line's breaking up.'

It was *the* car parked a few metres away. She was sure of it. Yes, she swore it was. The black four-by-four – a huge glossy Volvo – parked on a yellow line at the side of the promenade. And it was *the* woman, the glamorous woman with the blond hair, the one who was sitting next to the man who had honked her outside Tredower the first time she'd visited. The woman was handing a large brown paper bag through the rear window. A child's hands appeared and grabbed it. There seemed to be two children – boys? – their heads just visible.

'Mum, are you there?'

'Yes,' she managed to say, her voice high and odd. 'Um, Beth. Do you mind if I phone you back in one minute?'

'I'm off out,' said Beth, sounding a bit puzzled. 'Better speak later this evening. Tell Dad, yeah?'

'Of course. Don't worry about it. He'll be fine. It'll be fine. I love you.' April stood up from the bench and started walking slowly towards the car, not wanting to draw attention to herself in case they recognised her, but irresistibly drawn towards them all the same, as if she was being tugged forward on a mountaineer's rope. Her heart was jumping madly now. Yes, she was dead sure it was the same car, the same family. The woman got into the passenger seat, slammed the door. The car started to move. April was filled with a terrible longing to raise her hand and beckon them back. But her fingers just twitched helplessly at her sides.

Eighteen

Was that the grind of his Audi on the gravel? Please God, let that be the grind of his Audi on the gravel. I'll write my novel. I'll sweep the attic with a toothbrush. I'll never eat cooking chocolate again. *Anything*. Nell lay in bed with the duvet pulled up to her nose like a child, eyes squeezed shut. Please go. Please be gone. She listened to the sound of the car's engine receding. She opened one eye. Then the other. She glanced at the clock. Nearly ten. She'd finally fallen asleep only four hours ago.

What the hell had last night been about? The more she thought about it – and she hadn't been able to stop thinking about it – the weirder it seemed. Thank goodness she'd fled when she did, flicking his hand off her ankle and hurtling back into the house. What if she hadn't? What if she'd given in to those other urges? All those feelings that she'd thought had settled to the bottom of the big black pond that was Nell and Jeremy RIP. Those.

Nightmare.

Or was she reading far too much into it? Flattering herself? Jeremy had been a bit drunk and he always got horny when he was drunk. And that was the end of the matter. She rubbed her eyes. But then why would he say ...

'Shake those lazy old bones out of bed, sis,' bellowed

Ethan, rapping on the door. 'We've been up for hours!'

'Coming.' Nell threw on the quilted dressing gown. The moment she moved she felt terrible. Her head swam with lack of sleep. She rubbed some moisturiser into her face – she looked about 104 – and scurried past Cass's empty bedroom. 'Cass?'

There was a giggle. She peered into the twins' bedroom and saw a heap of children beneath a makeshift den of sheets and pillows and duvet covers, toast and croissants and glasses of orange juice scattered around them on the rug. 'You OK, Cass?' Or had the twins eaten her alive too?

'Leave us alone!' shouted Cosmo from beneath the den. Cue a lot of giggling. 'This is a grown-up-free zone!'

Downstairs, Janet was at the dining table, breakfasting on a fistful of nutritional supplements that looked like chicken-feed pellets. Her eyes were bright from breathing exercises and she wore tie-at-the-front white yoga pants, a grey marl vest and a biscuit Cornish tan. This all made Nell feel a hundred times worse.

'Help yourself to a croissant. They're good. I nipped out and got some fresh ones in Penzance this morning.' Janet grinned. 'Check you. Had a late one then, lady?'

Was Janet insinuating something about Jeremy? Did she *know*? Perhaps she'd heard something. 'Can't do it like I used to.' Nell lunged at a croissant. Carbs would help.

Ethan prodded his laptop, half asleep, his hair sticking out at right angles from his head. 'Practice, sis. All about practice,' he yawned.

'The day I reach your tolerance levels is the day I book myself in for a liver transplant,' Nell quipped, sitting next to Janet and tearing the croissant apart with her fingers. 'So Heather and Jeremy left early, then?' She didn't look up.

'You know what Jeremy's like about out-foxing the traffic,'

said Janet, eyeing her curiously, like she suspected something. 'Seemed in a bit of a tizz this morning.'

'Was Heather all right?' Through the dining-room door, in the kitchen, Nell glimpsed the solid form of her mother in her apron wielding a frying pan.

'Brittle,' said Janet in an offhand, slightly damning way. 'Touchy.' She lowered her voice collusively. 'I think she and Jeremy had a bit of humdinger.'

Nell felt a wave of guilt. But what did she have to feel guilty about? Nothing had actually happened. Still, she couldn't shift the guilty feeling. 'Oh yeah? What about?'

'Dunno. But you could cut the air with this butter knife,' she said, holding one up. 'Well, that's a taste of married life for you. She may as well get used to it.'

Ethan rubbed his eyes and yawned. 'It's not that bad, is it?'

Nell laughed. Janet didn't. Nell stopped laughing.

'More eggs?' said Valerie, emerging from the kitchen and wiping greasy hands on her apron. 'Toast?'

'Totally stuffed, Val,' said Janet, switching between husband-hating glare to mother-in-law beaming smile.

'Nell? Oh, you do look terrible,' said Valerie.

'Thanks.' She put the croissant down. It was repeating already. She couldn't eat another thing.

'Well, you can't wander around like that all day. You'd better go back to bed. I'll look after Cass. What if you get visitors?'

'Visitors?' said Nell puzzled. Had she missed something? 'What visitors?'

'Didn't I tell you that Michael chap from the café was asking after you yesterday? I bumped into him at the Spar. He said he might pop round.'

Michael? God, she'd forgotten about him since Jeremy

had been squatting in her headspace. 'No, no you didn't, Mum.'

Ethan whistled in a really annoying Ethanish way. 'Michael. The surf stud from the café.' He winked. 'Better do your hair, sis.'

Nell grinned. 'Shuddup, Ethan.'

'Hair? Somehow, I don't think that would be high on his list of priorities. Have you seen his?' Janet laughed, leaned back on her chair. 'Seriously, Ethan, can you see your clever metropolitan sister with some layabout surf dude? I think not.'

'He's not a layabout he's a . . .' said Nell quietly, wondering what he was exactly.

'A trustie, I reckon.' Ethan winked. 'Looking for a reason to get up the odd morning. Hence that swanky house on the hill. Hence the surf caff.'

Nell frowned. A trustie. Hmm. It made sense. Problem was it was one of her principles to dislike trusties. They were flaky. Your new best friend one day, a week later they'd forgotten your name.

'At least he's got a job, Ethan darling,' said Valerie. 'Women can't be picky, not when they're thirty-seven. Anyway, Michael seems a nice man, a very nice man.'

Nell rolled her eyes. She didn't have the energy for this. 'Mum, please. He is nice, but honestly . . . not like *that*.'

'Nell, I've always said, if you'd just let me fix you up on a blind date,' said Janet. 'I do know a couple of single blokes.' She stopped. Frowned. 'No, sorry. John's been taken. One single bloke. He's lovely.'

'You don't mean Terry?' groaned Ethan. 'You can't fix Nell up with Terry! You try and fix up all your single friends with Terry. They all hate him. He's even shorter than Jeremy. He's a dick. And he's called Terry.'

'Terry earns two hundred thousand a year,' said Janet

matter-of-factly. 'He has a three-bedroomed house in Holland Park.'

'And halitosis,' Ethan added.

Valerie put a hand on Nell's shoulder. 'Darling, this sounds like an opportunity.'

One hour later, Nell, Valerie and Cass stood by the front gate to wave Ethan and family off. As they stood there, Nell felt a wave of apprehension. She'd survived the week. Just. And now? Well, at least with the others her mother had been diluted, and Cass had had the twins to play with. Now it was just the three of them again: a series of mothers and daughters, like a collection of Russian dolls that didn't quite fit into each other properly. And they'd never got round to the attic. Which meant she had to brave the attic creatures alone.

Valerie tapped the back window. 'You tell your childish daddy not to speed, OK?'

'They scream when they want to go faster,' deadpanned Ethan from the front seat.

Cass ran towards the window and pressed a melancholy face up to the glass. 'I'll miss you,' she said.

Her beloved cousins stuck their fingers up their noses and waved bogies at her as the car accelerated out of the drive into the lane, leaving the Tredower sign swinging on its downwind. Monty chased after them barking furiously.

At eleven o'clock Valerie brought out the only biscuits to survive Nat and Cosmo's raid of the larder. She put them on a cracked floral china plate. The oak dining table suddenly seemed absurdly big for the three of them and without the raucous twins the house felt dead. Nell could only imagine what it must be like when her mother was on her own. Poor Mum.

161

Cass, reached for a biscuit. 'Can we go back home to London now, Mummy?'

Nell tried not to splutter her tea. 'You've been having such a lovely time!'

'It's boring without the twins.'

'Cass, that's rude to Grandma,' said Nell. 'Say sorry. And try not to talk with your mouth full.'

'Sorry, Grandma,' mumbled Cass, spitting out crumbs of biscuit and giving Nell a defiant look. 'It's boring without Uncle Ethan too.'

'Cass,' warned Nell in a low tone.

'Uncle Ethan is funny. He lets me have chewing gum.'

'He'd better not!' She'd kill him.

'*And* he hangs me upside down. You never hang me upside down, Mummy.'

So this is what she'd be talking about in therapy in thirty years time. 'I can if you like, Cupcake.'

'No,' she said thoughtfully. 'It won't be as good.'

Valerie laughed. 'Maybe we can find some other things for you to do? You could play dress up with all my old clothes and jewellery? Feed the chickens?'

A twitch of interest. 'Can I sleep in the chicken house with Henny Penny?'

'I don't see why not …' began Valerie.

'Mum! Don't be ridiculous! Of course she can't sleep in the chicken house.'

'Oh,' said Cass, face falling. She reached for another biscuit and munched it in silence, staring fixedly at Valerie. 'Grandma . . .'

'Yes, darling?'

'You are starting to grow silver hair like a ghost.'

'*Cass!*' said Nell, trying not to smile and undermine her own insistence on good manners.

Valerie touched her hairline. 'The thing is, Deng – you remember my marvellous Deng? – she used to dye my hair for me. But she's gone home for a while.' She dunked her biscuit in her tea. 'I can't manage it myself. But now that Grandpa's gone, I don't think anyone gives two hoots whether I'm grey or not, quite frankly.'

'I don't like it grey,' said Cass solemnly. 'It makes you look very, very old.'

Oh dear. It was going to be one of those mornings. 'Cass, everyone goes grey. I'll go grey. It doesn't mean you're old.' It did.

'No, Cass is right.' Valerie sighed dramatically. 'I am fading like an unlined curtain in the sun.'

An unlined curtain? Something twisted inside her guts. No mother of hers was going to fade like an unlined curtain! 'I'll do it for you, Mum,' she blurted. 'I'll dye your hair.'

'*You?* Dye my hair?' Valerie sat back in her chair, amazed, appalled, as if Nell had just suggested she operate on her frontal lobe with a fruit fork. 'You can do something useful and clear out the loft, if you're feeling energetic.'

'Mum, I used to bleach my hair when I was younger. I can't imagine it is *that* different . . .'

Valerie shook her head. 'I remember your bleached hair. No, darling,' she sniffed, 'I think not.'

'It's not good to look like a ghost, Grandma.'

'It is a very messy, smelly business,' said Valerie stiffly. 'Your mother would find it most unpleasant. She doesn't like getting her hands dirty.'

Right. That was it.

They washed the dye out over the bath. It looked like someone had thrown a cup of tea at the wall. Nell tugged an old wooden-handled bristle brush through her mother's wet hair, not wanting to hurt her, not wanting, actually, to touch her either. It was the most intimate contact they'd had for years. Her mother's scalp was not a pink healthy scalp like Cass's – and that's what she inevitably compared it to because she brushed Cass's hair every morning – but a chalky white. It unnerved her for some reason. She quickly brushed the hair down over it so she couldn't see it.

'Do remember the follicles are actually attached to my head, darling.'

'Sorry.' As she pulled her brush through again, slower this time, she realised that she could not remember Mum brushing *her* hair. Ever. She remembered Heather brushing her hair – they used to take it in turns, plaiting and brushing and adding bows made from wrapping ribbon. She remembered the series of homesick hairy-pitted au pairs doing it. But Mum, never. Tweezering splinters. Nit-nursing. Brushing hair. Never. And here *she* was all these years later . . .

'Can I have a go?' Cass perched on the side of the bath.

Nell willingly handed over the hairbrush. Cass began to brush tenderly, taking great care with the tangles. Valerie smiled and relaxed.

Nell watched them, the gentle little girl and the thawing grandmother and her eyes pricked at the quiet, unconditional connection that Cass and her mother shared. That she and her own mother had never had.

'You're doing a great job, Cass. Here, Mum, look.' Nell held up a small, oval hand-mirror so that Valerie could see the back of her head. 'Ta-dah! No roots!'

'You're not ghosty any more!' Cass tunnelled a finger into Valerie's newly dark locks. 'It's so pretty. Look!'

Valerie looked at the mirror. A slow smile spread across her face. 'Thank you, girls. Thank you very much.'

Nell couldn't remember the last time her mother had thanked her for anything, let alone in a way which seemed genuinely grateful. A surprising warm tender feeling began to uncurl inside. 'Do you want me to blow dry it?'

'No need.' Valerie stood up and towelled her hair. 'I'll sit on a deckchair in the garden. It's sunny now. It'll dry in no time. Oh, did you hear that? The doorbell. It'll be the postman. I'm expecting some new special inner soles for my garden clogs.' Valerie patted her hair carefully with the palm of her hand. 'Run! He won't hang around. He's Cornwall's most impatient postman.'

Nell took two stairs at a time. It was a pain to miss a parcel out here. The post office was miles away. She pulled open the door and put her hand out to accept a packet. Except it wasn't a postman.

'Right house, then.' The BFG grinned. He was wearing an orange sun-bleached surf T-shirt, his hands plunged deep in his jeans' front pockets, leaning forward in the manner of an eager, slightly nervous teenage boy.

She looked puzzled, trying to work out why he was here. Had she dropped her keys again? 'Hi!'

Michael scratched his jaw. 'I was wondering if you fancied a drive and a spot of lunch?' A flicker of shyness passed over his face. He scratched his jaw again.

'Me? Lunch?' Nell repeated in confusion. 'I'm afraid I've just eaten my body weight in digestive biscuits.' What a stupid thing to say! Why did she say that?

'Sorry, I thought you might be, you know, at a loose end, Cornish stylee . . .'

Why was he asking her out to lunch? She barely knew him. No, no, this would play into her mother's hands. She couldn't possibly go out. She wasn't dressed and she was still recovering from the bizarre episode with Jeremy last night. And she was wary about leaving Cass alone with her mother. Cass couldn't look after Mum, and if anything happened to

Mum, she couldn't look after Cass. 'It's a lovely idea but—'

'Nell!' Valerie shouted down the stairs. 'Is it the postman?'

'No, Mum.'

'The organic fish man?'

'No.' She smiled apologetically at Michael.

'Then *who* is it, dear?'

Something told her that this was going to deteriorate further. 'Michael.'

Valerie paused, her curiosity piqued. 'Michael? Who's Michael?'

Nell winced. 'Just the man from the café.' Oh dear that sounded terrible.

'Oh. That Michael!'

The unmistakable clatter of her mother's footsteps on the stairs. Valerie emerged into the hall with her damp, dark hair around her shoulders, finger drying it vigorously so it sprayed Michael's T-shirt.

He outstretched his hand. 'Michael. I don't know if you remember me . . .'

'I do indeed. Valerie. Valerie Stockdale.'

'I've admired this house many times, Valerie, driving past. It is absolutely beautiful.'

Nine out of ten for charm, thought Nell.

Valerie slipped on her impress-the-visitors persona, all long vowels and raised eyebrows. 'You know the Pattersons of Penzance, I believe.'

Nell braced herself. Oh no, she wasn't going to interrogate Michael? Of course she was.

'Yes, I rudely tried to buy their house from under their noses. And I'm now rudely pitching up and trying to take your daughter from under your nose for lunch.'

Valerie's face lit up. 'Lunch?'

166

'I was just saying it's not such a great time. I was about to go up into the attic and sort all that stuff out. Maybe in a couple of days . . .'

'Not such a great time?' repeated Valerie, looking at Nell in disbelief. 'Darling, what on earth are you talking about?' She nudged her sharply in the ribs, then beamed at Michael. 'It's the *perfect* time! The attic can wait. I'd love to spend some time alone with Cass.' She grinned at them both. 'Michael, my daughter would be delighted to accept your invitation . . .' she paused, as if her mind was whirring with infinite romantic possibilities – 'to lunch.'

Michael tried not to smile. 'If Nell—'

'Go! Go and get dressed, Nell.' Valerie leaned over and whispered loudly in her ear. 'At the very least put on some lipstick.'

Feeling like a humiliated match-made teen, Nell ran off to get dressed. She ripped off her hair-dye-splattered apron, checked for food between her teeth, wiped the hair dye off her nose and tried to smooth her fringe with her fingers. But she didn't put on any lipstick.

No, she wouldn't give her mother the satisfaction.

Nineteen

April studied herself in the pine-framed wall mirror in her B. & B. bedroom, trying to view herself dispassionately, like she might one of her paintings, in the hope that she could see herself as others might see her. Not a good idea. What she saw was a sprinkling of blond hair on her upper lip that she'd never noticed before. Crow's feet. Broken veins around her nose. The Cornish light showed up one's imperfections alarmingly clearly. She turned away, not wanting her confidence to sink further.

On the bright side, her hair was behaving. And at least Joy had a decent steam iron. She chose her clothes carefully: her best dress, a nautically striped jersey Hennes number that showed off her slim calves before they inflated into maddening thighs. Red patent sandals from M & S that didn't look M & S. The pink chiffon scarf that Beth had given her last Christmas gave the outfit a bit of colour – or panache, as Mum used to say. And she'd painted her toenails just the right pink to match the scarf. But still, frustratingly, she didn't look how she *wanted* to look, like the effortlessly glamorous thirty-something woman in that black four-by-four, or the kind of person who might visit a house like Tredower. No, now, more than ever, she felt provincial and the wrong side of forty.

It was tricky ageing. She'd always thought she was the type of woman to take it in her stride, down to earth, happily married, not particularly vain. But she was obviously vainer than she'd realised because she was finding it just the hardest thing. She'd upgraded from The Body Shop in the hope that something expensive packed with brutal chemicals might actually do something. She'd even Googled Botox, although she'd never dare do it in case Chris noticed. Despite all attempts to be philosophical – 'ageing is better than the alternative', 'forty is the new thirty' – whenever she woke up in the morning and saw a mark from the seam of the pillow bisecting her cheek like a scar, it was a downer. As was her neck. The weight had started to pile on too. She'd tried the Atkins diet, but it gave her terrible gas. She'd tried Spanx underwear but it redistributed the bulges and she'd get some odd lump midway up her back like a camel. She tried not eating. But she got hungry.

One of her favourite masochistic pleasures was sinking back on to the sofa with a nice glass of red and a packet of Pringles and watching the likes of Gok Wan and Joan Collins making over a woman, reassuringly fatter, and worse dressed than herself. Clingier, more colourful and a better bra seemed to be the gist of the advice, although it was obvious to April that in most cases losing a stone or two was all that was needed. Of course, once the programme and the Pringles had finished she'd feel an itch of insecurity.

Who was she to gloat? Her own wardrobe was dull. Too much black in the hope it was slimming. (Was it? Really?) Dresses that covered her upper arms. Hobbs and Jigsaw mostly. Shoes that didn't hurt because her feet were as wide as a yeti's. She didn't really do heels apart from at weddings and the like. Oh yes, and cardigans. She had tonnes of them. They hid all manner of sins.

Sometimes April would see an outfit in a shop window, a wholly impractical pink silk ruffled dress for instance, or a tiny skirt worn with ridiculous sky-high custard-yellow heels, and she'd catch her breath and be filled with this extraordinary *longing*. But she'd learned from expensive experience that if she did buy the outfit, she'd never have the guts to actually wear it. Her wardrobe was a tomb to such clothes. The hot-pink jeans she'd bought in Paris. The green silk top that was impossible to wear without bra straps showing, and gosh, if anyone needed to wear a bra . . . and, her favourite, the red-and-white fifties-style dress, all swishy skirt and tight bodice, that she loved, completely loved, so much so that occasionally she'd open her wardrobe just to gaze at it, like an art collector at their most cherished hidden masterpiece. But she'd never, ever worn the dress. It was a dress for another person. Someone more glamorous and daring, someone inside waiting to get out. Gok would probably say, 'Free her, girlfriend. *Be* her, girlfriend.' All very well. But he wasn't a forty-three-year-old mother of two, was he?

April tugged back her hair into a loose ponytail and pulled out some strands to soften her face. She sat on the edge of the bed with her hand-mirror and started to apply her make-up slowly, partly because it was so important that it looked absolutely right but mostly because her hands were a bit shaky and she was out of practice. She rarely even bothered with mascara at home. But today she needed to look her best. Her fear was that *the woman* – she couldn't even say her name yet, in case this might jinx it in some way – would answer the door, take one look at her and . . . No, she couldn't go there. She applied her lipstick. 'Sweet Hope' it was called. Fitting.

April could feel her whole body hesitating as she walked to the car, as if it wanted to do a moonwalk backwards. But she had come to the conclusion that she *had* to do this today, before Beth arrived. How could she tell Beth to be strong about the twins while she was such a chicken herself?

The road narrowed, the verges on the sides threateningly close. A ridge of grass seeds collected on the windscreen wipers as she turned into Prickle Lane. April's head started to pound, as if a migraine was coming on, and she was sure she was about to fail, suddenly and explosively. Soon, too soon, she was there, outside the swinging sign, turning into the drive, not, thank God, stalling or revving, but turning to the right like it was the turn she did every day of her life, hopefully, looking like a normal person, not some kind of deranged nutcase. Once she'd parked she had to sit for a few seconds to collect herself, her fingers drumming on the steering wheel, sweat pouring down her nose. After dabbing at her face with a tissue, she forced herself to pick her handbag off the floor. It was a new handbag, red with brass buckles, never used before even though she'd bought it in the Whistles sale with precisely this day in mind. It felt odd and stiff in her hand, like a bag that didn't belong to her. She had the same feeling looking at the house.

The gravel was awkward beneath her slippy sandal soles. This added to a growing feeling of disorientation as if she was walking on one of those moving treadmills at the airport and her motion didn't quite make sense. The closer she got to the door, to the doorbell, the odder she felt. As she neared the porch she had a strange sensation of looking down at herself from a few feet above the ground. She stopped, steadied herself with her hand against the wall, then, a few moments later, pressed the cracked china teat of the doorbell, barely daring to breathe. No audible ring. No footsteps. Relief. Then frustration. She supposed the bell must have gone off somewhere in the house. But, shit, what if it hadn't?

She'd always imagined millions of potential pitfalls but not this, such a small but potentially disastrous hiccup. She waited for a few minutes: still no sound in the house, no footsteps down the hall. This was a sign to cut her losses and call it a day, wasn't it? The other voice in her head defended its corner. No, come on, April, one more go. She rang the bell again, braced herself.

Then, magically, like she'd wished it into happening, the front door began to open. A tiny tanned bare foot. A gorgeous little girl with milk-blond hair and round, vivid green eyes stood there and stared at her indifferently.

'Hello, there!' A dog, a chocolate lab, pushed past her and sniffed her feet. 'Um, I was just wondering, er, does a lady, a lady called, er . . .' she was tripping on her words – 'Valerie live here?'

'Grandma lives here.'

Grandma. Of course.

'Is it the postman at last, darling?' a woman's voice called from inside the house.

April felt the blood rushing from her head. This was the moment. The one she had been dreading and anticipating. Now she was here she wasn't sure she could go through with it at all.

The little girl kept her eyes on April and shouted back over her shoulder, 'Not the postman. A lady.'

April sensed movement. Was a curtain twitching in the room on the floor above? A second later there was a dull thump, like a piece of furniture shifting.

'Grandma?' the little girl called, running back into the house.

Was everything OK? Should she ring the doorbell again? Where was the little girl? Not knowing what to do, April just stood there like a lemon. She couldn't walk right into the house. Or could she? The little girl was probably just playing a game. Yes, that was it. That was exactly the kind of thing Beth might have done when she was little, closing the door on a stranger, running off and forgetting all about it. She'd come this far . . .

April touched the door lightly. It swung open too easily.

Twenty

Michael opened his driver's window. The summer air blasted in. He glanced at Nell, smiled, pulled his eyes back to the road. 'Sorry if you got press-ganged into lunch.'

'Not at all. You saved me from clearing out the attic.' Nell wished she had put lipstick on after all. And maybe a dress. Anything other than these knackered old jeans and an old blue shirt. The strangeness of being in the car with him was gradually fading, softened by the familiarity of the surroundings and the unexpectedly lovely weather. If he was a mad axe murderer he surely wouldn't choose such a gorgeous day to chop her up and dispose of her body, would he? Besides, a mad axe murderer wouldn't wear an orange surf T-shirt. Nor would he be listening to The Beloved. He'd be listening to death metal. 'Where are we going for lunch?'

Michael tapped his fingers on the steering wheel. 'This we must debate.'

Debate? He had no plans? She immediately thought of Jeremy, the way he had plans for everything. He was the kind of man who pre-booked taxis at foreign airports before he flew. Pete had plans, even if it was to grab a Bloody Mary and one of her buttocks. All Londoners had plans.

'What do you fancy?'

'Um . . .' Totally blank. Besides, it was one of the ironies

174

of living by the sea, surrounded by fish and fields of fresh produce, that many of the local restaurants would still serve up a steak that tasted like a geography teacher's leather elbow patch and breaded fish from the freezer compartment.

'Do you like crab?'

'I love crab.'

Twenty minutes later they were sitting at an outdoor café beside a tiny fishing bay. The seating area consisted of four small round wooden tables overlooking the sea. Nell was surprised she didn't know about it. She studied Michael as he stood at the ordering hatch. Heinous raft shoes. Long, long legs in faded blue jeans, threadbare about the knees, with the rectangular bleached stamp of his wallet in the left back pocket. Coat-hanger surfer's shoulders. Small, round sybarite's tummy. Hair sun bleached at the ends. Curls crushed at the back of his head like he'd just woken up. He was the opposite of the metrosexually groomed Jeremy, or Pete. While the latter two looked like they'd walked out of a glossy ad for a designer kitchen, Michael looked like he'd rolled out from a month spent beneath a sand dune.

Nell felt an unexpected spark of sexual curiosity. Then caught herself. Michael was *married*. On no account must she forget this fact. Nor the fact that he wore rafting shoes. When you start fancying men in raft shoes you know it's time to return to the city.

Michael returned proudly holding aloft two white plates piled high with crab sandwiches, cut into quarters and scattered with cress, and two cold cans of pithy lemonade. Nell felt a shot of pity: he was blithely unaware that in his three minutes' absence from the table he'd been examined, assessed for potential and found wanting and damned for his choice of footwear.

'Bloody good, these,' he said, taking an enormous bite out of a sandwich. He slurped his lemonade to wash it down. She imagined he was the kind of man who'd burp in front of her, too. Everything about him was noisy and, she thought, noticing his big paw-like hands, strangely bear-like. 'Do dig in.'

'Thank you.' She picked one up daintily. Yes, good, very good. Michael had taste, in sandwiches at least. She secretly wished the café served wine. She had never, ever done a date without any alcohol units. But no! What was she thinking? This wasn't a date. Which was why it was sober. Only her mother thought it was a date.

'Are you around for the whole summer?' Michael asked hopefully, his eyes – nice, intelligent eyes, a dirty sea-blue – zigzagged across her face.

'Until September. My mum's not well, you see. Her carer had to go away. I'm filling her boots for the summer.' She pulled a frizzy chunk of hair out of her mouth. The chance that she was looking pretty and windswept in the manner of a Toast catalogue model seemed less and less likely. 'Long story.'

'Ah, a dutiful daughter.'

'Not exactly.'

'You're here, aren't you?' He took another energetic bite of his sandwich, taking out half of it. 'Although,' he added, 'if my mother lived in Cornwall rather than Cheltenham, even I might consider it. What price peace, eh?'

What price indeed. Nell wondered if Ethan was right. Was he a trustie? How could she find out? 'Pretty dead around here on the job front – well, on all fronts, really. If you're used to London . . .'

'And being fermented in a toxic metropolitan mix of stress and alcohol.'

Oh, definitely a trustie. He'd probably whip out a bongo and start telling her about the plastic bottle island in the Pacific in a minute. 'Well, I guess there's always the surf.'

Michael started to laugh, that warm, gritty known-you-for-ever laugh. And as he laughed his knee knocked against hers. 'Actually, I do get pretty busy down here,' he said, giving her an amused look like he knew exactly what she'd been thinking.

'Oh?' She'd never seen the café *that* busy. Still, all relative.

'Me and a friend have our own company, HQ's in London, although I can do quite a lot from Cornwall these days. We run a consultancy for virtual business . . .' He stopped. 'Oh, I know, it makes the best of us glaze over. But it's more interesting than it sounds. Promise.'

Nell felt a bit silly. 'How come you've got the café too?'

'I'd always dreamed of running a café on a beach.' He scratched his stubble lazily. 'You know, it was on the To Do Before I Die list and because the business was going well, finally, I thought, why not? I've paid my dues. Annie is the manager, but I'm afraid I can't help sticking my fingers in. It's my baby.'

Virtual businesses. People with futuristic-sounding jobs and renaissance lives made her feel antique and out of touch. What was the point in being a print journalist – *print*? Hello? – and scraping forty-five thousand a year when you could hold your jeans up with string, spend your time surfing, and pretty much retire before the age of forty-five doing something that nobody understood? Suspecting the career question was about to be deflected back to her she tried to think of a witty way to present her redundancy and couldn't.

'Are you with your daughter's father?'

Oh! Where had that come from? The question's directness

startled her. Most men avoided any subject that could be in any way linked with her role as a mother. 'No. It's civilised, though,' she blurted. 'Dean, he's a good dad. He's just married a dentist.'

'A dentist.' He did a comic shudder.

Nell laughed. 'She's very sweet.'

Michael raised an eyebrow. 'Sweet? Hmm. Bad for the teeth. It all sounds suspiciously civilised. Are there no bloody custody battles or anything?'

'Furiously civilised, I'm afraid.'

He narrowed his eyes, sizing her up. 'OK, so who's the lucky man, then?'

Nell grinned at his impertinence, and the assumption she wasn't single. 'I'm kind of seeing someone in London.' It felt really good to say this for once. Normally the answer was 'nothing doing at the moment'.

'You sound like my fifteen-year-old niece.' He chewed his last bit of sandwich and a bulb of pink mayonnaise appeared at the corner of his mouth. Nell was surprised that she didn't find it disgusting. Michael leaned back on the bench and stretched his tanned feet out, wiggling his toes in the raft shoes. He gazed at the sea, not looking at her but, she sensed, absolutely intently focussed on her all the same. 'Why bother, then?'

Yank up the defences! She hadn't come out to lunch to be interrogated! In fact, suddenly she wasn't sure why she'd come out to lunch at all. 'I'm not looking for a relationship, a proper one, not right now. Cass is still young.' She stopped: yes, she'd made her position quite clear! It was always best to get that bit out of the way first, just in case her mother had given him other ideas. 'What about you?'

'Ah.' Michael winced. 'Complicated.'

Well, of course it was. Bloody bounder. For some reason

178

she thought about Jeremy and a wave of crossness hit her.

He looked down at his hands. 'We're taking divorce one step at a time.'

Divorcing? Yikes. Baggage. What had he done? An affair probably. 'She's not here?'

Michael shook his head. 'No, London.' He smiled at her, his eyes warm, reconnecting with hers again. 'It's not really her thing, Cornwall.'

'Perhaps you should have chosen somewhere more exciting to set up a café. Hawaii? Bondi?'

'We have it all here. Surf, sun . . .'

She laughed. 'I beg to differ.'

'Come on, Nell. What are you lacking, right here, right now? What one thing would make the day better?'

The way he phrased the question, made it sound so ridiculously loaded, made her blush. To hide it she pulled at her fringe. Actually, when she considered it, there wasn't much else that could make the lunch better. Sure, she'd like not to be looking like a farm worker. And she could be holding a glass of ice-cold white wine. But apart from that even she had to admit it was a perfect Cornish day and she felt oddly at ease eating crab sandwiches – sober – with the divorcing BFG.

She liked Michael. There was something endearingly direct about him, kind of puppyish without being entirely stupid. He'd obviously make a terrible boyfriend – too much baggage, unforgivable footwear and facial hair, incomprehensible job, etc. – but he'd be fun to hang out with, a bouncy testosteroney antidote to the female toxicity of Tredower. She thought how much Ethan would like him and this made her like him more.

He raised his can of lemonade. 'To excellent company.'

Nell raised her can. 'To excellent crab.'

*

The afternoon got hotter. The heat slowed things down, made it harder to move, or want to go anywhere, in fact, certainly harder for Nell to make her excuses and rush home, as she'd planned. They sat in the lemony sunshine, hoovered up three sticky chocolate brownies between them, chatted about everything with that surprising frankness that could only happen between acquainting strangers. They joked and laughed, debated whether women should be banned from plumping up their lips and whether aubergine needed to be salted before it was cooked. It was silly, bouncy banter, like playing tennis slightly drunk. They walked off their brownies on the beach, shadows lengthening as the sun dropped and the sand slowly lost its heat like a cooling loaf of bread. Nell looked at her watch and was disappointed to see that the day was about to end. She imagined her mother jumping to all sorts of conclusions. She imagined Cass fractious, missing her and needing a bath. Her mother letting Cass sleep in the chicken house. And worse things: swallowing a laburnum pod, disturbing a wasps' nest, falling off a stile and knocking her front teeth out. God, the countryside was lethal. What was she doing?

'Would you like me to take you home?' Michael asked softly.

She looked up at him, surprised by his intuitive timing. The sunshine had gilded his tanned skin. His eyes danced. For a split second his ragged, almost-handsome face looked beautiful. And anything seemed possible. Then the sun slipped further and the light lost its gold. He was just the BFG in rafting shoes again. She was just Nell Stockdale, daughter, single mother, media reject in crap jeans. Tredower was waiting. 'I had no idea of the time,' she said, aware that her voice had become clipped, pulling away from him. 'Yes, I've got to go. I really must get back.'

Twenty-one

'Mummy!' Cass ran up the drive as Michael's car pulled away and large splodges of rain began to fall. 'Something's happened to Grandma!'

Nell stopped still for one second. Everything else fell away. Something's happened. Something's happened. The next moment she was on auto-pilot, rushing up the stairs with Cass, heart thumping, gripping her phone ready to call nine nine nine. 'Is Grandma OK?' she panted, taking two stairs at a time.

'She had a fall,' said Cass, trying to keep up.

Nell threw back the door of Valerie's bedroom. Mum was lying on her bed, white as a sheet, fully dressed, her eyes shut. 'Mum, are you OK?'

Valerie opened one eye. 'Perhaps.'

Nell instinctively put her hand on her head, as if she was a fevered child. She felt normal. 'Where did she fall, Cass?'

Cass pointed to the space beneath the window. Nell could almost see her lying there, leg stretched out, nudging the bottom of the peach curtains, the other bent; an outline of a crime victim chalked on a pavement. Oh God. What was she *thinking*, spending all afternoon on the beach with Michael? As if she needed further reminder that she wasn't on holiday. She looked back to her mother and felt a fresh wave of

181

mortification that she'd not been here when it happened.

Valerie opened the other eye. 'I'm not road kill, darling. Don't just stand there staring.'

'I'll call an ambulance.' She started to dial. Her hands were shaking.

'I don't need a bloody ambulance.' Valerie wedged herself up on her pillows. 'Not a stroke, before you ask.'

It hit her like a bus then. Her mother was going to die. Her maddening mother was going to die! Nell's eyes welled with tears. She wanted to shake her. Tell her not to die. Not to be ill. Not to be a burden. Not to be who she was. She wanted to tell her that she loved her and she hated her and to never, ever, ever do this selfish falling trick again when it was just her and Cass in the house. The thoughts shot out of her like lines of machine-gun fire. But she didn't voice any of them. Instead she said, in an astonishingly sane-sounding voice, 'Can you lift your arms above your head?'

Valerie lifted her arms above her head. 'See! I know when I've had a bloody stroke and when I've had a tumble. I'm not gaga yet.' She leaned back into her pile of white, threadbare, embroidered pillows. Nell studied her face for signs of droop or asymmetry. Nothing. Her words weren't slurred either. Touch wood, she was all right. Thank God.

Nell bent down to Cass's level, poor Cass, pale as an egg. 'And are you OK, Cass?'

Cass's bottom lip started to quiver. 'The door . . .'

'I should have eaten lunch,' said Valerie quickly. 'You know what I'm like when I skip meals.'

She sat on the bed beside her mother, holding Cass's hand. 'Did you bump your head?'

'I don't think so.'

'Which bits hurt?'

'Nothing.' Then, to Nell's horror, she started to sob.

182

'Oh, Mum.' Nell circled her arms around her. 'It's all right, Mum.'

In a terrible domino effect, Cass's face started to crumple too. 'Mummy . . .'

Nell reached for Cass. Now she had both of them wetting the pits of her elbows with tears. For a moment she was terrified, thrown by the responsibility of it all. This was so much harder than any job she'd ever done. Eventually, the tears stopped and they all just sat there entwined, snuffling and huddling together as the rain pummelled against the sash window. Over their heads – Cass's soft blond, Mum's coarse brunette with that tinny smell of dye – Nell looked around the bedroom, Grandma Penelope's old bedroom, and for a moment it summed up everything she was feeling.

When Nell had been a child, the room had seemed huge and regal to her; seeing it through adult eyes, the room seemed quaint and dated, like a bedroom in a three-star B. & B. The fireplace's stone surround was lined with silver-framed photographs of them as newborns with puzzled dark eyes. In the middle of these photos was a larger frame covered in white seashells. Mum. Dad. Confetti. Their wedding day. She'd always been transfixed by that photo – her mother's white lace veil, Dad's ridiculous boyishness – and the impossible idea that her parents had a history that predated her. Now, as she stared at the photo, it struck her with force quite how young her mother had been when it was taken. She was younger, much younger, than Nell now was. She, Nell, only had one child, and at times it felt impossibly hard. Her mother had had *three*. And, yes, she had Dad too. But Mum had been so young, hardly more than a child herself, young and badly suited to the post. Why had she never realised this before? The longer Nell stared at the picture, her mother, like the bedroom, seemed to diminish, shrink back in her arms to something on a far more human scale.

'Mummy,' said Cass, prising herself apart and shaking Nell out of her thoughts.

'What's the matter, Cupcake?' Poor traumatised child.

Cass looked up at her. 'Did you know that a group of ladybirds is called a loveliness?'

'No. No, I didn't.'

'Or that a group of butterflies is a rabble?' A thoughtful sigh. 'Grandma knows *everything*.'

Seven p.m. Still raining. Everyone had fully recovered. Apart from Nell. Cass was reeling off the list of collective animal nouns to Dean on the phone. Valerie was watching the news in the sitting room.

Nell had just about managed to rustle up a bowl of pesto pasta for them all and, on auto-pilot, had sorted out her mother's evening pills, fed the chickens, fox-proofed them for the night, bundled the mountain of weekend laundry into the capricious noisy washing machine that sounded like a cement mixer and smelled of damp tent, then finally collapsed with a bottle of cheap white wine on a chair in the kitchen. The idea that she'd been carefree on the beach eating crab sandwiches with Michael earlier that day seemed totally surreal. The idea that she'd once held a serious position on a newspaper and used to go to work in heels every morning was even more unlikely. Here she was, thirty-seven, with a freaky fringe, a sunburnt nose and her mother's hair dye under her fingernails, drinking wine alone and listening to the rain bucketing down outside. Her sister's fiancé had taken up residence in her head. Her arms were tired from loading laundry. Her stomach was still knotted by what could have happened – Mum falling over and hitting her head on a lurking iron, Cass being left home alone, a fire starting, social services getting involved – and what had happened. To make matters worse, Cass was now chirpily relaying the day's dramas to Dean on the telephone. She'd have to phone him back later and reassure him, try to explain why she was out when it happened, how nothing like this had happened before.

'Bye, Daddy!' she heard Cass say. 'Love you.'

It was when she went to round up Cass for her bath that she noticed it. A flash of pink snaking along the white skirting board in the blue hall. She bent down to pick it up. Funny. She didn't remember Heather wearing this. Janet's? But it didn't look like something Janet might own; the hot-pink was too shrill. She sniffed it. It smelled slightly of an unfamiliar perfume. Oh well. She slung it on a coat peg. It must belong to somebody.

Cass ran towards her, cheerily. Stopped. Looked at the scarf, puzzled.

Then she gingerly pulled it from the coat peg and looped it around Nell's neck like a ceremonial garland. 'Better,' she said, standing back, eyeing her coolly like a magazine stylist. 'I like it when you look pretty.'

Nell laughed. 'Me too. Must try harder.'

'Freya has a pink scarf too. *She*'s pretty.'

'Very pretty.'

Cass looked up at her with round, green, unblinking eyes. 'Mummy, I want to see Freya's bump. Daddy says the baby makes it jiggle.'

'And you will see it,' Nell promised, feeling guilty. What damage had she caused to the fragile psyche of her daughter by bringing her down here? What could she do to ease the transition of a sibling? Suddenly she had an idea. 'How about they come to the hog roast?'

185

'The pig party?' Cass's eyes lit up.

'That's the one.'

'I think the bump will like the pig party. Definitely.' Cass gave Nell one of her scrutinising adult stares, narrowing her eyes. 'Will you ever have a bump, Mummy?'

'Another baby, you mean?' She smiled and shook her head. She'd leave the sibling-making to Freya. 'I think that's unlikely, Cupcake.'

'Good!' Cass grinned. 'Let's just stay me and you.'

Nell laughed. 'Come on, bath time, young lady.' They clambered up the stairs hand in hand. 'Just me and you.' How gorgeous. But would Cass still want this closeness when she was older? Nell wondered, as they reached the bathroom. What would happen when she hit fifteen? Or thirty-seven, her age now? Then what?

'Can I have Henny Penny in the bath?'

'No!' She turned on the taps. Peaty water spurted yellow into the tub.

'Grandma said I could. She said Henny Penny likes baths. She said she's a very odd chicken, a Stockdale chicken.'

Nell laughed. 'That sounds about right.'

Cass looked up at her cheekily. 'Can I have Monty in the bath, then?'

'No!' She peeled off Cass's clothes. 'Look at the state of you. You're coated in sand and mud and goodness knows what.'

'I like it,' said Cass, daintily dipping one filthy foot into the tub. 'Grandma lets me get muddy. *And* she lets me touch slugs. Ow, it's hot!'

'Does she?' Nell pulled on the cold tap. She could only imagine what they'd got up to while she was out.

'I like touching the slugs, Mummy. They're soft. Like jelly babies. And the mud is nice. It's not dirty. Grandma said the city is dirty.' She crouched down into the bath and flicked the plug back and forth. 'I like it here by the sea with the mud and the slugs. I don't like cities.'

'You said you wanted to go back to London earlier.'

'I like it here now.' She lay back in the water. 'And we have to be here in case Grandma falls again,' she added matter-of-factly, with a childish compassion and simplicity that tugged at Nell's heart. 'So we'll have to stay here for ever, won't we?'

Later that evening, Cass settled, Nell attended to her mother. Valerie was still sitting on the brown velvet sofa, drinking sherry, staring morosely into the empty fireplace with the brow-furrowed intensity of someone glued to a gripping detective drama on telly. The Muffin catalogue was open in her lap.

'Mum, can I get you something?'

Valerie shook her head. She didn't look up.

Nell perched on the edge of a footstool beside her. 'Will you let me call the doctor? Give you the once over?'

'Absolutely not!' Valerie sprang to life. 'Talk about shutting the stable door after the horse has bolted. The less time I have to spend with doctors the better. You can light the fire, though. It's chilly. I feel a storm brewing.'

The fire was already stacked with logs and firelighters. Nell crouched down, struck a match, blew into the heart of it and watched the baby flames leap towards the breeze coming down the black chimney. 'Do you think it was just your blood sugar that made you fall?' The whole fall scenario still had a bit of a puzzling whiff about it. 'Maybe you've got a bug or something.'

Valerie frowned. 'Yes, it was a bit peculiar. The door went. I think I went to the window to see if it was the postman.

And I just got this feeling, a funny feeling . . .' She pressed her hands to her temples and looked confused.

Nell goosebumped. The doctors had warned her about moments like these, moments that sprang from nowhere, little discombobulations between events and her mother's brain's interpretation of them. Just when you thought her illness had gone away, there it was, knocking on the door, pushing it open, edging its way into their lives, reminding them all that it was going to eat their mother from inside out.

'It's started, hasn't it?' said Valerie, as if reading her thoughts.

Nell shook her head. 'I don't know, Mum.'

'I'm going to have a brain like a sprout.'

'You are a long, long way off being a sprout, Mum. You're not even a lettuce.'

'I don't know, Nell. Sometimes I think I'm imagining things that didn't happen.'

Nell sat back down on the footstool and touched her mother's hand lightly. 'Falls can do funny things. Maybe you did hit your head. Is there a lump there?'

'No, no lump. Nothing.' Valerie pulled her hand away, her fingers restless. 'Anyway, let's talk about something else. Like Michael. We'll talk about Michael. That'll cheer us up.'

She should have known that was coming. She steeled herself.

'Now, ignoring his hair, he seems very nice, a polite young man,' she said, expertly swerving away from the intimacy of their earlier conversation like a car between two lanes. 'I'd snap him up, if I were you.'

'We're friends.'

Valerie raised an eyebrow.

188

'Men and women can be friends, you know.'

Valerie took a sip of sherry. 'Not even me and your father were friends.'

Nell winced, remembering the blistering rows, the air-borne bits of Wedgwood, and then, sometimes, if things were partially resolved, the flight upstairs to the bedroom. They'd leave her, Heather and Ethan in the sitting room, playing Monopoly or Connect Four, and disappear for what, she realised now, must have been a make-up quickie. (Seventies parenting for you.) But Mum was right. They were never friends, not in a cosy, companionable way. 'We *are* friends, Mum. Anyway, he's married.'

Valerie sniffed. 'That never got in the way of your father.'

Nell stood up, split as always when it came to discussing Dad with Mum. She wanted to talk about him – it was through her mother that he seemed most alive – but didn't like to pick over his faults. It felt disloyal, even if the criticism was valid. OK, Dad was unfaithful, but as she'd got older, she'd realised that he had to put up with a huge amount and in his own flawed way he had stayed loyal to the end – well, his end anyway. Bless his tartan slippers.

'Don't waste too long being friends, though, Nell. Time. It goes' – Valerie snapped her fingers – 'like that!' She bent forward in her chair, as if imparting something import-ant 'All those things you shelve to "one day" in your head. Then, suddenly there is just a load of yesterdays and you didn't darn well do it!' They sat in silence for a few moments, staring at the flickering flames, tongues of hot orange, ice-blue at their core, much like her mother. Get too close, you get burned; stay far away, and you're frozen out. 'You've been lucky, Nell, in some ways. You've been lucky to have your baby and remain independent.'

Nell smiled, puzzled. Not her mother endorsing her career? Surely some mistake.

'But don't you feel something is missing?'

Right. She could see where this was going. Stock answer time. 'Mum, right now my focus is Cass. She's still little, very little, really. And she needs me. My job takes up so much of my time I have to devote the rest of it to her.'

'You don't have a job!'

Like she needed reminding. She tried to contain her irritation. 'Honestly, why does everyone assume my life is not enough? Why *should* I feel that something is missing? Other than my job and my favourite shoes that Monty ate and—'

Valerie laughed and looked at Nell fondly. 'Yes, I guess we're all missing something.'

'What are you missing, Mum?' Weirdly, the question fired out of her ready formed, as if it was something she'd always wanted to ask.

'Missing?' Valerie took a couple of seconds to think of the answer. 'Your father, I suppose. I miss him more than I thought I would.'

Nell smiled. This was as big a declaration of love as she was ever going to hear.

'The silly old sod.' Valerie became solemn again and stared into the fire. 'And I miss being young, Nell. Not because of my health, although it would be lovely to be young and fit and beautiful again like Heather.'

Like Heather. Thanks!

'But I miss the possibility of change.'

'That sounds a bit too deep, Mum. Not sure I get it.'

'When you age – and I'm talking mid-forties onwards, really – you start to hear a noise. Bang. Bang. *Bang*! Do you know what that sound is?'

'Middle-aged women shooting their husbands?'

'That, my darling, is the sound of doors shutting. That is the sound of your life being sealed like an old attic. The decisions you make when you're young are there *for ever*. You think you can undo them.' She shook her head. 'But you can't. It's just you don't know that at the time.'

Nell looked at the fire. Jeremy's face appeared in the flames. He flickered. He winked. He disappeared.

Twenty-two

Over the next few days, Nell started to experience two contradictory sensations. The first involved Jeremy. At odd hours of the day, for no particular reason, Jeremy memories that she'd successfully buried for years would hit her with the force of rogue unmanned surfboards travelling at seventy miles an hour. Wham! Straight in the head. And it was always a clear, vivid memory of Jeremy, something small, detailed and oddly particular like the way it felt to run her fingers along the hair that grew backwards up his neck like magnetised iron filings. Or how once, when she had really foul flu, the kind that makes you feel, and look, like a victim of the bubonic plague, he sat on the edge of their bed and cleaned her teeth and held out a plastic beaker so that she could spit out the toothpaste. He'd always loved her like that, vulnerable, girlish, needy.

If she was *really* careless, her mind would wander even more nomadically, going up the blind alleys of 'what ifs', the kind of 'what ifs' that any single woman in her late thirties must resist in order to stay remotely sane. Like, what if they'd slept through their alarm that morning five years ago and decided to ditch the hog roast? Or how about if Heather hadn't split up with Damian, and had been welded to *his* arm for the whole party?

And what if Jeremy had never said she was like her mother?

So this was one strata to the mental gymnastics of her day. But, increasingly, there was another.

Nell had started to experience an unexplainable sense of anticipation.

She'd be scissoring herbs in the garden or walking to pick up the papers or just doing that old-person thing of standing in a patch of sun, closing her eyes and enjoying the warmth, when she'd get this powerful sense of looking forward to something. Like you looked forward to a birthday. Or a party. Except her birthday was in November and the only party on the agenda was the hog roast, which she was beginning to dread because Jeremy was going to be there and it was galloping up on the calendar and nowhere near organised. So what *was* she looking forward to?

Hanging out with Michael. That was what, she realised on a sunny Friday morning, as the rest of the world got up and went to work and she and Cass stumbled down to breakfast in their dressing gowns and planned a hard day's work at the beach.

They'd met every day this week. He was proving a brilliant distraction from the shock-and-awe assault of Jeremy déjà vus, unemployment worries and family inheritance squabbles. (And the way her fringe had somehow begun to resemble a fisherman's beard sprouting from her forehead.) He always seemed interested in her life, however uneventful, but then again he was equally happy not talking at all. Better still, Cass thought he was the bee's knees because he owned a café – so much more impressive than Mummy's old job – with a real till that pinged and cake you didn't have to pay for.

Yes, Nell and Michael were becoming friends, good friends, which was a lovely surprise. (She hadn't made a new good friend since having Cass, maybe even before that.) Of course, occasionally, only occasionally, she wondered what it would be like to have sex with him, but that was an inevitable thought hoop to jump through when you were hanging out on a beach with a nearly naked heterosexual male with a surfboard. In fact, a sign of quite how platonic and genuine their friendship had become was that she had forgotten to suck her tummy in in his presence. Nor did she feel self-conscious about the big Ireland mole on her left shoulder.

They swam together. They ate. Swam and ate. Ate and swam. Even in the rain. Even when she wasn't hungry. Not even the prospect of wearing her olive-green Heidi Klein bikini acted as a deterrent to the shack's toffee ice cream. She'd become shockingly greedy, especially after swimming, and Michael, terrible influence that he was, always egged her on, joked that her willpower would always lose out so she might as well save herself the conflict and get on with surrendering to the ice cream straight away rather than in twenty tortured minutes' time. She tried to explain that she wasn't normally such a glutton. In London she'd been known to do the black grape, lemon juice and pepper detox. He said that she wasn't in London now and she didn't need to worry because she looked great anyway. If it wasn't for the extra squeeze around the waistline of her old jeans – old jeans never lie – she might have believed him.

'Mummy, there he is!' Cass shrieked, pointing into the crashing silver surf. Nell grabbed her hand as the water swirled fiercely around their ankles. 'Where?'

'There!'

Nell shaded her eyes, squinted into the sunshine and spotted him standing on his surfboard, body taut, leaning forward, tilting to steer the board, cutting the wave at an angle, rising up and up against the horizon as the wave swelled and crashed towards the beach. Moments later he was there beside them, laughing, shaking his wet hair all over her like a dog. 'Nice one,' he laughed breathlessly.

'Are you showing off?'

'That's nothing.'

Nell rolled her eyes. They'd slipped into the easy sibling banter that she enjoyed with Ethan. She rather liked it.

'Can I have a go? Please, Michael, please.' Cass tugged his arm.

'It's Mummy's turn.' Michael grinned.

'It is not!' Nell laughed. 'I am built for pleasure not speed.'

'Me, Michael! Me. Me. Me,' squealed Cass.

'Who again?' laughed Michael, pretending to look around him, and not see her.

'Me!'

Michael looked at Nell quizzically. Could he take her precious daughter surfing?

'You won't find it scary?' Nell asked Cass, marvelling at how much pluckier she had become. When they'd arrived from London she'd had to be coaxed into the shallows.

'I want to be a surfer,' Cass repeated determinedly.

'Go for it, Cupcake.' She looked at Michael. 'Not too far out, OK?'

Michael lifted Cass on to the surfboard, and pushed it gently from the back. He pulled her gently alongside the shoreline, careful not to go deep. Gradually, reassured that her daughter wasn't about to drown, Nell began to relax.

And a funny thing happened. As she stood there – the sun burning wrinkles into her face, crap fringe frizzing – a whoosh of feeling rose up inside her like the bubbles in a shaken bottle of Diet Coke. She wasn't exactly sure what the feeling was.

Only that it was fizzy and had an upward motion and was connected to the flooring realisation that right now, in this split second in her life, and perhaps for only this split second in her life, she'd rather be standing here in the surf than sitting in a features meeting in London. Or shopping. And she couldn't care less that her phone didn't work. That no one had offered her a job. That she hadn't even tried to write her novel.

Then she got a mad urge.

The urge was overpowering. It wrestled her backwards into the water, dunked her beneath the surf like a toddler. Freezing! Hilarious! The water funnelled up her nostrils, into her mouth, her ears, tore at her clothes, flipped her on to her tummy, tugged her across the sandy floor as she giggled, trying to keep her mouth shut.

'Nell!' Michael shouted. 'Are you OK?'

'Fine!' she gargled, managing to stand up, laughing, pulling her wet T-shirt away from her body so that it didn't cling over her bra. Bloody hell. What on earth had come over her?

Twenty-three

No, she could put it off no longer. The metal loft ladder shot out of the trapdoor like a piston and rattled to the hall floor, releasing a spume of dust from the attic and a vivid memory of her father climbing up this very ladder, a slim torch in his back pocket, his legs in his favourite cords, size eleven feet in their battered old school teacher brogues that got resoled year after year but never replaced. The memory of those shoes on the ladder rungs conjured Dad up with such visceral clarity that she missed him with a physical pang that left her almost breathless. She missed the way he said, 'You're a good girl, Nell,' even when she was a grown woman. She missed the way his eyes lit up when she returned home from London, the way he'd ask dozens of questions about her metropolitan life, bemused and fascinated. She missed the way he could barely boil an egg but he knew how to keep Mum from boiling over. And she knew he would have creased up in laughter to see her fully clothed in the drink yesterday. 'Wish you were here, Dad', she muttered. 'And I wish you were the one who had to clear this bloody attic.' It was all very well wanting equality but she drew the line at attics. Spidery, mousy attics. A man's job.

The ladder creaked with the first step. Was it really designed to hold a woman who'd ingested this much ice cream? She stood on the top rung and stared up at the fathomless black square above her head. Portal to Planet Stockdale. Lost world of discarded toys, clothes and family paraphernalia that had accumulated over decades. Crikey. She suddenly realised that the adrenaline-fuelled 'organise your life!' evangelism that she'd had when she'd first arrived in Cornwall was petering out. Why? Well, partly because she was getting lazy. But mostly because Tredower wasn't like her London flat. It was an endless repeating magic porridge pot of a house. She'd tackle one heap of crap only to discover another three she had not known existed. Rotting wellies in the cellar. Dead mice in the under-stair cupboards. Ancient *House and Garden*s in the pan drawer. Too much space. That was the problem. Basically, if you had the space, you filled it, in the same way a fat person had to eat both slices of cake if they were there, not just the one. That, and her mother's tendency to hoard. But she'd promised her mother she'd do the attic . . . Right. Deep breath.

She gripped her hands on the sides of the trapdoor, pulled herself up, and landed in a mushroom cloud of dust and dead moths. She coughed and tried not to inhale, swinging her torch around the vast empty black space, looking for the light switch. The torch's cone of light moved across the attic like a prison spotlight. She shivered, remembering the time that she and Ethan had naughtily crept up here once as children – the attic had been strictly out of bounds. When Mum had realised what they'd done, she'd closed the trapdoor behind them, letting them stew in their own thrilled, concocted fear in the pitch-black for what had felt like hours. Aha, there, thank goodness, was the light switch. The bare bulb hanging on a cord right above her head flickered on uncertainly, as if it might change its mind.

The attic was much bigger than Nell remembered, running

from one end of the house to the other, standing room limited to the centre of the vast room, the sloping walls pitch-black where they met the plywood floor. She never remembered it being this cluttered. An old broken chair. Oh, her old rocking horse! And what the hell was that? No, it was OK. Just a doll, one of those Hammer House of Horror ones with a china face. Blimey. Years and years of *stuff*.

She was surprised that Janet hadn't got here first, attached some crampons, swung up and done a fingertip search in case there was anything of value she could relocate to West London. Actually, hang on a minute. Nell stopped and stared at the floor. It *did* look like someone had been up here. There were smudged Scooby Doo-style footprints on the thick carpet of dust. She wondered whose they were. Maybe Janet had been up here after all. She wouldn't put it past her.

She picked a vase up off the floor and wiped it with her sleeve to expose pretty china, green hand-painted palms and parrots. Rather lovely, actually. Would look fab on her lime-green Habitat sideboard in London. She put it to one side – the 'keep' side to the left of the trapdoor. To the right of the trapdoor, rejects met their maker inside a black bin liner, and that's where the broken Melamine salad bowl was going right now and the battered, incomplete board games. She bent her head to avoid banging it on the rafters and walked towards the rocking horse, a lump in her throat. How she'd loved this horse as a little girl! She gently wiped off a lace of cobwebs and stroked its bedraggled mane. It wobbled on its rockers as if with pleasure at the warmth of human touch. She remembered it quite clearly in the nursery when they lived in London: a big square room on the ground floor with a bay window, full of light and noise and people. She smiled, remembering how Heather used to feed the rocking horse grass torn from the lawn, pressing it into its mouth with her little hands, so that it had a grass stain around its mouth like a green beard. No, she absolutely couldn't chuck the horse away now. Cass would love it. And what was this? Nell unwrapped a pretty pink china tea set wrapped in newspaper so old – 13 November, 1987 – and crisp it felt like baking parchment. One or two handles were chipped but the cups were adorable. Very Heather. She'd better keep it.

Nell pushed an old stack of yellowing papers towards the bin bag. She picked one off the pile and sneezed. School reports! Dare she? She picked up Ethan's, read it and started to laugh. 'Ethan is a very able child but easily distracted,' one of his teachers had written. Not much change there, then. She shuffled through to Heather's: 'A diligent student who puts great effort into her work.' Talk about damning with faint praise. Then her own: 'Nell has potential in spades but would benefit from improving her attitude towards those in authority.' What a cheek! She shoved the paper firmly into the bin bag, feeling a spark of teenage indignance towards the teacher. Then she tackled another enormous stack of papers, mostly letters. Did her mother not throw *anything* out? Old bills addressed to her father, opened, and, one would hope, paid. It was weird seeing her dad's name written on the envelopes, like he was still here and still getting correspondence from all those institutions – banks, building societies, tax offices – that proved you existed. She was reluctant to throw them away but it was senseless keeping them. She squatted down and pulled out another letter. This one was addressed to Valerie Stockdale. It looked new, unlike the others, the stamp still bright, the lettering clear, not bleeding with damp like many of the others. She flipped it over to see if it had a return address. Then the brick phone rang. She pounced on it with relief. 'Soph!'

'I manage to talk to you at last. I keep going straight to voicemail. How's it going?'

'Crawling around a hot attic covered in dust and dead insects and about fifty years' worth of family paraphernalia. You?'

'Picking up a deli box from Ottolenghi's, then a sneaky peek into Matches. Summer sales on, love.'

'Don't.'

'London misses you.'

'The feeling's mutual.'

'Babes, you OK? You sound kind of congested.'

'My nose is blocked by all this dust. But I'm fine. Very busy.'

Sophie laughed. 'Nell! How can you be busy in Cornwall? It must have the slowest pace of life in the country.'

'But there's so much to do, Soph. Planning the hog roast, clearing out the house, dealing with chicken poo. Man, have you seen the size of chicken poos? The logs are man-sized! I mean how is that physically possible?'

'Er, funnily enough, I've never actually mused on that one.'

'Also Monty needs walking, so does Mum. And there's Cass, of course, although she's less trouble than the other two.' She paused for a lungful of dusty breath. 'So that's what I do. Until I get to wine o'clock.'

'Blimey. Sounds like you might have to downshift back to London. No gossip?'

'I went for lunch with a man yesterday,' she said, deliberately casually.

'You *didn't*! Who? Tell me immediately!'

'Michael. Runs the café by Perranortho Beach. The new owner.'

'Michael, Michael,' said Sophie thoughtfully. Nell could

hear her tapping her fingers on a table. 'Shall I call my mum and get the lowdown?'

'Don't you dare! It'll be all over the valley in no time. My mother will start shopping for her peach mother-of-the-bride dress.'

'Deliver the lowdown.'

'Surfer. Ex-Londoner.'

'Promising.'

'Smoker.'

'You've been known to have a drunken puff.'

'That's social smoking. That's different. Anyway, he wears rafting shoes.'

'You can take him shopping.'

'Married.'

'Oh.'

'Although he is in the process of divorcing.'

'Whoa! *Not* negotiable. He'll be in crisis *and* on the rebound, looking to prove his manhood again or hurt a member of the sex that hurt him. Totally toxic.'

'Yes, you're right.'

'Even worse, he might try and make you work at the tea shack. Imagine.' Sophie laughed. It was one of those laughs that conducted firelight warmth right down the telephone line. 'Dare I ask, how was it with Jeremy and Heather?'

'Weird,' said Nell quickly.

'Bad weird?'

'Weird weird. It was late. Heather wasn't around and he started reminiscing about us.' She lowered her voice. 'He told me he missed me.'

'Jesus.'

'I know.' Something was happening in her stomach as she talked about it, a strange, liquid feeling, a mixture of dread, guilt and, shameful as it was to admit it, excitement.

Sophie blew outrage down the phone. 'The scallywag!'

His hand on her ankle. That throb of feeling up her leg.

'God, we need to talk properly. Don't see him again alone. *Ever*. Or this toxic divorcee. I'm going to have to come to Cornwall to supervise you.'

'Please do, at once!'

'Maybe I'll bring your Pete fellow.'

'Don't be silly,' laughed Nell, knowing that Pete would never come in a million years. 'Pete belongs to another life entirely. He exists on a different frequency.'

'And you need his vibrations right now, babe!'

'Yuck!' She pulled a large swag of web off her foot. 'Sticky spider web. Huge! It's like a trapeze net. Can I phone you back in a sec? I have to open my mouth to talk and I'm worried the spider will crawl in.'

'Don't say another word.'

Nell shoved the phone into her back pocket, swung her legs down on to the ladder, dragging her bin bag behind her. She'd done enough for today. Her eyes were sore and her nose was stuffy. She reached up and flicked the light off, shut the trapdoor, casting the brightly stamped letter addressed to her mother back into lonely darkness.

Twenty-four

April was hot with shame. She'd never stolen anything in her entire life. And now, of all people . . . What had she done? What on earth had she been thinking? Idiot! She sat forward on the bed and rubbed the glass that covered the photograph with the edge of her cardigan sleeve to clear the fingerprints. She'd been staring at this picture for the most part of the last three days, as if the longer she stared at the picture the more willingly it would reveal its secrets.

The photograph was shot in black and white, not big, about the same size as a small table mat. It showed a hand-some, tallish couple – early forties? – standing side by side in a garden. The woman was slim, with high cheekbones and dark curly hair. She had one of those proud, beautiful faces with a hint of suffering in the eyes, reminiscent of those sepia photographs of American pioneer women. She wore a floral dress, smocked at the top, an apron with a bulging front pocket, as if it might be full of apples. The man had a large, enthusiastic smile that showed a lot of teeth and a sunlit fuzz of hair that gave him a slightly nerdy professor look. The couple were not holding hands, but his hand was reaching towards hers and their fingers were just touching. Sitting on a log at their waist height were, she guessed, their children, or rather teenagers. Each resembled their parents in different ways. The boy – late teens? – was handsome, dark like his mother, a certain glint in his eye. To his right was a slight, notably pretty girl, blond, fragile, more like her father. To his left was an older-looking girl, dark haired, glowering, dressed all in black, heavy eye make-up, handsome rather than pretty. She was staring out of the picture accusingly as if she'd known then where this image would end up.

April sank forward, elbows on knees, resting her forehead in her palm. Chris had worried about this. That she'd come down to Cornwall and become someone he didn't recognise. And it had happened. How could she ever explain that she'd pried into a stranger's house and then grabbed a photograph off the hall table like a shoplifter? He'd demand she return home immediately. And who could blame him? She felt so alone, silly, horribly tarnished. Who was she kidding now? It wasn't about learning to draw again. Or finding herself. Having some time alone. Or flirting with that man in the beach café and feeling attractive again. It was about *this*.

This moment. This picture. That house. She dug into her handbag for her car keys. Enough.

The trees outside Tredower's front gate seemed thicker today, denser, more like a wall to keep her out. The house sign swung in the breeze, creaking on its hinges, and there was something about the sound that unnerved her.

April put on a sunhat to hide her face, just in case. She slid the picture into a plastic bag to keep it dry and tucked it beside the wrought-iron boot holder on the front porch. God knows what they'd think, but at least the photograph was back where it belonged, and she didn't have it on her conscience any more.

She glanced up at the house again – goodbye, house – walked quickly back to the car. It was then that she heard the slam of the front door. A child ran out into the drive. The little girl who'd answered the door! Then a woman with long, messy dark hair, a dog barking. April's heart stopped. It was *the* woman from the photograph, the teenage girl grown up, she was sure of it. A violent emotional reflex made her reverse, slam her foot on the accelerator, and screech out of the drive. She heard the woman shout something but she didn't dare look behind her.

Twenty-five

Nell lay back on the sand, pulling her yellow sarong over her face to protect it from getting more wrinkles. It was a stifling afternoon. And her brain was overheating, unsettled by the photograph behind the old iron boot stand that they'd found this morning. They hadn't even noticed it was missing. How long had it been there? It was possible the twins had done it – the incomprehensible kind of thing they'd do – and no one had noticed until today. Then there was that woman. Nell hadn't really clocked her face, it had been obscured by the hat. But Cass seemed to think that she was the same woman who came to the door the afternoon that Mum fainted. She sat up, whipped the sarong off her face. 'Michael, do you think *she* planted the picture behind the boot rack?'

Michael laughed, rested his foot on the ridge of his spade. 'Nell Clueso!'

'Michael,' said Cass. They were building the best sandcastle on the beach and she didn't want him distracted. 'Dig!'

'Sorry, Cass.' He dutifully carried on digging.

'But how on earth would that woman have got hold of it? No, it doesn't make sense.' Nell leaned back on to her towel, covering her face in the yellow dome of sarong again. 'I can't even follow the plot of *Lewis*, so, yes, this one has me foxed.'

Michael prodded her toe with his spade. 'What if . . .' he whispered, 'what if the woman was actually a maverick Cornish ghost?'

'Do ghosts drive Penzance hire cars?' she said, lifting a corner of fabric up. 'Fiats?'

'The twenty-first-century version of the headless horseman.'

Nell giggled. Increasingly Michael made her giggle a lot. She'd never thought of herself as a giggler. She wasn't that kind of woman, certainly not when she was in London. Employed. With a life. Sometimes she did actually worry that she was probably boring him senseless with the minutiae of Tredower. But he didn't seem to mind. Or did he? She lifted the corner of her sarong up again. 'Am I banging on, Michael? I don't mean to unload.'

'Unload ahead. You're not the only one,' Michael said, shovelling cool damp sand over her feet. 'I should get you all altogether and cut out the middleman.'

'What do you mean?'

'I get all sorts of ladies dropping in, pretending they're coming for coffee but really coming to hear my words of wisdom and check out my—' He stopped.

'Michael, dig!'

'Sorry, Cass, not paying attention.'

'Women won't leave you alone, right?'

'Fighting them off with clumps of seaweed.'

'That, I suspect, Michael, is more to do with the dearth of socialising opportunities here and less to do with your pull as a surf guru in yellow trainers, barista of the mean espresso machine,' she said, trying to sound wry and flippant and not quite pulling it off.

Perhaps Michael wasn't joking? Perhaps she was just one of many needy thirty-something single women who washed up on Cornish beaches like driftwood. Embarrassing.

'Don't move.' Michael brushed her neck lightly with the tips of his fingers. 'Wasp.'

'Thanks.' Was it her imagination or was Michael increasingly finding ways to initiate body contact? He started digging again. Her imagination, she decided.

'Cass, the moat is done and so am I. Do you mind if I sit down and talk to Mum for a bit?'

'OK.' Cass carried on digging.

'Move up.' Michael squeezed on to her towel.

'Argh! You're wet and amphibious!' Nell shrieked, rolling away.

He rolled towards her. She shrieked again. 'When can we get drunk together?' he whispered, pulling the sarong above his face too so that it was like they were in a private tent.

'We have something to celebrate?' she said in a particular tone of voice with a particular type of raised eyebrow. As she did so she thought, my mother does that. It's happened. I'm turning into my mother.

'Well, I'm off to London for a few days. Isn't that an excuse of sorts?'

Oh. What would she do if she couldn't hang out with Michael?

'And I'm going to open a surf school.'

Nell sat up and brushed sand off her legs. 'You and the rest of Cornwall.'

'No, Miss Cynic. This is going to be different. And don't say that's what they all say. Listen to Michael's master plan . . .' He leaned on to his side, rested his head on his hand. 'I'm going to aim it squarely at the city. All-in-one packages, fly the guys down to Newquay, house them up here somewhere cool, all catered locally . . .'

'Like it.'

Michael looked pleased to have her approval. 'I agree there is a contradiction between the flying down here and the eco credentials . . .'

His sincerity took her by surprise. 'I doubt it will niggle their consciences too much!' She smiled.

Cass squidged herself between them and spread sandy shells all over Nell's knees. 'They're for the windows, Mummy. Which is the best window, do you think?'

Nell picked up a dark grey shell. 'This one, perfect.'

Cass took it from her fingers. 'No, that's a door.' She looked up the beach. 'I want to ask Grandma about windows. Where *is* Grandma?'

'Walking Monty. She shouldn't be long.' Nell suddenly wondered whether she was giving Mum too much freedom. Heather would never let her go out for walks all the time on her own. Not that she'd be able to stop her. This particular solitary walk, Nell suspected, was done to make a point of her physical fitness and admirable stoicism since her fall. She'd been gone for a while.

Michael winked at Cass. 'And after you've added the door and windows, do you think we should have chocolate cake at the café?'

Cass leapt up. 'I'm done!'

They walked along the wet sand to the café and sat on the bench in the garden. At last Nell spotted the figure of her mother in her taupe billowing linens crossing the beach, throwing a ball to Monty. 'She's coming.'

'Shall I get her highness a cup of tea?' he asked.

'Milky. No sugar.'

Valerie panted up to the café and sat down heavily next to Cass. 'Goodness,' she said, looking at Cass's enormous oozing lump of chocolate cake disapprovingly. 'I can see you've inherited your mother's sweet tooth. That'll turn you into ten-tonne Tessie, darling.'

'Mum!' hissed Nell. 'Do you really want to give Cass food issues at the age of four?'

'Well, it's the truth. Monty. *Sit.*' Valerie pulled on his lead to stop Monty scoffing the crumbs beneath the table. 'You know me, Nell, I'll always call a spade a spade. I mean, dear me, just look at all these fat people,' she whispered loudly, pointing at an overweight sixty-something minding her own business at the neighbouring table. 'All this talk of big bones and metabolisms and what not. They are fat because they eat too much! Look, there she goes, forking more food. Stop, woman! For goodness' sake, woman, just stop eating!'

The woman, realising she was being talked about, stopped eating and started intensely reading a tourist leaflet about the Eden project.

'Mum! The poor woman is just eating a piece of cake.'

'My point exactly.'

'I like cake, Grandma,' interrupted Cass, staring puzzled at the innocent slice of cake on her plate.

'So do I, Cass,' said Nell firmly. '*And* so does Grandma, very much. She was just trying to point out that we should eat it in moderation with lots of fruit and vegetables. Green ones.'

'I like cake more than I like green things,' observed Cass digging into the cake again.

Michael came over holding a white mug. 'Tea, Valerie?'

'Thank you.' Valerie gave Nell an approving nod, as if he had passed some invisible test. 'How kind.'

'How was your walk?'

'Lovely, thank you.'

Valerie sipped her tea, studying him. 'Right,' she said, getting down to business. 'Nell tells me you're married.'

Nell groaned. 'Mum.'

'Just,' Michael said politely, taking it in his stride. 'We've split up.'

'What a shame,' Valerie said disingenuously. 'Recently?'

'Two years ago . . .'

Valerie tapped Nell on the arm and bent closer to her. 'Not *exactly* married, Nell.' She looked at Michael again. 'Divorcing?' she asked in a loud voice that made other café goers look over curiously.

'Mum, stop it!'

Valerie ignored her. 'Are your parents divorced, Michael?'

Jesus. She was unembarrassable.

'No, they're still together, Valerie. Very much so, as long as he doesn't forget their wedding anniversary or neglect the cat.'

Valerie laughed. 'Aha, a good example. You know, Michael, I wanted to divorce Nell's father so many times but I'm glad in the end I stayed with him . . .' she hesitated – 'all things considered. Anyway, we learned to tolerate each other, I think. I hope that Nell has learned lessons from that. The problem is that people have such high expectations these days. In my day, we all just accepted things. And I'm not sure we were less miserable for it.' She narrowed her eyes. 'Do you hope to remarry, Michael?'

No, no sign of let-up. Nell sank into her chair.

Michael paused awkwardly. 'Er . . .'

'Sorry,' Nell mouthed at Michael.

'It's good for men, marriage, you know,' Valerie went on. 'There are studies to prove it, I believe.'

Nell glanced at her watch. Three-fifteen p.m. There was a white strap mark next to her tan. 'Mum, I think Michael needs to get back to work.'

'Well, I hope you enjoy your—' began Michael.

There was a flash of mischief in Valerie's green eyes. 'Michael, I take it that girl, very young, rather pretty, I take it that wasn't your girlfriend, then?'

Michael looked taken aback. He laughed, puzzled. 'Sorry?'

'The girl I saw you with yesterday when I was taking a walk with Monty.'

Something in Nell froze. Had her mother's habit of blundering to the bottom of things revealed itself again?

Michael smiled – uneasily, Nell thought. 'No, just a customer,' he said quickly and nodded towards the café hatch where a huddled queue had formed. 'Now I must excuse myself . . .'

'And the lady with her, the pretty one in the orange anorak?' persevered Valerie, head cocked suspiciously.

Nell knew that woman in the orange anorak. Always walking quickly away from the café just as she arrived. They were obviously fated never to meet. Why was that?

Michael began to look a little bit flustered. 'A customer. I—'

'How unusual to find a proprietor *quite* so friendly with customers, don't you think, Nell?' Valerie smiled but her eyes didn't. Michael had let her down in some way. Her mood had shifted. 'Makes such a nice change.'

Twenty-six

Eight days later

The doorbell. Michael must be back from London! She'd missed their swims. Perhaps they could go now? She glanced at her watch. Yes, the final leg of the attic clear-out would have to wait another day. She ran down the stairs, opened the door. 'Oh.'

'Thanks for the welcome,' Heather said breathlessly, dropping an enormous Mulberry leather holdall to the floor.

'Sorry. I . . . I was expecting someone.' Nell was thrown. She hadn't been prepared for this. She had to scramble her defences together. Jeremy? She looked over her sister's shoulder, couldn't see him.

'Thought I'd surprise Mum. Had a window, grabbed it. Things are quiet at work,' Heather said, taking off her sunglasses emblazoned with the Chanel logo.

Nell felt a crackle of jealousy. She'd been the kind of woman who'd had spare windows occasionally too. Now her life was a formless open aperture. And her mother had sat on her nice shades so now she had to wear a crappy fifteen-pound pair from Boots. 'Come in. Do you want a hand with that bag?'

'No, I'm fine. Thanks.' Heather strained to pick up the

214

bag. She'd lost more weight, Nell noticed. She also looked immaculate in her camel-coloured shirt dress, pretty patent grey ballet shoes, swishy and shiny international hair. Her grooming and poise made Nell notice her own lack of both. She was, she realised, wearing old bootleg jeans that she wouldn't be seen dead in, in London, Monty-chewed flip-flops and a navy T-shirt of indeterminate ownership and age. She was turning into a tubster and wasn't even wearing make-up – not even sun block, which she applied religiously even on the cloudiest of days in London – and the salty air had given her hair the texture of a cactus. Her only concession to decoration was the thin, cerise scarf she'd found on the hall floor that day and had adopted as her own. Blimey. What had happened to her? She'd gone native. 'That's a bloody big bag, Heather. You moving in?'

Heather winced. 'Afraid not.'

'No, I guessed you'd have more sense.' Nell smiled. 'Welcome back to the pleasuredome.'

'What on earth are you doing here?' Valerie suddenly appeared in the doorway.

Heather's face fell.

'Aunty Heather!' Cass ran up behind her wearing an enormous straw hat, little feet slipping forward in a pair of Valerie's old court shoes. She looked around. 'Where's Mr Jeremy Fisher?'

Good question. Nell held her breath.

'Working. I've hardly seen him all week. Some heavy case going on,' said Heather quickly, pulling Cass's hat down further on her head and making Cass giggle.

'Yes, that's the flaw of every successful man.' Valerie nodded. 'Busy, busy.'

'Love the new hair, Mum.' Heather's dutifully leaned forward to kiss her. 'I told you I'd help out as much as

I can.' She picked up Cass, planting a kiss beneath the brim of her hat. 'I wanted to come down. I've got some ideas for . . .' She hesitated, glanced at Nell. And Nell knew she was about to talk Tredower plans. 'Look at you, Cass!' Heather changed the subject quickly, and looked at Cass. 'You're brown as a button, and so very glamorous! Quite the French starlet.'

Cass beamed. 'Aunty Heather, did you know that a group of crows is called a murder of crows?'

Heather looked a little startled. 'Is it? No, no I didn't. That's a bit gruesome.'

'And a group of ladybirds is called a loveliness?'

'Ah. That's sweet.' She put Cass down.

Valerie smiled at her granddaughter indulgently. 'Isn't Cass clever? After all these years, a child who actually listens to me!'

Heather bent down and rummaged in her bag. 'I've brought a few things. For you, Cass.'

'A headband!' marvelled Cass, holding a horrid plastic sequin strip up aloft like a trophy. Nell had not yet given in to the pink sparkly headband thing. Now the levees had broken.

'Sorry,' Heather mouthed at Nell. 'Couldn't resist it. For you, Mum. A blouse. Your kind of thing, I thought.'

Valerie took the smocked pale green silk blouse, sniffed it. She always sniffed new clothes. 'Very pretty.' Nell knew she'd forget all about it in five minutes' time.

She rummaged deeper. 'Ah, here they are. Wooden spoons from Divertimenti, to replace the ones that are rotting.' She passed over three spoons.

'What's wrong with my spoons, Nell?' Valerie looked puzzled.

Nell shrugged.

'And this . . .' Heather passed Valerie one enormous wooden spoon like a ladle. 'It's walnut; beautiful, isn't it? Thought we could use it to serve salad or something at the hog roast.'

Valerie frowned. 'But that's ages away . . .'

'Not that long, Mum,' Heather said gently, exchanging a look with Nell. 'We need to start planning the details.'

Nell felt herself bristle. *Start* planning? What exactly did everyone think she'd been doing down here, having hot-stone massages on the beach? 'I've done quite a lot of planning already, actually,' she said.

Heather blushed. 'Right, yes, of course. Sorry.'

They sat down at the table with a cup of tea. Nell could hear rustling as birds darted in and out of their nests in the house's beard of ivy. She tried to concentrate on this, not thoughts of Jeremy, what he'd said to her, what he must say to her sister . . . Valerie poured steaming Earl Grey into the three earthenware mugs. Cass fed Monty biscuits under the table. Heather sipped her tea daintily, glancing from Valerie to Nell and back again, like something about them was puzzling her. 'That scarf really suits you, Nell.'

Nell threw one end over her shoulder.

'In fact, you both look exceptionally well,' Heather added, sounding surprised.

'Were you expecting us to be walking around in muddy sarongs with a swarm of midges in our hair?' said Nell waspishly.

'No, it's just—'

'You're right, Heather,' mused Valerie. 'Nell does look well, doesn't she?'

'Not so tired.' Heather nodded.

'Younger. That's the Cornish air for you, darling. That and getting out of that ridiculous job. Biscuit?'

Heather shook her head. Nell didn't think she'd eaten a biscuit since announcing her engagement to Jeremy three months before, which was probably very sensible. Jeremy was not one of those men who preferred curves. A commitment to Jeremy would be a commitment to remain a size eight for ever.

'No job offer, then, Nell?' said Heather cautiously, unsure if she was allowed to bring it up.

'Tough out there, right now,' Nell declared in her businesslike older sister voice, omitting the smallish factoid that she had not sent so much as a workey networking email, let alone applied for a job for the last two weeks. Dynamic, go-getting journalist? Er, not.

'Well, it must be nice to have a break,' Heather said.

'A break?' Nell spluttered over her tea. 'Check out my hands!' She held her hands out over the table, to demonstrate the workhouse toughened skin but actually they just looked tanned, although thankfully there was a bit of damning mud beneath her fingernails. 'Labourer's hands.'

Valerie laughed. 'Nell is becoming acquainted with the vegetable patch, Heather.'

'No!' exclaimed Heather.

Cass grinned. 'We made Mummy touch a slug!'

'No!' gasped Heather.

'Yes!' chimed Valerie and Cass.

'And it was every bit as disgusting as I thought it would be,' said Nell quickly, lest Heather got the idea that they were having fun down here.

'So what else has been going on?' said Heather, catching Nell's eye. They were overdue for a chat.

'Grandma went to the doctor,' said Cass. 'He made her pee in a pot.'

'Cass!' Valerie gave her a pretend slap on the hand. 'Nice

218

things.'

'Can I tell Aunty Heather about when you fell over?'

Valerie tensed. Heather tensed; she'd heard already from Ethan.

'Not now, Cass,' said Nell firmly.

Cass rolled her biscuit along the table like a wheel. 'I'm not scared of the sea any more, Aunty Heather,' she added. 'The sea is my friend.'

Nell laughed and shook her head. 'She didn't get that line from me.' She got it from Michael.

'That's great,' exclaimed Heather. 'You'll be a little fish in no time.'

'*And* I ate a green thing,' enthused Cass.

Nell rolled her eyes. 'A pea. Note the singular.'

'A pea?' laughed Heather. 'And was it delicious?'

'It was OK. But I like cake more.'

'Me too,' said Heather, leaning over and giving Cass a spontaneous kiss on the cheek.

Nell felt a stab of guilt. Cass adored Heather. The adoration was mutual. And yet they'd barely seen each other for the last few years. Because of Jeremy. Everything was because of bloody Jeremy.

'Um, right, I've got . . .' Heather put her cup down and cleared her throat. She always did that throat-clearing thing when she was nervous. 'I . . . I've got some ideas, Mum. Some little ideas for Tredower.'

Nell's spirits plunged. All we need. The Inheritance Game. Come on down!

Valerie's face lit up. 'Really?'

'One sec.' Heather rummaged into the cave of her bag and pulled out a sheet of card with bits of fabric and squares of wallpaper stuck to it. She held it up to them. 'There!'

'What's *that*?' said Cass and Valerie in unison.

'It's a mood board!' declared Heather as if this was the most obvious thing in the world.

'A mood board?' repeated Valerie, looking puzzled. 'And what, pray, is a mood board?'

'Er, a visual representation of ideas, I guess.' Heather flicked a tongue of beige damask, stroked some metallic wallpaper. 'See.'

'I see silver wallpaper,' said Valerie.

'For the bathroom,' said Heather, trying to enthuse the blank faces.

'A bathroom? Why on earth would you wallpaper a bathroom? It'd get wet!'

Heather laughed. 'Lots of people wallpaper bathrooms now, Mum.'

'Silver?'

Heather nodded.

'How peculiar.' Valerie pursed her lips.

Peculiar indeed, thought Nell. We are looking at wallpapers that will repaper the house after her death. Bloody lovely.

Heather glanced anxiously at Nell, beginning to lose confidence. 'Well, my idea, my big idea – well, it's not such a big idea, Mum, but it is a beautifully simple one, I think.'

'Yes . . . ?' said Valerie impatiently. Nell felt sorry for Heather then. Mum had always treated her like she was a bit retarded.

'The idea is to *keep* Tredower as a fabulous family house but rent it out as a top-end holiday let. You can get over two thousand a week for a house like this in high season.'

'Two thousand pounds?' gasped Valerie. She looked at Heather doubtfully. 'Are you sure you've got this right, Heather?'

'If we spruced it up, sure.'

'For this old place! Goodness. It's a good thing your father never realised that or he'd have had us living in the fox's den at the bottom of the garden.' She patted the board. 'Maybe I could consider silver wallpaper in the bathroom after all.'

Heather's shoulders dropped. She smiled at Nell. 'Have you had a think about it too?'

'Well . . .' How to put this diplomatically?

'Nell disapproves of the whole thing, Heather,' interrupted her mother. 'She's being very censorious, Nellish and obstinate and refusing to participate.'

'I am not,' said Nell wearily. 'I just don't think it's a fair way of dividing up a family asset. And it's kind of morbid.'

Heather stared down at the tabletop. Nell looked out of the window. The conviviality was crumbling.

'But I look forward to Janet and Ethan's ideas. They're coming over this weekend too,' said Valerie closing the subject.

'News to me!' said Nell. 'Do you think you could let me know?'

'I did,' exclaimed Valerie.

Definitely did not.

'They're squeezing me in before they go to Jamaica. Isn't that sweet of them?'

'Ibiza, Mum. They're going to Ibiza, not Jamaica.'

'If you say so.' Valerie bit into another biscuit, caught the crumbs with the edge of her thumb. 'I must say, this is turning out to be a very busy summer. If I had known that Deng going away would have made you all rally around like this, I would have fired her years ago.'

'OK, you can tell me about the fall now,' said Heather as they sat in the conservatory looking out at a brilliant pink sunset later that day, eating Twiglets, and breaking open the second bottle of white wine, Heather having ditched the

221

detox for the night. As long as they didn't mention the J word it was OK-ish. Cass was in bed. Valerie was in the bath. And Nell had to admit that it was nice to have a bit of company at Tredower again.

'On the phone Ethan mentioned something about Cass saying there was someone at the door when . . .' Heather pulled an exasperated face – 'you know how completely hopeless Ethan is at remembering details. What happened?'

Nell shrugged. 'Well, it was all a bit muddled, to be honest. Cass said some woman knocked on the door asking for Mum . . .'

Heather started shovelling cubes of Nell's almond Green and Blacks into her mouth.

'Save me some.'

Realising how far she'd fallen, she crumpled the foil in her hands. 'Look at me! What a piglet!' She laughed. 'Gareth would not be happy.'

'Gareth? Who's Gareth?'

'My trainer.'

'The man responsible for your Hollywood arms?'

Heather blushed, waved her away. 'You were saying?'

'Well, that's it, really. There's not much to say.'

Heather grabbed her elbow. 'The woman,' she said urgently. 'You don't think it's the same lady who I saw *that* time. God. Do you remember? That woman I saw hovering outside the house?' She crushed her fingers against her mouth as if an awful truth had just dawned. 'And the photograph too.' She shuddered.

'That's what I'm wondering, actually. It's all mighty odd.'

'No, no, we're being silly.' Heather knocked back her drink.

Nell's skin started to goosebump.

222

'You know what, Nell? I'm beginning to feel a bit spooked. Kind of watched. Oh, I know that makes no sense. Not sleeping well. I keep getting these feelings of . . . doom.' She laughed shrilly.

'Doom? Oh dear.' Nell noticed that beneath the perfect make-up Heather did look strained. 'You're probably just tired. Stressed, you know, about the wedding and stuff.' Yikes. She'd mentioned the wedding. Quick, change the subject. 'I used to get those feelings all the time,' she added, realising as she said it that she hadn't felt them for a while. 'You know, that feeling that something was going to go horribly wrong.'

'But I know how lucky I am. It's silly.' Heather refilled their glasses. 'It's just . . .' She stopped, bit her lower lip. 'Nothing. Nothing.'

Nell was concerned now. She wasn't sure Heather had the right constitution for stressy feelings. 'You don't seem quite yourself.'

Heather raised an eyebrow. 'Well, no offence, Nell, but you haven't exactly seen much of me over the last few years. How would you know?'

Nell looked down at the tabletop, hurt. 'I still know you.'

'Do you?' Heather's bottom lip quivered. She gulped back her wine. Nell had never seen her drink so quickly.

'I miss Dad,' Heather said suddenly, her eyes brimming with tears. 'He'd know what to do.'

'About what?'

She rubbed her face with her hands, leaving a matt trail through her luminescent foundation. 'All of it. This.' She sniffed loudly. 'Us.'

Nell dropped her gaze. Us. She meant Jeremy.

'Why can't we just be a normal family, Nell? Why the bloody drama? I mean, take Mum, honestly.' She shook her

223

head. 'I don't know how you stand it here alone with her.'

'Oh, I guess, we've found ways of rubbing along.'

'When I first heard you were coming down here I thought it'd be fireworks all summer.'

They'd had their moments. Nell smiled. 'I think her gunpowder's got a bit damp.'

Heather held up her glass. 'Here's to you, Nell. I don't think anyone else could have done what you've done. I would have throttled her.'

'It's been a close call at times.' Nell smiled. Heather's acknowledgement felt good.

'I mean, bloody hell, if I was a mother – when I'm a mother – I'd be delighted if my daughter surprised me by turning up laden with goodies.' Heather's voice was starting to slur. She couldn't hold her alcohol. 'I wouldn't do that cool ice queen thing that she does. That kind of . . .' she lifted her nose in the air and sniffed, ' "Oh, what did the cat bring in?" voice.' She held out her glass and waggled it drunkenly. 'More wine, please.'

Nell looked at her doubtfully. 'Are you sure?'

'Well, Jeremy's not here, is he? I might as well let my hair down.'

Nell didn't dare probe further. It wasn't her place. Still, she wondered if Jeremy was doing his controlling thing again. He couldn't help himself. Yes, she was well out of it, she reminded herself. Well out of it.

'Have you ever done anything truly terrible, Nell?' Heather asked suddenly, staring straight into her wine as if searching for something at the bottom of the glass.

Not as terrible as you, she thought. 'How bad?'

Heather stood up and walked to the window, slumped against it and looked up guiltily from beneath her long eyelashes. 'Something *very* bad.'

'Now you are scaring me,' Nell laughed. 'What have you done this time?' She couldn't resist the 'this time'.

Heather's baby-blue eyes were following something or someone through the window. 'Someone's coming.'

'What have you done?' Nell asked more insistently.

'We have an interruption.' Heather hiccupped. 'Strange hairy man alert.'

Twenty-seven

'You're back!'

'Hope you don't mind me dropping by at this hour. I was cycling past.' Michael leaned his racer bike against the wall. His fluorescent cycle vest made his jaw glow orange. Nell kissed him on each cheek, catching the smell of him as she did so; a tang of fresh sweat and sea salt. He grabbed her surprisingly forcefully and yanked her towards him in a hug. In her open-mouthed surprise she got a mouthful of polyester.

'Easy, tiger,' giggled Heather, who was leaning against the hall wall, watching them, her head lolling back drunkenly. All the alcohol had hit her bloodstream at once.

'Michael, this is my sister Heather.' Nell gave her a stern look of warning. On the rare occasions that Heather got drunk she had the potential to be a *terrible* drunk. The kind of drunk who snogged taxi drivers then vomited on the taxi back seat. (On the way back from Trish and Andy's wedding, six years ago.) Or nearly drowned in a swimming pool. (Pattersons' house in Italy, ten years ago.) Or seduced someone else's boyfriend. (Hog roast, five years ago.) Yes, anything could happen when Heather got drunk. Nell knew she should never have opened that second bottle of wine.

Michael extended an arm. 'Delighted,' he said, suddenly

sounding consciously well spoken, as if he wanted to make a good impression.

'You're the café man, aren't you? I'm head over heels in love with your carrot cake.'

He laughed. 'Thank you.'

'But, you know what? My sister's been *very* quiet about your little friendship!' slurred Heather, prodding him in the chest with her finger. 'Most, most secretive.'

They stood there for an awkward moment, oddly paralysed, as if Heather's presence, a witness to what until this point had been a private friendship, had thrown their rhythm.

'Well, aren't you going to ask him in?' said Heather. 'Come in, Mr Café Man.' She started a come-hither beckoning action with her finger.

'Heather,' growled Nell under her breath. 'Stop it.'

Michael raised an eyebrow at Nell. 'I'm not intruding on a family thing?'

'If only you would,' laughed Heather.

Nell wondered what to do. Should she send Michael away and try to continue the conversation with Heather, who had seemed to be about to confess to something dramatic and bad and juicy? Or should she shelve it and see Michael? She'd missed Michael since he'd been off doing business in London. Really missed him.

She'd shelve it.

'Get inside.' Heather put on a bad West Country accent. 'We don't get many handsome men around these parts.'

'My sister is drunk. As you might have noticed.'

'Just a little tipsy.' Heather grinned, 'Can I get you a drinkie poos, Mikey?'

They sat in the garden and stoked a small fire in the barbecue grate. The logs they sat on were still toasty from the heat of the day. Heather made Pimms: eye-wateringly strong drinks swimming with enormous hacked-off chunks of cucumber and sprigs of unwashed mint covered in black fly that she'd drunkenly yanked up from the garden. She monopolised Michael, talking too loudly, ruching up the hem of her shirt-dress, asking him a series of questions he'd already answered. Swallowing gassy belches. Terrible drunk.

Eventually, finally, Heather began to lose steam. Her head lolled to the side. She rested it against the trunk of the apple tree. Her lids started to close slowly and heavily like a child fighting sleep. Then she succumbed.

'She's never been able to hold her drink.' Nell gazed at Heather's face. She looked so young and guileless asleep. It was the face on her pillow that she'd woken up next to as a child. It wasn't the man-stealing predator face that she conjured up with hate and fury when she thought about Jeremy. A sea breeze riffled across the lawns. She rearranged her sister's pashmina to cover up her bare (hairless) arms.

'It's cold tonight, come here,' Michael said.

Nell budged up closer on the log and they huddled up. He smelled of bonfire smoke. His body felt impossibly solid. A man. What a relief. Sisters. Daughters. Mothers. It was enough to make you want to bury your head in a hairy testosterone-soaked armpit or stick your nose in a bloke's trainer just to remain sane. 'So how was the metropolis?' She wanted to ask if he'd seen his wife. But she had to pace herself.

'Polluted, noisy, full of people buying crap they don't need.'

Nell sighed. 'Heaven.'

'You only say that because you're not there.'

She laughed. 'You don't understand. I've started browsing in the local Spar looking for Must-Have baked beans and pens in the colour of the season.'

'London has fashion, sweetie. We have the whole of the moon!' He nudged her. 'Check it out.'

Nell looked up. The moon was round, plump and white like a giant lychee. 'Wow.'

'A full moon is well known for sending all women doolally.'

'Not me.' She let herself slump closer into the comforting warmth of his ribs.

'It would take an eclipse for you to totally lose control.'

Oh. He thought she was a control freak. She bristled. 'Did you see your wife in London?'

Michael took it in his stride. 'Yup.'

'And?'

'Still mad at me.'

'OK, fess up, Michael,' she said, emboldened by the rocket-fuel Pimms. 'What did you do?'

'Shagged the mother-in-law.'

Nell jumped away from him. 'Oh my God! You . . . you *beast*!'

Michael laughed. 'Bad joke. Sorry.'

'Really bad joke.' Nell narrowed her eyes. 'Or a clever double bluff? Perhaps you're preparing the ground so that what you actually did seems less contemptible.'

Michael looked away. There was a vulnerability in him that she hadn't seen before. 'You really want to know what I did?'

'Only if it doesn't make me hate you.'

'I can't offer any guarantees.'

But her curiosity was piqued now. Of course she wanted to know what he did. 'Go on.'

Michael swallowed hard. 'I fell out of love with her.'

Nell winced. She tried to see it from his point of view. 'I suppose it happens.'

'I fell out of love with her before we were even married.'

'Oh.' Nell frowned and stared into the mothy dusk. It didn't make sense. And it didn't sound good. 'You were frogmarched down the aisle?'

'No.'

'Why did you marry her, then?' She had a bad feeling about his answer. There was clearly a risk that he'd tell her something incriminating and unsisterly and become, there and then, just another crap man. Like he was holding a sharp needle above the lovely soft big bubble of their summer friendship.

He took a deep breath. 'We'd been together for six years. Engaged for two. There was a lot of pressure. And I thought it was the right thing to do.' He pulled at his cheek with his hands, fingers grating through his stubble. 'Tania was lovely. Is lovely.'

Tania, thought Nell. The name made her more real. Lovely Tania. 'And?' Her voice was cooler now.

'At the time I thought that staying with a woman for six years and then dumping her at the age of thirty-five, just when I'd made a bit of money, just when she wanted a family, I thought that was a shitty thing to do.'

Nell struggled to take it all in. 'I'm not sure if you're the world's biggest arsehole or honourable, if horribly misguided.' She sipped her drink and felt something inside her claw away from him, as if she sensed his potential to hurt. 'It's bloody egotistical to assume a woman can't live without you, that no one else would want her at the ripe old age of thirty-five!'

She was thirty-seven.

Michael groaned. 'I fucked up. I know I fucked up.'

'If you're not in love with someone, they know.' She glanced at Heather. It felt strange, her sister being here, a dumb witness.

He drained his glass. 'We had sex once on our honeymoon.'

'Blimey,' Nell spluttered. But for some confusing reason she was pleased that his honeymoon hadn't been a bonkfest.

'Don't repeat that.'

'Won't.'

'Not the kind of thing a bloke broadcasts.' He stared at her for a few moments, the reflection of the fire embers alight in his eyes. She became conscious of his body next to hers, his breath in the air, like a warm current in a cold sea. A moment seemed to turn and twist between them, intimate, full of possibility. *Sexy.* Yes, he was kind of sexy. 'So did you leave your wife?' she asked briskly, crossing her arms tightly in front of her. Withdraw. Withdraw out of the danger zone. 'Did you meet someone else?'

He looked at her. His eyes were no longer so soft. The moment had gone. 'She met someone else, actually. At work.'

'Ouch.'

'She's an architect. He's an architect. Eyes met over the Apple Mac.' He kicked his feet out in front of him. 'Not the life plan, but there you go.'

Nell had a powerful urge to hug him in her arms and kiss him better. He *had* cocked up. And he was an idiot. But he was suffering, which redeemed him (almost). But she didn't hug him, in case she reignited that confusing moment again. They listened to the crickets and the hum of nocturnal life instead as the bats whizzed around them like dozens of tiny black question marks.

'It must be hard on your own,' he said, staring into the buzzing darkness. 'Being a single parent.'

'Dean. He's a great dad. I'm very lucky. And Cass is the best thing that ever happened to me.'

'That's because she's a wonderful child.'

This simple statement of fact made Nell's eyes water. She cleared her throat. 'She is.'

Michael brooded for a few moments, glanced at her a couple of times before speaking. 'So who is this man holding your heart in London, then? I guess he's insufferably successful and handsome?'

'Who?' she replied unthinkingly, swiping a mosquito away from Heather's sleeping head.

'How many are there?'

She laughed, realised her mistake. It felt as though Pete belonged to another lifetime. 'Pete's cute,' she blurted. Shit, that sounded even worse.

'Puppies are cute. I am relieved that I will never qualify as cute.'

'Your fluoro cycle vest will do it for someone.'

'Very funny.' He smiled. And there was *something* about that smile.

She remembered her mother's words. A ladies' man. Friendly with the female customers. And she'd had it with charmers. She knew from bitter experience where it could lead. 'OK,' she said, sipping her Pimms and getting a mouthful of scraggy mint. 'Who's the lucky lady?'

'You're very inquisitive suddenly,' he teased. 'Why should I tell you?'

'Because I'm your mate.' Something flickered across Michael's face as she said this. 'And I think there's something fishy, very fishy, about that pretty woman in the orange anorak? Mum says she's always at the café. And you know *nothing* happens in this part of Cornwall without my mother noticing. You can run but you can't hide.'

He smiled. 'You mean April?'

That smile again. April. Annoyingly pretty name. All

sunshine and rain and rainbows. 'Who is she?'

Michael laughed. 'Sweet. Down here doing an art course in Penzance.'

No flat denial! And 'sweet'. That's what men liked. Heather was sweet. Now April was sweet. Nell didn't think she'd *ever* be sweet. Did that make her sour, a caper to their honey?

'As it happens, April is the one who handed in your car keys.'

'Oh!' Life was weird sometimes. 'I guess I can take some responsibility for your . . . friendship, then.'

He laughed and prodded some embers with a stick. 'Come on. As we're on the subject, let's get raw and dirty, shall we? No more pussyfooting around. Confession time.'

Confessions made Nell feel uneasy. They made her think of Jeremy.

He looked up at her cheekily from beneath his mop of hair. 'Messiest relationship?'

'What is this? The truth game?' She wasn't drunk enough for a truth game. If she'd drunk enough for a truth game with Michael, she'd be as comatose as Heather.

'You bet it is.' He slapped a mosquito on his wrist. 'Got, you, you fucker!'

'Messiest relationship . . .' she repeated as if this was a matter for some musing, trying to ignore the one name flashing up in her head like a strobe. 'No, nothing comes to mind. All perfectly tidy in my garden.'

He playfully gripped her hand. 'I have ways of making you talk.'

She giggled and almost pulled her hand away but didn't. 'I can't tell you.'

'You can.'

'I can't,' she said coquettishly, still aware of his frisbee hand holding hers. 'You'd be horrified.'

He pulled her into a soft headlock.

'Ow!' she laughed. 'Stop it or I'll scream and wake up Heather and then you'll *never* find out.'

He let the headlock go but left one arm over her shoulder. It felt nice. 'I so want to be horrified by you, Nell.'

Dare she? She checked Heather. Yes, still snoring lightly. Oh, what the hell! 'OK, I used to go out with Jeremy, Heather's fiancé,' she whispered.

Michael's eyes widened. 'You didn't?'

'Shush! I did.'

'Jerry Springer!'

'Shush!'

'When? Ages before they got together?'

'No. He jumped off one bike on to another.'

'He didn't?' He whistled in amazement. 'And you two are *still* talking?'

'We weren't for a long time.' She stared at Heather sleeping and felt a trickle of something like tenderness. 'Avoiding each other hasn't been an option this summer because of the situation with Mum.'

'But you're so completely different.'

Nell grimaced. Chalk and cheese.

'Although same taste in men, obviously. Hats off to the guy. Must be some kind of stud,' he said wryly.

Nell laughed. 'He's a short arse and he wears pink shirts.'

'Jeremy!' Heather shouted, sitting bolt upright, eyes wide open.

They both jumped. 'Jesus, Heather?' said Nell, desperately hoping that she hadn't been listening in to their conversation. 'You OK?'

'I think I might be a little drunk,' she slurred, rubbing her eyes. 'Bed. I want bed.'

'Do you want me to take you up?' asked Nell.

'No. Just need bed.' She stumbled up and started wheedling her way along the path back towards the house. She stopped. There was the sound of retching. Cursing. Then more footsteps. More cursing. The sound of the back door slamming shut.

Nell and Michael exchanged glances and exploded into a geyser of laughter. Neither was really sure what they were laughing about.

'Oh dear,' said Nell, wiping her eyes, collecting herself a few minutes later. 'I'd better go and check on her.'

'Don't go.' Michael pulled her towards him. Straight into his testosteroney armpit. She looked up at him. He looked down at her. Everything freeze-framed. She noticed the shadowy dip beneath his cheekbone. The way his nose slanted a little to the left. The hair in his nostrils. The way his mouth was plumper than she remembered. His breath was coming faster. She felt it on her forehead, warm, Pimms flavoured. His excitement excited her. Something took over. She moved her face towards his and—

'Argh!' A loud bloodcurdling scream.

'Shit, that's Heather!'

They ran through the garden into the house. Heather was leaning against the closed front door, shaking, one hand pressed over her mouth, the other clutching an enormous lump of chocolate cake that was dropping crumbs all over her dress. 'Oh my God, oh my God,' she muttered over and over.

Nell put a hand on her arm. 'What happened? Are you OK?'

'There's ... there's ...' stuttered Heather, pointing at the door. 'There's someone in the front garden. I just grabbed a bit of cake from the fridge and then Monty wanted to go out and poo and ...' She started to gulp air again.

'What's the hullabaloo?' Valerie stood at the top of the stairs, blearily rubbing her eyes.

Nell forced a smile. She didn't want Mum spooked. 'It's fine, Mum. Heather thought she saw someone in the front garden. I'm sure it's nothing. You must go back to bed, Heather. Michael's here. He'll investigate.'

'A man in the house. Very good,' said Valerie as if this solved the problem, whatever the problem might be. 'He can deal with it. Do you want the shotgun, Michael?'

'Mum. Don't be ridiculous. Getting out Grandad's rusty old shotgun will just get us all arrested. Anyway, it's most likely to be some poor fox.' She realised as she said this that if the same thing had happened in London she would be anticipating a gang of knife-wielding hoodies. Why was she not being more paranoid?

'It wasn't a fox,' said Heather.

'Don't worry. I'll check it out.' Michael opened the front door and went outside. They waited a few moments. Nell heard the sound of voices. She opened the door and peeked out. In the dark, lit by the squares of light from the kitchen window, she could make out Michael and another figure at the front of the drive. They appeared to be talking. More worried now, she walked up the drive, stealing herself for some sharp words to a teenage-wannabe burglar. Oh. Strange. Michael was talking to a pretty, terrified-looking young girl.

'Everything OK, Michael?'

'Yes, don't worry. This is . . .' he stuttered, looking thrown.

'Are you OK?' asked Nell gently, taking pity on the girl. So young. Had something awful happened? Was she looking for help?

The girl nodded and stared at Nell as if awestruck.

'You gave her sister a bit of a shock, Beth,' said Michael.

Beth? He knew her?

'Sorry, I . . . I didn't mean to. I was just, like, checking out the . . .' Beth looked helplessly at Michael, then glanced over to where a car was waiting outside the front gate. 'Um, I was going past and I saw Michael's bike and thought . . .'

So she wasn't a young girl in distress. What the . . . 'Could someone explain what's going on?'

'*Beth!*' There was the sound of a car door slamming.

Nell jumped. A woman got out of the car. Her face was in shadow but her body language was agitated. 'Beth, come on.'

Michael looked bewildered. 'April?'

APRIL! The hairs on Nell's hands stood up. She stared at Michael angrily. What was going on?

Michael shook his head. 'No idea.'

'Yes, it's me,' the woman said quietly. Her voice was accent-less, soft, scared. 'I'm so sorry, Michael.' She twisted her hands together. 'We were just driving by and Beth wanted . . .' She stopped and spoke more urgently. 'Beth, please, we need to leave.'

Beth walked slowly towards the car, glancing back at them over her shoulder. Nell's mind began to race at a million miles per hour. What did she want with Michael?

When Beth got into the car the penny dropped. This was the car – that hire car – that had sped mysteriously, mentally, out of the drive a few days ago. She swore it was.

'I'm so sorry if Beth frightened anyone,' April stuttered. 'I'm so sorry.' Her door slammed. The car revved. And they were swallowed by blackness.

Twenty-eight

'Time to call the fuzz, sis?' said Ethan, wiping his Guinness moustache on the back of his hand.

'Nah, don't think so.' Having Ethan around made her feel normal again. Her brain had been whirring with all sorts of Wire in the Blood scenarios. Now sitting opposite her big brother in The Seagull's Nest, the events of two nights ago all seemed far less dramatic. Plus it was raining, which was reassuring in its normality.

'I don't like the idea of some odd woman stalking my little sisters.' Ethan kicked his neon high-tops up on to the wooden bar stool. The circle of bearded old-man drinkers on the adjacent round pub table stared. He still carried with him the otherness of London. Nell suspected she'd lost hers somewhere on Perranortho beach weeks ago. 'Who is she?'

'Some woman doing an art course down here. Heather's a bit spooked by her. But *I* think there's something going on with her and Michael. Maybe she's following him? She's realised I know him, hasn't she? She knows he visits me.' She shrugged. 'One theory, anyway.'

Ethan raised his eyebrow. 'Bunny boiler?'

'She doesn't look like one.' And there was something resoundingly normal, familiar even, about her voice.

'They don't all look like Glenn Close.'

Nell smiled. 'Guess not.'

'We don't want Mum worried by all this. Not after the fall and stuff. Does she know?'

'She thinks it was a fox. I bluffed it.'

'Nice one.' Ethan sipped his Guinness, thoughtfully. 'Has Mum got worse, do you think, sis? The stuff the docs warned us about. Wandering out in her dressing gown, going to have tea with the Queen in the woods?'

'No.' Nell grinned. 'Give her time.'

They sat in silence for a moment. And Nell knew they were both struggling with the same thing.

'I still can't believe she's going to die,' said Ethan quietly.

Nell looked down at the stained wooden tabletop. She'd got better and better at blocking it out. She concentrated on getting stuff done, the daily routines of pills and meals and walks and swims. 'I try not to think about it.'

'Lucky you. It's there when I wake up, when I go to bed. Fuck. I mean this inheritance issue doesn't help, does it?' Ethan sank his head into his hands. His fingers ruched up his skin and suddenly he looked his age. And this was wrong. She wanted Ethan to be a boy for ever. She felt a nostalgic pang for the spirited children they once were. The fights, the laughter and the camaraderie forged against the dysfunctions of their family life.

'Man, Janet's become obsessed with it all,' groaned Ethan. 'The future of Tredower! Her new project. I can hardly bear to talk about it.'

'Well, don't, then. I refuse to, Ethan,' Nell said defiantly. 'I think what Mum's doing is wrong.'

'Isn't it also wrong not to give Cass a shot at inheriting Tredower one day?' Ethan shook his head at her principled naïvety. 'It's a tough old world out there, Nell. We need everything we can get and it's going to be even harder for the next generation.'

'It's divisive and it's wrong. If I inherited it, and there is no chance of that, I know, I'd sell it and divide the proceeds anyway.'

Ethan laughed.

'Why are you laughing?'

'Because everyone *thinks* they'd do that.'

'You don't?'

'Janet wouldn't let me.'

Was he joking? Probably not. 'Can't you get Janet to cool it just a little bit? If none of us participated, then—'

'More chance of flogging her wedding ring.' He snorted. 'Not that that's so unlikely.'

'What do you mean? Is everything OK, Eth?'

For a moment Ethan just stared at her as if he was trying to decide whether to tell her something. Then he looked down at his pint. 'Fine.' He drained his beer. 'Tricky summer, eh?'

Nell studied him, trying to work out what was going on. 'Yes, tricky summer.'

Ethan glanced around the pub, a little uncomfortable at the turn in conversation.

She wasn't going to let it lie. 'Is Janet OK?'

Ethan sighed wearily. 'She wants another baby.'

'Ah. Right.' Nell smiled. 'And you don't?'

Ethan groaned. 'Those twins, man, I love them, totally love them, but they're such bloody hard work. I've aged a thousand years since they were born.' He pulled back his hair to show his receding temples. 'I mean look! Bald! Every sleepless night took a fucking follicle. The baby thing again? I'll be bald as a monk. And to think we could have more twins! More boys! Jesus. It doesn't bear thinking about.' He shook his head.

240

'You know, sis, I want my freedom back . . . one day.'

Nell laughed. 'Your freedom's long gone, Eth.'

Ethan rolled his eyes. 'You're looking great on one child, anyway,' he said, changing the subject.

'I look like a country bumpkin.' She scooped out an ice-cube from her glass and sucked on it.

'The most relaxed I've seen you in years. Not this nutty thirty-something in silly heels rushing manically around London.'

'I liked being a nutty thirty-something in silly heels. It beats being a Cornish-something of indeterminate age in Mum's muddy old Birkenstocks.'

He looked down at her feet in amazement. 'You're not joking, either. So your ankle tendons didn't snap when you put on flat shoes?'

'Funnily enough, no.'

He flicked his beer mat. 'Someone else looks close to snapping, though. Heather can't sit still. What's eating her?'

'Freaked out by all the comings and goings the other night, I guess.'

Ethan shook his head, leaned forward and spoke con-spiratorially. 'Problems with Jeremy? Has she said anything?'

Nell rolled her eyes. 'You reckon she'd confide in me about him? Ethan, the fact that we have salvaged *some* of our old relationship this summer is a near miracle. But I'm afraid there's still some way to go.'

'Pre-wedding tension, Janet reckons.' He glanced at his watch. 'Oh shit. We're going to be late for lunch.'

Ethan drove too fast. Nell was relieved when they pulled safely into the drive. Rain slid off the ivy in sheets, dripping from leaf to leaf then to the ground like an intricate water clock. Nell picked her way over a fallen army of muddy green boots in the hallway, poked her head round the door of the playroom where the twins were wrestling. No Cass. The dining-room door was ajar and she could see Mum at the head of the table, Janet on one side – a vision in an emerald-green silk blouse and dangly coin necklace. Heather sat next to her, fiddling with the buttons on her shrunken pink cardigan, biting strips of skin off her lower lip.

'Hi, guys.' Nell flicked her soggy fringe out of her eyes.

Ethan kissed Janet's cheek. Janet turned away slightly. 'Sorry . . .'

'You're late,' interrupted Valerie. 'You've missed Jeremy's asparagus soup.'

Nell froze. *Jeremy?* Asparagus soup! Janet nodded discreetly to the kitchen.

Jeremy put his head round the door. He gave her a handsome white-toothed honey-I'm-home smile. Like his fingers hadn't been on her ankle. Like he hadn't said he missed her. Like nothing had happened. 'Hi.'

'Hi.' Nell tried hard to look like nothing had happened too. But the heat started to rise on her face. 'This is a surprise.'

'Managed to get away from work early,' he joked. 'Broke the shackles.'

Nell looked around the table. 'Where's Cass?'

Cass's impish face appeared round the door. 'I'm helping Mr Jeremy Fisher, Mummy. I'm eating all the carrots. Carrots are orange.'

'We're quite a team, aren't we, Cass?' said Jeremy in a way that made Nell feel sick. How could he be so *normal*? So sickeningly brother-in-law-like after what happened last time he was here?

242

Maybe she'd imagined it after all.

'Take a look at this, Nell.' Valerie stroked a spiral-bound folder. It had clearly indexed pages marked in an assortment of neon colours. 'Plans for Tredower! Marvellous plans by marvellous Janet.'

What fresh hell?

Janet swiped the folder off the table and quickly shoved it into her tan handbag. 'Let's not bore the ladies with it now, Val.'

'Janet has got wonderful ideas for a sculpture garden,' enthused Valerie, waving her fork around like a baton, oblivious to the crackle of tension. 'Arty festival open days. Which we could actually charge for! Imagine. And that money could be ploughed back into the house . . .'

Nell poured herself a glass of wine. Anaesthetise, anaesthetise.

'Mum,' said Ethan gently, touching her hand and trying to stop her.

She carried on relentlessly. 'The house could be a –' she made quote marks with her fingers – ' "self-sustaining eco-organism," as Janet says. I *adore* that idea, Janet. And I am also rather tickled by the idea of teaming up with the Muffin catalogue in some way.'

Oh so now Tredower was to be a marketing vehicle for Muffin? Now why didn't this surprise her? Heather and Nell exchanged alarmed looks. Janet coloured guiltily beneath her tan.

'As for . . . the wind turbine!' Valerie puffed, awestruck. 'Now, that *would* give the village ladies something to get hot under the collar about.'

Heather looked like she wanted to stab Janet in her yoga-toned thigh with her fork. 'Wind turbines are ugly.'

'And we're in a valley,' Nell pointed out.

'Besides, if we did art events here, we'd get besieged by hundreds of tourists coming in just to use the loo,' added Heather, wrinkling her nose.

'Heavens,' said Valerie, putting her hand over her mouth. 'Yes. I hadn't thought of that.'

'Or nick the sculptures,' added Nell mischievously.

'Grandmother Penelope wouldn't approve. She wasn't into that sort of thing,' added Heather with a note of finality.

Janet cleared her throat. 'From what Ethan tells me,' she said slowly as if addressing a class of remedial six year olds, 'your grandmother *was* interested in art, Heather.'

'Seascapes. Pictures of seagulls,' said Nell, reaching for some bread. 'Not your kind of thing, Janet.'

'Well, yes, I was thinking something more modern. Tatey stuff. New art school graduates.'

'It's a good idea, Jan,' Ethan said loyally.

'It is.' Valerie sighed. 'And you're quite right, Janet. My mother *did* like art. She occasionally even picked up the paintbrush herself.'

'Not sure I remember that.' Ethan scratched his head.

'That's because you don't remember anything pre-1992,' quipped Heather. 'I've seen them. They're OK. Watercolours and stuff. Up in the attic somewhere.'

Nell fleetingly wondered how Heather knew where they were.

'Daddy was a bit less interested, to put it mildly,' Valerie mused. 'He liked stamps and trains and collecting old Bibles . . .' She flexed her hands, her sinewy arms extending from the circles of her navy sleeves. 'Those bloody Bibles.'

'Those bloody Methodists.' Ethan grinned. 'Bet he had a secret collection of naughty nudes stashed somewhere. Probably up in the attic too, if you dig hard enough, Nell.'

'He didn't have any stuff like that. Goodness, no. They

were from another era, really.' Valerie knocked back a gulp of wine. 'I believe the word is stiff.'

'It's fascinating, Valerie, all the history here,' said Janet, twisting her gold coin necklace with her fingers anxiously, knowing she had to win them all back round. 'Tredower must feel like it is part of you, Val. Kind of cool, really. I can't imagine living in the house I grew up in. We moved six times before I was ten.' She sighed. 'I guess living here makes it easier to hang on to the happy memories.'

Valerie was silent for a little longer than was comfortable. Everyone started to feel twitchy, the silence broken only by the noise of Cass and Jeremy clattering pots in the kitchen. 'Happy,' Valerie shrugged, pouring water from the green water jug. 'Sad. It doesn't matter. When you get older, it's harder to differentiate between the two.'

Unexpectedly Nell got an overpowering sense that she'd always remember her mother as she was then, sitting on that ladder-back chair, matriarchal, holding the bright green water jug. It was like the lens of her brain taking a picture. A new memory at its moment of creation.

'Nell, as we're having a nostalgia trip here, did you find my old table football in the attic?' said Ethan. 'I'd love to reclaim it.'

'I didn't,' said Nell, relieved at Ethan's intervention. When Mum started talking about the past she always started to look so sad. 'But I'll have a look for it next time I'm up there, if you like.'

'Glad that you're putting your intrepid journalistic nature to some use at last, sis,' Ethan winked.

'That's right, Ethan. The attic is not for pussycats who shake at the sight of a harvest spider.'

Ethan puffed out his chest. 'I presume you're talking about Jeremy.'

Everyone laughed. Janet leaned forward over the table. 'What else have you unearthed up in the attic, Nell? Treasure? Antiques?'

'Cobwebs, wallpaper, chipped vases . . .'

Janet looked unconvinced. 'Just junk? Really?'

'One man's junk is another's—' Nell suddenly remembered the letter. The letter with the bright stamp. The one addressed to her mother. She must bring it down.

'Ta-da!' said Jeremy, walking into the room with Cass, their faces obscured by puffs of steam. He placed an enormous bubbling lasagne and a dish of perfect buttered beans on the table.

Yes, it smelled good. Jeremy was an annoyingly good cook and had seduced her with many a meal when they first started dating. She watched him dish up the lasagne with one of the new Divertimenti wooden spoons Heather had brought. Those big hands with their blue-vein piping. The square knuckles. The index and forefingers practically the same length. She'd recognise those hands in a line-up. They'd caressed her once. Now they caressed her sister. She had to stop herself from thinking further.

'A rainbow!' Cass yelled, pointing out of the window. 'A rainbow!'

They all turned their heads in unison. Sure enough, through the frame of ivy, a bridge of colour arched over the trees, appearing to deposit its pot of gold somewhere near the vegetable patch.

'I knew the rain would clear,' said Valerie, scooping up the runner beans. 'Who'll join me for a dunk in the sea after lunch? Jeremy?'

'I might take the dunk on a towel-with-beer option,' said Jeremy.

'Pussy,' mumbled Ethan.

'Guys, it's a beautiful day. The surf will be amazing,' said Nell. Did she just say surf? She'd obviously been spending too much time with Michael.

'Who needs Ibiza, eh, Ethan?' said Heather.

'Oh yes, I'm sure he'd rather be here than surrounded by topless supermodels,' quipped Nell.

Janet visibly bristled.

'*I'd* certainly rather be in Cornwall,' said Heather. 'Much rather.'

'Me too,' said Nell with a mouthful of lasagne.

Everyone turned to look at her in amazement. What had she said?

'Whoa!' Ethan whistled and banged his water glass with his knife. 'Important announcement! After thirty-seven years Nell has finally fallen for Cornwall.'

'You announce nothing but your own idiocy,' laughed Nell.

Valerie dabbed at her mouth with a napkin and her eyes flashed with mischief. 'I fear that there are other reasons for her change of attitude.'

'Hang on a minute, what change of attitude?' said Nell.

Ethan banged the water glass again. 'Shush, Nell! Continue, Mother.'

Valerie smiled. 'Might a certain café owner have anything to do with it?'

Nell felt herself blush, a great sizzling blast of a blush. You could have fried prawns on it. Jeremy's eyes were drilling into her. She had nowhere to hide.

'The surfing trustie!' honked Ethan.

'He's *not* a trustie, he's got a . . . a . . . virtual business,' Nell said, annoyed with herself for making his business sound silly when it wasn't.

'Virtually employed, even better.' Ethan winked. 'Nice work, if you can get it.'

'Oh for goodness' sake! Why can't I be friends with a guy?'

'Not a denial, not a denial!' hooted Ethan.

'I met him,' said Heather. 'He's very sweet.' She started to giggle. 'If . . . a little hairy.'

'Is he a . . . bearded love-god?' teased Ethan.

'He's not bearded!' Nell leapt to his defence. 'It's stubble.'

Janet nudged her and whispered, 'Can feel rather nice in certain places, if you get my meaning.'

Suddenly there was a screech as Jeremy pushed back his chair along the flagstone floor. 'Excuse me,' he glowered, 'I've got to make a quick work call.'

Twenty-nine

Nell could see straight away that Michael wasn't in the café. The goth girl was there, serving frothy coffees on her own, nose ring blinking in the sunshine like a solitary fairy light. Maybe he was up in London working? Maybe he was with April? Something twisted in her stomach. Well, at least Ethan couldn't say something loud and embarrassing. And Jeremy wouldn't get a look at him either. Nell could just imagine what Jeremy would think about someone like Michael. He'd think he was a waster.

Ethan stood at the serving hatch and ordered a selection of goodies – cakes, juices, crisps – to complement his crate of beer. He turned to Nell. 'The bearded love-god isn't here,' he whispered.

'I'll kill you.'

Jeremy strode away quickly, crossly, Heather having to almost run to keep up. Cass yelped as the cousins tugged her towards the beach. Nell resisted the urge to call her back. She wanted her to have some freedom. Soon they'd be back in London. Back to parks and fenced playgrounds and organised play-dates.

They found their spot. It was one of Nell's favourite spots at the top of the beach near a cluster of cockle-free table-shaped rocks. Valerie changed beneath her white towel, flashing bits of her white bare bottom. Valerie strode purposefully down to the sea in her turquoise swimming costume. They all watched her go. Monty ran along beside her, tussling with seaweed.

'Oh God, Nell, she shouldn't be swimming,' said Heather, gazing after her anxiously as she shook out her towel. 'The sea's really rough today.'

'The doctors say she's meant to exercise.' Nell shrugged. Mum was now a small, dark silhouette, walking slowly into the waves, shaking her hair with her fingers. 'I can't stop her.'

Heather held her straw hat to her head with one hand. 'I suspect the doctors mean something like yoga.'

'Ladies, she's a marvel,' sighed Janet, propping herself up on one hand. 'You've got to admire her chutzpah, no?'

'And Monty's inventiveness.' Jeremy smiled. 'Look at that. He can make a sex doll out of seaweed. Quite something.'

Nell glanced at Jeremy quickly. His dark skin already looked a couple of shades darker than it had done earlier in the day.

There was a fizz, a pop, as Ethan ripped open his first beer. 'Ah, the sound of sunshine,' he said, tipping it back into his mouth. 'Help yourself.'

'I'd prefer something soft,' Heather said, reaching for an apple juice.

Ethan whistled. 'Oh, don't come over all teetotal with us, Heather. I hear you were drunk as a skunk the other night.' He looked at Jeremy and winked. 'See what she gets up to when you're not around, mate.'

The corners of Heather's mouth twitched with a smile. 'I always forget quite how strong wine is these days. I'm not used to it.'

'Yeah, right,' said Ethan, nudging her leg playfully with his bare foot.

'It's something to do with Tredower.' Heather put the straw of the juice carton to her rosebud lips and sucked, knowingly Lolita-ish.

'The house made me do it!' said Ethan. 'It'll be mixing double-strength vodka and tonics next, slipping them to you as you sleep, sis.'

'We do all drink too much at Tredower,' said Nell. 'I'm feeling perfectly pickled.'

'Whenever I think about Mum . . .' Heather stopped and looked sad. 'It makes me want to drink.'

'And eat chocolate,' added Nell. 'Preferably drink and eat chocolate at the same time. That's my excuse and I'm sticking to it.'

Janet, lain out on a towel, the latest copy of *Vogue* covering her face from the sun, reached out and put a hand on Nell's knee. 'I've got these brilliant Tibetan milk thistle pills back at the house. Perfect for overworked livers.'

'The devil's own,' quipped Ethan, swigging back his beer. 'Don't do it, sisters. Not while we're sharing a bathroom, anyway.'

Nell sipped her beer, enjoying the cold bubbles breaking against the back of her throat in the heat. 'You know what? I might take my chances with the time-tested hair-of-the-dog method, thanks all the same, Janet.'

'And I tell you what,' said Ethan solemnly, stretching his hairy legs over Janet's smooth calves. 'If this summer's taught me anything, it's that life's too short. Something's going to get you, isn't it? You spend your life worrying about skin cancer and you get run over by an ancient Datsun on your way home from the gym. You stop drinking and it's that mole that gets you. It's impossible to know. Something will take us all out.'

'Jeez. I'm feeling happier already, Ethan,' said Heather.

'Ethan's right,' said Jeremy, leaning his head back on his arms gracefully, making his biceps bulge. 'Valerie should absolutely be swimming in fearsome seas and drinking like a pirate if that's what she wants to do. So should all of us.'

'But Jeremy . . .' said Heather, puzzled. This was not like her Jeremy. Nell gave him a sidelong glance too.

'You live once, don't you?' Jeremy looked at Nell. 'Seize the day and all that.'

Nell became clammily aware of Jeremy all over again. The distance between their bare feet. The blackness of his eyes beneath those long lashes. The way his eyes looked closed but weren't. She knew he was looking at her.

She wished she was wearing a better bikini. Not the frumpkini beneath her sarong. It was navy and low legged, masquerading as a sports bra and big knickers, one of those bikinis that was meant to disguise the saggy bits but somehow just drew attention to them, and made it look like you had body-esteem issues to boot.

Janet, however, was not wearing a frumpkini. She did not think she looked fat. Nor was she in the least self-conscious. She kicked off Ethan's legs, stood up and bent – bikini-clad bottom in the air! – over her towel on her hands and breathed noisily. No one knew where to look.

'Jesus, you're giving us indigestion, Janet,' giggled Heather.

Janet peered through her legs – 'Valerie's survived the swim, guys' – and gently stretched out her downward dog until she was lying flat on the towel again, as if impromptu near-naked yoga in public was entirely normal. Heather looked horrified.

'Gosh! That is a rough sea today!' Valerie sat down beside

them, breathless, exhilarated, spraying Nell with icy seawater as she towel-dried her hair. 'Wonderfully exhilarating! You lot are missing out. I'll have one of those, darling,' she said, nodding at the beer.

They all hesitated.

'Will someone please pass me a beer?'

It was Jeremy who passed her one in the end. Probably trying to kill Mother-in-law-off, Nell mused.

The sun sank lower in the sky. They all went for a swim – apart from Nell, who was engrossed in her book, and Jeremy, who had taken himself off on a cliff walk – then come back to eat. Valerie pulled out a loaf of crusty white bread and potted mackerel paté, which was immediately crusted in sand by Nat, Cosmo and Cass running past – naked – high on the endless sandy space and the sun and the happy possibility of ice cream. After the gritty sandwich, Nell flipped over to her front and opened her book again. Enjoying the warm sunshine on her back she lay there reading for a good forty-five minutes, looking up every so often to check on Cass. She'd managed to persuade Cass to put her bikini bottoms back on, thinking that Dean might disapprove, but the boys were still joyfully naked.

'One last swim,' said Valerie, putting down her news-paper. 'Then we can think about supper. All these meals, all this food. Goodness . . .' She stood up. As she did so, she faltered and reached out for Jeremy's shoulder for support. 'Oh!' Her face went pale. She squatted back down on the sand.

'Mum!' shrieked Heather.

Nell squatted down next to her. 'Mum? You OK?'

'Jesus! Is she having a stroke?' gasped Janet. 'Ethan! Grab my handbag! The Rescue Remedy!'

'Call an ambulance! Call an ambulance!' shrieked Heather. 'Jeremy, *do* something!'

'I can't find the bloody phone,' said Jeremy, frantically rifling through the pile of towels.

'Guys, calm down. Mum?' said Nell gently, realising that her mother was pinking in the cheeks again and giving them all a reassuringly indignant glare. 'You OK?'

'I'm bloody well not having a stroke!'

Nell smiled. That clarified that, then.

'I think you should be checked out anyway, Mum. I'll drive you to hospital,' said Ethan.

'Don't be ridiculous. You can't take me to hospital every time I burp!' She frowned. 'It's the beer, probably. I've never been good at daytime drinking.' She looked up at Ethan. 'Will you take me home?'

'Of course.' Ethan rubbed his sandy hands on his swim shorts. 'Janet, honey, will you round up the troops?'

'I'm coming too,' said Heather firmly, reaching for her sun hat. 'Let's go.'

'You really don't need to . . .' protested Valerie.

'Well, I *am* coming,' said Heather, taking her mother's arm and pulling her up gently.

Valerie's face fell. 'I don't want to spoil things. It's such a beautiful day. Nell, you haven't even swum yet. Nor have you, Jeremy.'

'Oh, that doesn't matter,' said Nell, looking around for one of her flip-flops.

'I refuse to be a burden!' Valerie said. 'It is my human right not to be a burden.'

Nell and Ethan exchanged amused glances.

'OK, if it makes you feel better, Valerie, Nell and I will stay and have a swim,' said Jeremy matter-of-factly. 'Nell definitely deserves one.'

Nell looked at him in horror. A swim? With Jeremy? Think not! 'Oh no, I should get Cass back. It's getting late.'

'Oh, don't you worry about that, Nell,' said Janet. 'Val's right. We don't all need to go home. I'll pop Cass in the bath with her cousins. And I promise to supervise.'

Nell felt a rising panic. She didn't want to draw attention to the fact that she didn't want to stay here. Alone with Jeremy. But. Lord. No! 'That's very sweet of you, Janet. But—'

'Janet is more than capable, darling. Don't be so controlling,' said Valerie, brushing sand off her skirt. 'That's an old office habit.'

Controlling! Who was doing the controlling here! 'I've drunk too much beer and the sea's rough.'

'Oh for goodness' sake, it's not the local authority swimming pool,' said Valerie. 'I've never heard such nonsense. Enjoy your swim, Nell.'

As Jeremy and Nell waved the party off, Nell suddenly became horribly aware once more of the frumpkini, thus far artfully hidden, lurking beneath her sarong.

'Shall we?' Jeremy's black eyes danced. He was amused by her. He knew she didn't want to be here alone with him. He was playing with her. Bastard.

'You hate swimming in the sea,' said Nell, clutching the sarong against her body for dear life. Her body must have changed so much over the years, especially since having Cass. She hated the idea of Jeremy looking at it and comparing it to what it was, or, worse, her sister's younger, non-pregnancy-marked body.

'It's what your mother wanted.' He peeled off his T-shirt. 'Come on.'

Nell hesitated.

'You never used to be a girl to chicken out of a rough sea.'

Nell dropped her sarong to the ground. Frumpkini be damned. Jeremy be damned. She wouldn't have him think she'd lost her nerve! 'Come on, then.'

The surf was rough indeed. She threw herself into it. She squealed. Jeremy stood in the shallows, the water only over his knees.

'It's colder if you just stand there,' she laughed, enjoying his townie torment. A wave thumped over her head.

'It's The Perfect bloody Storm!'

'Pussycat!' Nell laughed, flicking her legs off the sand. She threw herself in deeper. As the thundering water closed over her shoulders she felt a burst of happiness, closely followed by a déjà vu so powerful it made her choke. God, here they were again, just like the first time she took Jeremy down to visit her mother, made him go swimming and he'd groaned and declared the sea unfit for purpose. Then they'd had sex in her car in a perilously windy deserted car park at the top of the cliff. To get rid of this particular image she took a huge gulp of air and sunk her head beneath the waves. The sea roared up her nostrils, tunnelled into her ears, and flung her forward, then back, the current pulling her fingers apart, starfishing her hands. A strange series of images pixelated against her squeezed-shut eyes: Michael on his bike, April standing at the gate in the dusk, her mother striding out into the sea in her turquoise swimming costume, and suddenly she couldn't breathe and the water was pulling her under, pulling her out to sea like a hundred tiny mermaids' hands. A rip tide. Shit. She was in a bloody rip tide. She panicked. More pulling, then rotating, something spinning her round and round as if she were stuck to a wheel. Where was Jeremy? Where was up? Where was down? She struggled to raise her arms above her head, alert someone to her distress. But she couldn't. Then the pulling again, the suction down and out, out, out to sea. Taste of blood in her mouth. A moment of calm: so this was how it was going to end. Not cancer. Not car crashes. Drowning. In a frumpkini. A loud whooshing noise deep inside her head.

Blackness.

Thirty

Wolvercote, Oxford

Beth lay back on the sunlounger, huge pink sunglasses obscuring her face, arms stretched languorously above her head, looking like she'd been parachuted in from an American rap video. She had a streak of fake tan over her tummy, April noticed from her adjacent deckchair – were you allowed to fake bake when pregnant? – and her tummy was definitely getting bigger by the day. Beth's thick dark hair looked thicker than ever and shone glassily. Yes, she'd definitely bloomed in Cornwall. There was a strange natural affinity between the sea and a pregnant woman, April decided.

'Stop staring at me, Mum.'

'I was just admiring your belly.' She'd love to draw it. She missed the course. It already felt like a lifetime away, even though she'd only got back yesterday.

'Well, don't. It's totally gross.'

'It's gorgeous.' OK, not the moment to suggest a sitting. 'I'm not sure you're allowed to sunbathe pregnant, love. It overheats the baby. Sorry, babies.'

'Can't do bloody anything, can I?' groaned Beth, reaching for her T-shirt.

She'd been in a funny mood all morning, April thought.

Skittish and irritable. Hormones, probably. 'Language.'

'Can't drink. Can't smoke . . .'

'You don't smoke!'

'No, I don't,' said Beth, quickly. 'But you know what I mean.'

'It's only nine months.' April flipped the page of the baby catalogue and studied the double pushchairs. The pushchairs cost *how* much? The cost of the baby gear – and so much of it – was eye-watering. Clearly, the only drawing she'd be doing now was on her chequebook stubs.

Beth pushed her sunglasses up into her hair. 'A girl at antenatal told me it's actually ten months. Imagine! Ten months,' she sighed incredulously, as if it were ten years. 'Unbelievable.'

'Not with twins, it won't be. They like an early entrance.'

Beth sat up on the lounger, crossed legs, hands cradling her belly. She hesitated, her face softening. 'Mum, there's something I wanted to talk to you about.'

Oh? April gave her an open ask-me-anything smile. She hoped it was a pregnancy question because she'd discovered she rather enjoyed offering Beth pregnancy advice. It felt nice, a transaction of knowledge from mother to daughter. And it was the one type of advice that Beth would actually listen to, even if she pretended not to. 'Go on.'

Beth hesitated. Her fingers drummed on her glossy tanned knees.

That moment Chris put his head out of the kitchen window. 'Tea, ladies?'

'Not for me, Dad, I'm meeting Claire in Starbucks.'

'I'd kill for a cup.' April turned to Beth. 'How well trained he is since I've been away.' She called back at him, 'Quite the domestic goddess!'

Without warning, Beth leapt up and hugged April tightly, burying her head in her shoulder.

'What's that for?' April combed Beth's hair with her fingers, relishing the feel and smell of her. Beth was like a cat, only wanting affection when *she* wanted it.

'Nothing.' Beth unwrapped herself and smiled sheepishly. 'Look . . . I . . . well, I'd better go or I'll be late.' She started walking down the garden path.

'Bye, sweetheart. Take care in this heat. Drink lots of fluids,' April called after her. It was only when she heard the front door slam that she realised Beth hadn't asked that pregnancy question. Damn.

A few minutes later, Chris brought out her mug of tea and sat on the edge of Beth's vacated sunlounger. 'It's good to have you home. You look beautiful, April.'

'Beautiful?' Her days of looking good in her bikini were well and truly over. She should be wearing a one-piece. What the hell. She grinned.

'You got a great tan in Cornwall.' He stood up behind her, gently pressed his thumbs into the pressure point on her neck. 'And, I don't know, all that painting must suit you. Something about your eyes.'

She felt different too. More connected with something. Maybe it was the actual doing something she'd always wanted to do that made the difference, rather than just talking about it. Or maybe it was because she loved the fact that the more she practised her art the better she got. (Not a rule that applied to other things such as parking, meringues, or blow drying her hair.)

She looked up at Chris. Framed by the rear of the house, he seemed so extraordinarily familiar it shocked her. It was silly, but when she'd first got back from Cornwall she was surprised that everything was as it always had been, like she'd

260

never been away at all even though so much had happened. Same niggly old details: piles of washing, a stack of unopened post, an invitation to Louise's birthday party upstairs at The Perch – she had to go to that one, first since Louise's divorce – and so it went on. Her life in small, domestic, insignificant increments. Whereas in Cornwall everything had felt dramatic and cinematic. Had that really been her? The woman who stole the photograph. The woman who'd confided her hopes and dreams to some guy she'd met at a surf shack. The woman who could talk about art in a group setting (without blushing or apologising) and had got up at five a.m. to swim naked – naked! – in the sea.

Chris stroked his fingers up her hot neck. He cleared his throat nervously. 'Didn't Beth tell you, then?'

She let her head loll against his soft belly. 'What?'

There was a silence. His fingers froze on her neck.

Puzzled, she turned round. 'What was she going to tell me?'

Chris winced. 'She's mortified, that's why she still hasn't said anything. But she promised me she'd tell you this morning. Shit.'

'Mortified about what?' said April impatiently. 'Tell me, Chris.'

'Beth told someone, April.'

'She told them . . .' She filled in the blanks. 'Oh no.' She pinched the bridge of her nose and closed her eyes. 'Whom did she tell?'

He frowned. 'Some guy called Michael.'

Thirty-one

A pair of hands yanked her up by the armpits. Nell came spluttering and gasping up to the surface. Her body felt weirdly floppy. Alive? Dead? Anxiety dream? She belched up a mouthful of water. Alive.

'Fuck, Nell,' panted Jeremy, grasping her tightly. 'Are you all right?'

'J–J–Jeremy?' She looked at him, rubbed her eyes. Stingy from salt. The sun was a spike of brightness. Jeremy's face was very close. She slowly became aware that they were lying on the beach, sea lapping against them, bodies entwined, his knee between her thighs, pressing up against her crotch. 'Did you just rescue me?'

Jeremy flicked his black wet hair out of his eyes. 'At your service.'

'Like *Baywatch*.' Through her gasps Nell started to laugh, hysterically, on the verge of tears. Then she belched up another mouthful of seawater, wiped it off her chin with the back of her hand. 'Sorry.'

'And I thought *you* were meant to be the top swimmer.'

'The beer wasn't a good idea. In hindsight.' In fact, she felt stoned, buoyant, as if she was still in the water, spinning around. As if all the details of the day, the year, their particular awkward circumstances, were melting away and everything was just reducing like sauce in a pan, reducing to large swathes of colour and flavour. The intensity was paralysing. She could not move either her eyeballs or her legs, not right this second, not at this moment, with the sun and the sky and the water still in her head. A cold flush of seawater trickled out of her left ear. She gazed at Jeremy.

The sun shone through his wet eyelashes, casting a filigree shadow on his cheek. Nell, viewing him through giddy My Hero goggles, was struck by how handsome he looked with his hair wet and gleaming like a seal's skin, his chest heaving with exertion.

'What does it feel like to drown?' he asked eventually, resting his head on his hand, gazing at her just as intensely.

'Lonely.'

Jeremy moved his leg a fraction, pushing his knee harder against her groin. It sent a wave of desire pulsating down her thighs. Her body recognised him as an old lover immediately, the exact density of him, his dispersal of body hair, the over-showered smell of him. She shifted away, and bent up her neck so he could remove his arm from beneath it. But he didn't move his arm. Instead Jeremy leaned his face closer to hers so that he was peering down at her intently. His pupils spread to big, black cosmic holes.

'If you had drowned . . .'

A wave smacked against the soles of her feet.

'Oh, Nell.' He started to stroke her hair.

The stroking was oddly hypnotic. She was a tickled trout, lying there helplessly on the beach. And the way he was looking at her, pinning her to the sand with those dark, intense eyes. Hungry. They were hungry. They sucked you in. They stripped you naked.

Out of the corner of her eye – movement. She had a strong sense that someone was watching them. She broke free from

263

Jeremy's hypnotist's stare and looked out to sea. Someone in the surf. Michael. Coming towards them on his surfboard. Shit. Awkward. Somehow she had to explain why she was lying on the sand with her sister's fiancé like something from a Sandals ad.

She quickly staggered up to her feet.

Pulling his surfboard up the beach, Michael looked anxious. He nodded at her and Jeremy. Jeremy stuck out his hand. 'Jeremy.'

A small volt of surprise flickered in Michael's face and Nell knew he remembered Jeremy's name and who he was. Shit.

'Well, we were just—' she blurted and made everything so much worse.

'Nell,' Michael said, his face not revealing anything. 'I need to speak to you.' He looked at Jeremy. 'Sorry. In private, if you don't mind.'

Ten minutes later, sitting on a rock beneath a cloudless sky, he dropped the bombshell.

Thirty-two

'Thanks, Heather. If you're sure . . . OK, goodbye.' April put the phone down, amazed that she'd actually sounded vaguely normal, that any sound at all had escaped through her mouth. It was as if her brain hadn't caught up with the significance of the call that had come out of the blue this warm, sunny Saturday afternoon, rearranging her life for ever. She crushed her hand over her mouth and turned to Chris, eyes widening as the impact slowly hit. 'Did that phone call really just happen?'

He nodded. 'What did she say?'

She felt unsteady on her feet, sat down on the edge of the sofa next to him. 'She says she's sorry. Terribly sorry.'

Chris frowned. 'For?'

'Whoa,' she exhaled, 'whoa. Seriously . . . I – I – I'll try to explain, sorry, bear with me, I feel kind of strange.'

Chris put an arm round her waist. It felt like a seat belt, the one thing that was stopping her flying off this sofa into the air, catapulting out of the window into the flower bed, the street, the stars. She swallowed hard, tried again. 'Heather said her older sister Nell – she's called Nell – had called her in a terrible state because Michael, that's the guy who owns the beach café I told you about, had told her because—' she gabbled.

'Beth told him.'

She nodded. What had possessed Beth to tell Michael, she'd never really know. Maybe it was the hopeful clarity of youth that had inspired her to take the plunge on her mother's behalf just when she had given up. Bloody Beth. Beautiful, brave Beth. She still believed in fairy tales.

'But how did this woman get your number?' Chris frowned.

'The letter. She'd copied it down before hiding it.'

'She *hid* it?' He shook his head. 'Bloody hell.'

'In the attic. Valerie never saw it.' April closed her eyes for a moment. Anger sparked inside, threatening to ignite. All the agony and the waiting and the guessing that wouldn't have happened had Valerie received the letter. Her letter. Not Heather's.

'She sounds like a piece of work. Why did she hide it?'

April blew a lungful of air out, collected herself, started to speak. 'At first Heather said she thought I was a nutter, OK, fair enough, but then she admitted that she did wonder if it was true. She said she felt jealous. *Jealous!*' April's face was very pale. 'Can you believe it, Chris? Heather was crying on the phone. Actually crying. I think she's genuinely remorseful.'

'As she bloody well should be.'

They sat in silence for a few moments trying to take it all in. April nestled into the safe cocoon of his arms. She couldn't blink back the tears. He kissed them away one by one.

'What do I do now, Chris? What?' She pulled away from him, heavy, burdened with a terrifying new power. 'I don't want to ruin their lives for ever.'

Thirty-three

The curtain around Valerie's bed was blue and green check, splattered with unidentified substances the origin of which Nell didn't want to dwell on. Worrying groans bubbled up from the other five beds in the ward as she passed, feet and handbags of visiting relatives poking out from the bottom of curtains. One old lady – the only one not curtained off – was sleeping, snoring loudly, a spittle of dribble on her chin, her uneaten lunch tray still on her bed. There was a smell of boiled cabbage and disinfectant. Nell fought back her tears. She hated the thought of her mother here, knowing how much she herself would hate it. However kind the nurses were it was dehumanising, there was no getting around it. And she knew the sight of Mum lying here would have broken Dad's heart too, which made it all the worse somehow, even though he was not here to see it.

A curtain by the window-side bed clattered back on its rails. Heather emerged, red eyed and porridge faced, closing the curtain behind her.

'Is Mum OK?' Nell asked stupidly. Of course she wasn't OK. She was in hospital. She'd had a stroke and collapsed in the strawberry patch.

Heather crushed her hand to her mouth. 'I'm getting a tea. Do you want one?' she croaked. 'I need a bit of air.'

Nell shook her head. She didn't think she'd be able to stomach anything. She walked slowly over to the bed, took a deep breath and pulled back the curtain. She was startled by what she saw. Her mother was asleep, plugged in to an assortment of monitors, beeping, electronically alive, but otherwise as still and pale as a corpse. She sat down next to her and held her hand. It felt fragile and limp in hers and the site of the drip needle was disturbingly raw. Wearing the regulation nightie, she looked like a patient. Just another patient. Not her mother. She gulped, tried to speak. 'Mum?'

No response.

'It's Nell. You're going to be OK.' But not even the doctors knew that yet. They couldn't be sure if there was any lasting damage. The signs weren't great. 'Mum, are you there?'

Valerie's left eyelid twitched. Life! She was there! Maybe she was even listening! She stared at her mother, mesmerised and horrified. She was still in shock from what Michael had told her, like him, unsure whether to believe it. It seemed so preposterous and yet . . . and yet . . .

The only person who knew the truth was Mum. And now. She might never speak again. It broke her heart into a million pieces to think that she might die never knowing about April. She started to sob. 'Mum, why did you never tell us? *Why?*'

There was a rustle behind her. Ethan pushed the curtains apart. 'Hey, sis, come on, sis. Don't cry.' He put his arms round her and they hugged. 'Just popped downstairs to grab a sandwich. Cheese and pickle or ham. Do you fancy?'

Nell shook her head. They shared the one hard plastic chair beside the bed, wedged up close, studying Valerie, glancing anxiously at the monitors that seemed to let out a series of alarming beeps for no reason. 'Her heart!' gasped Nell, looking at the monitor that seemed to have flat-lined. 'It's stopped!'

'No. That's her heart one,' he said, pointing to a computer with a jumpy-looking graph on it.

'Jesus.'

'It's like being at mission control. All these tubes and things. I wish I could just pull them all out and take her home.'

'I'm sure she'd prefer that.'

'The doctors said she *could* make a full recovery,' he said, as if trying to persuade himself. 'There's a chance she won't be brain damaged. There's a chance...' Then his voice broke.

Nell hadn't seen her brother cry since he was in a school uniform. He sobbed on her shoulder like a baby. 'Hey, come on, Eth.'

Ethan wiped his eyes. 'I'm not prepared for this. I thought I was but I'm not.'

'Nor am I.'

'I feel like I should be doing something. But there's nothing I can do and ... and ...' His voice broke again.

'Let's try and be positive. Come on, we've got to be strong. She's as tough as old boots, you know that. She'll be so cross about being in hospital that she'll make herself better out of sheer bloody-mindedness.'

'Yes, you're right,' said Ethan, pulling himself together. 'She'll be fine.'

'She will,' said Nell, trying to convince herself. She had to tell Ethan what Michael had told her before ... well, before Mum died. If she died. He was the only one out of the three them who didn't know. The timing was *so* bad. But he'd kill her if she kept it from him. 'Ethan—'

'At least it happened before I left for Ibiza. At least we're all here.'

'Ethan, there's something you need to know.'

Thirty-four

Chris hugged her as close as the jutting armrest would allow but, even so, every time the train pulled into a station April had almost got off. That tang of seaside – fishing boats, chips doused in vinegar, wet swimwear drying in the sun – filled her with fear. However many times she went to the toilet she still needed to pee.

The train ground to a halt at Penzance. Here already. She and Chris exchanged looks. The families in the carriage bustled about, yanking down luggage on to their heads, gathering up Nintendos and puzzle books, announcing their arrival loudly on their mobiles, their children rushing towards the doors like puppies, eager to escape after the long confinement. Normal people on normal journeys.

April checked her watch. 'Shit. We're late, Chris.'

'Three and a half minutes late.'

The doubts reared up again. What if she wasn't waiting? What if she hadn't turned up? April couldn't go through with it. She just couldn't.

'Please ensure you collect all your belongings and leave the train . . .' an official voice boomed over the loudspeakers, as if issuing instructions directly to her.

Chris pulled April up and they started to walk down the narrow empty carriage together, stepping over crisp packets

270

and squashed juice cartons. Then they were on the platform. Sticking their tickets into the machine. A whirr and they were through. No way back now.

'Are you absolutely sure you want to do this alone?'

April nodded. She thought of Beth. She would be brave like her daughter. 'Yes.'

'You don't want me there to crack a few bad jokes and lighten the mood?'

April almost managed to laugh. 'Not this time.'

'Call me afterwards.' He squeezed her hand. 'Good luck.' He turned and went out of the exit on his own. She waited a few moments, wondering if he'd spotted her on his way out or whether she'd just look like another face in the crowd. She checked for food between her teeth with her tongue then headed to the exit. She looked up. The station clock. She was not here. Her spirits crashed.

'April?'

Nell was as April remembered her from that encounter at Tredower, tall and handsome, wearing tight grey jeans, one knee ripped, and a white shirt, like something a man might wear, white plimsolls, dark wavy hair tied back in a messy ponytail. She looked notably tired, her eyes red rimmed like she might have been crying. The dog leapt up at her and pawed her jeans with mud.

'Down, Monty!' Nell grabbed him firmly by the collar. 'Sorry, your jeans . . .'

'Oh it doesn't matter, not at all. Really.' April smiled at Nell. She had no idea what kind of smile it was.

'Can I carry your bag?'

'I'm fine, fine, really,' she stuttered.

'It looks heavy.'

Not sure of the etiquette – was there an etiquette for such a situation? – April passed it over. Their hands brushed each

271

other. She felt a little jolt of something in her fingers. 'Thank you.'

They stood there for a moment, staring at each other, wondering what to do next. 'A cup of tea somewhere?' Nell asked.

'Yes, that would be lovely. Thank you.' She spoke politely and carefully, in the manner of her mother, wanting to make a good impression, knowing that Nell would be sizing her up trying to work out if she were real or a stalker. She wanted Nell to like her so much she knew she was bound to make a gauche blunder.

'There's a nice little tea shop . . .' Light glinted in Nell's eyes. 'Or something stronger? I could do with a drink myself, actually.'

April felt a surge of relief. If ever she'd needed a bit of Dutch courage. 'Yes, please.'

'Before I forget . . .' Nell dug into her handbag and pulled out the long, pink scarf. 'Yours?'

Evidence of her loony stealth and photograph-nicking episode that, oh God, she'd have to somehow explain. 'You keep it,' she blurted, cheeks burning.

Nell didn't argue. Her hands clasped the scarf tightly as if she were drawing something from it, then she pushed it back into her handbag. There was a moment's awkwardness as they hesitated, waiting for the other to start walking.

'I'm sorry. This must be the last thing you need right now,' said April, flushing again.

Nell just shook her head, as if she wasn't listening. She was just staring and her pupils were dilating, the eye shape changing minutely, as if a million thoughts and feelings were piping through them in that very instant.

April winced, steeling herself for the rejection, the under-standable rejection. She couldn't just barrel into strangers' lives and expect a warm welcome. She desperately didn't want to upset Nell, or anyone. She wished Chris was with her now.

'My God,' Nell said slowly, not taking her eyes from April's face. 'It all makes sense. It's . . . it's . . . almost like I've always known.'

April felt a wave of self-consciousness. She had no idea what was coming next.

'You know the weirdest thing? When I met you at the gate of the house that time, you reminded me of someone and I didn't know who. And now it's so obvious, so obvious. You are the spitting image of Grandma Penelope.'

Who was Grandma Penelope? She had so many questions. But she didn't have the courage to ask them, not here, not now, maybe not ever. She just smiled politely, unable to think of anything smart or remotely relevant to say. 'Oh.'

Something softened in Nell's face. 'I believe you, April.'

April let the words sink in. She blinked furiously. *Do not cry, do not cry.* 'Thank you. Thank you so much.'

'I think we should find a drink immediately or we're in danger of causing a scene.' Nell slipped her arm through April's. 'Come on, there's so much I need to tell you.'

April looked down in astonishment at the arm then up at Nell's strange-familiar face and they walked, quietly at first, then talking and talking, on and on through Penzance's narrow back streets, along the sun-bleached promenade, no longer strangers. Sisters.

Thirty-five

Janet slammed her water glass on the oak table. 'Gold-digger!'

'Come on, Janet. She didn't know Mum was ill. How could she have known?' Even though Nell had barely touched her glass of wine she felt drunk, disorientated, as if the compass to her life – the certainties, the north, south, east and west – had been turned on its head. April rewrote everything.

'Er, because this April character has been snooping around Tredower all summer like a freaking stalker? I think Heather's gut instinct was right,' sniffed Janet. 'Heather should have burned the letter.'

'No, I shouldn't have hidden it.' Heather blew her nose loudly into a bit of loo roll.

Too right, thought Nell. Still, this was no time for recrimination. They all knew that this could blow the family apart. More than ever, they needed to come together.

Heather sniffed again. Jeremy put an arm round her shoulder. Nell looked away. She couldn't help wishing that she had someone to put an arm round her shoulder, too. It was one thing being single and strong when Mum was fine. But now that the world had fallen in on their heads? She suddenly yearned for someone to be there.

'Has she got proof? A birth certificate or something?' demanded Janet.

'She says she has. Look, guys, I was totally in shock seeing her, what with Mum in hospital and everything. I didn't ask her as much as I should have asked her. It's just that I didn't want to interrogate the poor woman . . .' explained Nell, wishing she had her clear-thinking London head on. That head would know what to say, what to do. But it had gone walkabout.

'You should have,' said Jeremy, annoyingly weighing in with his measured lawyer voice.

Nell felt a wave of righteousness on April's behalf. It was wrong to gang up on her. 'Honestly, guys, when you really look at her, she's the spitting image of Grandma Penelope.'

'Bollocks.' Ethan rubbed his face and exhaled loudly. 'Has life got any more cards it wants to put on the table? Fucking hell. Bring it on.'

Janet made a harrumph noise in the back of her throat. 'Well, thank goodness Ethan has power of attorney. At least he'll protect you from yourselves.'

'Listen, Janet,' said Nell, fighting to remain civil now. 'We all need to withhold our judgement until we know more.'

Ethan slumped forward on the table. 'She's right, Janet. And I don't know why, but on some weird level it makes sense, doesn't it? I mean if Mum did have a baby and gave it away, then it would explain her depressions, everything . . .' His voice trailed off and his forehead furrowed. Unimaginable, yet . . .

Heather started to sob. 'That's what I'm thinking.'

'*If* April is some love-child from an affair, it's going to be messy, guys, it's going to dig up all sorts of shit from the past,' muttered Jeremy sagely.

'Thank God Dad never knew,' sniffed Heather.

'Maybe he did,' mused Nell. 'Maybe he knew there was someone else.'

'Fuck.' Ethan dragged his fingers down his face. 'The implications are just . . . just massive.'

'Not least regarding your inheritance, I'm afraid,' said Jeremy dryly, pouring himself a glass of water, wearing his stony lawyer face.

Nell wished he'd shut up.

'I told you she's a gold-digger,' Janet muttered under her breath, as she inspected her nails.

Ethan glared at her. 'Will you stop it, Janet? Will you just fucking stop it? This is about family.'

There was a stunned silence. No one had ever heard Ethan shout at Janet before.

Janet went pale. Then she went puce. 'Don't you dare speak to me like that,' she hissed, standing up from the table. 'You! *You!* Pretending to be the righteous one! Perhaps you should look a bit closer to home for your charity?'

Ethan blushed. He never blushed. Nell and Heather exchanged puzzled glances. What was going on? Nell had a horrible feeling that April's appearance had somehow set in motion something none of them could now stop.

'I think everyone's feeling the strain here,' said Ethan quickly, who seemed to have actually shrunk on his seat. 'Why don't you take some time out, Janet?'

Janet prodded his chest violently with her forefinger. 'Don't try and make out this is my fault!'

Nell frowned. 'What's going on, Ethan?'

Janet looked at him accusingly, her eyes bright with tears. 'Tell her, go on. I dare you. Mr fucking family man.'

'Ethan?' said Heather in a worried voice.

Ethan sank his head into his hands, revealing a coin-sized

bald spot on his crown. He had the look of a man about to be publically flogged.

'Ethan had an affair,' Janet said quietly.

'You didn't!' gasped Nell and Heather in unison, glaring at their brother.

Ethan looked up, winced. 'It wasn't an affair. It was one night. It was a terrible, terrible mistake.'

'He slept with a girl on a film set.' Janet's eyes were bright and pink with hurt. 'And before you say anything, Ethan, being coked up doesn't excuse it.'

'Two years ago.' Ethan paled. 'And I've been paying the price ever since. That's why I couldn't come down this summer, Nell. That's why Janet wants Tredower.'

'You owe me,' Janet said tearfully. 'You promised me you'd try and get Tredower. Considering . . .'

Nell and Heather exchanged horrified glances. Nell had a sense they were dangling over an abyss. She couldn't believe Ethan had had an affair. He was meant to be one of the good ones.

'Guys, shall we just talk about April?' said Jeremy in a patrician tone.

'Fuck this April! Whoever she is,' Janet shouted in a shrill, un-Zen-like voice none of them had ever heard before. 'And fuck you, Stockdales! You're all mental. Totally mental. Every single of one of you! And Jeremy, you're a . . . a . . . a prat!' She ran from the room and slammed the door behind her.

They all turned slowly to look at Ethan.

'She doesn't mean it,' he said sheepishly. 'She loves you all.'

'I haven't been called a prat since I was at least twelve,' marvelled Jeremy, staring at the slammed door.

'Oh it's all going wrong.' Heather started to sob again. 'If we turn on each other, it will finish Mum off. It will.'

Ethan stood up jerkily. 'I better go find my wife.'

'One sec, Ethan,' said Nell, gentler now. Despite everything, she felt a little sorry for him. He looked stricken and had clearly created a terrible marital debt that would never be repaid. 'We need a plan. I think we've got to tell Mum about April as soon as possible.' The very thought made her feel sick to the pit of her stomach.

'If she comes round,' sniffed Heather.

'*When* she comes round,' corrected Ethan.

'Which of you is going to do it?' asked Jeremy, sitting back on his chair, the only one of them cool and collected while they were unravelling around him.

'Ethan's the oldest,' said Heather. 'You're her favourite,' she said, turning to Ethan.

'You hid the letter, Heather,' said Ethan. 'Maybe it's best it comes from you.'

'She'll hate me for it,' Heather shook her head. 'If April's really her daughter, Mum will never ever forgive me.'

As Nell listened to them talk and thought of Mum lying there motionless on the hospital bed, she became aware of a new emotion beating in her chest. Something brave and dutiful. She swallowed hard. 'I'll do it.'

Thirty-six

The Seagull's Nest, eleven in the morning. Rain smashing against the mottled windows. Wet feet. Bra strap digging into her back. Head buzzing with lack of sleep. Enough small talk. Nell knew she had to ask *the* question. The others were at home sitting around the home phone, waiting, waiting, waiting. If she didn't get on with it, they'd all end up barrelling round to the pub. She took a deep breath, locked her eyes with April's. 'There's something we need to know.'

'Yes?'

Nell took a breath. 'Who's your biological father?'

April looked surprised by the question. 'Actually, I was wondering if your mum could tell me.'

'You don't know?' gasped Nell.

April shook her head. 'I'm so sorry. I know this must be really hard to get your head around. If I'd had any idea your mum was ill . . .'

Nell was struck by how both loaded and banal the language was. Biological father. Biological mother. It sounded like different types of washing powder. 'How old are you again, April?'

'Forty-three.'

'So Mum must have been pretty young.' Nell racked her

brains. Where had Mum been then? Cornwall, certainly. She'd have been a teenager.

'I've clung on to that bit. I hoped that it wasn't that she didn't want me. More that –' April's voice broke. 'Things were different in those days, weren't they?'

Nell nodded, reached out and touched her arm lightly. They sat there for a few moments in silence, brains spiralling with possibilities. Nell couldn't take her eyes off April, fascinated by her face, the code of lashes and eye colour – hazel, edged with green – the way the muscles in her face pulled her mouth into a very particular smile, Grandma Penelope's smile. It was weird but the longer they sat there in silence the stronger the connection. And she instinctively liked her. There was something grounded and warm about April. Something refreshingly normal, despite the extraordinary circumstances.

'I had to find out, you see. I've been a bit obsessed.' April sipped her white wine neatly. She had pretty, neat fingers. Heather's hands. 'I always hoped that Valerie might contact me through an agency. She never did. But there was a paper trail back to Tredower House. She was living there when I was born, you see.'

Nell's head started to swim again. To think of her mum living in the same house where she'd given up a baby years before. How could she? 'April, I can hardly remember anything you told me when we first met. My head was all over the place. So, forgive me if you've already told me, but where did you grow up?'

April smiled. It was an easy, uncomplicated smile accompanied with unflinching eye contact. No looking down at the table. No grimace. Nell knew she'd been OK.

'I was adopted by a librarian and a teacher . . .'

'Yes, I remember that because my dad was a teacher.'

'And I grew up near Oxford.'

'Where you live now with . . .'

'My daughter, Beth, Corin when he's back from uni – he's off travelling around Africa at the moment for the holidays – and my husband Chris, whom you met earlier . . .'

Chris, yes. He'd seemed nice, clearly protective of April.

April smiled. Nell was struck by how pretty her ordinary face became when she smiled. 'Dad lives in Spain now. He and Mum emigrated a few years ago. Mum died last year of leukaemia.' She looked down at the table.

'Oh no, I'm so sorry.' It was strange the things they had in common, Nell thought, then wondered if these were actually the things that women the world over had in common; ageing parents, trial by children.

'I didn't want to hurt her feelings by looking for my biological mother. We were close, very close, although . . .' she paused – 'very different.' She smiled and looked a little wistful. 'It's funny, I always felt different, cut from another cloth. I could never tell Mum that, although Dad always knew.'

Nell didn't know what to say. She couldn't imagine.

'When Mum died I felt OK about finding out more about my birth parents. That's when I sent the letter.'

Nell winced. 'Yes, the letter. God, I'm so sorry. Heather's not a bad person, April. She's really not. She has issues with Mum that go back years. We all have. She's totally appalled that she hid it.'

April smiled softly. 'I know. It's OK.'

'You must have thought—'

'I thought maybe I'd got the wrong address but that seemed unlikely. Or that Valerie was dead. Or' – April tried to smile – 'that Valerie had received the letter but wouldn't acknowledge it. So, in a way, finding out that Heather had hidden it was a kind of relief.'

'You know what, April? You're brave. I'm not sure I'd have had the guts.'

'I'm not brave. Not at all. I put it off for a long time, tried to forget about the letter.' April's face softened. 'When Beth got pregnant I knew that I had to do something. I want my grandchildren to know where they're from.' She stopped and laughed again, more nervously this time. 'I'm sorry. I sound silly.'

'You don't.'

Nell smiled, studied her thoughtfully. 'Was your childhood happy?'

'Yes,' said April, not missing a beat. 'Not perfect. But happy, mostly.'

She suspected as much. April had that solidity about her. 'You're lucky.'

April looked puzzled. 'Lucky?'

'It hasn't always been a happy house here, April.'

'Oh.' April was clearly disappointed. 'But it looks so . . . so idyllic.'

How to put this? 'Mum's quite a tricky character, April.' Nell closed her eyes and thought of her mother beeping into all her machines on her hospital bed and felt guilty for not giving her better press. 'She was worse when we were growing up; depressed a lot, I guess, although no one mentioned that word then. She's mellowed with age but I still don't know how she'll react to . . .'

April wiped a tear from the corner of her eye, trying to catch any smudged mascara with the edge of her finger. 'I realise that Val— your mother may not want to know. I'm prepared for that.'

Nell wished she could reassure her. But the truth was that she had absolutely no idea how Mum would react. If she'd kept this a secret all these years, it did suggest that she wanted it buried. Maybe it was all too painful to exhume. And then there was the chance that she wouldn't recover from the stroke at all. There was a very high chance it wasn't going to end happily. How to put this? 'I'm afraid the stroke might have –' The words stuck in her throat.

'Nell, I don't expect anything. I never thought in my wildest dreams that I'd be sitting here having this conversation with you. Just this. It means everything to me.' She looked up at Nell and smiled that wide, transformative smile.

Nell felt a rush of warmth for her. Hadn't she always yearned for an older sister? And here she was. The missing bit of the jigsaw.

'Do you mind if I ask you something?' said April shyly.

'Anything, go ahead.'

'Do any of you lot paint or anything?'

'Paint? No. Why?'

April blushed. 'Sorry, it's silly, I—'

'Wait a minute.' Nell sat bolt upright. 'Grandma Penelope was a bit of an occasional amateur painter. Watercolours, things like that.'

April grinned. '*Really?*'

'Of course, you're doing this art course and—'

'Oh, I'm completely rubbish,' April said quickly. 'But I used to be good when I was younger, you know, good as in scraped an A in my art A level rather than being Picasso, then I neglected it, of course. My parents always thought art should be kept as a hobby, nothing more.' She rolled her eyes. 'They didn't think it useful.'

Nell smiled. 'It must feel good to be picking it up again now.'

'Yeah ... you know what? It really does. I feel, um, reconnected. That's the only way I can describe it.' She looked down at the table, as if slightly embarrassed by her candidness. 'More like myself.'

283

There was a silence which might have got awkward if April hadn't broken it. 'I'm so sorry that you had to hear it through Michael like that,' she said suddenly, looking up. 'I had no idea that you two were close.'

Michael! April mentioned his name with such warm familiarity – something knotted inside Nell's throat. All this stuff was bigger, far bigger than him. And yet . . . she felt a flash of sudden, uncharitable jealously. 'We've been hanging out all summer.'

'So have we!'

'You found my car keys.'

'I know. Isn't that the oddest thing? We must have come so close to meeting so many times.' April smiled, looked down at her hands, twisted her gold wedding ring round her finger. 'Michael's amazing, isn't he?'

'He's . . .' Nell felt uneasy discussing him with April for some reason. She really wasn't sure quite how intimately April knew him. This conversation could end badly. 'He's great. Look, I'm going to have to go. Cass—'

'Please, of course.' April sprang up. 'Your little girl will be wondering where you are.'

Nell hesitated, unsure how to close things.

April seemed to sense this. 'I've got to go home tomorrow night. I promised I'd be at my daughter's antenatal scan.'

'That's so exciting!'

'And just a little terrifying. It only seems like yesterday I saw *her* on a scan!'

'And you'll still meet Ethan and Heather tomorrow?'

April's smile froze. 'After breakfast.'

'Ethan's a pussycat,' Nell reassured her. 'Heather is wracked with guilt about the letter. And when she's guilty it makes her kind of defensive. She's in a real state about Mum as well. Don't take it too personally if she seems distant.'

'Honestly, I understand.' April pulled on her cardigan briskly.

'Well,' they both said in unison, then laughed, suddenly both shy.

'It's been mad,' said Nell, feeling a roll of sadness and relief that they were parting ways.

'You've got my number.'

Nell tapped her head. 'In here.'

April swung her handbag over her arm. 'Will you call if anything changes with Valerie?'

'I promise.'

Nell kissed her on both cheeks. There was something so familiar-smelling about her skin it startled her. She stood back. 'What do we do now? Shall we hug? Or would that be weird?'

'Let's hug.'

Thirty-seven

Five days passed. Valerie remained in a coma. They took it in turns to sit by her bedside. Heather lost half a stone. Ethan gained half a stone and took up smoking. It was all too much emotional crackle for Jeremy, who fled to London, much to Nell's relief. Janet dangled healing crystals around Tredower and attempted to run Muffin from her laptop while looking after the children, which, obviously, was impossible. So the children were mostly left to their own devices and grew wilder by the hour. A perilously unstable tree house was constructed at the bottom of the garden. Monty was forced into the indignity of wearing a pair of Cass's frilly knickers as a sunhat (although he didn't put up much resistance). A frog was dissected and cooked on the barbecue by Nat. Cass didn't go near a bottle of sun-cream for days. Her skin was deep tan, her white-blond hair dreading at the ends, her feet crusted in chocolatey soil.

Somehow into all this chaos came an offer of work. Work! Real work for Nell. A maternity-leave cover at a glossy. A good job, not much money, but better than nothing. Nell stared at the email in disbelief. Work? Her? Surely some mistake. Obviously news of the fact she had no brain cells left hadn't yet reached London. She remedially read through the email again. Oh. Shit. She had to start now? Like next week now. And she had to have responded to them two days ago. She quickly emailed back – rewriting the email a dozen times, she'd lost her touch – but it turned out the job had already been snapped up. Inside, secretly, she felt a fluttering of relief.

Nell visited the café most days when she had a chance, telling herself she needed sea air but really trying to bump into Michael – she hadn't seen him since that time on the beach with Jeremy. So much had happened since then. But nose-ring Annie told her he'd returned to London for business. Something stopped her from phoning him, worried about the reception she might get. She missed him. She missed their swims, their surfing, their easy silences, his non-judgemental, intelligent perspective. She missed the way when she was with him she was present in the moment and the noise faded away. But he wasn't here and so there was no respite.

Bad weather in the brain, that's what. The past howled incessantly. Morbid thoughts – What did dead people actually look like? What would Mum look like dead? – rained down while the future loomed uncertainly, like an unsettling yellow sky. She couldn't stop thinking about April. Or what April meant. All of them were in a state of limbo, unable to fully believe her until their mother had woken up and explained everything. The problem was she might never wake up. Or she might wake up a loon. So they'd never know the truth.

As the days passed, everyone in the house started to vibrate on the same, restless frequency. Ethan cancelled Ibiza (no refund, Janet loudly pointed out, six thousand pounds down the toilet) and Heather took compassionate leave from work and her life with Jeremy.

It didn't take long before they slipped naturally into a routine of sorts. When not beside the bedside, they'd take it in turns to plate up fish and chips from the local chippie, or, if they were feeling particularly energetic, some pasta pesto. They got through crates of wine and beer. Although they all made an effort to keep the vegetable patch slug-free and watered – this seemed important for some reason – none of them had the energy or inclination to clean the house. Nell watched all those hours of frenzied organising and clearing undoing themselves; the alphabetised books returned to their random homes on bathroom floors and wardrobes as if poked around by a maverick poltergeist, the kitchen cupboards were gradually scattered with tobacco pouches, mouse droppings and toy cars. She no longer cared.

It wasn't long before they all began to unravel too. Baths got less frequent. Toenails began to curl over dirty toes. Even glam Janet became wind blown, salt soaked, and matt haired. Collectively they resembled a rabble of festival-goers who'd lost their tents and lift home.

But, as yet, they hadn't argued. Bloody miracle, Nell thought. Somehow Ethan, dressed down, his philandering exposed by Janet, had become, almost overnight, a humbler person. He was rising to the family crisis, taking charge and – finally! – acting like a responsible older brother, rather than just a lovable rogue who wouldn't grow up. While Janet, exposed as a wronged woman, no longer carried off that air of untouchable superiority that she'd nailed so irritatingly well. She seemed genuinely touched and surprised by Heather and Nell's sisterly solidarity and their gratitude for her free-spirited child-caring. (Although her crystal waggling remained really annoying.)

And Heather? Heather was an issue. They were all worried about Heather. She wasn't coping well at all. Barely eating. When she wasn't at the hospital, she'd retreat to private dark enclaves of the garden for hushed phone conversations. Nell wondered what she and Jeremy were talking about. She wanted to reach out to her but felt the barrier of Jeremy between them like never before, like one of those big concrete blocks that sat outside parliament to absorb car bombs.

On Friday, the man himself roared into the drive. He was still in his work suit, clean, shiny eyed and shaven, incongruous against the mess of Tredower. He swaggered into the dining room, pulling out his shirt from his trousers. 'Shit, it's hot.' He looked around. 'Where's Heather? I can't get hold of her.'

'She's at the hospital,' Ethan said, digging into a late lunch of Chocolate Digestives and flicking over the pages of yesterday's newspaper. 'Her phone will be turned off.'

Was it Nell's imagination or did Jeremy look a bit relieved?

Jeremy ruffled his dark hair. He had a V of sweat down the spine of his shirt. He smiled at her. 'Looks like you've thrown a wild party in here.'

'Hardly,' said Ethan, not looking up.

Jeremy put up his hand in apology. 'Sorry. I didn't mean it like that.' He poured himself a glass of water from the green jug on the table. Mum's old jug. Nell watched him, warily. She needed to talk to him about Heather. Tell him how worried she was. Maybe she'd have a chance later.

Jeremy raised a wry eyebrow. 'Ah, I see April hasn't got her feet under the table yet. Thought I might find her here too.'

Ethan rubbed his new Grizzly Adams beard. 'She's back home now.'

'For the moment,' said Janet waspishly, picking at a bowl of dry Cheerios with one hand, prodding the laptop keyboard with the other.

Nell stood up. 'I'm going to check that the children haven't dissected the dog.'

Jeremy looked at her intently. 'Oh. I was hoping you'd come for a walk.'

'A walk?' she repeated, as if he'd suggested a weekend in Paris. 'I . . .'

'Perhaps you want to get a bit of sea air after being in the dank depths of the hospital?' He held her gaze. His eyes were trying to tell her something. She wasn't sure what.

'The thing is—' Nell began.

'Good idea, Jeremy.' Ethan licked his cigarette paper. 'My sister could do with an airing. She's been a star – she deserves a break.' He looked up at Nell and smiled. 'You should fill him in about what's been going on with . . .'

Heather. Yes, of course. Good idea. Nell nodded. 'OK. Let's go.'

They stood at the top of the cliff, gazing down into the spit-hole above Perranortho Beach. Below them waves roared and collided, their explosive white spray sparkling in the sun. The wind whipped over the cliffs in a frenzy of oxygen. Nell breathed in deeply and felt as if the wind was inside her too. She could see the cheery blue roof of the café from here and it already seemed symbolic of happier, simpler times.

'Fucking beautiful up here,' said Jeremy, sitting down on the ledge by the edge of the hole and dangling his feet over it.

'Careful.'

'You live once.'

'And not very long, if you fall down there.'

Jeremy shaded his eyes with his hand. 'I'll take my chances.'

Nell sat down on a smooth, warm rock a safe distance away. 'You sound uncharacteristically reckless, Jeremy. Water?' She threw a bottle of mineral water towards him.

'Thanks.' He swigged. Then he peeled off his shirt, exposing a bare brown chest. Nell looked away. 'I'll come to you if you won't come to me.'

Nell budged up on her rock, relieved that he'd moved away from the edge of the spit-hole. Their bodies touched, the skin of his arm sticky against hers. 'Heather's not in a good way, Jeremy.'

Jeremy looked surprised that she'd mentioned Heather. 'No? No, I guess she's not.'

'I know it's been so difficult, the last week, but even so she seems very . . .'

Jeremy turned to face her and put his finger very gently on her lips. 'Shush.'

'What are you doing?' she mumbled beneath his finger. Her heart started to slam.

'I don't want to talk about Heather. Not now. Not yet.'

The sun seemed to get hotter. And hotter. The sweat popped on his Roman nose. He removed his finger, devilishly slowly. As he did so she remembered him making love to her. She remembered how those fingers had been in every nook and cranny of her body. And her sister's. A seagull swooped close to their heads. The sea roared. Her head roared louder.

'Don't look away, Nell. I need to talk to you. I desperately need to talk to you.'

She looked at him, eyes full of tears. Whatever he was about to say, she didn't want him to say it.

'This summer has changed everything,' he said, his eyes evangelically bright. 'Your mum's stroke. April turning up. It's been like a wake-up call for me.'

'Why?'

'The fragility of life. Wasted years. Time running out.' He rubbed his nose, a little embarrassed. 'All that stuff.'

'You put it so succinctly.' She tried to defuse his sincerity, blow the moment out of the water.

'I mean it, Nell. I'm deadly serious.'

Nell frowned. There was something unsettling about the sincere, philosophical Jeremy.

He grabbed her hand. 'I wish Cass was mine.'

'*What?*' she spluttered. 'Where has that come from?'

'Seeing you with her . . . you're so lovely together. You're an amazing mum, Nell.'

Nell couldn't help but feel flattered. 'I muddle through.'

He cocked his head on its side, studied her for a few moments. 'She's not mine, is she?'

'Cass?' Nell laughed. How could he think her milk-blond daughter was his? 'No, God, no. She's Dean's. Can't you tell? I would have told you, Jeremy. I'm not that much of a cow.'

'It's just that it all happened quite quickly. You and me. Then . . . him.' He spat the word 'him' out like an olive stone.

'Tell me about it.'

He gazed at her intensely and for one, awful second she thought he was going to burst into tears. 'We fucked up, Nell. We never should have split up. I was too goddamn proud to try and get you back and then you were pregnant and it was too late and—'

She wanted to put her hands over her ears, tra-la-la. 'Jeremy, please. Old ground.'

He swallowed hard. 'I dated Heather to punish you, do you not realise that?'

Nell shut her eyes tight. She had the strange sensation of her life funnelling down to this one point like the final grain of sand falling through the aperture in an egg timer. 'That's sick, Jeremy.'

'Sick?' He laughed. 'I *am* sick. Sick to the pit of my stomach that I'm about to go walking down the fucking aisle with the wrong sister! The wrong sister.' He dropped his head into his hands and pulled his fingers down his cheeks. 'Fuck.'

He went out with Heather to punish her? Oh no. Please don't let that be true. Please. 'She loves you so much.'

'I love her,' he said quietly. 'She's a honey. And we stayed together because it was easy, Nell. We get on. We want the same things. We don't fight like you and I used to fight. Jesus, do you remember our fights?'

Nell bit her lip and nodded.

'But the mad thing is I still want what *we* had.'

Nell shook her head, sniffed back her tears. 'That's gone, Jeremy. Everything's completely changed.'

'Tell me you haven't thought about me all summer? Tell me, go on. You can't, can you? I can see it in your eyes, Nell. I can smell it. I can smell your love for me. It never went away, did it? Did it? You still want to fuck me, don't you? Do you remember how fabulously we used to fuck, Nell? How I used to make you come and come until you couldn't take it any more?'

'Stop it! Stop it!'

His face was inches from hers now. 'Let's start again, Nell. Please don't shake your head. I know it looks impossible. Don't cry, darling. Don't cry. Nothing's impossible. We can all start again. It's not too late.'

She turned her head away from him. He brought it back firmly with his hand on her jaw, forcing her to stare into those black, black hypnotic eyes. And then suddenly his lips were on hers. His tongue was in her mouth and his hand slipping between her thighs.

'No!' Nell broke away, horrified at herself, at both of them. She pressed her fingers against her lips as if burned. 'No, Jeremy.' Her head was exploding. Her heart was exploding. The drop of the spit-hole was beckoning, that long drop down, into icy, sparkling oblivion.

'Nell, come back!'

She ignored him, started to run before she did anything stupid, cantering down the steep twisty narrow path. She slipped, lost a Birkerstock, grazed her knees. Pulling herself up again, she lunged forward and ran . . . straight into an orange polyester cycle vest.

'Michael!' she gasped, looking up at his full height. He was back! 'Where have you been?'

Michael stood there, eyes blazing.

'Michael?' she asked, puzzled. Why wasn't he smiling at her?

'I came to find you to say goodbye.' The wind blew his stack of hair wildly.

'Goodbye?' she gasped. 'But so much has happened that I need to tell you about—' He didn't even know about Mum.

'I've got to go to New York,' he interrupted. 'Big business deal.'

'But . . . but New York's so far away.' He couldn't go away! Not now. She needed him around. 'When are you going?'

'This afternoon. I'm late already. I've got to leave now.'

'Oh no. When are you back?'

'I don't know.'

She wanted to hug him goodbye but his body language wasn't making it possible. His hands were glued to his sides, fisted. His eyes, which were normally so warm and glittery, were cold and still. There was an awful silence.

And she knew then. She knew that he'd seen.

Thirty-eight

Nell collapsed on a rock on the beach, the seawater up to her ankles. The tide was coming in but she couldn't move. She couldn't do anything. Jeremy had turned her world upside down. And the kiss had been *witnessed*. By Michael, of all people. Michael who was leaving for America. Leaving and thinking she was a hussy, not knowing about her mum, anything. She'd never felt more wretched or more alone. If it wasn't for Cass, she suddenly wasn't sure she'd have the energy to go on. What was the point? A warm hand covered her eyes from behind. 'Surprise!'

The hands lifted off her eyes. She swung round. 'Soph! Oh my God. What are you doing here?'

Sophie hugged her tight. 'Thought I'd come down while your mum was in hospital, see if I could help out.'

Nell burst into tears. 'Thank you, Soph. You have no idea how pleased I am to see you. I'm in danger of losing the plot here.'

Sophie hugged her against her yellow sundress.

'We must get you out of those muddy shorts and into a glass of dry white wine immediately,' Sophie said, holding her by the shoulders. 'We've got too much to talk about. But first I need to warn you . . .'

'Not more shit?' She groaned. 'I'm not sure I can take any more stuff falling on my head today.'

'It's Pete,' Sophie hissed.

'Pete?' What was she talking about?

'*Pete*. Your Pete.'

'Eh?'

'He's here in Cornwall.'

'No!'

'I'm not joking. I met him on the train this morning. He'd decided to come down to see you.'

'Some mistake. Pete wouldn't come to see me. We haven't spoken for ages. And, well, he just wouldn't.'

Sophie smiled. 'I wasn't hallucinating, Nell. Look, I explained about your mum, how it might not be the best timing, but . . .'

Nell was stunned. 'Oh. My. God. Where is he now?'

Sophie winced, nodded towards the slipway.

And sure enough a man *was* walking towards them. Deafeningly pink Hawaiian shorts. Short-sleeved yellow shirt. That John Wayne walk. Oh no. She turned to Sophie aghast. It was like a holiday fling turning up in your real life. This kind of convergence never happened to her. Ever. She'd fallen into a Bermuda triangle of romance. 'What the hell am I going to do with Pete in Cornwall?'

Sophie shrugged. 'Lend his shorts to the emergency services as a visibility aid?'

'Give us a kiss, Nell-Not-a-Tube-Station!' He whipped her round by the waist as if she were weightless, then planted her, giddy, breathless and stunned, back down on the sand. 'Babes, so sorry to hear about your mum.' He studied her, taking in the muddy shorts, the ancient Birkenstocks, the crappy vest top. The last time he'd seen her she was wearing a pencil skirt, leopard-print blouse and heels. 'Geez, you look,

296

er, kind of different. Where's that cute little school-girl fringe?'

'I forgot to get it trimmed.'

He cocked his head on one side, sizing her up for a moment. 'You know what? I think I kind of like your new rough and ready look, Foxy.' He swung a palm at her bottom and squeezed her right buttock. She got a blast of aftershave. He pulled her towards him and caught her in another bear hug.

'Don't mind me,' laughed Sophie, standing up and picking up her beach bag. 'Perhaps you two should go get a room.'

At that moment, to her horror, over the bristling hairs of Pete's left shoulder, Nell glimpsed Jeremy cantering down the cliff path like a bat out of hell. Her heart missed a beat. She pulled away. 'No, we mustn't. Not here . . .'

Jeremy was walking towards them now, big angry strides across the sand.

'Oh no,' muttered Nell under her breath. 'Now the shit's really going to hit the fan.'

'What?' said Sophie, following Nell's sightline. 'Jeremy? Eh? What's he doing out here?'

'Don't ask,' said Nell. Oh God. It could not end prettily. It could not. Pete put a hand on her bottom again and left it there. She tried to shake it off, wiggle away, but it stuck to her butt cheek like a limpet to a rock.

Then Jeremy was standing there. 'All right, Sophie,' he growled.

'How are you, Jeremy? It's been . . . um, ages!' Sophie looked to Nell for help, wondering what was going on.

Jeremy turned towards Pete, his face tightening like a fist. 'And who the fuck are you?'

'Jeremy!' said Nell. She put a hand on his arm to silence him. He shook it off.

'What's your problem, mate?' said Pete, chest swelling beneath his Hawaiian shirt.

A muscle twitched in Jeremy's cheek. He looked at Nell. And it was *the* look. That look of possession. Of control. 'Let's go, Nell.'

Now Nell really was scared, scared she might obey him.

'Um, what's going on, Nell?' said Sophie, searching Nell's face for clues.

'Nell. *Now*,' ordered Jeremy, a deep red flush rising up his neck.

'Nell?' said Sophie.

'Nell?' said Pete.

Time seemed to stand still. And she could no longer hear the sea. Or the seagulls. Her brain emptied of thoughts. Shit, shit, shit.

'Don't make the same mistake twice,' said Jeremy. It sounded like a threat. It was a threat. 'Don't.'

And in that split second she knew. She knew exactly why she'd finished the relationship all those years ago. And she knew with absolute spine-tingling clarity that she could never, ever, choose him over Heather. It would break her sister's heart. No, he wasn't worth it. He was never worth it. 'I'm staying here, Jeremy.'

'Listen, mate, you heard what the lady said,' said Pete, stepping forward. 'I don't know what your problem is but—'

'Piss off, twat,' hissed Jeremy.

Pete swung a fist. It landed with a horrible click on the side of Jeremy's jaw. Jeremy stumbled backwards, righted himself. He put one hand to his cheek. He lowered his head. And without a word he charged at Pete. Pete stepped neatly aside like a matador. Jeremy thundered past, just missing him.

'Stop it!' shouted Sophie. 'For God's sake. Both of you stop it.'

Jeremy stood dead still now, panting, sweating, veins throbbing in his neck. 'Nell,' he gasped, one hand holding his thumped jaw. 'Don't you dare walk away, Nell. Don't you dare.'

'Ignore him,' instructed Sophie, slipping an arm through hers and yanking her forward. 'Ignore the little bugger and just walk.'

Nell put one foot in front of the other and Nell walked. This time she didn't look back.

Thirty-nine

Two hours later, after depositing Pete at a B. & B. – well, he couldn't exactly stay at Tredower, could he? – and telling everything to a gobsmacked Sophie, Nell pulled into the drive. She felt a disorientating swell of anxiety as she walked up the garden path. What if Jeremy tells Heather? He'd do it. She was sure of it. He'd do it to punish her. Oh God.

But what if he didn't? That might be *worse*. She'd be forced to watch her younger sister comforted by Jeremy, kissing him, walking up the aisle towards a man who didn't love her, not as her sister, any woman, deserved to be loved. What the hell should she do? If she told Heather, Heather would think she was a crazed jealous monster. And if she said nothing then she was complicit.

'Mummy!' Cass bolted out of the door and into her arms. Nell sank her nose into her downy blond hair and inhaled. The smell of Cass's hair always calmed her down. It simplified things. Cass was the only person who really mattered. The rest was noise. 'So sorry I'm late, Cupcake.'

'Nat ran naked into the shop!' giggled Cass.

'He didn't!' A door slammed behind them. Jeremy? She swung around. No, thank goodness, Ethan.

'I need you, sis,' he hissed, beckoning her over. He looked stressed and ragged. 'Quickly.'

Oh no! He knows. Heather knows. Everyone knows. 'Is everything OK?' Stupid question.

'Nat is doing a nudie, uncle Ethan,' giggled Cass.

Ethan looked at Nell. 'We've got bigger problems right now. Something's going on with Heather. Something messy. She and Jeremy have obviously had a terrible barney. He's only gone and stormed out!'

She knows. She knows. She knows. 'Where's Heather?' she asked weakly.

'Down by the pond. Sobbing her heart out.'

She definitely knows.

'She's inconsolable. She even told Janet to fuck off.'

Nell steadied herself with a hand on Cass's shoulder. It was a matter of time. Minutes before the whole family exploded like an egg in a microwave.

'She keeps asking where you are. Will you go see her, sis?'

Nell took a deep breath and nodded.

'Can I come?' chirped Cass. 'I can kiss Aunty Heather better.'

Nell hugged Cass very tight and took one last inhalation of her hair. 'Not this time, Cupcake.'

Nell walked slowly, very slowly, to the dark triangle of green at the bottom of the garden, through the dappled light and shade of the trees, the fuzzy seeding grasses tickling her bare calves. It was the longest walk of her life. As she broke through the undergrowth she hesitated a safe distance away behind the prehistoric leaves of giant rhubarb. And she could see her then, her little sister, chin on hand, framed beneath the wisteria-wrapped pergola, blond hair trailing over her heaving shoulders, looking like a wounded goddess on a Tarot card. Nell fought back her own tears. She wasn't sure how she was going to do this. What would Heather do when she saw her? Scratch her eyes out? Try to drown her in the pond? 'Heather . . .'

Heather looked up anxiously, her face puffy and pink. She didn't say anything. She didn't need to.

'Can I come and sit with you?' Nell whispered.

Heather almost nodded, a slight downward twitch of the head. Daring to take this as a yes, Nell sat gingerly beside her on the bench, feeling the fragile energy around her sister crackle like dry tinder. Neither of them spoke. They stared at the pond. A dragonfly. Three skaters. Air bubbles breaking the surface.

'Do you want to talk about it?' Nell said eventually when she could bear it no longer.

'The wedding's off.' Heather spoke deadpan, not taking her eyes from the pond.

'I'm –' Her voice broke. 'God, I'm so sorry, Heather.'

Heather made a snotty gurgling sound in her throat and turned to face Nell with an accusing stare. 'Are you?'

Nell dropped her head into her hands. Bring it on. She deserved it. She *had* been thinking of Jeremy all summer. She'd been thinking of him so hard that she'd brought the kiss into being. It was all her fault. What a godawful mess. 'It was never going to work out, was it, Nell? I guess you knew that. Bad karma. I . . . I should . . .' she started to cry again. 'I should never have nicked your boyfriend.'

Whoa! Nicked? *The* confession. Nell was stunned. She never thought she'd ever hear those words. Weirdly, they weren't as gratifying as she'd imagined they would be.

Heather sobbed. 'I wanted him because he was beautiful and clever and . . . and, maybe, just a little bit, because he was yours.'

Nell closed her eyes. Oh no, this was dark. They shouldn't go there. 'Don't, Heather. Please don't.'

'You had everything I wanted and you didn't even want it! It came so easily to you.'

'That's not true, Heather,' gulped Nell. Whatever had happened, she suddenly knew that she didn't want to lose Heather forever. She wanted her little sister back.

'You were cool and clever and funny. I had to work so hard for everything, for the grades, for Mum's attention.' As soon as she mentioned Valerie her voice wobbled and she started to sob again. 'You didn't have to try.'

'Heather, Heather, you're remembering it all wrong!' Nell yearned to hold her but knew that Heather would shake her off. 'You were the beautiful one, the gorgeous little girl. Mum, Dad, they completely adored you.' How could they both have had the same childhood but remember the fundamentals so differently? How could Heather, perfect Heather, ever have coveted what *she* had – or, mostly, hadn't? It didn't make sense. She'd never seen herself refracted through Heather's eyes.

Heather wiped her nose on the back of her hand. 'Mum and Dad treated me like a silly doll.' She let out an unhinged, mirthless laugh. 'Jeremy used to call me his doll too, you know.'

Nell shuddered. He'd called her doll, too, on occasion.

'I think that's why he liked me waxing my arms.' Heather sniffed. 'It hurt, you know. More than the Hollywood hurt and that was like being skinned alive. But, do . . . do you know what was the worst thing?'

Nell shook her head. It was stirring. The deadly fury. She could feel it, like the minutes before a ferocious thunderstorm whipped in off the sea.

She paused. 'Sometimes he called out your name when he came.'

Nell shut her eyes. Oh God.

303

'I pretended I didn't hear. I never said anything.' She looked up at Nell intently, her pale blue eyes shining with tears. 'You've no idea how much I despise myself for not saying anything, for allowing myself to be second best.'

'Oh, Heather.'

'I was second best to Mum, and Dad. You were Dad's golden girl. And I was second best to Jeremy too. It doesn't take a fucking psychoanalyst to make the connection, does it?' She dropped her head into her hands. 'I don't know why it's taken *me* so long.'

'Heather. I think we were all second best to Mum. The baby she lost . . .' Lost. She couldn't bear to say 'gave away'.

Heather shook her head. 'Why should we excuse her, Nell? Why? Anyway, I'm not sure I have the strength to believe April's story any more. It's so . . . mental.'

'But you've seen the birth certificate.'

'Jeremy said it could be forged.'

'Well, duplicity is his thing, isn't it?'

Heather covered her face with her hands and stared through the gaps in her fingers at the black pond.

'Heather . . .' She stopped. How could she explain? How could she explain without obliterating what remained of Heather's self-esteem?

Heather took her hand from her face and turned to look at Nell intently. 'Don't you see, Nell? I've never done anything brilliantly, not like the rest of you. Ethan always got away with murder. Despite his crapness he's ended up with a great career and a family. He always falls on his feet.'

'I think we have Janet to thank for that.'

'Janet.' Heather rolled her eyes. 'Yeah, I suppose we do.'

'And I don't think anyone would see my life as ideal.'

Heather frowned. 'Why not? You manage to juggle single motherhood with a great career.'

'I *managed* it. Past tense. And it nearly killed me at times.'

'Even April is sorted, you know, marriage, kids, a nice normal life, the kind of life, if I'm being totally honest, I wanted.'

Nell bit her lip hard.

'What am *I*, Nell?' Heather went on, wiping the tears off her cheek. 'Not academic. Not a fancy media person like you or Ethan. Working in a bloody shop. What am I good for, if *not* marrying a city lawyer like Jeremy?'

'You mustn't think that, Heather.'

'Jeremy makes me feel secure.' She glanced at Nell, snorted. 'Well, he did.'

Nell studied her hands through the milk of her own tears.

'Finally, after all the wobbles of our family, he was someone solid, successful, strong. He made me feel safe.'

That was what Nell had felt once too. Jeremy had been her rock. Then he'd turned out to be quicksand.

'I always thought it would all work out. That he'd love me as much as he'd loved you. Once he saw me in my dress.' She made a strange gurgly sound. 'It's a beautiful dress, Nell. It's called Norma.'

'Norma?' Something about the wedding dress having a name meant that Nell could hold it back no longer. The tears started pouring down her face. Oh God, Norma. Like Norma Jean.

'Wedding dresses have names. Like handbags.'

'I . . . I . . . I never knew that.'

'You'd love Norma. Gives me proper cleavage and everything. I chose it on my own. I could have asked a girlfriend, or Mum, I suppose, but I only wanted it to be you. I wanted my big sister to be there but . . . I couldn't ask you, could I?'

The image of Heather shopping alone for her wedding dress was too much to bear. Nell dug her fingernails deep into the palm of her hand and felt like the world's most wretched excuse for a sister. She should be dunked in the pond as a witch. 'Oh, Heather, please stop.'

Heather reached for Nell's hand. Nell looked down in amazement, Heather's hot, tiny and surprisingly strong hand. It was the first time they'd held hands in years. 'How can I not blame myself?' blurted out Heather. 'It should have been enough for me. And it *had* to be worth it because I'd lost you when I got him. But it wasn't, Nell. And you know what?'

Nell squeezed Heather's hand. 'What?' she said weakly.

'I *did* mind waxing my arms. And doing stupid dinner parties for his stupid city colleagues. And, you know what? That life in Surrey. I thought it's what I wanted, I really did. I thought it's what we both wanted, but we're miserable, totally miserable, and scared of admitting it to each other. He talks about his old flat in Fitzrovia like an old lost love.'

Nell nodded – yes, that made sense. She'd always doubted his potential for the suburban dream.

'I'm like a fish out of water, Nell, the childless woman on a street of families and school run gossip, the woman waiting for all that *stuff*, stuff that Jeremy doesn't really want, I know he doesn't, waiting in that big empty house for marriage and babies while Jeremy works later and later. We shouldn't be there, not yet, we should be living . . . I don't know, in Belsize Park or something. And the whole set-up makes me want to howl. It makes me want to run down the street naked waving a pink rotating vibrator in the air!'

Nell smiled. 'Jeremy's an idiot, Heather.'

Heather studied Nell's face. A small smile twitched at the corners of her mouth. 'You don't get it, do you, Nell?'

Nell took both of Heather's hands in hers and looked at

her pleadingly. 'Look, I know this is a really fucking horrible situation and I don't know how we're meant to get through as sisters, but I know that we will somehow, and that—'

'Nell, I *told* him . . .'

'You told him what, Heather?' Suddenly nothing was making sense.

'He came back from the beach in a really bizarre mood today. The way he looked at me. God, it was like he *hated* me, absolutely hated my guts. And then when I ate a mini Magnum – a mini! – he told me that I'd regret putting the weight back on. I don't know why, Nell, but I just snapped then. Something in me snapped, when he said that. So I screamed it all out. There and then.'

'What did you tell him?' said Nell, confused. What on earth was she going on about?

'About Gareth.'

'Gareth? Who's Gareth?'

Heather looked down at their clasped hands. 'My trainer. The guy I run with.'

'I don't understand.'

Heather took a deep breath. 'I've been sleeping with my trainer.'

Nell's mouth dropped open. '*Heather!*'

'Judge me all you like, Nell!' Heather's eyes glittered defiantly. She took her hands away and sat up straight. 'I know what everyone will think. Gareth is not rich. He doesn't have a first from Oxford. He lives in a one-bedroom flat. But he makes me feel loved and wanted and beautiful. All the things that Jeremy doesn't.' She was smiling. 'There, I've fucking said it!'

'Oh. My. God.' Nell couldn't take it in.

'I've been denying my feelings for Gareth for months, and then, just before I came back down here, it happened.' She started to cry. Nell reached out and hugged her tight. 'And I feel so ashamed and so guilty but it was just so ... *so* beautiful all the same, the best sex I've ever had,' Heather mumbled into Nell's shoulder. 'Oh God, Nell, I've been so confused. I've felt like I was going mad, totally mad. And there's only been one person I've wanted to ask for advice and that's you. But I couldn't. So I've been sitting at Mum's bedside, talking to her, telling her everything, and going over it all in my head, and she doesn't speak or do anything. But seeing her like that made me realise that one day I will get old and ill. And when I do I don't want Jeremy at my bedside.' She sat up and looked her in straight in the eye. 'And I want to have known a big, sizzling love before I get old and wrinkly!'

'God, you really have got it bad.'

'Gareth,' said Heather, her eyes softening as she spoke his name. 'Gareth Anders.'

Nell started to laugh. She tried to hold her laughter back but the giggles came faster and faster. 'Oh, sorry,' she gasped, trying to get the words out. Then Heather started giggling too and they were setting each other off, heaving, snorting, on the verge of peeing their pants, just like they did when they were little girls. 'I ... I can't stop,' heaved Heather. 'Make me stop laughing ...'

'You ...' Nell held her back with her arms. 'You enjoy every minute with Gareth. And don't feel guilty. You break free and live your life and you love like you've never ...' She stopped and laughed. 'Oh dear, I feel that old cliché coming on.'

Heather giggled. '... been hurt before. Dance like ...'

'... no one's watching.'

When they regained their composure Heather looked coyly at Nell, head tilted to one side. 'So when are you going to fall in love, Nell?'

'Me? Oh, I don't think I can . . .' she started to say but stopped because she was simultaneously whacked by two realisations, like cricket balls hitting the back of her head. The first was that this was the day she'd got her younger sister back, just when she thought she'd lost her for ever and that was totally marvellous. The second was that this was also the day she, Nell, *had* lost something. Something else.

And that something was her story. The insightful, juicy journalistic narrative that explained who she – Nell Stockdale – was and the autocue she read from every time a man showed interest in her: her spectacularly fucking up the relationship with Jeremy, Heather's betrayal, Jeremy's betrayal, the rebound sex with Dean that got her pregnant . . . This was her story and it had given her an excuse for years not to get intimate with anybody. But it turned out that Jeremy, flawed, messed-up Jeremy, had loved her all along and had taken the darkest route of revenge possible. And that when presented with a chance to return to her old love, she discovered that the love was no longer in her after all. He wasn't the one who got away! He was the one she'd escaped.

And, maybe, just maybe, he'd created a vacancy.

Forty

'Room OK?' Nell asked. The B. & B. smelled of a swimming pool changing room. She felt a fresh pang of guilt that she'd shoved Pete into this damp little cottage.

'It's better with you in it, babes.' Pete was sitting on the edge of his single bed, his bare chest adorned with a gold necklace, and, yes, there was no other way of describing it, a small, gold medallion.

'I'm sorry I can't be more hospitable. But it's a tricky time.'

Pete shrugged. 'I should have given you some warning. Stupid of me.' He patted the bed. She sat down gingerly beside him. He wrapped a thick tanned arm round her waist. It felt warm and comforting to be held firmly by Pete. There was something of the bulky Antipodean male about him; blokey, straightforward, protective. 'You didn't tell me you had another bloke down here, though.'

'I don't! Oh, it's a complete misunderstanding. My time in Cornwall has been chaste, ridiculously so, which is why this is all so . . . so totally bizarre.' She felt silly explaining this: they didn't have a vow of fidelity after all.

'Hey, it's all right, Foxy. I know you're not a nun.' He plucked the waistband of his shorts to make room for his obvious growing erection. 'I don't expect you to be a good girl.'

Euw. She'd forgotten Pete's tendency to walk that very fine line between cringe-making corniness and sex talk.

'I can't expect you to be faithful. Not when I . . .' He cleared his throat and grinned boyishly.

'What?'

Pete scratched his nose. 'It's been a long, long summer, babes.'

'Oh. Right.'

'You're not jealous, are you?'

Actually, no.

He plucked her knicker elastic but it didn't ping because the knicker elastic had been knackered in Tredower's mincer of a washing machine. 'Remember that time I forgot you weren't there and went round to your flat and Miranda—'

'Miranda?' Her *neighbour?*

A cheeky grin. 'I was thinking that we could all get together when you get back . . .'

'Yuck! Get lost.' She pushed him away.

Taking that as a green light, Pete pulled them backwards on the bed and sandwiched her with the weight of his brawn. The bed creaked.

He pressed his hand against the gusset of her knickers. 'You're not wet.'

'Pete!' His hand felt like an invasion, an uninvited guest. It was not, she realised, absolutely not the hand she wanted near her knickers. She wriggled away from him. Sex and death. Might work for some people. Not her. 'Pete, stop . . .'

Pete withdrew his hand, puzzled. 'Whassup, babes?'

Nell sat up on the bed and primly rearranged her skirt. 'I can't do this.'

'You don't fancy me any more?' Pete frowned, as if struggling to comprehend what he was hearing.

'It's not that.' But it was that. She didn't fancy him any

more. He was the same old puppyish Pete. But something in her had changed. She didn't want a non-committal fuck with Pete. And she certainly didn't want a committal fuck with Pete either. There was no grey area. 'Look, you're lovely.' Lovely? No man wanted to be described as lovely. 'I'm just not . . .' She was about to say, not in the right head space for all this, but that was the wanky kind of thing men said.

She'd spare him that indignity. 'Sorry.' She stood up, picked up her straw beach bag off the floor. She glanced at him. He looked crestfallen and still had a bulge in the groin of his shorts, which made it worse. 'I've really got to get to the hospital.'

'You don't want to meet later for a bit of slap and tickle?' One last try.

'I'm really sorry, but I don't think I do.'

'Right.' He got up from the bed, readjusted his shorts, looked up and gave her a charmingly resigned smile. 'Have a nice life, Nell-I'm-Not-a-Tube-Station.'

Forty-one

Free of Jeremy! Free of Pete! Goodbye and goodnight. She fled from the B. & B. to the beach. She needed to see the sea. The sky. She needed time on her own to mentally prepare herself for seeing Mum again, before having a quick coffee with Soph – on her way apparently – and heading up to the hospital and taking over from Ethan. She parked appallingly, ran up to the café.

The blue shack glowed in the sunshine. It seemed the focal point of the whole landscape. The slant of the cliffs, the stacks of clouds, they all seemed to converge at this one point, the bright blue box with the steep roof. She stopped by the gate. Even though she knew Michael was in New York a little part of her hoped that he might, by some miracle, be back.

He wasn't.

Nose ring Annie smiled quickly, then turned her back on her and busied herself with other customers. A bit off? Jeremy and Pete had clashed publicly on the beach and nothing stayed a secret in this area for long. Or maybe Michael had said something. Her heart sank.

She sat down heavily at the bench at the bottom of the café garden with a coffee that she didn't touch, beneath the tree where the blue tits sang, where she'd first met the BFG. The heart-pumping adrenaline that had sustained her throughout the last week had gone and she was engulfed by a terrible flatness, a weightiness, a kind of gravitational pull towards the earth so strong she could barely move her feet.

Thinking of him, his yellow Converse trainers, his terrible fleeces, his Atlantic grey eyes, the way he'd filled her summer with unexpected happiness . . . she had to summon all her strength not to sob her heart out. She needed him. *Why* was he not here? How could their friendship end like this? She looked up at the sky. Fast high winds were pushing the clouds along like brushstrokes. The sea shimmered. It was unspeakably beautiful, perhaps the most beautiful thing she'd ever seen. A deep love for Cornwall washed over her, drenching her like a freak wave she hadn't seen coming.

She sat there, unable to move, hearing only the pulse of the waves hitting the beach, and she was overcome by this strange sensation – it was like she was hollow and was being filled up through a hole in her head. And she could hear his laugh again. She could feel the splash of icy seawater on her face, his frisbee-big hand on her bum as he pushed her up on to the surfboard. And she ached for him like she'd never ached for anyone. Acute homesickness, only for a person not a place.

She knew then.

She knew completely, without doubt, and the knowledge now learned couldn't be undone.

She gasped, pressed her hand to her mouth in amazement. How could it be *possible*? How could she not have seen this coming? Hadn't she protected herself against it? She'd tried so hard for exactly this not to happen.

'Sorry I'm late. You all right, babes?' Sophie walked towards her, licking an enormous ice cream and wearing a cherry print bikini. She held out her ice cream. 'Lick?'

Nell shook her head. 'No thanks.'

Sophie sat down next to her. 'Any change with your mum?'

Nell shook her head. 'No, no. It's not that.' She turned to face Sophie. 'Soph, something has happened.'

'Oh no. What?'

'It's Michael.'

Sophie looked puzzled. 'Your mate, Michael? The guy who runs this place? The married guy?'

Nell nodded, still astonished. How on earth could she tell Sophie? How could this be happening?

'What's up with him?'

She turned to face Sophie, eyes shining. 'I . . . I . . . I've got a horrible feeling that I'm in love with him.'

Sophie sprang off the bench. 'You're not!' She let out a loud, high squeak and jumped up and down on the spot. 'Eeeek!' She fluttered her hands in front of her face to cool herself down. 'OK, let's calm down here. Calm down. Calm down.' She took a deep breath. 'Let's think this through before I get too excited. Right. OK. The situation with your mum means it's understandable if you've gone a bit doolally. No one could blame you.'

'I don't think it's—'

'We need a way to get to the bottom of this.' Sophie looked serious. 'OK, listen. You must answer my questions. Do not hesitate. Speak from the gut.'

Nell laughed, put a hand on her belly. 'From my gut.'

Sophie cocked her head on one side. 'Do you want to undress Michael?'

'I want him to undress me.'

'Do you still find his raft shoes offensive?'

Nell shook her head.

'His fleeces?'

She thought about it, shook her head.

315

'You don't want to change him in any way? Not even take him shopping?'

'I don't think I do, no.'

'Oh. My. God. Hell has just frozen over.' She raised her ice cream up in the air like the Olympic torch. 'You *are* in love! And now . . . yes, it's obvious. Look at you! You're wearing crap clothes and your fringe has gone completely mental and you're spending your time in stinky depressing hospital wards but you look incredible!'

'I do?'

'You do! This is wonderful!' Sophie stopped, wrinkled her nose suspiciously. 'So why aren't you jumping for joy?'

'Well . . .' It was wonderful. It was also a disaster. A total disaster. She was in love with someone who did not, could not, ever love her back. She'd blown it before it had even started.

'Ah, yes.' Sophie put a hand on her mouth. 'He's married, isn't he? For a moment there I forgot.'

Nell sighed. 'The divorcing bit is not the problem.'

'It's not? What's the problem, then?'

Nell's eyes filled with tears. 'He saw me with Jeremy. Twice. He thinks I'm the world's biggest fuck-up.'

Sophie sat down next to her again. 'Ah, OK.'

'I haven't had a chance to explain anything. He's gone to New York on business. And now . . . oh . . . what am I going to do?'

'But he must love you! He must! It all makes sense, Nell. Why else would he bother teaching you to surf? You're a crap surfer. You're hopeless. And . . . and . . .' Sophie had forgotten about her ice cream in her excitement and it was dripping down the cone on to her hands. 'When is he back from New York?'

'He doesn't know. I guess it could be days, weeks.'

'*Weeks?*' she squealed. 'Oh, for God's sake. We need him here!'

Other café goers turned to stare.

'Shush,' hissed Nell.

'There's nothing for it. You'll have to fly to New York!'

'Sophie, don't be ridiculous!'

'OK, OK. You need to be here for your mum, I guess.' Sophie hushed her voice and spoke urgently. 'Who knows him well, apart from you? Is there a middleman here? We need a middleman. Jesus, he must have friends? People who would *know*.'

'Honestly, Soph. Leave it. I've got bigger things on my plate at the moment.'

'Bigger things?' Sophie grabbed Nell's hands and pressed them to her bosom. 'I'm sorry but *nothing* is bigger than Nell Stockdale finally falling in love! And you know that your mum would totally agree with me. She'd be packing you on a flight to JFK as we speak.'

There was a ringing from the sandy depths of her beach bag. Nell rustled through it, pulled out the brick and clamped it to her ear. 'Ethan, hi.' She tried to sound vaguely normal. 'How is she?'

Nell jumped two red lights, screeched to a halt in the hospital car park, ran through the waiting room and the maze of pale-lemon corridors and bumped smack into Heather outside the ward. They bundled in together and both nearly collapsed with the shock of seeing their mother sitting up in bed looking like she'd awoken from an afternoon nap.

'We have company, Ethan,' said Valerie quietly. The droop on the left side of her face had disappeared. The corners of her mouth were moving upwards. She was smiling!

'Mum!' Heather barrelled into her arms.

317

'Easy,' laughed Ethan. 'She's still attached to the mission control board.'

Relief shuddered through Nell's body in waves. 'Mum, you're back!'

'What made you wake up, Mum?' gasped Heather.

Valerie looked puzzled. 'I just had this sense that I had to wake up. That someone was waiting for me.'

They all exchanged glances.

'The doctors can't believe it,' said Ethan proudly putting a hand on Valerie's shoulder. 'You're a medical miracle.'

Valerie frowned. 'Are you sure I've been out for six days, Ethan? *Six?*'

'You have.'

'Really? I can't believe it.' She shook her head. 'And I'm not a sprout up here?' She tapped her head.

'No,' Ethan grinned, 'seems not.'

'And I haven't missed the hog roast?'

'No. We were about to cancel it anyway,' said Heather, stroking Valerie's hand. 'Don't worry about that.'

'Cancel the hog roast?' She looked at them all as if they were mad. 'But why?'

'Mum . . .' Ethan said hesitantly. 'I don't think—'

'Ethan. Am I dead, yet? No, there you go. It will go ahead.'

Heather's mouth opened and shut in silent protest.

Valerie looked at Nell and smiled. 'Now have I missed anything else at all? Do tell.'

'Er . . .' There was no easy answer to that question.

Forty-two

Valerie, who had lost the mobility of her right leg, arrived home in a wheelchair, rolling down the ramps of the ambulance like a battered old ship into dock. Ethan christened the wheelchair Fast Harry. The twins plastered it with Ben Ten stickers and launched Grandma on hair-raising freewheels down the slope in the garden. Valerie didn't care. She was just thrilled to be out of reach of those pesky doctors who had saved her life.

Nell, Ethan and Heather circled around her constantly, driving her back and forth to hospital for regular checks, bathing her, wooing the physiotherapist to compensate for her general non-compliance, and, of course, wondering when it was time to drop the A bomb. The doctors had said she was still weak and might have another stroke. They were nervous of taking any chances.

But time was running out.

Nell looked anxiously at her watch. April's train would be coming in soon. She'd said she'd text when she was here. Sophie had sweetly offered to meet her at the station while they all prepared the ground with Mum. The plan was that April would stay at a B. & B. in Penzance ready, when and if, Valerie agreed to see her. Nell was relieved that April had

319

Beth and Chris with her. She was going to need them.

'Nell! Nell!' Valerie was beckoning her into the garden.

'Look!' Valerie was holding a small wicker basket containing two speckled brown eggs on her lap. 'Eggs!'

'Eggs?'

'Cass is a wonder, Nell!' Valerie's eyes were shining. 'Henny Penny's laying eggs again!'

'Amazing,' Nell said, remembering the time she'd eaten eggs Benedict after surfing with Michael. 'Where's Heather?'

Valerie raised a waspish eyebrow. 'Having *another* marathon phone chat with that young man, Gary . . .'

'Gareth.' Nell couldn't help noting how Michael was a much better name than Gareth.

Valerie shook her head. 'You girls, honestly. What can I say?'

'You're not too put out?' said Nell, puzzled at her mother's easy acceptance of missing out on being mother of the bride. 'Heather was worried you'd be hugely disappointed.'

'Well I certainly do not relish having two unmarried daughters in their thirties.'

I don't care about being married. I just want to see Michael.

'And' – Valerie sighed – 'Jeremy never did get on with Cornwall, did he? I was always a little concerned about that. And of course he was terribly short.'

Nell laughed. Michael was not short. Michael was tall and hairy and beautiful and he surfed like a demon. Jesus. She must stop this immediately! Why had Michael taken residence in her head! It was driving her insane. He was following her around like a shadow, striding beside her in his orange surf T-shirt, always almost there on the horizon, whipping through the surf, muscles rippling in the sun.

Except, heartbreakingly, he wasn't.

Valerie reached out and touched her arm lightly. 'It is very sweet of you to give Heather the keys to your flat, Nell.'

'Well, she can't exactly carry on living in Surrey now, can she?' It was the least she could do really. The flat was empty and as she was in Cornwall for the foreseeable future – waiting for Michael, shit there she went again – there wouldn't be too many squabbles about who finished off the hummus or who put the pink knickers in the white wash. And the rent would certainly help. The redundancy money wasn't going to last for ever.

'All right, ladies.' Ethan walked towards them, swinging a naked, nut-brown twin from either arm. 'Deng just called.' He winked at Nell. 'You're going to like this, sis. Listen up.'

'Deng? How is she?' Valerie gripped the sides of her wheelchair.

Ethan paused. 'She's changed her plans. She's coming back to work next week, Mum! For the hog roast.'

'Oh! Oh how wonderful!' Valerie clapped her hands and Fast Harry nudged forward.

'Civilisation calls, sis!' Ethan whirled the twins around by their hands. 'The land of black cabs and sushi is yours again.'

Oh.

Deng was back. Next *week*? She could go back to London and pick up where she left off, get a new job, get on with the future. No more dilly-dallying around on beaches with Cass, surfing, eating crab sandwiches. Back into heels again. Nannies. Alarm clocks. Real life. The summer was over. Her eyes welled with tears.

Ethan and Valerie looked at her, puzzled. 'I thought you'd be pleased, darling.'

'I am, I . . .' But the words didn't come. All she could think was, Cass will miss this place. She bit her bottom lip. And I

321

won't see Michael when he comes back from America. Nell desperately tried not to cry. Be strong. This was fate. It was fate's way of telling her to move on and leave Michael alone.

'Don't get sentimental, darling. We both know you've been desperate to leave since the day you set foot here.'

'I . . . I . . .' How could she explain? How could she explain that she was walking around cupping this fragile love in her hands like a baby bird fallen from the nest?

'And think of all those men, darling. Such a shortage of decent single men on the coast, everyone says so.'

Nell's spirits sunk even further. To stop the tears she had to bite her lip so hard she tasted blood.

Ethan slung an arm round her shoulder. 'Your work here is done, sis.' He gave her a squeeze. 'Brilliantly.'

Valerie beamed. 'Hear, hear.'

'Thanks, Mum.' There was a whoop of delight. Nell looked across the garden and saw Cass's shiny blond hair flicking in an arc as she cartwheeled across the lawn. 'I'd better break the news to Cass.'

Nell sat cross-legged on the lawn. Cass sat in the cradle of her lap eating a handful of freshly picked strawberries. Monty dozed beside them on his front paws.

'Cupcake, do you remember Deng, the nice lady who looked after Grandma?'

Cass nodded.

'Well, she's coming back. And this means we can go home, sweetheart.'

'Home?' Cass's face scrunched up, puzzled.

'London.'

Cass was silent for a few moments. 'But I like the beach. Henny Penny and Monty will miss me.'

'We can visit lots.'

'But it's so far away. And London makes me wheezy.'

'You'll see more of Daddy there.'

Cass looked unconvinced.

Nell played her ace. 'By the way, Daddy's coming back from Italy this evening. *And*, Cupcake, he's coming to the hog roast.'

Cass grinned. This was more like it. Then, as if following another train of thought, she frowned. 'What about Michael? Will he come to London too?'

Her heart leapt at his name. 'I'm sure we'll see him again.' But she wasn't so sure now. Not at all.

Cass leaned back into Nell's lap, licking her fingers. They swayed gently from side to side, watching Janet in the distance moving deftly through the vegetable patch in her green dress, stooping down slowly, rhythmically, picking up strawberries and dropping them into the wicker basket which she held against her hip. Nell's eyes watered. She'd miss Tredower. Her brother. Heather. Maybe Janet. And, yes, actually she might even miss her mother. A little bit anyway. God, what had happened to her? She'd gone gooey as a marshmallow. She'd better pull herself together and fast if she was going back to London in a week. And she'd better bloody wax her legs too. Shocking.

'Are you crying, Mummy?'

'Hay fever.'

'Do you want my last strawberry?'

'No thank you, Cupcake.' She sniffed. 'Very kind of you though.'

Cass looked worried. 'Mummy, when we go back to London will you go away again?'

'What do you mean?' But she had a horrible feeling that she knew exactly what Cass meant.

'To your job.'

Nell pictured herself flung back on to the hamster wheel, blotting her lipstick while gulping back coffee, hopping round the flat, one heel on, one heel off, trying to find her laptop and her iPhone, calling a list of requirements over her shoulder to the nanny as she scrambled towards the door, telling herself over and over that Cass didn't need her just so she could do this every day. 'Not like before, no.'

'Really?'

'Really. I'll be around more. I'll fix it somehow.'

'Do you mean you will give me tea sometimes?' Cass asked incredulously.

'I do.' She'd work something out. She'd start freelancing with a vengeance. She'd write that damn book. She'd do anything to stay out of that nine-to-seven office. 'Promise.'

Cass looked at her a little warily, as if assessing the implications of her mother looking after her every day. 'You won't make me eat broccoli though?'

'I might.'

'I don't like sweetcorn, remember.'

'I remember.' She didn't remember.

'Or those little baby yoghurts you used to buy.'

Did she mean Petits Filous? She'd always thought Cass had loved them.

'But I do like fish fingers with ketchup and peas, but only the baby peas. I will eat peas now,' she declared solemnly. 'Even though they're green.'

'You've got yourself a deal.' Nell smiled, shut her eyes and hugged Cass. She'd always imagined that making a decision to step off the corporate career ladder would be a struggle, one that involved a huge amount of stick beating and sacrifice and Mumsnet hand wringing. But it didn't feel like that. In fact, right now, in the sunshine, with Cass sitting on her knee, it didn't even feel like a decision at all. It was just the way things needed to be. After years of viewing school gates and their incumbent mothers with a certain amount of dread and, in all honesty, snobbery, she was surprised that she was actually looking forward to meeting them. She could do with meeting some other mothers. You never knew, maybe there would be one or two who could become friends.

'Mummy . . .' Cass sat straight up on her knee and peered over her shoulder.

'Mmm?'

'Your phone is flashing.'

She picked it up. A text from Sophie, who was at her parents' house, to tell her that April had arrived. Shit. It was time.

Forty-three

'OK, darling. Let's talk hog roast.' Fresh from her siesta, Valerie sat up in bed with her notebook flipped open, Biro poised. Soft afternoon light flooded in from the bay window catching spirals of dancing dust. 'Suckling pig? A nice plump fellow, I hope. Should be here Friday?'

Nell nodded. She wondered if Ethan was listening at the door. She'd left them all in a state of jittering high anxiety downstairs, biting their nails and pacing the floor, while she'd been sent upstairs to do the deed. Even Sophie was waiting by her phone. She felt the weight of the world on her shoulders.

'Too big for the fridge, it can go in the garage cool box. Pete and the boys from the village are in charge of the spit roast, as per usual. As long as they don't hit those ales. I do worry about Pat's son though. He's barely old enough to get served, is he?'

'No, he's fourteen, Mum.'

'We'll all have to turn a blind eye.'

'Mum, can we—' Nell attempted. She sat on the edge of her bed.

'Now the village ladies are doing the potato salads, under the orders of General Nancy Trelawney. I fear they think I'm far too ill to do my own potato salads and just this time, darling, I'm not going to contradict them. Such a bore scrubbing all those spuds.'

'Mum—'

Valerie flipped over the pages of her notebook. 'Now, what else? I thought you could pick up the glasses from the pub on Thursday, give them a polish, you know I'm a stickler for sparkling glasses. Oh yes, and Heather's ordered tonnes of strawberries and cream and some pecan pie, which is unnecessary. I didn't want to upset her, not after everything with Jeremy, so I've gone along with the pie, although I know that the village ladies will miss my banana bread. And, of course, Ethan insists on doing the music, so we'll all just have to speak a little louder like deaf people. Janet is in charge of . . .'

'Mum I need to—'

'. . . the booze, which should arrive Thursday.'

'We need to talk,' said Nell more firmly.

'We are talking, darling. Now, have I given you the soft-drink list?'

'We need to talk about something else. Not the hog roast.' She began to feel sick.

'What on earth are you rattling on about, Nell? You do look ever so grave.'

'I don't know how to say this.'

'Darling, *what* are you talking about?' She propped herself up on her pillows. 'I really need to focus on the task in hand. We've got fifty-four people coming for lunch in six days' time.'

So Nell told her. Directly. As matter-of-factly as she could. Just what she knew, what she'd seen, nothing more, nothing less. It took less than a minute. To her horror, Mum didn't react at all. She froze like a stone bust. Had she died there and then? 'Mum, Mum, are you OK?'

Finally, Valerie turned her head very slowly and stared out of the window.

'Mum? Please say something. Anything.'

'Does she have blond hair?' Her voice was so quiet and husky Nell could barely hear her.

'Brownish, highlights.' So it was true. Of course it was. Nell gulped. Tears caught in her throat. April! April was definitely her sister!

Life flickered back into Valerie's features. She turned to look directly at Nell, her eyes blazing with an emotion that Nell had never seen before. 'What's her name?'

'April. April James.'

'Pretty name.' Valerie swallowed. 'Is . . . is she nice?'

'I like her very much.'

Valerie started sobbing, quietly, then the sobs became deep growls, more animal than human. Nell hugged her tight but the noise kept coming. She wondered whether she should call up her reinforcements. She was scared.

'I . . . I . . . I didn't dare hope,' stuttered Valerie. 'I never thought. I never . . .'

'It's a big shock . . .' Nell cradled her mother's head in her arms, and felt as helpless as she'd ever felt. She couldn't reach her. She couldn't reach into this experience. How would it feel to give away a baby? How? The very idea of losing Cass made her heart scrunch into a ball. She sniffed back her own tears. Must be strong for Mum. Must be strong for Mum.

'They took her away. I had her for two weeks,' Valerie sobbed, twisting her hands together in her lap. 'She was so pretty, so tiny, my little girl with little pink fingernails and blond curly hair. She didn't even cry. Then this lady came and they took her away . . .' Valerie started to tremble. 'I signed the forms. They took her away.'

Mum's trembles passed into Nell's body like transferred pain.

'They told me I couldn't keep her, Nell.' She looked up

now desperately, pleading for understanding. 'I was just 19, and an immature 19. We had nothing. Nothing. No money or independence. We weren't married. You've no idea how different it was. My parents thought I'd committed the most terrible sin, brought shame on the family. My pregnancy was hidden. No one knew. And when she was born my mother wouldn't even touch her.' Valerie's shoulders began to shake uncontrollably. She buried her face in her hands.

'My mother said that the only way I could atone was to give the baby up, start again, give the girl a chance with a . . . a . . . a . . . proper family, not a harlot like me.'

To her horror Nell felt like her mother was dissolving in front of her eyes. Layer and layer of her peeling back, rawer and rawer, until there was just this kernel of a person, no longer her mother, but this tiny, scared, vulnerable girl she barely recognised.

'I wasn't like you, Nell. I didn't have your balls to do it on my own.'

'Things were different for me, Mum,' said Nell gently, trying to stop her voice choking up. 'I was in my thirties. I had a job.'

Valerie closed her eyes, raised her hand as if to hide her face in shame. 'You kept your baby, Nell. I didn't. You have no idea how much I envy and admire you for that.'

And all this time she'd thought that Mum disapproved of her bringing up Cass alone.

'Did she get a nice family? Do you know?' She asked in a very quiet voice.

'Lovely parents, she said. Her mum died last year but her dad lives in Spain. She has a son of her own now.' Nell smiled through her tears, trying to sound cheerier and to reassure her mother. 'And a daughter, Mum, a daughter who's expecting twins.'

'Twins!' Valerie smiled for the first time. 'Gosh. Like Ethan.'

Nell stroked Valerie's hair, pulling it off her face. 'April had a happy childhood, Mum. She seems like a happy person.'

'Oh, thank God,' Valerie exclaimed. 'Thank God. I wished so desperately that she was having a nice life. You know, I'd go down to the summer house and stare out at the moon, Nell, and I'd always wonder if my baby was looking at the same moon and I'd pray and pray that she was happy.'

So that's what Mum was doing. 'But why did you never tell us? Why?' Nell felt a flush of anger.

'Because it was a terrible thing to do, what I did. I wanted to forget it. And I didn't want you all to hate me.'

'We would have understood. We would.'

Valerie shook her head. 'No child would understand that. How could they? I thought maybe I'd tell you when you were older but it never seemed the right time . . .' She stopped, tried to collect herself. 'I've missed her every day for forty-three years, you know.' Valerie wiped tears away with the edge of her finger. 'And I can still feel the down of her hair, the way she gripped my little finger, like she couldn't bear to let go.' She started to sob harder. 'I still hate myself for handing her over, for giving in to my bloody parents . . .'

'Shush,' said Nell, trying to calm her down. 'It's OK.'

'When your father and I got married, I thought it would make things better in some way, then I could have more children. But it didn't make it any better, Nell,' she said desperately. 'It made it worse, much worse. We tried to find her. We tried to get her back! But they said it was final. I'd signed the forms. That was it. It was too late. Too late.' A strange cry leapt from her throat. Nell hugged her closer. 'I promised myself I'd never put myself through that pain again. I'd never try and find her any more. I'd let the poor baby be.'

She sighed heavily. 'Then I had Ethan. He was a boy.' She swallowed and looked at Nell. 'And then I had you.'

Nell wasn't sure she wanted to hear the rest of it. It was all so obvious now. She was a replacement. Only she could never replace April. No one could.

'And you came out dark, darling, with this olivey skin, long limbs, wiry, alert and feisty, and so different from the word go. I wasn't expecting that, you see. I thought you'd come out the same.' She shut her eyes. 'But you came out different.'

Nell tried to speak but the words wouldn't form. This was far, far harder than she had imagined.

'I've been a beastly mother to you. Beastly. And none of it was your fault.'

Nell rocked her from side to side.

'I'm so sorry.'

They sat like that for a long time, the evening sun falling through the bay window, the twitter of the birds in the ivy outside, the yelp of the children in the garden. And in that moment, in the afterglow of her impossible mother's apology, Nell felt something inside her shift. It was a physical sensation, a twisting and turning and tugging, as if she was trying to pull off a tight dress that didn't fit her any more. And she suddenly knew that she was different, fundamentally different, irrevocably different to the person who'd walked into this bedroom minutes before. She pulled away from Valerie. There was one more question. 'Mum, I've got to ask you, who is April's father?'

Valerie looked startled by the question. 'Why, your father of course.'

'Dad?' The sun lowered, filling the room with its light and heat.

'There was never anyone else, darling.'

Forty-four

Dizzee Rascal's 'Bonkers' trembled the Union Jack bunting on the gate, rolled out over the apple trees, tunnelled down the long, narrow lane, deep into the surrounding countryside, out to sea. In the breaks a loud hum of voices and laughter ballooned up above the tree canopies. Beneath the oldest, gnarliest apple tree Ethan's tattooed back gleamed in the sunshine as he stood at the decks. He cradled the headphone between ear and shoulder, prodding the record with his ring-stacked middle finger. Deeper in the garden, beneath the umbrella shade of giant rhubarb leaves, the doomed baby pig hissed on its spit, orange in its mouth, its underage roasters drunk on ale, serving strips of pork belly sloshed in grainy local mustard to a snaking line of guests. Ladies gossiped beneath wide-brimmed straw hats. The men, all wearing their worst summer shirts and with sunburnt noses, sank brown beers and eyed up the feast of flesh and distractingly short dresses.

Sophie's cleavage was a guest in its own right. It shuddered when she laughed and swelled every time someone congratulated her on her unexpected betrothal to The Shagster, while her shy actor boyfriend smouldered and smoked in a cinematic fashion beside the pond. (Monty, totally smitten, refused to move from his side.) The Sweets' Wedding – already

332

so called – had gone *some* way to placate the locals, who were reeling from the news that Heather's wedding was not to be, as well as the presence of Gareth – five shades darker than anyone else south of the Tamar – at the party and as closely entwined with Heather as was humanly possible without their actually being conjoined.

Everyone marvelled at Valerie's Blitz spirit in the wheelchair. They marvelled at her ability not to be embarrassed by her feral grandchildren, as Nat and a naked Cosmo led astray spumes of crazed young followers and crashed through the crowds on their rusty toy tractor, sending drinks flying. They marvelled at just how pretty and slim Freya looked pregnant and what a nice man That Lovely Dean was as he swung Cass round and round by her arms so that her white frilly dress flew out like the ribbons from a maypole. But most of all they marvelled – and felt just a little bit irritated – at Valerie's ability to keep her dark, shocking secret from them for *so* long. The rumours that had rumbled over cups of tea from the late 1960s to the present day, passed between mother and daughter, as both gossip and salutary warning and moral fable, were true! Not only were they true but *she* was also here, brazenly walking amongst them in a red and white dress!

So while the party appeared to progress as summer garden parties normally progress – everyone getting drunker and more sunburnt and feeling slightly queasy on the undercooked meat – really it was all just a dance around April James. Nothing could compete. Not Sophie's engagement. Not even quiet little Heather going AWOL.

Marjorie Patterson's lips started to twitch with the effort of tact. How she wanted to interrogate April! Heels drilled into the lawn as women strained and pivoted for a view of the long-lost daughter or, almost as good, her husband and

– sharp intake of breath – the pregnant teenage daughter. Every time one of *them* – or were they really one of us? – went to the toilet or journeyed from one side of the garden to the other, dozens of eyes followed, feather fascinators trembled, and all the hats tilted in the same direction like angled satellite dishes on a terraced street.

Nell stayed protectively close to April. 'You bearing up to the scrutiny?'

'Well, the Pimms helps.' April smiled. 'At least I survived an assault by tractor.'

'It's being steamrollered by Mum's friends you need to worry about.'

April laughed. She looked different already, Nell thought. Maybe it was her dress, red and white flowers, swishy, full skirted, a bit of a 1950s Hollywood musical dress. And maybe the dress was so noticeable because up until now she'd only ever seen April in conservative clothes or an anorak. But there was something else too. A sparkle in the eye. Something she couldn't quite put her finger upon. April's apologetic hesitancy had been replaced by a self-possession Nell had not been aware of before. Was this because of the presence of Chris? Nell wondered. April was holding his hand tightly, leaning into his body, and they looked, Nell thought with a happy–sad pang, about as together as anyone could decently look after twenty odd years of togetherness. Let alone a couple preparing for their precious (and clearly headstrong) teenage daughter to give birth to twins. They were inspiring, that's what Heather had said, and Nell had to agree. There was something enviably complete about Chris and April and she found it hard to imagine that they'd ever struggled or doubted their marriage, as April had confided that she had.

It still felt like five minutes ago that Sophie had driven an ashen-faced April to Tredower on that drizzly Friday morning.

Nell, Heather, Ethan and Janet had taken turns to wish her luck. Heather had engulfed her in a teary hug. Janet had pressed a crystal talisman into her palm. Ethan gave her an emotional high five and she, Nell, had squeezed her hand and led her gently towards the sitting room where Valerie was waiting in the glinting hulk of the wheelchair. April had stood uncertainly at the doorway, pale in the rainy yellow light, looking terrified. Nell's heart was in her mouth as she'd watched April walk slowly towards the wheelchair. She choked up as Mum's wrinkled sun-spotted hand arced slowly towards April's cheek with the tenderness of an old gorilla reaching out to its young. Feeling like a voyeur of an almost unbearably private moment, she'd shut the sitting-room door, slipped away and, overcome with emotion, sobbed on to Ethan's shoulder, ruined for the rest of the afternoon.

April had come over every day since that momentous one. Sometimes she'd visit with Chris and Beth. Sometimes on her own. Within a few days the extraordinariness of it all had became almost normal. April had somehow filled a hole in the family that they had always sensed was there without knowing why.

Nell was optimistic. OK, these were early days – the honeymoon period probably – and there was so much to learn about one another and maybe trickier times ahead, but right now it had gone as well as any of them could have dared to hope. Chris was such a nice person to have around, unassuming, intelligent. Nell liked him more each time she met him. Beth was a hoot – Valerie was enchanted – and a great leveller for April, her cool teenage wisecracks defusing things when they got too heavy and emotional. Like when Valerie had given April Grandma Penelope's seascape watercolours – Nell had finally located them beneath a stack of old wallpaper in the attic – and April had started to cry.

Beth had said, 'Come on, Mum, they're not that good.' (Valerie had thought this hilarious.)

Best of all, with all the commotion, Nell hardly had the space to think about Michael. When she fell off the wagon and did think of him and her heart scrunched, she sternly reminded herself that what was happening to the family was bigger, far, far bigger, than any romantic fancy. Michael was just a man after all. And she'd survived on her own this long . . .

'Rock out, people!' shouted Ethan, forming a rapper's fist in the air.

Dizzee Rascal faded into Rod Stewart's Maggie May. There was a whoop of approval from the revellers, as the ladies unplugged their heels from the lawns and shimmied (closer to April).

Sophie and Janet danced up. 'Ladies,' laughed Janet, twirling her coin necklace in her hands, 'shall we disco?'

April looked at Chris who pushed her gently forward. 'Go on!'

'Only if Nell joins me,' said April.

Janet and Sophie pulled Nell and April towards the trampled bit of lawn in front of the speakers. April started dancing, shyly at first, swishing her skirt to the music, slowly gaining confidence.

'Woo woo woo!' squealed Sophie, doing her Sophie dance-floor thing, holding up her skirt, can-canning her legs. Janet grabbed Nell's hands, then April's hands, forming a bridge between them, wiggling their arms in unison.

'Beth. Over here, join the middle-aged groovers immediately!' shouted Sophie, kicking her shoes off into the awe-struck crowd and gyrating barefoot. 'Being up the duff is absolutely not an excuse. No, not even with twins, girl.'

Beth, neat bump now obvious, walked over reluctantly.

Sophie grabbed her and shoved her into the line.

'She won't forgive me for this,' April whispered to Nell. 'This will be, like, beyond embarrassing.'

They snaked their way around the garden, picking up Heather on their travels, reclaiming Beth from an attempted escape, all of them giggling and dizzy with the silliness and the sunshine until the record changed and they collapsed in a sweaty heap beneath the pear tree.

They looked up to see Chris wheeling Valerie towards them in her wheelchair. 'Hi, girls.' She beamed from beneath her blue hat. 'You look like you're having fun!'

'Hi,' they all chimed together. Nell, like everyone else, wondered how to extricate herself and leave April and Mum to it. These last few days of the summer didn't belong to her. This hog roast didn't either. It belonged to April and her mother. Everyone knew that.

Valerie smiled at April. She couldn't stop smiling at April. She was besotted. 'April, will you come with me? I'd like to introduce you to my very old friend, Marjorie Patterson.'

April leapt up. 'Of course.'

'Don't let her talk you into visiting Penzance, whatever you do, April,' muttered Heather under her breath. 'She'll force-feed you her infamous scones and your digestion will be shot for weeks.'

'I heard that,' said Valerie over her shoulder as April wheeled her to the top of the garden where Marjorie, beside herself, was waiting, cracking her knuckles in excitement.

The music got louder: Florence and The Machine's soaring vocals.

Janet groaned. 'Ethan obviously thinks he's in Ibiza. The poor old dears with the hearing aids are getting feedback.

337

Sorry, ladies, excuse me. I'll tell him to turn it down.' Janet went over to the deck, whispered something in his ear, nuzzled her head into Ethan's shoulder.

'They seem to have sorted it out,' Heather whispered into Nell's ear. 'Thank goodness.'

'Is it just me or is Janet looking kind of . . .' Sophie wondered, sizing Janet up.

'Fat?' said Heather. 'Just what I was thinking.'

'And the tits! OK, bet's on for a spring baby?' said Sophie, putting her hand out. 'Tenner!'

'Shush!' said Nell. 'The trees have ears.'

They looked around and a huddle of women standing behind the tree quickly looked in the other direction.

Gareth appeared. Sophie nudged Heather in the ribs. 'Lover boy.'

'Shuddup, Sophie,' Heather hissed under her breath.

Gareth grabbed her hands, pulled her up. 'A dance?'

'Blimey, I've never seen Heather dance like *that* before!' whistled Sophie, as they watched the couple clinch and shake around the lawn. 'Ditching Mr Jeremy Fisher has given a new lease of life to her hips.'

'Hasn't it?' Nell smiled.

'Snatched from the jaws of Surrey in the nick of time, just before she started doing the suburban foot shuffle.' Sophie put an arm around Nell's shoulder. 'And April is completely lovely, isn't she?'

Nell glanced over to where April was being interrogated by Marjorie and a growing crowd of gawping ladies. 'She is. I'm so pleased you two get on. It would be a disaster if you didn't.'

'Yes, we get on very well. I took her for a drink, you know. I thought I'd check her out for myself.'

Nell laughed. 'Poor April.'

'Well, she passed the test. With flying colours. Not a bunny boiler. Not a gold-digger.'

'Yeah, yeah, I know that, Soph.'

'And not', Sophie declared emphatically, 'the type to have an affair with Michael, for God's sake, Nell! Had you gone completely barking?'

Nell winced. 'Now I've met Chris I confess I feel a bit of a dork for entertaining that idea.'

'Just because one of your sisters ran off with your man it doesn't mean April will too. That said …' Sophie's voice went all sing-song and pleased with itself.

Nell narrowed her eyes. 'What?'

Sophie shrugged. 'She *is* friendly with Michael. I know this because we had a good chat, a very good chat.'

'Sophie, you're up to something.' Nell grabbed her arm. 'Confess, Sophie Sweet, or you're for it. I'll wear a peach polyester matron-of-honour dress to your wedding.'

'Tra la la la!'

'I'll read one of those dreadful Internet renta-poems at the ceremony. I'll sing "Angels".'

She winked. 'April had his number.'

'Soph!'

'Oh, April and I have been very, very bad.'

Nell shut her eyes in despair. Sophie's meddling always ended in disaster. 'I'll kill you, Soph.'

Sophie laughed. 'The execution must wait.' She nodded behind her. 'You have a gate crasher, Nell. Fresh off the plane.'

Forty-five

Nine months later

The days were getting longer again. Nell gazed out of the window. It was a restless dappled May sky, almost an exact match with April's watercolour on the wall. From the long stretch of lime-green sofa, perched on the top of the cliff above the bay, Nell could waste hours sky-gazing, weather-watching. The window, which folded back in summer, stretched from one side of the sitting room to the other like an enormous cinema screen. Except it wasn't a screen. It was real. All real. She still found it hard to believe.

She looked up at the wall clock. OK, an hour before it was time to pick up Cass from school. She pressed save on her laptop. She had almost finished the masterpiece that was to be the final full-juice Stockdale Express round robin but she'd hit a conundrum. Which address should she put on the top of the letter?

Her London address? No, Heather was living there now. Still deeply dippy about Gareth, she had a new job managing a small boutique in Notting Hill's Ledbury Road, which she loved, as did everyone else because it meant they got a 30 per cent discount. She was now new best friends with Miranda the ceiling destroyer from 1B and, best of all, like Nell herself, thoroughly cured of Jeremy, who, after the wedding fallout, had suffered a bona fide midlife crisis, grown a beard, resigned from his job, and set off round the world on a Harley, last heard of somewhere near the Colombia-Brazil border.

Or should she put Ethan's address at the top of the letter? But . . . no, Janet would never forgive her for making their stylish West London home an annual target for dozens of robin-in-the-snow Christmas cards. (There was no chance they'd move to Cornwall. Since the Muffin catalogue went bust and the much-longed for girl, Florence Aida Stockdale, was born – as Ethan's loins had once damned him, they now redeemed him – Janet had fallen abruptly out of love with the slow-cook pace of life of Cornwall, and anything faintly eco. Florence offered a whole new set of darling shopping opportunities, for one thing. And the London Prius had been nothing but trouble.)

What about *this* address? Nell tapped her fingers on the edge of the laptop. Hmmm. This glass-box house – no draughts, no damp, no spidery attic! – floating above the world still felt private, new, tender. Lots of wonderful things had happened here, not least the fact that it was within these walls that she'd written her novel and actually finished it! (Trying out different titles in various fonts and text sizes was her favourite chore-displacement activity. At the moment *It Happened One Summer* – Helvetica, Italic, size 16 – was her favourite.) But wouldn't it look a bit presumptuous to put this address at the top of the letter?

April. What about April? No, she couldn't put April's address. She wouldn't do that to her. She'd be besieged by terrifying invitations from Mum's friends and rellies. And, knowing April, she'd be too polite to say no. Bless her. Nell smiled. She knew April much, much better now. They spoke most nights on the phone and had discovered many shared passions – cherry Coke, Mad Men, Primark T-shirt bras – and dislikes – geometrical-patterned fabrics and wallpaper, sickly over-iced cupcakes, *A Place in The Sun* when Amanda Lamb wasn't presenting it – and odd, spooky coincidences – it turned out they'd holidayed in the same village in the south of France one year and their favourite song was 'Perfect Day' by Lou Reed. April was a revelation, really, the warm, grounded antidote to Stockdale dysfunction, bringing all of them closer together in unforeseen ways. Not least about their inheritance.

In the end there were no squabbles. Without fanfare Valerie had quietly altered her will: Tredower would be sold – to a wealthy surgeon and his family who were relocating from London – and the profits divided equally between the four of them. Even Janet accepted this. The problem, when it came, was an unexpected one: April gratefully accepted a couple of old family pictures, a small Victorian brooch of Valerie's, even a sun-faded velvet chair (Janet nabbed the prize furniture pickings, no one else had the space), but she absolutely refused point-blank her share of the money. It was not hers. It was theirs. She'd never, ever wanted money, only knowledge of who she was. It was Ethan who finally persuaded her to use the inheritance to buy a small Victorian cottage in Wolvercote for Beth, Duncan and their twins, Max and Edie. Beth, of course, had been frenziedly grateful. The financial security meant she could start a part-time degree course at Oxford Brookes university the following autumn and her life wasn't, like, totally over.

Nell stood up. Pressing her forehead against the window's cool glass, she gazed at the beach, torn between wanting to imagine her mother on it, wading out in her turquoise costume, and wanting to see it just as a plain beach, washed clear of the past. When Deng had found Mum in bed on that sunny late November morning, she'd thought at first that she was sleeping. But the Big One had come stealthily during the night, as Mum had always said it would, claiming her back from the room in which she'd been born decades earlier. It was as good a death as she could have hoped for, given the circumstances: Nell was sure that would have been Dad's practical take on it. Mum had always wanted to be remembered not as 'a Brussels sprout', but for who she was, Valerie Florence Stockdale, marvellous and flawed. For a life lived, if not always well, at least cogently. Nell took much comfort from this and the fact that, shortly before she died, Mum had told her that that autumn was the happiest time of her life. Anyone could see that April's appearance, and April's unequivocal forgiveness, had changed her mother, softened and quieted her, finally given her some peace. In those final weeks, Nell was certain that Mum had become the woman she was meant to be had her life not been framed by a misguided decision she'd made as a terrified teenager.

Nell's grief still came and went during the day, every day, almost as if it were tidal, but the full disorientating whack had passed. The fact that she was no longer anyone's child made her feel very vulnerable. But it had made her grow up too. Made her realise many things. That downshifting wasn't the same as burnout. That Daisy Lowe fringes are not compatible with a Cornish climate. And that love, *this* love, was worth the risk. She heard the back door click.

'Meet your supper, sweetheart.'

Michael. He always surprised her with the realisation that he was just as gorgeous as she remembered. Although she was less sure about the plate-sized wriggling brown crab in his hand. 'Jesus, it's alive! Put it down!' she shrieked, getting tangled up in her leopard-print scarf as she leapt off the sofa. 'It'll have your fingers.'

He dropped it into the sink. There was an alarming clatter of claws. 'Whoa, that's one feisty lady.'

He walked over to Nell, grabbed her by the waist and nuzzled his nose into her neck. The slightest of his touches still made her flesh tingle. 'News?'

'Finishing the round robin.' She smiled, rolling her neck into his kisses. 'Thinking, very creatively and very intensely, about our surf weekend biz and, well . . .' she laughed – 'kind of idling.'

'Idling? Not my Nell, surely.'

She stepped back, wrinkled her nose. 'Yuck. Michael, you smell fishy.'

He pulled her close again and inhaled her frizzy, salty hair. 'And you, sweetheart, you smell of home.'